KU-710-154

WoA

PENGUIN BOOKS

The Swimming Pool

Louise Candlish studied English at University College London
and worked as an editor in art publishing and as a copywriter
before becoming a novelist. Though her stories are about people
facing dramatic dilemmas, she tries to live an uncomplicated
life in London with her husband and daughter.

The Swimming Pool

LOUISE CANDLISH

PENGUIN BOOKS

PENGUIN BOOKS

UK | USA | Canada | Ireland | Australia
India | New Zealand | South Africa

Penguin Books is part of the Penguin Random House group of companies
whose addresses can be found at global.penguinrandomhouse.com.

First published in Great Britain by Michael Joseph 2016
First published in Penguin Books 2016

005

Text copyright © Louise Candlish, 2016

The moral right of the author has been asserted

Set in 12.82/15.23 pt Garamond MT Std
Printed in Great Britain by Clays Ltd, St Ives plc

A CIP catalogue record for this book is available from the British Library

B FORMAT ISBN: 978–1–405–91987–6

www.greenpenguin.co.uk

MIX
Paper from
responsible sources
FSC www.fsc.org FSC® C018179

Penguin Random House is committed to a
sustainable future for our business, our readers
and our planet. This book is made from Forest
Stewardship Council® certified paper.

For John Candlish

Prologue

I am running naked through the streets of Elm Hill.

It is late evening, summer's end, and the streetlamps burn synthetic holes in the darkening sky. Deep in the rack of streets on the east side of the park, the mild air feels hostile, the near-silence thunderous.

I am trembling badly. The arm covering my breasts has begun to spasm and both knees are buckling. Blood leaks from my right foot where gravel has sliced the sole. But none of that distresses me as much as my face, the grimacing, primitive feel of it, as if I've been robbed of all that makes me civilized.

He has done this to me.

A sign for Wilson Road slides into view and I feel a sudden ache of hope: where I started is farther from me now than my front door. Just a left turn here, a quiet stretch of residential road, and the high street will be ahead. This *will* end.

A woman approaches, lifts her eyes, and I see the same startled expression and flash of high colour as in every other face I've encountered, all mobility arrested by the shock of seeing a nude woman loose in leafy Elm Hill. They suspect I'm insane – there is a secure mental-health facility at Trinity Hospital a mile or two away – and are afraid to help in case I turn savage.

But there's a flicker in this face that prompts me to speak for the first time since this nightmare began. 'Please, can you lend me something?'

'What?' She's stunned by my addressing her – and by my accent. It's worse to know that I'm educated.

'To cover myself. Please.'

'I don't think I've got anything . . .' She looks down at her cotton dress and gestures helplessness. It's balmy: no one is carrying a scarf or a jacket.

It strikes me that I'm thinking normal thoughts. I'm still rational.

'Oh,' she says, and suddenly she does have something, screwed up in her handbag, a light cardigan of some sort.

'Can I borrow it? I'll return it if you –'

'Keep it.'

With shaking hands, I tie the garment around my lower half, then tighten my arms over my chest.

'Look, hang on.' The woman takes a purposeful step towards me, her gaze lingering on the bruises that bloom on my arms. *His* fingerprints. 'My name's Beverley. You don't have to tell me yours, but something has obviously happened, hasn't it? Come home with me and –'

I interrupt: 'Where do you live?'

'Broadwood Road.'

I know it: no closer than home. 'No, thank you, I'm fine.' I sound polite, as if declining the offer of a drink.

The awful thing is she's relieved. She did the right thing and now she can scurry away with a clear conscience and a story to tell.

On the move once more, I slam my left toes into the raised edge of a paving stone and cry out at the pain. Raising my free hand to my face to wipe away tears, I catch a scent beneath the sweat, a scent that only makes me sob harder: chlorine and sunshine, scrubbed stone and suburban grass. Swimming pool.

I'll never go back.

At last the high street blazes in greeting, the Vineyard bar directly opposite the junction at which I've emerged. I falter. I'd forgotten about the pavement terrace, its crush of smokers: I'll need to pass right by it to reach Kingsley Drive. From a standing start, I sprint across the traffic lanes and meet the shockwave, the universal bewilderment that erupts into laughter.

'Who booked the stripper?' a man's voice calls out, and a second round of laughter volleys into my back. 'Bit long in the tooth for that, aren't you, love?'

I sense rather than see the phones in their palms. There will soon be pictures circulating, if not already, attracting likes and shares and re-tweets, comments that make this man's sound tender.

I'm on my street. The pain in my damaged toes is ferocious, consuming the foot and calf, causing me to limp. My building is in sight: four featureless storeys, the night sky above. It's nearly over, nearly over.

And then I see him. He stands by the building doors, watching, waiting. My knees roll and at last I sink to the ground, powerless. Because I know he'll watch for ever – he'll wait for ever.

It will never be over.

I

She coughs in her sleep.

I spring to her bedside to check that her chest is rising and falling as it should, that her pulse is steady and her skin warm. In the dimmed light, I can see the vestiges of stickers glued on the headboard in younger years, pictures of kittens and ponies and love-hearts: all things nice. Children grow and it strikes the parent as both miracle and loss.

The coughing subsides, but I remain on my knees, vigilant. I haven't watched over her like this since the night she was born, when I stayed awake, enchanted and petrified, ready for her cry. At least Ed is with me this time. Thirteen and a half years ago, he wasn't allowed in the maternity ward after visiting hours but was sent home with the other fathers, ready or not.

I don't suppose Lara Channing had to stand for *that*. She would have been in some posh clinic for the births of Georgia and Everett, installed in a private room with Miles at her side, the recipient of privileges she'd assume came as standard. 'You are an angel,' she would tell the staff, in her smoky, intimate way. 'I mean it, an *angel*.' And she would say it like she really meant it.

But I mustn't think ill of Lara. Not now.

'Here, this should sober you up.' Ed comes into the room with mugs of black coffee – as if adrenalin had not annihilated the alcohol hours ago, pinned open our eyes and cleansed our ears.

I return to my seat on the little pink sofa by the door, take the coffee in both hands. The smell is instantly comforting. Though there is space next to me, Ed chooses not to take it, perching instead on Molly's desk chair under the window. 'Is she sleeping a bit better, d'you think?'

'Yes. I'm glad we brought her home.'

We speak in whispers. Until the last half-hour she'd fought sleep, like an infant, her distress slow to fade, and since then we've hardly dared exchange more than a syllable.

'She needed to be in her own bed,' I add.

'You're probably right. It's good you insisted.'

You insisted, this should sober *you* up: it destroys me, the way he speaks. If never again, surely tonight we should be united. 'She was completely hysterical, Ed. We know how to deal with that better than anyone. And it's not like we've snatched her from intensive care and absconded, is it?'

He lifts his glasses from the bridge of his nose, replaces them a second later. He is not quite looking at me. 'No, but the paramedics were pretty clear about wanting to take her in for observation.'

'We'll observe her here,' I say.

6

He nods, lets it go. To the right of where he sits, Molly's school uniform hangs on the wardrobe door, a scholarly silhouette with regulation tights dangling low. New shoes sit on the carpet below. All ready for the first day of term on Wednesday. I wonder if she'll be well enough to go back or if we should keep her at home for the week to recuperate fully. To think how we used to dither over arrangements when she had a day off sick, debate whose turn it was to cover, like it actually mattered!

All three of us were different people then.

'Ed?'

'Hmm?'

'I wish I'd never . . .' I pause, struggling to subdue the what-ifs, to keep them from massing and charging.

'Wish you'd never what, Nat?' *Now* he looks at me, direct and eager, almost with a sense of daring.

I lose my nerve. 'Nothing.'

And I think how wrong people are when they say you should never regret, I think how unrealistic that is – dangerous, frankly. Personally, I regret almost everything, including and especially these last months. Even the parts when I was so happy I thought I might levitate, when it felt as if I'd never before known what summer was, what pleasure was, what it meant to live life to the full.

Mostly, I regret ever laying eyes on Lara Channing.

2

Sunday, 21 June – ten weeks earlier

I happen to know that the sun rose at 4.42 the morning I first saw her. It was, in fact, the longest day of the year, with sixteen hours and thirty-eight minutes of daylight.

I'm guessing it was past eleven by the time I logged on to the Elm Hill community website and saw her photograph, possibly even closer to noon. Sunday mornings were sacrosanct in the Steele household: all three of us being in full-time education, we time-tabled down-time and this was our prized weekly triple period of laziness, the only blank box on the kitchen calendar.

Pleasantly indolent as I sat at the kitchen table, mug of green tea cooling in front of me, all I had in mind was to check if it was the right week for the farmers' market on the high street, but as soon as the homepage appeared I was waylaid. With her blonde tresses falling to her breast and her slender, burnished limbs, with a smile broad enough to post a letter through, she eclipsed quite effortlessly the competing items. Missing moggies and pedestrianization schemes, forget them, look at *me*! Listen to *my* news!

There was a second figure in the photograph, a newer, fawnlike version of the first, a teenager who looked older than Molly by two or three years. A mother-and-daughter shot, then, like one of those pictures you see of 'ageing' supermodels and their mini-me progeny on the beach in St Barts, the kind that make you wonder how each party *really* feels about the other's beauty. The caption read:

Brave locals Lara and Georgia Channing prepare for this morning's Dawn Dip at the new Elm Hill lido.

Ah, of course. Now I noticed the band of cyan water at their feet, the festive triangles of bunting above their heads, the blurred rainbow in the background that must be the row of changing huts I'd heard about, each door painted a different shade of art-deco pastel. In tribute to the 1930s origins of the site, mother and daughter had attired themselves in swimwear from the period: high-necked, low-legged, this was a style that flattered few. Luckily for all concerned, these two *were* the few.

The mother was quoted in the accompanying report: 'To have such a beautiful pool on our doorstep is a gift. This is going to be the best summer Elm Hill has ever had!'

And, against my better judgement, the words stirred excitement in me, causing me to turn to the kitchen window and check the sky above the plane trees: yesterday it had glowered the grey-black of a mussel shell, but today it shone blue and unblemished, a perfect June day.

If I opened the window I'd be able – almost – to smell summer. Teachers exist in a perpetual mode of count-down and I didn't need the calendar to tell me there were less than three weeks till school broke up (four for Ed and Molly, an inequality that neither had any intention of letting me forget); maybe it *was* going to be the best summer we'd ever had. Maybe, after all our careful avoid-ance of the new neighbourhood facility, it was going to be possible to enjoy it.

Then again, I thought, sensing resistance in the seat next to me, history suggested otherwise.

'Four forty-two, good Lord!' I swivelled the laptop to show Molly, who glanced up from her DS.

'Four forty-two what?' Her face was expressionless as she registered the image. With her straight brows and small mouth, she did impassivity well – even when wear-ing a Dalmatian-print onesie.

'That's what time these two crazies went swimming this morning, and a whole lot of other people as well. It's midsummer. The new pool has opened.'

Molly made no comment, which was not unusual even when the subject was to her taste. I loved her reflec-tiveness, a quality I believed to be deepened, if not outright caused, by her being an only child. Not that I wasn't sometimes tempted to project my own thoughts on to her, of course.

'Maybe next year that will be us,' I said, keeping the mood casual. *Never judge, never blame*, the last therapist but one had said, a little mantra for us. In the end, he had brought nothing new to the table, but I didn't judge or blame him for that.

Molly glanced again at the photo, raised her eyebrows. 'To be brutally honest, Mum . . .' – that was what the girls her age were saying at the moment, *to be brutally honest* – '. . . I don't think that kind of swimsuit is, uh, your style.'

I narrowed my eyes at the screen, failing to diminish the backlit glamour, the pull of the Channing woman's energy. 'You're probably right. Maybe I'm better sticking to the one I've got. Bland, conservative, modest . . .'

'I'm not even kidding,' Molly said, another current teen favourite (what did it 'even' mean? An expression of agreement, I gathered, or possibly contempt). Infants modelled their turns of phrase on their parents', but at this age they could come from anyone.

Not only do you have to let them go, my friend Gayle said, but you get no say in who influences them instead. On matters to do with parenting Gayle was my touchstone. The day I dismissed her advice was the day I lost faith in common sense.

I closed the laptop and returned to my tea, feeling – and I know it sounds trite – different. Inspired. So the lido had opened at last – re-opened, to be precise, following a closure that had lasted nearly two decades and at least three fund-raising campaigns that had bitten the dust before this last successful one. Each delay had been met with disappointment by the local community; only Ed and I had wished it would never happen, that the funding would fall through once and for all, or some

11

stalemate develop between builders and conservationists. That it would be left for the skateboarders or graffiti artists or clubbers or whoever else had been making use of the derelict site during the dark, dry years.

But secret wishes were dandelion clocks to the force of nature that was Lara Channing, for, as I would soon learn, it was she who had driven the project. From the very day she had moved into her parkside house and eyed the abandoned beauty from her terrace, she had made its resurrection her mission. She'd personally overseen the procurement process, the bid to the Lottery Commission, the final restoration; she'd even interviewed the lifeguards.

'People don't turn Lara down,' Miles Channing told me once, and his eye lingered on me long after he'd made his point.

Saturday, 27 June

Well, we were only human and, intrigued, Ed and I strolled down to have a look at the new pool the following Saturday morning when Molly was at her tennis lesson. Of course I'd passed the abandoned building countless times over the years, but such was its design – squat brown brick walls with enclosing curved corners, a horizontal strip of windows too high to see into, entrances and exits that had been boarded up more securely with each trespasser's breach – that, prior to its reopening, it had been impossible to get so much as a glimpse inside. Now the plywood frontage had been replaced with a stark glass entrance, the reception area beyond a temple of flawless pale stone and polished wood. Signs in art-deco font directed arrivals one way to the changing rooms, the other, through a long sky-lit corridor, to the renovated poolside café.

There was already a queue for tables when we arrived, but fortunately the manager, Liam, was the partner of a colleague of Ed's and he offered to squeeze us in on the sundeck. 'We'll need the table back at twelve,' he warned. He had the look of a man whose brakes had failed and we stepped quickly out of his way, seating ourselves before minds could be changed.

'Table back?' we grumbled. 'What is this, the Ivy?'

But at the first turn of my eyes my cynicism vanished. It was as if a large nut had been cracked open to display its fruit – and the fruit was liquid blue, shivering with its own freshness. I had to shield my gaze from the sheer dazzling beauty, from the transforming, sun-spangled glamour of it. With the photogenic length of multicoloured huts and the candy-striped deckchairs on the upper terrace, it might have been Miami Beach or the Côte d'Azur. Only the smell was English, not of swimming pool yet, but of the park beyond, of sap-drenched leaves and cut grass; green and lusty and alive.

'It's so huge,' I said to Ed, slightly idiotically. The shallow end, a riot of flailing limbs and shrieking mouths, seemed a field's length away. 'I can't take my eyes off the water, can you?'

'Humans have an inbuilt attraction to it,' he replied, his words scarcely audible above the raised voices of a group of children setting up camp on the other side of the railing. 'They've done a nice job, haven't they?'

'Nice? It's *glorious.*'

Ed registered the word – not one either of us had used in years, if ever – before shaking straight his newspaper. That Saturday *Guardian* symbolized many things for him. It spoke of who he was: a left-leaning man who still took the time to read the news in print and in full, at least once a week. Others might have downgraded their engagement with current affairs to a quick scroll on their phones as they jostled commuters on train platforms or jay-walked their kids across perilous roads, but *he* was still willing to give it the time and attention it deserved. Even if his wife would have preferred a conversation

After we'd ordered I scanned the other tables for familiar faces. As a teacher at one local school and a parent at another, I was confident there'd be several. There was Molly's chaotic chum Rosie and her family – we exchanged waves – and Gayle's neighbour Ian, dressed for once in jeans and a shirt, not his customary Lycra (a keen cyclist, he was one of those hovering spidery types who, you suspected, had only themselves to blame when caught in a skirmish with a motorist); and Annabel from the kindergarten at Elm Hill Prep, in my opinion not so much teaching assistant as holy being.

As a member of staff at the largest senior school in the postcode, Ed, were he to look, would recognize more Elm Hillians still (recent incomers had led a movement to call us Elm Hillbillies but the old guard had squarely rejected *that*). Though not, I guessed, the woman my gaze fell on next.

She was at the table closest to the water and the best on the deck, glamour radiating from her and rendering the rest of us mere extras in her scene. Her clothes were exotic (to my eye, anyhow; doubtless they were workaday to her): a pink silk shirt-dress with a woven silver belt; flat snake-print sandals, the kind you might wear on a luxury safari or for a stroll through a hilltop village in Umbria. Oversized sunglasses with amber-coloured frames covered much of her face, leading the eye down a small kittenish nose to an insolent Bardot mouth.

Irrationally, my brain ordered my pulse to leap.

'There's that woman,' I said to Ed in an undertone.

He didn't look up. 'What woman?'

'The one I told you about, with the matching daughter. I can't remember her name.'

That was a lie: I didn't want to utter it for fear of being overheard by its owner. It was only six days since the sunrise photo shoot, but already Lara Channing had become the de facto face of the place, her photo gracing the leaflets posted through doors and even appearing on the features pages of the *Standard* to illustrate a piece about the new heyday of London's lidos.

She was not with her daughter this morning but with a man I assumed to be her husband, given their idle tapping of iPhones and sporadic, inattentive conversation (at least he had not, as Ed had, placed a partition of newsprint between the two of them and kept it there even after their orders had arrived). I couldn't see his face, only the back of his head, the still-dark hair fastidiously cropped, the strip of neck between hairline and box-fresh cotton shirt expensively bronzed. On the table, alongside the phones, were a black coffee (his) and a green smoothie (hers), the antioxidant one with kale and kiwi that I'd not ordered myself because I thought £4.99 was scandalous for a soft drink – and even if I didn't Ed would.

'They're locals, apparently,' I said, prodding his newspaper. 'Though I've never seen them before, have you?'

'Hmm.' He lowered the paper to reveal a chewing jaw, his plate of sourdough toast almost finished. He was famously hard to engage in gossip even when he wasn't trying to read. Careless talk costs lives: he would have led by example quite beautifully in wartime. 'The daughter's not at All Saints, is she?'

'I'd be amazed if she was,' I said. With or without the staff's dedication, All Saints (staff nickname: All Sinners) was not the school of choice for any known elite, and if I took anything from this first in-the-flesh impression of Lara Channing it was that she belonged to an elite. With those enticing looks and that media-magnetism, she was a breed apart from the mothers of Elm Hill

Prep, BMW-driving, gem-set-watch-wearing creatures of privilege though they were. Even the way she looked out at the water suggested a satisfaction more personal, more nuanced, than mere inbuilt human response.

Giving up on Ed, I spooned my granola, enjoying the erogenous touch of the sun as I continued to watch. But it was a risk to scrutinize someone in sunglasses when you were bare-faced yourself and, sure enough, she soon sensed my attention and returned it, even lifting her sunglasses in a playful peekaboo gesture. I blushed. Never in my life had I so regretted not making an effort with my appearance. My skin was makeup-free – caked in foundation during the working week, I tended to let it air at weekends, hardly noticing after all these years the looks that strayed to the birthmark above my right eyebrow; my hair was limp and in need of a wash, with a rather Tudor centre parting I didn't normally wear; my clothes were shapeless and unflattering. Not at all the right look for Miami Beach, for the eye of Ms Channing.

There was worse to come. I became aware of her husband/companion twisting in his seat to stare across to our table – at exactly the moment Ed happened to glance behind him with a frown. As I squirmed, mortified, there was a sudden heightening of energy at the other table, an exchange of urgent mutters, before Lara's laughter sprayed the air, musical and delighted and, it seemed to me, a little contrived. I adjusted my seat so that Ed blocked my view of them and theirs of me, my heart stuttering as if something significant had just occurred.

'What?' Ed said, seeing my face. His expression softened. 'Thinking about Molls? You're allowed to like it, you know.'

'Like what?'

'This. The pool. There's nothing to stop *you* coming here.'

'I know.' I didn't say that I hadn't been thinking of Molly at all.

We'd hardly finished eating when the bill came, unbidden. 'I think Liam wants the table back,' I said. 'Look, the queue's out the door. Shall we go?'

Ed sighed. 'If this is what it's going to be like, I don't think I'll come here again.'

But we both knew it was a moot point for soon his Saturdays would not be his own. Change was afoot in the Steele household: this summer, he would be offering himself as a private maths tutor, to continue at weekends during the autumn term and until the entrance exam season in January. If it went well, it was possible he might be able to do it full time from the 2016/17 school year, and as a family we would prioritize this mission. All Saints, like any conflict zone, was no place for middle-aged men.

In any case, once Molly's term-time Saturday-morning tennis finished and she was free to join us on such outings – well, this was the last place she'd want to come.

*

18

I remember exactly how I felt as we strolled home from the lido that day, a restless blend of exhilaration and frustration that struck me as overdue, even inevitable. I remember thinking how effortlessly I could predict the unfolding of the day and how it might be more interesting if, for once, I could not. Molly would arrive back from tennis and hole up in her room – she had the larger of the two bedrooms: we'd recently swapped after she'd accused us of never using the superior square footage while conscious, which was more or less true – or at the kitchen table where the laptop and other electronic devices lived. (None was allowed in her bedroom, a child internet-safety rule and school recommendation we obeyed religiously.) Later, she'd hang out with a local friend, probably at the friend's since that was more likely to be a house with a garden, siblings and pets, amenities we couldn't offer.

Meanwhile, Ed had year-ten exam papers to mark, and I, having risen early to take care of next week's lessons preparation, thought I might steal a march on the laundry (racy stuff). Later, I would pay a call on our upstairs neighbour Sarah, whose recovery from hip-replacement surgery was proving slower than hoped. Ed and I often ran errands for her or popped in for a cup of tea. Homework and chores being duly completed, we would then slide pizzas into the oven (nutritionally supplemented with broccoli spears or sliced peppers) and gather as a three to watch TV or a film. Ed and I would share a bottle of red and Molly would have a fizzy drink of her choice. It was that kind of life: casual on the surface but orderly, strictly managed. Rules were in force, standards upheld.

'Is it me or does it feel very small in here today?' I said, as I plucked back the curtains to expose the very edges of the windowpanes. Our flat, on the first floor of a 1980s block in a quiet lane off the high street, was north-facing and, though it was bright outside, the light in the living room was indirect and dreary. Even our furniture felt wintry: the indestructible Indonesian wood that had been in vogue twenty years ago and never replaced (a victim of its own success); the brown leather sofa that had looked so stylish in the store but leached the light like a plug hole sucked bathwater; the glass vases that held fresh flowers far less frequently than had originally been intended.

'It *is* small,' Ed said, 'but there are plenty of migrants who'd consider it palatial.'

I'd noticed before that this was a difference between us – he always compared down, I up – but today it felt defining. It felt problematic.

The flat had been ours long enough for us to feel as if we owned it, though it was in fact a housing association sub-let, the reason we could continue to afford to live in a suburb like Elm Hill since an upgrade of the overland line had caused both house prices and private rents to rocket. These days, when people remarked on how the place must have tripled in value since we'd bought it, I simply nodded, weary of explaining again our tragic missteps in the London property dance. At the beginning, we'd saved and sacrificed like normal couples, had been mere months from having the deposit for the modest terrace of our ambitions, when all at once prices had begun to race out of reach. It was no more than a fever, we told each other: best to keep our cool and wait it out. By now, of course, the deposit that might once have bought a terrace was barely sufficient for a one-bed. We'd still look at the property websites sometimes, watch the numbers rise and rise. It was like hyperinflation in the Weimar Republic, we would say.

But we were not the only ones in this situation, and if you were in the mood to count your blessings you could find plenty of them. There was the relatively modest rent, of course, which had saved us thousands of pounds over the years; the park was a ten-minute stroll away; Molly took the bus to her school, while Ed and I walked or cycled in separate directions to ours. I had nothing to complain about.

Why, then, on that Saturday afternoon, as Ed frowned at his malfunctioning All Saints software and I lugged the laundry hamper from bathroom to kitchen, was I suddenly feeling so discontented with my lot?

'I bet they live in one of those big houses on The Rise,' I told Ed.

'Who?'

'The Channings.'

'Who are the Channings?'

I sighed. 'It doesn't matter. I'll ask Gayle. She'll know.' Indeed, Gayle kept herself so thoroughly abreast of local gossip that when we'd worked together at Rushbrook Primary I'd sometimes had to tune out of her bulletins to keep myself from spontaneous combustion.

Definitely The Rise, I thought, closing the washing-machine door with a mildly resentful thump. Overlooking the southern edge of the park and with views of the city, The Rise was hands-down the best street in Elm Hill and the new lido would raise its status even higher. I had visions of snakeskin sandals kicked off in a huge central hall, a softly lit mirror for the adjustment of blonde loveliness on departure. There would not be, as there was in our entrance nook, a noticeboard pinned with calendar, timetables and a chore schedule, set dead centre above a shoe-storage unit checked daily for dis-orderliness. (About as welcoming as an army barracks, my mother said, the last time she visited, adding, 'I don't know who's worse, you or Ed.')

'I think our focus needs to be our pensions,' Ed had concluded eventually on our prospects for home ownership.

Imagine being (relatively) young and your husband saying that! And imagine being able to suggest no better idea for a shared *raison d'être*, not when you were as busy as you were pairing shoes, separating coloureds from whites and generally bringing control to bear on systems that would have thrived perfectly well on their own. It was pitiful, truly.

All of this is, I think, important background.

3

Sunday, 28 June

'You know what?' I said to Molly. 'How about we just do this straight away before it becomes a big thing?'

Honed over the course of a decade, my tone neither coaxed nor demanded, only neutrally suggested – 'big thing' was not 'Big Thing'. Her objections I pre-empted deftly: 'Just you and me. No little exercises. We'll sit right at the back and we won't stay long.' I no longer made such rookie errors as asking what the worst that could happen was. As far as she was concerned, it was the *very* worst.

Even so, I wasn't expecting her to agree quite so readily to a trip to the lido.

'Fine,' she said, with a sigh forceful enough to lift a strand of hair. (Like mine, hers was neither dark nor light, neither straight nor curly; recently she had begun blaming me openly for its lack of distinct identity.)

'Really? That's great, darling.' I guessed she must have been expecting the proposal and had decided that if she humoured me this once I might not ask again and she'd have her summer to herself.

In the same spirit of getting it over and done with, I drove, which was a mistake because the roads off The

Rise were fully parked and soon we had circled almost for as long as it would have taken us to walk. As I hunted, Molly gazed into her lap, ominously silent. Her chin sank low, fringe dipping over her eyes; it was as if she hoped it might cover her whole face and screen her from the rest of the world. At last, I spotted a Fiat 500 vacating a space by the side wall of one of the large villas I'd ascribed to Lara Channing, and reversed my old Mazda into it.

'Finally.' Molly groaned with a world-weariness I knew to conceal nerves. Delays did not sit well with her: they were unscheduled minutes in which she might work herself up to a change of mind. As we approached the lido entrance, she remained a careful pace behind me. You could already hear the screams.

Inside, the terraces teemed (I read later that a thousand people went through the turnstile that first full weekend), almost every square inch patch-worked with towels and bags and picnics, and the general explosion of paraphernalia that came with a family day out. It felt more like a lake than a pool, so vast was that expanse of aquamarine, its straight edges made jagged by the heads and shoulders of bathers clinging to the side rail. I had imagined us taking a pair of deckchairs, Molly's angled strategically away from the water, but all were occupied. We settled instead at the rear of the far terrace next to the exit turnstile, Molly sitting with her back to the wall, as if the pool were a terrifying precipice to be kept at extreme distance.

Which, to her, it was: 50 by 25 metres of water, with a depth that increased from one to 2.5 metres. I had no idea of the cubic volume but suspected that she did: before this outing, she would have armed herself with all published facts about Elm Hill lido. I suspected, too, that she was itching to get up and give the turnstile a push, check that it was in working order in the event of an emergency evacuation. And the reason her gaze strayed frequently to the gate that divided the café from the pool area? She was scanning for the nearest alternative exit route, having noted that re-entry to the reception area was impossible, thanks to steel barriers.

It goes without saying that she was the only young person here behaving in this way. The rest thronged at both shallow and deep ends, noise levels pitched somewhere between frenzied and hysterical.

'No wonder everyone's screaming,' I said. 'It's only eighteen degrees in the water, according to the noticeboard.' I spoke in a we-know-better tone, as if the temperature were the reason she wouldn't be going in. Enabling, a therapist would call it, or collusion, as Ed would have it, but for God's sake, wasn't it really just compassion? *Love?*

'OK, Molls? I'm so glad we've come.'

She must have noticed the gratitude in my voice because she gave me a co-operative half-smile before extracting her book from her bag. Without further comment, I began pulling off my clothes. The sooner I swam on our behalf, the sooner we could persuade ourselves that it was acceptable to leave, in spite of the steep entrance charge that had encouraged others to make a day of it. For us, thirty minutes would be a success.

Dodging the pumping legs and wayward elbows of small children, I lowered myself into the shallow end, sucking in my breath as coldness crept over my bottom half. Across the water on the café terrace, vast umbrellas swelled with the breeze; overhead, a plane scratched a pale line across the blue. Still delaying, I waded to the roped swimming lanes with my arms held high, as if navigating a river with my possessions balanced on my head, and only when laughed at directly by a group of teenagers, who might or might not have been past pupils of mine, did I submerge fully.

There was an instant surge of pleasure. In the last ten years, when I'd all but eliminated swimming from my life, I'd forgotten its curative charms, the optimism it stirred; I'd forgotten that I associated it with joy. Holidays in Devon when I was very young and my parents still enjoyed each other's company; my honeymoon in Greece, with that mesmerizing blur where turquoise infinity pool met the silver-blue of the Ionian Sea; and, steeped in nostalgia of a more unsettling kind, the summer spent in my grandparents' village in Hampshire, when a neighbour's daughter and I had disappeared for hours every day to the bathing pond in the woods.

After the first length, I looked across to check on Molly, glimpsed her face in profile, her expression stoic rather than miserable, which was as much as I could hope for. She could break through at any time, the therapists said. Never give up. And yet, with each new expert, we *had* given up.

Resting already, I touched my midriff under the water, felt the extra inches I affected not to loathe, evidence of another long winter – and spring – of staff-room snacking, birthday cake after birthday cake, Friday treats every day of the week. At Elm Hill Prep, Christmas and Easter meant high-end chocolates from twenty-four sets of top-earning parents and, well, it was rude to refuse them.

I was pitifully out of shape and managed only four or five more lengths before, afraid my lungs would burst, I climbed out.

It was as I was drying myself – casually out of range of Molly, who had been known to shrink, even scream, if dripped on – that I saw Lara Channing again, passing through the gate from café to sundeck with a boy of eight or nine by her side. Her hair was piled on her head in a careless beehive, thick fringe tumbling over the gold-rimmed mirrored aviators perched on her nose. She wore a pale-blue sarong crossed at the chest and tied behind the neck, a style that accentuated her well-toned shoulders and delicate collarbone. I wanted both to watch and avoid watching when she removed it for swimming and revealed that photogenic, age-defying figure, the kind I had never come close to owning even in my twenties.

I focused on Molly. 'What are you reading?' Then, when she showed me the somewhat juvenile title: 'Didn't you read that years ago?'

She shrugged, didn't need to explain. Re-reading books for younger children was a comfort, a safety behaviour. An imagination alert to danger – hypervigilance, they called it – could not cope with anything too complicated and now was not the time to begin *Crime and Punishment*. Her posture was even tenser than on arrival, sweat visible on her forehead and lip, and I felt the rush of tenderness I always did when her fear became tangible, the longing to draw her close and murmur protective words. But I'd learned she didn't like that.

'I had an idea,' I said instead. 'Dad knows the café manager, Liam. Why don't we ask him to arrange a behind-the-scenes tour? See how it all works? They'll have state-of-the-art systems, I'd have thought, or maybe they've restored the original plumbing.'

Her expression was unyielding. 'You said no little exercises, Mum.'

'It's not an exercise, I just thought it might be interesting. You know, historically.'

'*Historically*,' she echoed, with teenage disdain.

'Well, it was just a suggestion.'

It was then that I became aware of a pair of bare feet at the edge of my outspread towel. They were narrow and fine-boned with pretty little toes and nails painted a glittering black. Above, silver and green threads had been worked into the blue fabric of the sarong, a raised

28

woven texture that I wanted to rub between thumb and forefinger.

'Hi again,' a voice said and, though I'd never heard it before, I would have known even without those visual clues that it belonged to her. It was the sultry, rough-grained voice of a lifelong habitué of some smoke-filled speakeasy – or at least a woman with a sore throat – a voice that didn't try to please so much as expect to.

I looked up, unable to make direct eye contact thanks to the reflective lenses of her sunglasses (Ray-Bans; the ones the previous day had been Gucci – evidently there was a collection). By her side, the small blond boy smiled down at us with the self-confidence of a young ambassador. I was familiar with the type from my year-four class.

'We saw you in the café yesterday,' she said. 'I was here with my husband, Miles.'

'Oh, right. OK.' Under her deluxe gaze, I adjusted my sitting position so my thighs didn't splay so much, sucked in my stomach, which barely helped; you could suck in muscle but you could not suck in adipose tissue. My swimsuit was royal blue with white piping and now I wished it was plain black or, better still, that I was not fat. I'll swim every day, I resolved. I'll come after work – no, not enough time, plus there was Sarah's dog to walk. When term breaks up, that's when I'll start. Every morning, no excuses.

While these thoughts chased one another in circles, Lara had begun smiling in a perfect pink crescent that made dimples. '*Your* husband is a teacher at All Saints, they tell me. I bet the girls love him.'

'Well . . .' Though I didn't look at Molly, I could easily imagine her expression at this declaration, not to mention the suggestive tone. 'As much as any maths teacher can be loved.' I wondered how Lara Channing knew Ed was a teacher at All Saints. She was not a parent there, of that I was more certain than ever.

She tipped her head a fraction, as if I'd tempted her to break an important confidence, which caused strands of blonde fringe to curve over the sunglasses. 'He looks a bit like Alain Delon, we think.'

We think, *they* tell me. She was utterly self-assured.

'Has anyone else said that?' she demanded. 'I like to think I've got a bit of a gift.'

'I'm not sure. I don't think people know who Alain Delon is, these days, do they?' Indeed, I had only the vaguest notion myself: a French film star with dark hair and moody attitude. In any case, it seemed unlikely that Ed resembled a film star of any nationality or vintage. If he did, he'd hardly be married to someone like me. He'd be married to someone like her.

'He was a famous actor in the sixties,' Lara told Molly, who was regarding her with admirable sangfroid. 'He was kind of like a young Michael Caine or maybe Terence Stamp. Cool, *very* cool. He's in one of my all-time top ten French films from the sixties.'

Cultured though I liked to think I was, I wasn't sure I could name more than a handful of French films I'd seen in my whole life, much less be able to pick out ten favourites from a single decade. Nonetheless I sneered secretly at the phrase 'all-time top ten', which struck me as rather adolescent. Molly, meanwhile, only nodded, her expression knowing, even faintly doubtful, as if she watched Terence Stamp and Michael Caine films every day of the week and had her own opinions on them.

'*Belle de Jour*?' I suggested gamely. 'The one with Catherine Deneuve?'

Lara raised her pretty chin and laughed. It was a beautiful thing, melodious and commanding, and even amid the general clamour people turned their faces to heed its call. Her teeth were large, white and imperfect, with little gaps, and even that was charming, as if she had no time for impeccable dentistry, life being the carousel that it was. 'No, he's not in that. That was Jean Sorel, I think. The one I love is *La Piscine*.'

'I don't think I've seen it,' I said, grateful at least to be able to explain to Molly that *la piscine* was French for swimming pool.

'I know,' she replied crossly. 'I'm not an idiot.'

I sucked back a reprimand, mindful of the circumstances.

'Well, you must see it,' Lara told us. 'Lust and deception in Saint-Tropez. Alain Delon and Romy Schneider. A classic.'

At this the boy spoke for the first time: 'My sister's middle name is Romy.'

31

'Exactly.' Lara looked delighted with him, as if he'd named the capital of Mauritania. 'After the actress, that's why. *Your* middle name, my love, was inspired by Sinatra. Everett Frank Channing.' She stooped to kiss the top of his head, and as her sunglasses slid down her nose, I caught a glimpse of oversized dark eyes smoky with kohl. She winked at me before pushing the sunglasses back into place. 'Miles and I did look up whether Frank and Romy ever slept together. Hard to verify, it *was* the sixties, but if they'd ever been a proper couple, well, that would have been too weird.'

Unlike discussing the sex lives of dead celebrities in front of small children: *that* was not weird. Clearly this woman did not buy into the prevailing parenting cult of the appropriate, which I had to admit Ed and I had raised to an art form. (Was it appropriate to give appropriateness quite so much value? Might it not on occasion be helpful to be *in*appropriate? This, genuinely, had once been a debate in our household.)

Beside me, Molly's cool had slipped and she was starting to gape – good news in that it meant she was being properly distracted from her preoccupation. The boy, Everett, likely used to this sort of talk, was less riveted. With a kindly pat on his mother's hand, he left her side to stamp across people's possessions to the pool's edge and cannon-ball into the deep end with a tremendous splash. We were too far back for the spray to reach us but still Molly flinched.

'You don't like the water,' Lara said to her, more in observation than query.

'No. She hasn't since she was little.' I spoke for Molly even though Ed and I had agreed to stop doing so because she wasn't an invalid, and if you couldn't speak for yourself at thirteen, your parents had done a pretty poor job raising you. 'So, this is quite a crowd, isn't it?' I said, changing the subject. 'A runaway success, I'd say.'

'It certainly is.' With a languid movement, Lara brushed her hair from her eyes to view the crush. 'But, my God, it's been a long time coming. There were so many times I almost threw in the towel, no pun intended.'

That was how I understood that she had been not only the most photogenic participant of the inaugural swim but also instrumental in the restoration project as a whole. And yet she did not make her remark as a boast or even with any particular pride, only in the casual assumption that I would know full well who she was and what it was she had done. She was less queen bee than citizen queen.

'I'm not sure I know your name,' she said, and when I told her she was unexpectedly pleased, clapping her hands together and lacing her fingers in delight. 'Well, there you go! His first wife was called Nathalie! The one he left Romy for.'

I looked at her, bewildered.

'Delon, I mean. Poor Romy, she was *utterly* heart-broken. I don't think she ever really recovered.' Her attitude was one of true sorrow, as though these people were good friends of hers. She was, I thought, quite bonkers. 'Did *your* Alain leave someone for you?' she asked.

'Not that I know of, no. And he's called Ed, actually.'
I cleared my throat. 'Will your little boy be all right in the water on his own?'

She didn't turn a hair. 'Oh, totally, he swims like a fish.'

'And is your daughter here with you?'

'Somewhere, yes, with her little band of chumettes.'

'We saw you in the paper,' Molly piped up to my surprise. 'You were wearing those old-fashioned swimsuits.'

'We were!' And Lara rewarded her with the same dazzling smile she'd bestowed on her son for remembering his sister's name. 'Not a bad shot, was it, but I'm a bit ambivalent about it now, to tell you the truth. Apart from anything else, it's only gone and brought another scout out of the woodwork.'

'Scout?' I assumed she didn't mean the ever-prepared kind that camped in the woods and strove to make the world a better place.

'Yes, bloody model agencies. You know, she's even been approached getting on the school coach. She's barely fifteen! It should be against the law. It's hardly better than pimping or grooming.'

This was too much. Quite apart from the fact that Ed and I raised such adult and unsavoury subjects with Molly only after careful rehearsal, how much more arrogant complacency could one parent fit into a statement? A daughter so beautiful that model agencies fought over her, pestering her as she boarded a private coach to an

34

independent school (only the independents had their own coaches, the termly cost being considerably more than was allocated by the state for a child's lunch); and a parent so well off, so principled, she could afford to be dismissive of such approaches.

'My heart bleeds,' I said. 'What a terrible cross for her to have to bear.'

'*Mum*,' Molly objected and I bit down my smile. The little betrayer was already siding with some beautiful stranger against her own flesh and blood.

She needn't have worried, however, because after a tiny moment of surprise Lara began giggling. 'I think I'm going to get on very well with you, Natalie,' she said, in a flirtatious drawl, and I undid my previous good work by being thrilled that my little rebellion had impressed her.

As a sudden afterthought, she asked, 'Are you a teacher as well, Natalie?'

'I am, actually.'

'At All Saints, like Alain?'

'Ed. No, I teach year four at Elm Hill Prep.'

'Oh, yes, across the park. I've heard good things about it.' And she gave me a last interested look before taking her leave.

Out of the corner of my eye I saw her trade kisses with a couple at the edge of the café terrace before joining a female friend at the same plum table she'd occupied the day before. Its surface was scattered with phones, ashtray and cigarettes, ice bucket with champagne bottle and several glasses – no kale smoothies today – and all of this, along with the small dog sitting on the friend's lap in defiance of the no-dogs signs around the site, conferred an aura of roped-off VIP glamour on the arrangement.

The supervision of her son was evidently to be managed from afar and with a drink in hand. As the waitress approached to refill their glasses, Lara beamed up at her with exaggerated gratitude – 'You're an *angel*!' I lip-read – and her shoulders sagged like Odysseus returned, though all she'd done was pick her way across the decking to Molly and me and make a few eccentric remarks.

I didn't ask myself why she should have done this when she didn't know us, any more than I'd questioned with any real weight how she'd informed herself of my husband's profession and place of work. No, her idiosyncratic line in conversation was enough to tell me she did as she pleased and that, thanks to the dumb luck of being more attractive than the rest of us at an age when only the attractive retained any societal relevance, she got away with it.

Which both irritated and impressed me.

That evening, Molly and I Googled Alain Delon, and the images we found made us rock with laughter. To think of Ed being likened to this brooding Gallic god! Then I thought to bring up images of Delon at the age of forty-five and I saw there *was* a likeness of sorts: Ed could have been his less blessed, less tormented brother or cousin, an offering from a low-grade lookalike agency (perhaps a scout – someone with a 'gift', like Lara's – would approach him as he boarded the number 68 bus).

'We met a fan of yours at the lido today,' I told him, when he came into the kitchen to see what all the hilarity was about.

'Who?'

'Lara Channing. The one sitting near us in the café yesterday.'

'I don't remember.'

'You *do*. I showed you her picture in the *Standard* last week?'

'Oh, that one. The self-publicizing blonde.'

'Exactly. Well, she's decided you look like that old French movie star, Alain Delon.'

'She said that,' Molly confirmed. Sometimes she and Ed double-checked information with one another as if I were not a reliable source in my own right.

Not that Lara had been the first to note Ed's relative good looks – he *was* a little more handsome than most men of his age and type, and I don't deny there was a reflected glory in that, especially when meeting new people. There must be something about her if she's with *him*, they thought. But once they got to know us they understood the true inversion: in spite of his handsomeness, Ed behaved as if he were no less ordinary than his wife. 'He distrusts flamboyance,' his late mother had told me, on our first meeting, and the manner in which she said it – shrill, provocative, loud enough to be heard in the next street – made no further explanation necessary.

37

As for *my* first impression: with reasons of my own to desire conformity, a lack of exhibition, I'd known an exact match when I'd found one.

'Let's have a look.' Ed viewed the images with commendable bafflement, enlarging one in which a sunlit Delon, hair swept casually from a furrowed brow, cigarette between his fingers, glowered menacingly into the mid-distance. 'I think she must be overdue an optician's appointment.'

I laughed. I'd never given my style of laughter a moment's thought, but now it struck me as inferior to Lara's ringing instrument, expressive not so much of pleasure as of a mean-spirited crowing. How had I not noticed before? Was that how I'd sounded to Lara?

'We talked to her at the lido today,' Molly said, her pride unmistakable. It struck me that it was the first time I'd heard her utter the word 'lido'.

'Oh, yeah?' Ed said. 'What's she like?'

'She's really nice.'

'She's very . . .' I searched for the word, careful not to criticize in front of Molly '. . . she's very boho.'

Ed made a face and closed the image of Delon to expose the wallpaper image of a pre-pubescent, pre-sarcastic Molly that never failed to cause a sentimental pang. 'Beware of boho,' he said. 'It's just another word for immoral.'

'Her daughter's a model,' Molly said, undeterred.

'Could be,' I corrected, 'but not allowed by her parents.'

'Pleased to hear it,' Ed said. 'Modelling is not a career to aspire to. It totally destroys your value system. Brains are what count.'

Until you get Alzheimer's, I thought, but since Molly's grandparents and even a great-grandmother were still of sound mind I had yet to have occasion to explain *that*.

One human tragedy at a time, Gayle always said, and it was as sound a parenting philosophy as any other I'd heard.

4

Monday, 31 August, 1 a.m.

'What happened tonight?' Ed asks, and he speaks under his breath as if he has no real expectation of being heard, much less answered. Then, more forcefully: 'I'm not sure I understand, Nat.'

Here we go. I press my fingers into the plush of a soft toy on Molly's sofa – Rabbit, one of the few to survive the cull of puberty – before settling on my response. 'She could have drowned, that's what happened.' And before I can help it, I'm bristling: I'm blaming him for what happened because he was there when I was not. He could have kept her closer, kept her safe.

But, of course, he thinks the same of me. He always has.

'No, I mean, where were you before that? I was looking for you – I looked everywhere.'

I sit Rabbit on my lap. 'It was a big crowd. I couldn't find you either.' My eyes return to Molly's resting form. Her rumpled sheet rises with each pull of breath and she has writhed free of her blankets. Is she warm enough? The paramedics wrapped her in hypothermic blankets – should we have asked to keep them? Her party clothes were in a dripping bundle by the front door. 'We need to concentrate on making sure she's OK,' I say. 'And I don't just mean physically.'

He looks grim. 'Well, this is going to be a setback, to say the least. Maybe take us back to square one.'

'If we're lucky.' And we *are* lucky, I remind myself, compared to the Channings. At the thought, my heart begins to pound, a huge and frightening sensation. As if in objection, Molly's breathing grows a little more insistent and our heads turn instantly to monitor it. Only when it quietens again do we continue.

'Seriously,' Ed says, 'it would have been better if she'd never stopped being terrified. Then she wouldn't have been there in the first place.'

None of us would.

There is silence, broken by a hungry grumble from the hot-water pipe.

'Where were you?' he asks again. 'Who were you with? Obviously not our daughter.' And I catch a faint note underlying the suspicion, a note of patience run dry, of love lost.

Undone, I mutter that I need the loo, an easy way to end this before I say the wrong thing. Before I give myself away. Stepping from Molly's room into the hallway, the flat feels foreign, as if we've borrowed it from strangers, as if there are corners and shadows I've never noticed before.

In the bathroom, the first thing I see is the dress I wore to the party, sitting in a heap on the tiled floor. I changed it for jeans and a shirt at the first opportunity, hours ago, or perhaps minutes, I'm not sure. Time is different tonight: it thickens and clots, rolls and spins. I can't trust it.

Who were you with? Obviously not our daughter.

And now I think the thought I've been suppressing these last hours: This is twice I've let you down, my love.

Twice I've not protected you as I should.

5

Tuesday, 30 June — nine weeks earlier

On weekdays after work, Ed and I took it in turns to walk Sarah's cockapoo, Inky, for her, mostly to offer practical assistance during her recuperation, partly to assuage our sporadic urges to acquire a pet of our own. Because we all knew *that* wasn't going to happen — we would never be able to suffer the hairs and the dirt.

As with most other Steele activities, strict protocol was in force and whichever one of us did not dog-walk was expected to cook dinner and take care of any other domestic chores. When my mother had made that comment about not knowing which of us was worse, the answer was easy: neither, because Ed and I liked order equally. The difference was in motivation. For him, it was about efficiency, time management. Divide and conquer, he would say, whenever we drew up schedules or cross-referenced diaries, sometimes punching the air for effect. (When he did this, I could see how he might be mocked by his students if he wasn't as nice-looking as he was.)

Keen for her to benefit from the fresh air, I always invited Molly on my walks, though she invariably declined on homework grounds (what parent who happened also to be a teacher was going to challenge *that* excuse?). Gayle sometimes came, however, depending on whether or not she was on a weight-loss mission, and this evening, with the school holidays only weeks away and the new parading ground of the lido on our minds, we both were.

'Weight doesn't mean a thing,' she said – with two teenage daughters she was as vigilant as I was about judgements on body image. 'But I'd prefer it to be ten stone that doesn't mean a thing, not thirteen.'

'I agree.' Actually, I liked Gayle the way she was, approachably sized and animated of feature. She had a heart-shaped face and narrow nose that flattened slightly at its tip, and the kind of faintly bulbous eyes that looked wonderfully emphatic in heavy make-up (though bare, as they were this evening, gave the unsettling impression of their owner being caught mid-throttle).

'Do you think we should sign up for this early bird aqua-aerobics?' she asked, a little out of puff as we took a break at the lido noticeboard. It was an uncomfortably humid evening, the slow-rising, ripe-smelling humidity that you know isn't going to break in time to deliver a good night's sleep. The buttercups, normally on springs in late June, were heavy-headed. 'Eight a.m. isn't *too* crazy, is it? The café won't be open that early so there'll be no one to witness the horror of our exposed flesh.'

I remembered the teenagers laughing at me on my first outing, and my shame under Lara's gaze. 'Well, we could certainly try,' I said. A few weeks ago, I would have scoffed, referenced one of our failed pursuits of previous summers (Zumba, transcendental meditation, bridge), but now I felt only the same gush of optimism I'd had on seeing the picture of the Channings on the community website. How lucky we were to have the long holiday ahead – that sacred stretch when hope triumphed over experience to make you believe you'd be free for ever.

'Of course, you'll have the place to yourself soon,' Gayle said. 'How long between your lot breaking up and the release of gen pop?' (*Gen pop*: general population. American prison parlance was used often at All Saints and even at Rushbrook, though not at EHP. The day I heard my new head, Mrs Godwin, referred to as a screw would be the day the British monarchy was overthrown.)

'Just over a week and a half,' I said. 'We'll be here with our verbal reasoning papers and iPhones and I don't know what else – cellos? This sounds good, Gayle, look – a Last Day of Summer party.' I pointed to a poster for a ticketed event to be held on the August bank-holiday weekend. *Cocktails ... Live music ... Limited tickets still available!*

'Dress code: the French Riviera,' Gayle read. 'Hmm. The last time Craig and I went to the South of France it rained and we wore anoraks. I seem to remember he slipped and twisted his knee.'

'Do you think you'll come, Natalie?'

'What?' I was startled both by the question and the sudden quickening in my veins. 'Oh, hello, Lara.'

Presumably having emerged from the nearby exit turnstile, she had come to a halt rather close to us, near enough for me to catch the scent of chlorine on her skin. I had not seen her face uncovered before, or at such close range, and I experienced for the first time the kind of persuasive velvet-brown gaze that sells washing-up liquid and frozen peas, its blink designed not for the owner's physiological needs but to give the beholder a moment's relief.

'How are you?' I said, and – I couldn't help it – I felt a shiver of proprietorial pride.

'Exhausted.' Lara took an illustrative deep breath. 'I've just done fifty lengths.'

'Wow.' Remembering the measly six of my own first effort, I didn't need to pretend to be impressed by this.

A second blonde strolled up alongside her, possibly the friend I'd seen cradling her dog like a newborn. While not in the same league as Lara in appearance, she was certainly in the one above mine, her figure the right side of athletic, jawbone enviably sharp. The whites of her eyes were pink from the water, the irises glowing the pale blue that can look unearthly, even sinister, if the emotion is wrong.

'This is my friend Angie,' Lara said. 'We've been toasting ourselves all afternoon.'

'In both senses of the word,' Angie added, miming the raising of a wine glass, and I stopped myself voicing the hope that they'd done their swimming before drinking, given that alcohol was a contributory factor in at least twenty per cent of deaths by drowning.

Both women were in waffle robes, as if leaving a hotel spa for their guestrooms, which appeared to confirm my hunch about a residence on The Rise. Since it was a weekday in term time, I deduced that they had neither conventional jobs nor any requirement to be at home feeding children or supervising homework. In Lara's case, perhaps the head-turning teen broke away from practising poses in the mirror to put fish fingers in the oven for the little boy. More likely there was an au pair or a housekeeper – no, both, a whole staff of helpers.

I introduced Gayle, who gave a grudging smile, and at once Lara returned her attention to me. 'So you'll come to the party?' she said, and I noted the 'come' instead of 'go', as if the invitation were personal. 'I'm helping organize it,' she explained. 'You and Ed should definitely come. And Molly too, of course. We want a family vibe.'

I was flattered that she had remembered Ed's and Molly's names – and mine, for that matter. Perhaps it was the effects of exercise, perhaps the contrast with her tipsy friend, but she had a less capricious air about her today, and the sincerity of her invitation prompted an unusual honesty in my response. 'I'm not sure,' I said. 'I'd like to, but we don't come to the pool often, not as a family.'

'Why not?' Lara and her friend waited, confident that there was no problem I could propose that they couldn't solve on the spot. By my side, Gayle was restless, poised to move on. She didn't expect me to explain my family difficulties to members of a different tribe, especially not one so remote from our own. As if to reiterate our less upmarket credentials, Inky strained the lead to sniff a patch of half-dried urine at a nearby bin.

'It's Molly,' I said. 'She suffers from aquaphobia.'

'Aquaphobia? What – is that like hydrophobia?' It was Angie who spoke, her forehead crinkling only at the hairline, which pointed to Botox or some other desperate measure.

'Not quite. It's a fear of being in the water. She's still willing to drink the stuff, she just doesn't want to get into it.'

'But that's *terrible*.'

Lara's reaction was rather more contained. 'Oh, yes, you said before she didn't like the water. Is it really that bad, Natalie? An actual phobia?'

'It's pretty bad. But it could be worse. It could be severe allergies. Or agoraphobia would be more restrictive.' My brain held a league table of phobias, ranked not only in order of severity of risk to life but also of hardest to hide.

'So how does that work with swimming at school?' Angie asked.

'There *is* no swimming at her school,' I said. That was hard for them to understand: the independent schools their kids likely attended would have sports facilities galore, including an indoor pool. 'It's not compulsory at state secondary schools. In primary school, she had a medical exemption.'

'What about when you go to the beach?' Lara said, in an earnest tone. 'Is it the same in the sea?'

Sensing Gayle smoulder, I knew she had automatically interpreted this as some superior allusion to Mauritius or Antigua, exotic family idylls thrown off kilter by the inconvenience of a reluctant snorkeller in the family. And yet intuition told me that Lara was not completely ignorant of the hardships of other people. Her eyes were unusually expressive of empathy, expressive in fact of considerably more pain than I was currently feeling.

'It's the same, I'm afraid,' I said. 'To be honest, we don't go. We try to work around it, have different kinds of holidays.'

Angie continued to frown. 'But wouldn't it be better to tackle it head-on than avoid it like that?'

Gayle made a disapproving huffing noise just as Lara said, 'Poor you,' and placed a hand on my upper arm. Her touch was very gentle, the thumb moving in a faint, comforting caress, and I felt myself colour at the intimacy. 'And Ed, of course. That must be very difficult for both of you, very worrying.' She sighed, as if personally burdened, before withdrawing her hand and stepping from us. 'Anyway, we'll leave you to it. I'm sure you don't want to be waylaid like this when you're walking your dog. Isn't he adorable? So *bouclé*.'

Our parting left me with the absurd sensation that I'd received the healing touch of Mother Teresa.

As Gayle and I strode off, legs working far faster now (there was nothing like an encounter with richer, thinner women to urge you towards the pain barrier), I didn't have to wait long for her explosive verdict.

'Who do they think they are? "Tackle it head-on"! Like you haven't thought of that yourself. You're the girl's mother!'

'They meant well,' I said. 'It's hard for people to get to grips with Molly's situation when most kids love the water so much.'

Gayle changed tack. 'Seriously, though, she spoke as if she knew you really well. I can't bear that kind of overfamiliarity, can you?'

Seeing her scowl, I felt an unexpected flare of impatience. She had a tendency to condemn everything that failed to conform to her life view; Ed was the same, always so sure of his position. Normally I went along with them, today I thought, hang on, wasn't this a case of inverted snobbery? No more attractive than the conventional kind, at the end of the day. 'Well, we did chat at the lido on Sunday, so I suppose it's not *that* overfamiliar.'

'That explains how she knew Ed's and Molly's names.' She tutted. 'She was like the lady of the manor checking on her peasants. Your dog is *bouclé*! I mean, come on, why do they feel the need? No wonder the other Westbridge mums call them the Noblesse.'

I chuckled. 'That's a good one.' Westbridge was a more-expensive-than-most private school in Battersea with a liberal-arts bias, just the kind of school I would have expected the Channing children to attend. 'Every school gate has its alphas,' I added, 'even Rushbrook. How do you know all this, anyway?' (A ridiculous question: Gayle knew everything.)

'Are you kidding? Everyone knows *Lara*. She's our new local celeb. You know she helped get the pool reopened?'

'I gathered that, yes.'

'Apparently she was some sort of competitive swimmer before she was an actress, hence it being her pet project.'

'She's an actress?'

'Well, *was*,' Gayle said, with a faint sneer. 'Don't you remember, she was in that mermaid film in the early nineties? A kind of British *Splash*. She was still a teenager. And then she was in a soap briefly, plus those nauseating ads for some bacteria-fighting yoghurt.'

Not frozen peas, after all. I did some quick arithmetic. 'So she must be, what, early forties now? Not much younger than us.'

'Looks *a lot* younger, though,' Gayle said crossly. There'd been a stinging incident recently when her electrician had mistaken her older sister for her younger. 'Must be all that swimming. Fifty lengths? That's two and half kilometres and she didn't look remotely knackered. Life's not fair, is it?'

But I refused to admit defeat so easily. 'Come on, we'll be getting just as much exercise in the holidays when we start our regime. It'll be a fresh start. Oops, not by the picnic, Inky . . .'

Gayle watched me scoop Inky's poop as a pair of picnickers averted their eyes in disgust. 'Anyone would think you liked them,' she said. 'Lara and her friend.'

'Well, I see no reason to *dis*like them.'

'You don't?'

And for the second time in five minutes, I had cause to note my surprising change of position. After all, hadn't I been suitably snarky to Lara during our first conversation? At least until she'd said she liked me – *I think I'm going to get on very well with you, Natalie* (yes, I remembered the exact phrasing). Was that all it had taken to win me over? All the advice I gave Molly about beauty being only skin deep and the evils of vanity, and here I was in my mid-forties, responding to the fleeting favours of the pretty girls in the most predictable fashion imaginable.

Or maybe I was just keeping an open mind. Harnessing that new optimism.

'I don't know,' I told Gayle truthfully, and dropped the bag of dog poo into the nearby bin. 'I haven't decided yet.'

July 2003

Molly's was not an inexplicable problem: it had its known beginning. What we did not know, and what made it so difficult to manage, was how it would end. Whether or not it *would*.

It had begun when she was eighteen months old, with an incident in a toddlers' pool in a park in the Surrey town where I'd grown up and where my mother had remained after her divorce from my father.

Molly had been paddling happily, playing with her stack of plastic pots, filling and pouring and splashing. It was her favourite activity, the pool a perfect mid-calf depth, and when visiting Mum in good weather we came at least once a day. Seated at the edge with my feet in the water, aware of the deepening midday heat, I reached behind me into my duffel bag for my phone and saw that it was time for us to leave and return to the house for lunch. Tugging at the towel, rolled up tight and crammed into the bag, I paused, distracted, before adjusting the toggle and pulling it free.

When I next looked, the world had tipped. Molly was no longer standing but lying on her front, her left arm by her side, the right bent but too weak to lift her body on its own. Her head was twisted to the side and raised in a bid for air, ear and cheek exposed but nostrils submerged. The roar of adrenalin was as powerful as a jet engine. I leaped forward and scooped her up, clumsy but fast. 'Molly? Oh, God! What happened?'

In my arms her body was rigid and her face contorted with such terror it seemed to alter her identity and I stared for a second as if at a stranger's child. After a pulse-stopping delay, she opened her mouth and wailed.

It had an alien new sound to it, a tone of primal shock, almost like the first scream after birth.

'Is she all right?' A woman had appeared next to me, her own child in her arms, dark splashes of water on her clothes from having dashed across the pool to help.

'I think she's fine,' I said, pressing Molly to me, 'just a bit upset.' Blood churned in my head, made our voices remote and unreal. 'She's coughing. That must be a good thing?'

That was when the trembling began, huge, wild convulsions, as if her muscles had a life of their own, her flesh as hysterical as her voice.

'I wonder if you should get her checked out at A & E,' the woman said, 'just to be on the safe side. Who knows what bugs there are in this water?' The kind soul even offered to drive us, saying her car was right near the gate, but I knew I wouldn't be able to bear a chaperone and, crying my thanks through Molly's screams, tore the greater distance to my own car. I drove to the hospital barefoot, my pumps abandoned by the pool.

'Her face was only submerged for a few seconds,' I told the triage nurse, then the paediatrician, over the continuing wails.

'She's had a shock,' came the reassurance, 'but she's absolutely fine physically.'

I knew what Ed would ask first, was only grateful he didn't ask it in front of the hospital staff when he came to meet us, fear pinching his face and squeezing his voice. Or before Molly fell asleep, passing out in her car seat as we left the hospital grounds. 'Why weren't you watching her?'

'I was,' I said. 'I was right there, a foot away from her. I only turned away for a second.'

It was the sort of plea you might hear at a trial – or an inquest.

'So how did she come to be under the water?'

'I don't know. She must have lost her balance. Maybe she reached for one of the pots and fell sideways.'

'OK. So it was longer than a second.' From the driver's seat, he turned his eyes to me, then back to the road, as if to demonstrate the acceptable length of a break in concentration. 'I'm not having a go at you, Nat. I'm just trying to understand.'

'It was a couple of seconds,' I admitted. 'I glanced at my phone, then my bag's toggle got stuck so I couldn't get the towel out. Maybe four or five seconds.'

I couldn't tell him that three of those seconds I had spent immobilized, that the act of retrieving the towel, of plucking rugged fabric with damp fingertips, had caused a sensory memory that had torpedoed me. That a face I hadn't seen for at least three decades had sprung into my mind, so vivid, so three-dimensional, I'd thought it was real, that she was standing in front of me.

I couldn't tell him that it had felt like a haunting.

More than that: a warning.

6

Saturday, 4 July

Nineteen degrees. One degree warmer than the previous week and yet I could have sworn the water was five colder. As I slithered in up to my waist, the entire surface of me pimpled, even my ears. Then, nailing the crucial shoulder dip, I felt pure shock, rather as revival by CPR might be: cardiac arrest followed by the restoration of spontaneous blood circulation.

'It's about the same temperature as the Atlantic,' a passing swimmer told me, and his comradely tone implied either 'Aren't we lucky?' or 'Aren't we mad?'

Mad, I decided.

Predictably, I was alone, Gayle having insisted her fitness campaign begin strictly with the school holidays, Ed busy at the All Saints summer fair and Molly at tennis. Perhaps that was why I was experiencing the horrors of submersion so acutely: without her to monitor, I could concentrate on myself – and on the muscular low-hanging legs of a male lifeguard, in his raised seat, who, I noticed with a second, smaller, shock, could not have been out of his teens.

From the café terrace came the metallic clatter of cutlery on plate, the chime of coffee cup on saucer, the rise and fall of conversation. It seemed a heroic leap to make in a single week, from granola with Ed and his *Guardian* to solo cold-water swimmer, and I had a sudden image of myself springing to my feet at the table, vaulting the rail and crashing into the water fully clothed. The thought made me laugh at just the wrong moment and I took in a large mouthful of water.

'All right there?' In a trice, the lifeguard was down from his chair and at the water's edge. His reflexes were impressive, even if they had caused an embarrassing number of fellow swimmers to look over in concern.

'Fine, thank you,' I spluttered. 'I just swallowed some water.'

Resettled in his chair, he kept an eye on me, his red torpedo aid held benignly across his lap. Even when I swam into another zone, he glanced over regularly – I was one to watch. Still, I of all people was not about to fault him for his conscientiousness.

He really was remarkably good-looking – I could just picture the girls who'd be crowding the sundeck today, hoping to catch his eye. To think of all the young passions that would ignite on these terraces over the course of the summer, requited or otherwise – what a heroic thing Lara Channing had done if this were to become the meeting place for young people. A place of wholesome exercise and cleansing summer sun (provided they remembered sunscreen), better than some dreary shopping centre or, worse, a social media page and the ghastly, compulsive totting up of likes and shares.

Pausing mid-length to recover my breath, I saw that the café table Lara had occupied last weekend was in use this morning by a family I knew from Rushbrook. The mother, Jo, and I had worked hard to help Sam progress in spite of his ADHD and dyspraxia. In the sunlight, strands of her hair glinted silver and when she bent her head you could see a thick band of pale roots along the centre of her skull. Her body language spoke of defeat. Mothers were so senior now. Lara Channing was a rarity in more ways than one: she couldn't have been much older than twenty-five when she'd had her daughter.

I decided not to wave to Jo and draw attention to myself. It threw parents off balance to encounter a teacher in the wild, especially the more formal ones like me. To them, I belonged in the classroom, all humanity suppressed but for the parts useful to their children, of course.

That's what you think, I thought. In less than a week I would be off duty and not due back in the classroom for almost eight weeks. Fifty-five days. Life was too short to work out what that was in hours.

I managed ten painful lengths before calling it a day.

Tuesday, 7 July

Before Lara, I had no illusions as to how I was perceived by the people in my life. Middle-aged, middle income, *middling*. I was a primary-school teacher, a good citizen, the sort you'd want to witness your signature on a pass-port application, not enlist to get the party started. I was Old Elm Hill, a known quantity, part of the furniture.

Recently, I'd given myself a bit of a buffing by leaving Rushbrook, the local four-class entry state primary, to take a post at the well-regarded independent Elm Hill Prep, a move driven by the desire for a less chaotic working day rather than any political realignment. In environment alone, it was a serious elevation. Rushbrook had been built in the 1970s on the site of a former rubbish tip and sometimes, when the windows were opened in the summer term, I'd fancied I could catch a whiff of the original malodour rising from the foundations. In con-trast, Elm Hill Prep had begun as an Edwardian vicarage, every subsequent extension either faithful to the original period or conceived in bold contrast, and its parkside location was idyllic. In the whole of my first year there'd been only one less-than-fragrant incident: when the flor-ist was late in delivering the weekly bouquet for Reception and the previous week's lilies were slightly on the turn. By break, they'd been removed, the air freshened with citrus and lavender.

My year-four classroom was on the second floor. With its polished parquet and shining, smear-free window panes, it was just the sort of classroom in which *A Little Princess* might have found herself, the kind in which we would all wish our children to learn their les-sons. Most did not, of course, Molly included, what with the fees being five thousand pounds a term.

'And who can tell me what kinds of things were rationed?' I asked my class, that Tuesday morning, half of whom were restless as lunchtime approached and half enfeebled by the heat. It was the warmest day of the year so far, the air entering the open windows too soupy to give any relief. We were in danger of being gelatinized. Indeed Sophia, leaning against Theo, had lost control of her eyelids and fallen asleep. I thought of the clean cool water of the lido across the park and wished I could break my class out and take them there. 'I'll give you a clue,' I said. 'It was all the fun things.'

Now they began to call out.

'Toys!'

'I Phones!'

'Pokémon!'

'They didn't have mobile phones or computer games in the 1940s, did they? Think about what people like to eat and drink . . . Sophia?'

Her lids twitched, but I didn't have the heart to insist.

'Cakes!' Theo suggested.

'Good. Eggs and butter were rationed.'

'Chips!'

'Actually, potatoes weren't rationed here, so you could still have your chips, so long as you had the fat to fry them in.'

'Chocolate! Bread! Coffee!'

'Coffee wasn't actually rationed in Britain, but do you think it was always the nicest kind? Like the coffees your mums have in La Tasse or Carluccio's?'

'No, it tasted disgusting!'

'If they didn't have real coffee, they drank ersatz,' said Alfie Mellor, who, it was fair to assume, would one day appear on *University Challenge*, cutting in on starter questions with crisp, faultless answers.

'What's ersatz?' the others wanted to know, and my unprepared definition made me feel like an ersatz teacher.

I was saved by the scheduled knock at the door: a tour for prospective parents hoping for a chance place. These occurred considerably more frequently than the places came up, but Mrs Godwin had never been known to burn a bridge and was scrupulously gracious to all-comers. This morning, there were two couples. One comprised the familiar pairing of mother in her thirties at the peak of her ambitions and father in his forties at the peak of his earning power, each as eager to give a good impression as to gain one. The other, unexpectedly, was Lara Channing and her husband, Miles.

My energies stirred at once. 'We've got visitors, guys!' I sang and, though the children were taught to proceed with lessons as if uninterrupted, their eyes settled immediately on Lara, who wore a thigh-skimming black sundress with heeled sandals laced to the knee. Over her shoulders was draped a fringed canary-yellow shawl.

'Hello, Natalie,' she called to me, and the use of my Christian name caused the children to snicker and me to redden under my make-up. 'Sorry, I mean *Miss*. We know each other from the lido,' she told Mrs Godwin, as if confessing to a terrible indiscretion.

'We're great supporters of the lido here,' Mrs Godwin replied. 'The children did a sponsored silence for it, as I remember.'

'Which just happens to be my all-time favourite way to fundraise,' Lara said. 'I salute the genius who thought of *that*.'

Mrs Godwin allowed a rare public chuckle, causing the other mother to eye Lara with that mix of resentment and admiration that one-upped parents customarily extend to the one-upper.

As Mrs Godwin pointed out various features of the classroom layout, I took the opportunity to study Lara's husband. He was about my age, his face unremarkable in feature and colouring, at least from a distance, and his expression effortfully neutral. I guessed he was impatient to be done with this and get to the office, as most of the fathers I dealt with were. Likely he was one of those workaholic, socially disinterested husbands you often found with glamorous women; opposites on the colour wheel. He was to be commended for wearing a suit in this heat. I caught his eye and offered a sympathetic smile, but as I did so I thought I saw a flicker of query in his gaze, a flicker that caused an involuntary raising of my fingers to the right side of my forehead, masked though the skin was by concealer.

'Mrs Steele, please don't let us interrupt you,' Mrs Godwin told me, in the way she had of disguising an order as an apology. 'It sounded as if you were having a discussion about the Second World War, were you?'

'We were,' I agreed. 'I was just about to ask everyone what they might wear to the end-of-year party next week. The theme will be VE Day.' Not the Riviera, I wished I could add for Lara's benefit, and I had an involuntary image of myself arriving at her party in the kind of glamorous, structured dress I had never owned.

'Gosh, I don't hold out much hope for the catering,' she said, favouring a succession of pupils with an individual beam. Sophia, among the lucky ones, had sprung awake and begun slurping from her water bottle. A girl who liked to touch things she wasn't allowed to, she probably longed to finger the silky fringe of that yellow shawl.

'It's going to be rock cakes,' I said, warming up now and smiling directly at Lara.

'They're not *actually* rocks,' someone told her, and Alfie looked disgusted that such a statement should need to be made.

Miles Channing checked his watch. It was only when he slipped, phone in hand, behind another male adult, that I remembered the other couple were there and that I should spare them a little attention. If they hadn't already enquired, they'd be hoping the Channings' child was not in the same year group as their own because, if he was, it was a foregone conclusion as to who'd be offered any available place.

At the end of the school day, I dropped by Mrs Godwin's office. Originally the vicarage's drawing room, it had a beautiful bay with French windows to the grounds. I imagined the smaller pupils appearing at the glass, mouths agape, then fleeing from it at the first sign of a raised eyebrow. I knew, even within a year of employment, that I would never come to occupy this room.

'I was just wondering how the rest of the tour went this morning?' I said.

'Oh, it was fine. All very smooth.'

'It was a shame you didn't come by two minutes earlier. You would have caught Alfie Mellor using the word "ersatz".'

'Yes, that *would* have been impressive,' said Mrs Godwin, and we exchanged looks that concurred it was just as well he was precociously bright because his parents wouldn't be satisfied with anything less.

'Which year are their children in?' I asked.

'The Wilkinsons have twins for year two. They've moved back from the Far East unexpectedly and are in a bit of a panic. I've just come off the phone with Mrs Wilkinson, actually, and she has accepted the places.'

'They're lucky two came up at once.'

'Well, with Isabella moving out to Hampshire and Harry switching to City, they were in the right place at the right time.'

'What about the other couple? They've got a little boy, Everett, I think he's called.' Just as I had in the park, I felt a thrill at being able to claim prior acquaintanceship with the Channings, but told myself that at least this time I recognized the vanity of it. After all, it was self-awareness that separated us from the chimpanzees (and not, as Gayle claimed, Netflix). 'He's at Westbridge, I think.'

'That's right,' Mrs Godwin said, 'he's just finishing year three. That was why I brought them to see a year-four class.'

I was pleased by the coincidence: somehow I wouldn't have liked to know that Lara had toured the premises and I'd missed her. Odd that she hadn't mentioned her planned visit when I'd told her my place of work – then again, even boho mothers knew that, when it came to school selection, discretion was the better part of valour.

'I'm not sure they're serious about moving him,' Mrs Godwin said, 'which is just as well since we're full in year four for September. I did tell them that before they came.'

'I wonder why they're even considering it,' I said. 'Westbridge is just as oversubscribed as we are, isn't it?'

'Mr Channing is in insurance. Perhaps he wants something more traditional for his son.'

We exchanged another coded look. Neither of us had the spare hour needed to scratch the surface of what fathers might want for their sons or mothers for their daughters or any combination thereof. Suffice to say that what all parents wanted was to have a silk purse made out of a sow's ear, while at no time acknowledging responsibility for the sow's ear. Well, we did our best at EHP (school motto: *Semper excelsius* – always higher). We couldn't perform miracles, but we certainly couldn't be accused of not giving our cause the Blitz spirit.

'Where's Isabella moving to?' I asked. 'You said Hampshire?'

'Yes, it sounds like a delightful little place. Stock- or Stone-something, perhaps?'

'Not Stoneborough?' I felt a tingle of dread – troubling that it should start at the mere mention of the place, and *my* mention at that. 'How funny, my grandmother lives there. My mother too, actually. She moved down there a few years ago.'

The forwarding address was, of course, at Mrs Godwin's fingertips. 'Not Stoneborough, Stockbridge, that's right. On the river, I think they said.'

Behind her, light exploded through the glass and it took me a moment to understand the simple consequence of cloud sliding from the sun. Relief did that to you: it disconnected your brain. I wouldn't have been able to pick little Isabella out of a line-up, but it was unconscionable to me that anyone connected with EHP should have the opportunity to fall into conversation with someone in Stoneborough who might remember me.

'Sounds idyllic,' I said.

First at the lido, then in my classroom: she was like a word you've never heard before that people are suddenly saying everywhere you go, until pretty soon you forget there was ever a time when your vocabulary lacked it.

The next reference came the following evening from Sarah, surprisingly so, since she was housebound to all intents and purposes and therefore cut off from the local gossip – except for that which visitors like me shared. Actually, now I think about it, it was I who brought Lara up.

Having given Inky his lap around the park, I returned him to his home on the third floor and stayed for a cup of tea. Sarah's flat was exactly the same size and design as ours, but it never ceased to surprise me how much more light was gained by two storeys' elevation. Above the treeline, the sky was closer, almost touching distance, aglow that evening with July sun. After a run of hot, stagnant nights, there was at last enough breeze to disturb the foliage; we would sleep better tonight. Though muted, the TV was on in the corner, playing the unmistakable images of summer: white figures haring across green grass, rows of sunhatted spectators gasping as one. It was Wimbledon, rain had not stopped play, and therefore all must surely be well with the world.

'Seen any murders recently?' I asked Sarah, for her chair was right by the window, angled in such a way as to give her an unobstructed downward view into the loft bedroom of a thirties semi.

'No, but I've read plenty.' She gestured to the towering pile of crime thrillers that had been her saviour during her recuperation. Though she'd greyed noticeably during the last few weeks, and necessarily slowed physically, her spirit had remained indefatigable and I had nothing but admiration for her.

'Not in here, I hope?' I held up a copy of the local magazine *Elm Life*, which inevitably had a shot of the new lido on its cover, and settled on a footstool to leaf through. My fingers paused at a double-page spread. 'Lara Channing, who else?' I said.

'Indeed.' Sarah sighed. 'St Adjutor herself.'

I looked up, curious. 'St Adjutor? Who's that?'

'The patron saint of swimmers. A very minor saint.' Sarah eyed the magazine in my hands. 'More people have heard of *her*, I would guess.'

I checked the issue date: May. It must have been printed well before the opening of the lido. 'I'm starting to wonder if I'm the only person in Elm Hill not to have heard of her until the last couple of weeks.'

'Oh, don't worry, I didn't know her from Adam until I read this. Now I know she absolutely adores pralines dipped in white chocolate. Or is it white chocolate dipped in praline? One of the two.'

'I've met her a couple of times,' I said, studying the photo. 'There's no way a woman in *that* kind of shape is gorging on chocolates.'

'She must be re-launching her acting career,' Sarah said. 'Why else would she want her face all over the place like this?'

I thought about the children at Rushbrook, the yearbook produced by the year-six teachers as a farewell gift. Under 'Career Ambition' a troubling number had put 'To be a celebrity' or 'Get a million views on YouTube'.

'Gayle doesn't like her,' I said.

'Does she know her?'

'Neither of us does, not really. But I must admit I'm intrigued. It's easy to mock, but what she's achieved with the pool, it's pretty incredible.'

'I agree,' Sarah said. 'She's obviously a woman of great energy. I'd be very happy to have her hips – and I don't mean for the lack of cellulite.'

As we chatted about her physio exercises, my phone buzzed. 'Dinner's ready, I have to go. Would you like to join us? Or can I bring you up a plate?'

'No, thank you,' said Sarah. 'My sister's coming over with her granddaughter and they're bringing me a chopped salad, whatever that is.'

'A salad in which all of the ingredients are chopped?' I laughed. 'The sort of thing Lara Channing really eats, I'm guessing.'

Gayle and I wondered sometimes how it would work if everyone were allowed to ditch their own parents and adopt ones more to their taste (she made no bones about her willingness to jettison her own father in favour of Michael Palin). Sarah was the mother I wanted, though I was not so naïve as to misunderstand that, if she *were* the woman who'd raised me, then by now I'd find her kindness cloying, her equanimity provocative. Meanwhile the criticisms sent my way by the woman in Stoneborough might, from the lips of a neighbour, be considered bracing and entertaining.

'I've got another new student,' Ed announced, as we took our seats at the kitchen table. He had made spaghetti carbonara, a favourite of Molly's when she was little because of the way he served each portion with an egg yolk for you to stir in yourself. He'd forgotten that she'd recently come to consider this practice both childish and gross.

'Raw egg makes me heave,' she informed us, then, seeing my face, chanted a childhood rule: '*I know*. If someone's gone to the trouble of cooking for you, the least you can do is go to the trouble of eating it. Yeah, yeah.'

'Get on with it then,' I said. I was surprised, even slightly delighted, by my excellent mood.

Ed, also buoyant, returned to his news. 'Can you believe how quickly it's all happening? I haven't even started yet and I'm almost at the point of having to think about a waiting list.'

'Amazing,' I said, though it really wasn't. The ambitious zeal of the current generation of middle-class parents was well documented, Thatcher's children overinvolved in their own kids' lives to the point of dysfunction. Hypocritical though it might sound for Ed to be catering directly to it, he would, I knew, do all he could to help relieve the pressure on his students, not add to it.

'Who's the new one?' I asked, twirling sticky strings of pasta around my fork.

'A girl at Westbridge High. She's just finished year ten. Didn't do well enough in her end-of-year maths exam, apparently, and screwed up the statistics GCSE she took early. The parents want two hours every Saturday, starting this weekend, then twice a week once school breaks up. They want her back on track for GCSE year.'

'I'm sure they do'. I smiled at Molly's exaggerated grimace.

'Izzy says private tutors get, like, a thousand pounds an hour,' she said. 'They work on yachts.'

'If that's the case, then please tell Izzy she's welcome to act as my agent.' Ed chuckled. Excitement was causing him to talk with his mouth full, a crime no doubt clocked by Molly and stored away for when one of us next chided her for the same. 'Mind you, this one did offer to up my rate when I said I might not be able to do the hours she wanted. They live around here. The kid's got one of those American place-name names, Atlanta or Savannah or something.'

'Not Georgia?' I said. 'Georgia Channing?'

'That's it. How did you know?'

'The mother's the immoral blonde at the lido, remember? How funny. I was just talking about her with Sarah.' Professional discretion prevented me adding that Lara had been into Elm Hill Prep for a tour. 'I wonder how she heard about the tutoring.'

'From me. We got chatting at the summer fair last weekend.'

I was astonished. 'Lara Channing was at the All Saints fair? Why didn't you tell me?'

'Was I supposed to? She didn't call to book me until today.'

'Why was she at the fair, anyway?' I asked. 'Promoting the lido?'

Ed shrugged. 'Maybe she was just supporting her local school.'

'We should Google her,' I suggested. 'Find out all about your new client.'

'I don't see why. I haven't Googled any of the others,' he said.

In the end, I did it myself. I sat down and investigated Lara in exactly the prurient and painstaking fashion that twenty years ago would have roused the suspicions of the police but was today not only acceptable but encouraged.

She had been born Lara Markham in June 1973 and was forty-two. A competitive synchronized swimmer, she'd represented Great Britain in a number of events before missing trials for the Barcelona Olympics owing to illness. In 1992, at nineteen, she'd left the sport – and full-time education – to star in *Mermaid on Mulberry Street*, a role for which she'd been handpicked after the director had spotted her when watching a televised synchro event with his daughters. The film was a moderate success and, as it would transpire, represented a career pinnacle for Lara. Still in her twenties, she'd gone into semi-retirement when she'd married Miles Channing and started a family.

Since her fame predated the digital era, older images were limited, but there were clips from the mermaid movie, as well as the original theatrical trailer. Even allowing for the hair and make-up enthusiasms of that era, she was stunning, with those doe eyes and that erotic mouth. Her face was more familiar than I might have expected, given that I'd never seen the film, until I remembered the daughter in the picture on the Elm Hill website and in the lido's publicity material. Of course: the teenaged Lara looked like her daughter did now.

On Amazon, I scanned the customer reviews for *Mermaid on Mulberry Street* and found them at best lukewarm:

– Not a patch on *Splash*.
– Bring back Daryl Hannah, all is forgiven!
– OK family viewing, but not a classic . . .
– Someone should have given the girl some acting lessons – Lara Markham is embarrassingly bad!

I felt quite defensive on Lara's behalf and would have considered ordering the DVD in solidarity were it not extortionately priced at £16.99.

I wondered what she would say if she knew I was occupied in this way. She'd be flattered, perhaps, or validated. I snickered to myself at the unlikelihood of *her* researching *me* – or even being struck by the thought that she'd bumped into me rather a lot lately. To even things up I Googled myself: *Natalie Steele teacher.*

There was nothing much. My entry on the Elm Hill Prep website was the first of very few:

With almost twenty years' experience in primary education, Mrs Steele is our newest member of staff, teaching her first EHP year-four class this year.

Favourite subject: history.

Favourite EHP moment: 'Taking the boys and girls to the *Golden Hinde* and learning about Sir Francis Drake.'

An unflattering headshot accompanied this, my hair stripped of warmth, plenty of putty-coloured foundation on my face. As I've said, I always covered my skin for work. Disfigurements tended to distract pupils and distractions were frowned upon by parents.

It was Nathaniel Hawthorne, if I remembered correctly, who said about birthmarks, 'It may be the stain goes as deep as life itself.'

I sincerely hoped not.

7

To still the mind, focus on the physical.

In the bathroom mirror I inspect my birthmark as if for the first time. I can't pretend I don't know why it interests me afresh, why, after the four and a half decades I've lived it suddenly has new significance. The size of a dog's pawprint, it has browned with age from the livid raspberry of my childhood, when I would scrutinize it daily, judging it a disgusting flaw, an impediment to future happiness. As a teenager with an allowance, I learned to conceal it with make-up, a ritual that continued daily, on weekdays at least, right until these last transcendent weeks, when I've come to think of it as a mark of distinction, perhaps even grace.

Tonight is different. Tonight I think it's how they would identify me on the mortuary slab.

Georgia, I remember, and the memory of her damp, blanched face makes my body temperature drop by a degree.

'Nat?'

I jump, like a criminal, drop my hand from my face.

Ed is in the hallway, watching me from the shadows.

'You gave me a shock. What is it – is it Molly?'

'No.' Only his feet and legs are lit by the bathroom light spilling through the open door, his voice disembodied; the effect is eerie. 'I just wanted to say, if you won't talk to me about tonight, fine, I can hardly force you. But you do realize you'll have to talk to the police?'

In an instant my cheeks are aflame. 'What do you mean? The police won't want to speak to us.'

'I think they will. If I were them, I'd be very keen to know why the parents of a child with her medical history allowed her anywhere near a swimming pool.'

I swallow. 'The parents', he said, but what he means is 'the mother'. No matter how hard I've tried, no matter how controlled I've been, I've always been the sinner in this family.

'I've almost finished in here,' I say, keeping my voice steady, and I close the door on his shadow, stand with my back against it, facing the room.

My eyes land again on the dress. As I reach to scoop it from the floor, my senses are waylaid by memory: a white bedroom of filtered afternoon sun, palazzo doors meeting with a kiss, the scent of something rarified and intimate and sweet.

You will wear it, won't you? For me?

Handling the dress with fingertips only, as if the fabric is on fire, I drop the thing into the bin, trying but failing to ignore the smell of shame.

8

Thursday, 9 July, seven and a half weeks earlier

Somehow I was not as surprised as I might have been when, on the penultimate day of term, just as I had five minutes to myself, my mobile rang and it was her.

'Listen,' she said, 'I've found you a therapist.'

'Hello? Who is this?'

'It's Lara.' Of course, *silly*. 'So I've asked around and she's supposed to be the best.'

'The best?'

'You know, for the aquaphobia. I spoke to the therapist and she says she's treated it before and had great success.'

I struggled to find a clear response. It appeared that this near stranger had taken it upon herself to make medical investigations on behalf of my daughter, a girl she'd met for about five minutes. On the one hand it was intrusive, not to mention naïve that she should think Ed and I lacked the wherewithal to 'ask around' on our own; on the other, I was touched. Most people's good intentions began and ended with kindly incomprehension.

'That's very thoughtful of you, Lara, and I don't mean to sound ungrateful, but we really have tried everything already.'

'You haven't tried *her.*'

Indeed, when she gave the name of the therapist, I didn't recognize it. 'You're right, we haven't, but I'm guessing that's because she doesn't do NHS referrals and is too expensive, in which case we're not going to be able to see her now.'

'It's not as expensive as you'd think,' Lara said, though vaguely, and I remembered Ed's report of her having offered him a higher rate to meet her tutoring require-ments. 'Just promise you'll phone her. I'm determined to get Molly in the water,' she added.

Again, the audacity of it – and the generosity. I didn't ask how she'd got my mobile-phone number. Perhaps from the school office. They weren't supposed to release staff contact details but I had a feeling Lara would know how to get people to do things they weren't supposed to do.

I relayed the exchange to Ed.

'You mean she's the same one who's just signed up for tutoring? The woman I met at the summer fair?'

'Yes, she seems to be our new fairy godmother. Maybe she feels bad for having helped open a pool in our neigh-bourhood and making Molly's life a misery.' I remembered Molly at the lido that time, hunched against the wall, emotion locked behind her eyes, released from her tor-ture only when Lara entertained her with her chatter.

'But she can't feel personally responsible for the opening of a public swimming pool, can she? Only a complete megalomaniac could take that position.'

Ed smirked. 'Megalomaniac, fairy godmother: same thing.'

'Cynic,' I said, chuckling.

Summer 2003

Molly may have been fine physically after that shocking afternoon in July, but she was not otherwise. Water, from that day onwards, was the enemy. Bath time, which had previously delighted her, became so fraught I would dread it all day, prepare at length my strategy, my calm, only to abort the task the moment she felt liquid creep over her skin and began yelling to get out. Ed fitted a new, lower showerhead and we washed her in the lightest of sprinkles, careful not to allow water to fall on her face.

Subsequent expeditions to any swimming pool, large or small, indoor or out, raised hysteria as awful as the original. A paddling pool, even a bucket, provoked the same distress. She began to refuse to go near the duck pond in the park near our flat, screaming herself into a frenzy each time we tried to coax her towards it, digging her fingers into our flesh, both desperate for our protection and terrified we would not give it. I tried not to notice that she always reached for Ed first, tried not to think that she had good reason to trust her father over her mother. During these episodes she suffered nausea, palpitations, diarrhoea and, worst of all, hideous choking convulsions, though there was never any obstruction in her throat.

As her speech developed, so did her ability to describe her fear.

'What do you think the water will do?' I asked her once.

'It will swallow me,' she said, and a grotesque image spilled into my consciousness, an image of hands tearing at blonde hair, of desperate eyes still open under water. I purged it at once, like bile in the gullet.

Seeking advice online, we came upon the glass of water test, which involved turning a glass upside down and plunging it into a basin full of water. 'See, the air is still inside the glass,' I told Molly, though she could hardly bear to look, doing so only through splayed fingers. 'The same thing happens when you put your head under water. You see, it can't go inside you! The air prevents the water flowing into your nose.'

'So long as you don't tilt your head back,' Ed said.

'Ed!'

Molly tilted back her head and cried.

Swimming lessons, conducted by instructors experienced with nervous pupils, were, without exception, disastrous. However thoroughly we briefed the teacher, however specialized he or she claimed to be, it made no difference to the strength of Molly's aversion, the depth of her anguish. It was heartbreaking, over and over.

On good authority, we tried a lake instead of a pool: no sudden drop, no queuing or climbing required on exit. We tried to tempt her to the water's edge with a chocolate finger for each step taken. There would be a toy, we promised, if she just put her toes into the water. She became hysterical, straining against our grip to escape us and calling out that we were hurting her, which drew concerned approaches from bystanders. We concluded that we – like the swimming teachers – did not have the necessary expertise to tackle what must surely be a form of post-traumatic stress disorder: a psychologist would succeed where we were failing, an expert in childhood phobias.

That was when the word 'aquaphobia' entered our vocabulary, as did the necessary definition for explaining to others how it differed from hydrophobia. (Very occasionally, word leaked that poor Molly had rabies.)

And so to the years of therapists, so many I lost count. The process never varied: waiting for the referral to reach the top of the waiting list, waiting for the next appointment, waiting for advice about subconscious learning and empowerment through knowledge. The Archimedes Principle was discussed, the buoyancy laws we'd demonstrated so unsuccessfully in the bathroom basin explained over and over. Hippocrates came up (so, once, did *Jaws*). We were told that instead of following our teacher's instinct patiently to detail time and again the technical reasons why a situation was safe, we were simply to say to her, 'You know the facts.' And yet the facts included statistics that made Molly's fear so understandable in the first place – and stirred our own, frankly. People *did* drown, thousands a year worldwide, about four hundred annually in the UK; and for those who could not swim, the risk was considerably greater, making our daughter's condition a catch-22.

'What do we do?' I asked Ed.

'We get on with it,' he said. 'With the rest of life.'

Not all of it, however: for one thing, there would be no second child until we'd fixed the first, until I'd stopped blaming myself, stopped declaring myself unfit. But how could I stop when I knew that Ed had not? Even the least educated or experienced of parents knew you didn't take your eye off a toddler in water, however shallow; a teacher of young children and possessor of an up-to-date first-aid qualification had no excuse. There were times when I allowed myself to be overwhelmed by the fear that he might believe complacency had caused me to reach too sluggishly for that towel or even – on ghastly nights when I couldn't sleep – that he thought I'd toyed with risk for the perverse thrill of it.

'Poor thinking', the therapists called this sort of thing: feelings of helplessness on the parents' part that served no one, least of all the child.

Finally, there came a new approach. 'This is a childhood fear that has not been outgrown – yet,' said the last therapist. 'I suggest you let nature take its course. Pools can be avoided easily enough, can't they?'

Well, yes, we'd managed by then to avoid them for years. Moving to Elm Hill when Molly was three or so, we'd been relieved, if not attracted, by the absence of a duck pond or lake in our new park. That crumbling old lido was *never* going to reopen.

We agreed to take a year off from therapy and revisit on Molly's thirteenth birthday. ('Not literally on her birthday,' Ed said. 'That'd be no treat.')

'So long as we crack this before she reaches the age of independence, we'll be fine,' the therapist said. 'After that, she's less likely to want to communicate with you about it.'

Which brought us to the present day. We hadn't cracked it, we'd reached the age of independence, and as to whether she still wanted to communicate with us, well, she was a teenager now and the odds were not exactly in our favour.

Friday, 10 July

'A *hypnotherapist?*' Gayle said, looking up from her salmon in watercress sauce with a short-tempered frown. She said it exactly as you might *exorcist* or *warlock*.

'A hypnotherapist,' I confirmed. The sight of a rogue flake of fish inside her open mouth reminded me that the light was much too bright and I rose to dim the spots. I should have lit candles, created an ambience, but our dinners with Craig and Gayle were so easy and frequent that we often didn't shop specially for them or make any particular preparations. At least we could speak freely, Molly being at Izzy's for a sleepover and Gayle and Craig's two girls having long since established social lives of their own.

'She's called Bryony Foster. I checked her out online.' It was only right, I had felt, that I should pay Lara the respect of taking her recommendation seriously, if for no other reason than that when our paths next crossed I wanted to be able to give an informed reason for my failure to make the appointment.

It had come as no surprise that the therapist was based in Harley Street. That she was a hypnotherapist, well, maybe that hadn't come so left of field either: what I'd seen so far of Lara Channing did not suggest a rigid adherence to convention. But there were stranger therapies in the world and it was certainly worth sounding out the notion on parenting forums. There, I discovered that Bryony Foster was considered the best in her field.

– I heard she's a total genius. We tried for Lucie's bedwetting but there was a six-month waitlist!
– Keep trying! We got a cancellation, so lucky! Charlie's anger issues have been completely cured.

What Molly had, however, was nothing like bedwetting or anger issues. It was a chronic and debilitating phobia. When I'd phoned the previous morning, Ms Foster's receptionist had made no mention of a waiting list. 'Oh, yes, Mrs Channing contacted us about Molly a few days ago. We'd be pleased to help. We have a cancellation next Tuesday at five? Does that give you enough time to get here after school?'

It would be a scramble, but only that first week: we'd be more flexible once Molly broke up for the summer on the Friday. I was surprised to find myself already thinking in terms of multiple visits. 'How much does it cost?'

'The standard fee for a private session is a hundred and ninety pounds.'

'And how many sessions do you think she'll need?'

'It's impossible to say without meeting Molly, but the average is five or six.'

Quick mental arithmetic told me that even at the full price the sessions would be more or less the same as the fees paid by the Channings for Georgia's twice-weekly tutoring.

'I'll take it,' I said.

Now, salmon finished or abandoned (it wasn't my finest culinary hour), Gayle and Craig looked to Ed for a rational explanation of so lunatic a leap of faith.

'We've tried everything else.' He shrugged. 'There's only alternative therapies left.'

'So you have to pay for it?' Gayle asked. 'Hypnotherapy's not available on the NHS?'

'No, but it's acknowledged by them as a treatment for phobias, addictions, a lot of stuff.'

But Gayle was not convinced. 'What would *she* know about phobias, anyway?'

Craig exploded with laughter. 'Listen to that *she*. Always a sign that you've got it in for someone.'

Gayle shot him the kind of fiercely contemptuous look that was more common than you'd think between spouses of two decades' standing. 'Seriously, Nat, you have no personal connection with this family, how can you trust their recommendation?'

This was getting unduly obstructive, almost as if Gayle were hoping Lara's therapist would fail like all the others. That Molly would never be cured. 'We have no personal connection with anyone we go to for help,' I said mildly, 'and referrals by medical professionals have so far been one hundred per cent unsuccessful. As Ed says, we exhausted mainstream options long ago, and time's running out. This could be our last real chance.' Just saying this caused a twinge of anxiety, and I knew instinctively that it had been right to take the appointment. 'Besides, we do have a connection now. Starting from tomorrow, Ed is the Channings' daughter's new maths tutor.'

'Ah,' Gayle said, somehow both pleased and displeased by this information. 'I get it. You scratch my back and I'll scratch yours.'

'Yes,' Ed said. 'Though I'm hoping no spinal injuries will be sustained in either activity.'

At the mention of tutoring, we'd arrived at the well-trodden subject of escape routes from the System, of teaching having become a minority pursuit, most of our time spent writing up notes in one form or another for some phantom authority who would never read them.

Gayle drank her Oyster Bay with the gusto of the institutionalized. 'Is it *really* too much to ask that I be allowed to prepare a lesson, teach it, and then start preparing the next?'

'I think we'd all like that,' I said, and was met with the now-familiar humouring nods of those who did daily battle with a grisly crew of between thirty and forty pupils while I swanned about with my selective intake of twenty-four. I felt selfish relief that Ed had made the first step towards bridging the divide.

Evidently Craig was thinking the same thing. 'So you're joining the dark side as well now,' he said to Ed. 'Never thought I'd see the day. *Et tu, Brute* and all that.'

'You should consider it yourself,' I told him. 'The demand for private tutors has never been higher.'

'I don't know. I've heard a lot of scare stories,' said Gayle. 'One on one, it makes you very vulnerable.'

'I wouldn't risk it, personally,' Craig agreed, and we all nodded, downcast. In my eagerness I'd forgotten that two years ago he had been investigated following a complaint made by a male pupil about his relationship with the boy's on-off girlfriend, a classmate. Rumours of teacher-pupil fraternization were fairly routine. Every year, there would be at least one girl at All Saints who eschewed her peers in favour of a teacher her father's age (Ed, with his allegedly Delon-esque bone structure, had been the object of his share of crushes) and the issue was often escalated unnecessarily, thanks to parents drawing fire before listening to a word of evidence.

What had been less routine in Craig's case was the parents making a complaint to the police. Eventually, it had been dismissed and the accuser suspended, but it had been a frightening experience for Craig and his colleagues.

'Under-fourteens will come with a parent,' I said. 'We'll use the living room as a waiting room.'

'Fat lot of good that does anyone,' Gayle said. 'Parents never have a clue what's going on, even under their own noses.'

There was a brief silence as each of us wondered what we might not be noticing under ours.

'Kids have got us over a barrel,' Craig said. 'There'll come a time when we're not allowed to make eye contact with the buggers.'

'The answer is robots,' Gayle said. 'TeachBots. I'm going to apply for a patent.'

I began to stack the plates. How many times had the four of us had this conversation? Friendships were built on this, I supposed, on the comfortable familiarity of a shared script. Perhaps it was the completion of my first year on 'the dark side', as Craig put it, but I felt detached from the collective sensibility, even liberated.

'Anyway, the downside to all this is I'll be working through the summer while you lot are free to malinger,' Ed said.

'One of us already is,' I said from the counter, where I unboxed and quartered a readymade apricot tart. 'I didn't want to rub it in, though, so I haven't displayed the twenty-four thank-you cards I received this week.' One from every single child in the class, mostly hand-crafted: the rich were different indeed. 'But I know you'll appreciate the Fortnum & Mason chocolates we're having with coffee. I've got kilos of them.'

'So how did you spend your first day, Nat?' Craig asked.

'Toasting at the lido mostly.' Hearing the echo of Lara and her friend, I wondered if Gayle had too. I added dollops of crème fraîche to the tart and began passing the plates to the others. 'You know what my ambition is this summer? To forget that I'm a teacher – who cares what kind? I know, I know!' I raised my voice above their cries. 'I wouldn't be "malingering" at home if I wasn't one. I'd be chained to a desk in town somewhere with a week's leave if I was lucky. But I'm still going to try. I'm going to live this summer like . . . like a civilian.'

There was brief silence, then Craig and Gayle broke into laughter, raising their wine glasses to me and crying, 'To Nat, the civilian!'

Only Ed looked perturbed, even a little fearful. 'Good luck with that, Nat,' he said.

9

Saturday, 11 July

If Lara traded on one brand of persuasive charm, her daughter Georgia, I discovered, was the agent of quite another. I'd like to say I happened to be at home for her first session with Ed, but the truth was I deliberately returned from errands in good time to be there.

When I arrived, they were in his study. ('Study' was perhaps overstating the definition of a zone that had previously been a cloakroom. All it needed was bars across the tiny square window and a slop pot in the corner and it would have been an authentic cell.) The door was ajar and I could see on the small desk a stack of sample GCSE papers, along with the stapled assessment Ed had prepared. Over this a blonde head was bent, long strands veiling the details of her face. She was a dainty girl, I could tell that much, and graceful: the way she drew up an ankle and tucked it under her, as if her limbs were made of more pliable materials than the rest of ours, spoke not only of good genes but also of a decade's worth of dance or gym classes – or perhaps synchro, her mother's sport.

After the session, they came into the living room, where I was reading a novel and Molly socializing online with friends who lived so close by she could virtually have conducted the conversation from her bedroom window. Ed made the introductions and Georgia regarded us with well-mannered ease. We were all standing.

'Hello,' I said very brightly. 'I've met your mother, but not you, I think.' It was unconvincing, the notion that I might not remember her, and I hastened on: 'Would you mind passing on our thanks for her recommendation?'

As Georgia widened her eyes I noted that the irises were paler and more golden than Lara's. I knew from the photograph, of course, that she was a pretty girl, but what the image had not conveyed was the frankness of her appeal, the lack of embellishment. She was devoid not only of make-up and other adornments, but also of the twirling and flicking of hair, the twisting of ear studs, common in adolescent girls. Her clothes appeared to have been selected if not for camouflage then for comfort, light cotton garments that skimmed the sharp symmetry of her hips and elbows and collarbones. Not so like Lara then, after all, with her tousled up-dos and fringed shawls and kohl-smudged gazes.

'If you just say that, she'll know what it means,' I added. I didn't want to be more explicit about the hypnotherapy in front of Molly.

'Sure.' She gave an elegant half-shrug. 'I like your top,' she said, and I was about to thank her when I realized she was addressing Molly. She liked Molly's high ponytail, as well; in fact, now her attention was on Molly and not me she was far more forthcoming. Her voice was standard posh girl, with an endearingly earnest quality. 'Don't you sometimes wish you had a younger sister so you could do her hair for her? I do. Like my mum used to do mine.'

I imagined Lara and her sitting in front of the mirror brushing that spun-gold hair, mother and daughter Rapunzels who could never be lonely while they had each other.

'My mum thinks it's vain to spend hours on your hair,' Molly told her. This was a new habit: to present opinion that might not be entirely generous-spirited as mine, not hers. Whereas in the past she'd have looked to me for reassurance in the presence of an affecting new acquaintance like Georgia, lately she'd become dismissive, keen to disassociate herself from me. It was classic stuff, just another signifier of growing independence, but that didn't mean I had to like it.

'You can probably tell that just by looking at me,' I joked.

'I think spending a *little bit* of time on your hair is acceptable,' Georgia said, glancing politely from Molly to me. 'It's social grooming, isn't it? Primates do it. It's not just about hygiene, it's about bonding and communication. It's not like we're trying to look like some Disney princess.'

Goodness, had she read my mind about Rapunzel? My hand sought the corner of the sofa, anchoring me.

Georgia's presence was starting to cause a strange uncertainty in me, making me tongue-tied, a little soft-kneed, and the trigger seemed to be her unselfconscious beauty. After all these years, might I have got it wrong? Might being pretty be important, after all? As the thought developed, I felt a terrible plunging sensation: since I was feeling this with Georgia when I had not with Lara, who was as beautiful as her daughter, if not more so, did that mean my issue was not with beauty but with youth? I must be experiencing the terrible midlife realization they say awaits us all, that the departure of youth is not some temporary wheeze, like when you have flu and look a decade older in the bathroom mirror, but is permanent, gone and never coming back. And every day that passes takes you further away from when you had it, every day that passes carries you *closer to the end*. Like Gayle and Jo, with her stripe of white roots, I was far closer to Sarah and her worn-out joints than I was to Georgia and her elastic, peak-condition anatomy.

How horrendous: a midlife crisis right there in my own living room. Curious though I'd been to meet Lara's daughter, I was grateful when she left, frankly.

'Do you think she's one of those teenagers with a totally secret other life?' I asked Ed later, when I'd recovered from my turn. 'You know, that whole cliché? She seems all sweet and simple on the surface but in reality has a career in underage porn and a crack habit?'

'I actually think she's the real deal,' said Ed. 'A genuinely nice kid.'

'Then maybe it's a case of role reversal. The parents are free-spirited so she plays it by the book. Is she bright? She seems it. I bet she doesn't even need extra tuition.'

'I'll have to mark her assessment,' Ed said, 'but I'm guessing she needs it no more or less than most of them. But you know how it is, they infect each other – even the hippie ones.' He meant mothers. Mothers spread infection. FOMO, they called it: fear of missing out. They saw another mother pushing ahead and they thought they ought to push ahead too, the inevitable result being that everyone remained the same as everyone else, just in a new, more expensive way. A way that placed children under greater strain – particularly, I'd observed, girls.

Once, I'd left school early during term time to go with Molly to see a psychotherapist at the Maudsley Hospital. Arriving back in Elm Hill, I'd taken her to La Tasse on the high street for a hot chocolate. All around us women chattered about themselves – even the staff in the place comprised opinionated females – and I'd had a sudden sense of being in a piece of science fiction, a world in which men had been eliminated from society.

'Well, they pretty much have, haven't they?' Gayle said when I told her about it later. 'In Elm Hill, anyway.'

I laughed, amused and a little smug, because I had no reason to doubt that my own place in the matriarchy was assured.

At least, not until Georgia Channing came along.

Mrs Bryony Foster, HYP, Dip Hyp, GQHP, and various other qualifications of the sort I'd grown wary over the years of accepting as evidence of anything much, greeted me with the calm, inclusive air I recognized from Mrs Godwin and other successful negotiators of the modern middle-class family. Even the environment resembled Elm Hill Prep, with its restored period features and wittily contrasting soft furnishings, presumably selected to remind paying customers of their own homes.

'Are you coming in too, Mrs Steele?' she asked.

'Well, yes.' I hesitated. 'Or am I not supposed to?' It had not occurred to me that Molly should attend the hypnotherapy session without me.

'I'm happy with whichever you decide.' She glanced at Molly with just a trace of significance. 'It can sometimes make older children self-conscious to have a parent there. Molly might feel more relaxed if she's not observed.'

'I'd like to go in on my own, Mum,' Molly said.

'Really?' She had a purposeful expression that I didn't think I'd seen in previous times, though it was possible she was simply a better actor now that she was older. Whole days, perhaps weeks, of my life had been spent debating with Ed whether or not our daughter 'really' wanted to get better, so fiercely, so enduringly, did she fight the prospect of going near water. (Another fear birthed in those lightless, insomniac nights: did her continued suffering express some subconscious need to punish me?) We agreed that she did, but that time and again the phobia proved too powerful, the evil twin that perpetually triumphed.

'Okay,' I said, and that was that. How tall and solid she was as she walked from me into the consulting room, the opposite of a waif like Georgia Channing; from behind, from a distance, you could be forgiven for mistaking her for an adult.

I waited with a copy of a health and fitness glossy, listening for the screams that told of unnatural goings-on, of confirmation that I had made a terrible mistake in letting her go into a room with a hypnotherapist, in coming here, in taking Lara's advice in the first place. Gayle was right, what did *she* know about phobias? Her self-confidence was practically sociopathic, her own off-spring demonstrably flawless. And hadn't she said the recommendation had come from 'asking around'? Around whom, exactly? Doubtless a circle of other privileged numpties with new-age leanings, women like Angie, who walked the streets in waffle robes and booked Reiki sessions for their dogs.

I imagined Bryony's voice on the other side of the door, chanting in Molly's ear: *Ignore your mother, she let you down very badly* . . . What would emerge from Molly in return? She'd been too young to retain conscious memory of the original incident, all previous experts had agreed on that, but were they about to be overruled? This was a regressive therapy, after all.

Then, inevitably, almost as if those maternal concerns had assembled expressly to conceal the thought: *What if it were me in there?* If experiences you genuinely couldn't remember were extractable in this way, what about those you deliberately sought to suppress?

Conveniently, I would require no answer of myself on this score for Bryony's door was opening and Molly came strolling out. She looked undamaged, even cheerful.

'How was it?' I asked, noticing she held a cup of water and wondering if it had been used in the therapy.

'It's only been half an hour, Mum.' She sipped the water.

'It went very well,' Bryony said, joining us. 'Molly will tell you about it herself, but I'm confident we're going to be able to make progress together.' When Molly excused herself to visit the bathroom, she added, 'I gather you have a new local pool. My advice is that you don't take her there again until she suggests it herself.'

I was heartened by the use of 'until' when she could have opted for the less committal 'unless'. Paying, rebooking, I recognized old feelings, the foremost being gratitude that the burden of worry was being shouldered by someone better qualified than me. Was this, then, no different from the others? A necessary attempt at a cure rather than a faithful one?

As always, the only true belief that mattered was Molly's.

'So was it like falling asleep?' I asked her, as we walked towards Oxford Circus for the bus home.

'It was more like feeling sleepy,' she said.

'What kind of thing did she say?'

'Stuff.'

(Stuff: the noun-sibling of 'Whatever'. 'We'll assume you're more willing to elaborate in your English essays,' Ed would say.)

'Are there any exercises to do?'

'Not really.'

'And you're sure you're happy to go back?'

'Yeah.'

It was a while since I'd been in the West End during rush-hour and, though there was movement and action in every direction, the clamour was less than I remembered. Black cabs moved with an almost sinister noiselessness and there was a marked absence of conversation since nearly everyone we passed walked with his or her head bowed, attention riveted to a phone screen. I was struck by how young the faces were – some looked only a few years older than Molly – with their smooth foreheads and richly pigmented hair. I wanted to urge them to look up and appreciate the world while they had attention to spare. Enjoy it! Discuss it! Then, all at once, I had a flare of the same fear I'd felt with Georgia, the sensation of hurtling away from my prime and towards death. I felt almost dizzy.

It was the sun, I decided, surfacing. In the suburbs it consoled, here it punished, oppressed. I saw that Molly had shaken me off and was walking ahead as if alone. About to cross a one-way street, she too was looking at the screen of her phone, oblivious to those silent taxis.

'*Molly!*' I called in warning and she turned, cross with me for having fallen behind, cross with me for catching up. 'Careful of the traffic,' I said, falling into step again, slightly breathless.

'I'm not a child,' she protested.

'People of all ages can get run over.'

Just like people of all ages can drown.

And the way she reacted, with a scowl of near revulsion, made me wonder if I'd said it out loud.

Saturday, 18 July

Not quite the early birds we'd aimed to be, Gayle and I met at eleven thirty on the first Saturday morning of the state-school holidays, some three hours after aqua-aerobics had finished. A veteran of four previous dips, I was not as melodramatic as she was in my assessment of the temperature.

'Did you put a couple of tons of ice cubes in here before we arrived?' she called to the lifeguard, as she inched along the edge, arms and shoulders still exposed, a method that I'd kindly pointed out only prolonged the agony.

'It'll warm up by August,' he told us. He was the same good-looking one who'd approached me before, thinking me in difficulties, though I saw no reason to relate that humiliation to Gayle.

'That's no use to us now, is it?' Her manner was flirtatious, and seeing the boy's polite lack of understanding made me feel pity for her, for both of us.

I was not the only one who'd put on weight over the long months of winter and spring, and we made heavy weather of the ten lengths we asked of ourselves. As we broke the surface and clambered out, I tried not to make associations with large, possibly injured, marine mammals. Sitting on our towels with coffee from the snack bar, both virtuous and miserable because we'd denied ourselves a flapjack to go with it, we had our backs to an excitable gaggle of teenagers on the edge of the sundeck. Into a sudden lull came the voice of the lifeguard we'd spoken to and, turning, I saw that he was issuing stern advice of some sort to the group. 'No more, all right? I don't want to see that kind of thing here again.'

One of the boys, about sixteen and with the narrow waist and muscular development of a trained swimmer, glanced about to see who might have heard and caught my eye briefly before returning to his cohorts. The way he disregarded me was familiar to me from other encounters with young people who did not know me as a teacher or as the mother of a friend: just a forty-something woman of limited or no relevance.

The lifeguard retreated, his face flushing, a reaction to the confrontation, I assumed, until I saw Georgia Channing hurrying towards him. She moved with a silent and arresting grace, rather like a sprite, and he couldn't take his eyes off her.

'Hi, Matt!' she sang, then, glancing over her shoulder, 'Oh, hi, Natalie!' Reaching the noisy group, she came to a halt, smiling hello. Without discussion, the kids gathered her into their heart and rearranged themselves, as if her presence had been required before they could properly settle.

'Isn't that the Channing girl?' Gayle said.

'It is. I met her the other day.'

'She's quite the queen bee, isn't she?'

Though this echoed precisely my own prejudices before I'd met her, I protested, 'She's actually very sweet. Not what you'd think at all.'

'Really? I don't believe that for a moment. She'll be a member of the Noblesse in the making.' Gayle made no attempt to disguise her dislike. It appeared that, on the matter of the Channings, she had made up her mind in advance.

'Oh, Gayle.'

'You said that exactly like you say "Oh, Ed",' she said, laughing.

'How do I say "Oh, Ed"?'

'You know, fond but dismissive. As if he's a lost cause.'

'That's not true,' I said.

'It is! Not that I'm one to talk. It's a miracle I haven't murdered Craig – he's always so *negative*.'

Not knowing quite where to start with those remarks, I took the path of least resistance and said nothing.

On our way out, we happened to catch the eye of the young lifeguard, back in his chair, and I asked, curious, 'What were they up to, that group over there?'

He followed my gaze to the sundeck. 'They play these stupid breath-holding games. I've had to tell them about it before.'

'What – you mean swimming under water?'

'Or just ducking under for as long as they can. Some of it's swim-team stuff. We used to do it at my club – the coaches encouraged it to build lung capacity. But now we know it can cause shallow-water blackout.'

'Sounds dangerous,' I said.

'It is. That's why I'm here.'

In spite of his elevated position, he spoke to us with the deference of a young man trained to respect his elders, and whereas in the past I would have appreciated the courtesy for the rarity it was, this time it was somehow dismaying, coming as it did so soon after the younger boy's indifference.

'What's the longest someone can go?' Gayle asked. 'I don't think I could hold my breath for longer than thirty seconds.'

'My record was almost three minutes.' If he was proud, it was only in a dubious, self-knowing way. 'That's about the limit without hyperventilating first. You have to bring your pulse down to do it for any real length of time. You know some German free-diver just did twenty-two minutes?'

'Twenty-two minutes under water without breathing? I don't believe that for a moment,' Gayle said briskly.

'It's true,' he said. And he almost added 'Miss', I could tell. Though I didn't recognize him as a former pupil of mine or Ed's, somehow he seemed to know we were teachers without needing to ask.

'We're old,' I said to Gayle, as we were propelled through the turnstile. I had never seen the park so bucolic: the trees' foliage was full, thick as wigs, the nettles temptingly velvet-soft, lethally chest-high. A suburban jungle. 'I don't know why I'm suddenly so aware of it, but I am.'

'Baring all in public will do that to you,' Gayle said. 'But if it means remembering to breathe in and out at the correct intervals then I'm very happy to be old.'

A sudden outburst of excitement followed us through the turnstile and I knew without looking back that it was Georgia's group.

10

Unsurprisingly, Molly had made no request to return to the lido since our brief excursion together in June. When we walked past the main gates of the park together at the start of the holidays, I marvelled aloud at the trail heading towards it, its pilgrims' shoulders heavy with swimming kit, supermarket carrier bags full of picnic lunch: 'It's like the path to the cathedral of Santiago de Compostela.'

'Huh?'

'You know, in Spain. It's a really famous pilgrimage.'

'It's just a pool,' Molly said and her words, emotionless and hollow, made me shiver slightly. There not yet having been a second session with Bryony Foster, it was far too early to discuss progress and I was certainly not going to tempt Fate by voicing expectations. In any case, there were plenty of places for Molly to be besides the lido. As the daughter of teachers, she had no assumptions of her school holiday being idle. The first part would include a week of tennis, a stack of French worksheets (a holiday staple after it had been discovered that my year fours at Elm Hill Prep were as advanced as her year-eight class) and, naturally, extra maths. Later, in August, there would be a holiday with us in the New Forest and a week on her own in Stoneborough with my mother and grandmother.

Needless to say, she objected to every last bit of it. 'Can't you just leave me alone to do what I like? Can't I just go wild, like you used to in the olden days?'

'I never went wild,' Ed said, and then, when we accepted this without argument. 'No need to protest *quite* so passionately, girls!'

'We know *you* were a model citizen from birth,' Molly drawled. Sometimes the adult-sounding intonation caught me unawares and I would startle, scrutinize her features, check she was still our child. 'But Mum was naughty, wasn't she?'

'Oh, yes, your summer of sin,' Ed said, smirking at me. 'You were about Molly's age, weren't you?'

'I think I was a bit younger,' I said vaguely, though I knew very well I'd been exactly the age she was now. My ancient unease, usually suppressed, had prickled close to the surface lately. I didn't like where this conversation was headed.

'You were so lucky to be *free*,' Molly proclaimed.

'I was unsupervised,' I corrected her, 'and that's not a good thing. I didn't see my mum and dad for a month. I felt insecure, like no one would care if I got into trouble. Once I was back home again, I was fine.' Was it only me who heard the rampant self-justification in this summary?

Molly was watching me. She knew even less than Ed did about that 'summer of sin' and it was as easy for her to dismiss it as it was to profess a desire to emulate it. 'You hung out with Mean Mel, didn't you?'

'That's right.' I couldn't remember whether Mel had been awarded the sobriquet at the time or merely acquired it in the retelling, but she'd earned it all right, just as I had Nasty Nat.

'What kind of trouble did you get into?' she pressed.

'I told you before: shoplifting, smoking . . .'

'Note that it put her off both activities for life,' Ed interjected.

'What else?'

Vigilant now, my mind sifted the minor crimes. 'We played chicken with the traffic – *that* was stupid. There was one kid who very nearly got run over and the driver threatened to call the police, which gave us all a scare. And once we broke into a building site, climbed the scaffolding and dared each other to jump down on to a big mound of sand. It must have been twenty or thirty feet. We were very lucky we didn't break our ankles.'

'That was trespassing, by the way,' Ed said. He liked the learning to be quite clear. 'They could have got into trouble with the authorities even if they didn't kill themselves through sheer idiocy.'

'Yeah, right,' said Molly. Talk of death did not put her off. For someone afraid of the bathtub, she was ghoulish in her love of other brands of misadventure. 'So what were you *meant* to be doing?'

I paused before admitting, 'The adults thought we'd gone to the pond in the woods to swim. That's where we went most days.'

There was a catch in my voice – to speak of the pond was to have the empty spaces in me fill with anxiety sharp as hunger – and judging by Ed's quick look, he had heard it. Of course he would think I was being careful not to insist on how much fun it was to go swimming with your friends and blurt out my wish that Molly could enjoy it too, though I was not. (In any case, the pond had had dark water, water you couldn't see through, with a soft, muddy bed that your toes couldn't rely on, and the expert in me knew that dark water was a whole other potential fear, more closely related to agoraphobia than aquaphobia.)

'That was when you hid all the boys' clothes, right?' Molly said. 'Even their trunks.'

I forgot now why I'd once shared that particular detail – in warning, presumably, or in one of my talks about the developing body and respecting others' privacy. 'Only one boy at a time,' I said, smiling both for her benefit and in the hope that it might trick my mind into subduing the agitation. 'I'd hold him down and Mel would pull the trunks off. He'd have to beg, borrow or steal to get them back.'

As a half-repellent nostalgia settled on me, I surprised myself by chuckling. For all the insecurities I'd experienced that summer, for all my shame and dread about the way it had ended, I retained a clear memory of laughing, and especially when torturing boys, of laughing so hard my whole chest ached. I could hear Mel's voice, deepening with giggles as she swore at me to sit harder on our victims. I don't think I had sworn before that summer.

'Did the boys cry?' Molly asked.

'Once or twice, if they couldn't find their clothes.'

'This is starting to sound like my stag night,' Ed said.

'More like *Lord of the Flies*,' Molly said, earning an approving look from Ed for having begun the reading list for year nine. 'I think that was really horrible, Mum. Why did you do it?'

'Because they teased us,' I said truthfully. Somehow she was extracting more information than I normally gave, but this was not the dangerous part, I reminded myself. This was not so different from climbing scaffolding and stealing cigarettes. 'They teased Mel about her turned-up nose and me about my birthmark. They called us names.'

'What names?'

'Snout-nose and Pock-face. Also the Ugly Sisters. One boy called me Two-face, that's a character in *Batman* who has acid thrown in his face. I remember I'd never heard that one before.' I'd learned that you never forgot hurtful nicknames, from however long ago; I hoped Molly had none to remember.

'Maybe what you did was fair, then.' She had an air of respectful impartiality, like a coroner. Perhaps it had developed to balance the irrational energy of her phobia or perhaps it was simply her father in her.

Ed and I often discussed whether or not our parents would even have noticed if we'd had a phobia like Molly's, whether we would simply have hidden it. After all, it wasn't so many generations ago that to have learned to swim was the exception to the rule, not the other way around. We always ended up drawing the same conclusion: even if we hadn't concealed it, they wouldn't have noticed. Because, back then, stuff got overlooked, which had done our generation a great disservice.

On the other hand, well . . . it had done us a bit of a favour, too.

In my case, certainly.

Wednesday, 22 July

It was only when Georgia Channing was next in our flat that I thought again of the lifeguard's talk of shallow-water blackout – I'd developed a memory for the names of disorders and had no trouble recalling it – and I discreetly read up on it while she and Ed worked. In short, it was when a swimmer passed out under water as a result of a lack of oxygen to the brain, sometimes, as the lifeguard had warned, after having purposely engaged in breath-holding exercises. There being no warning signs and a very limited time frame for possible resuscitation, it frequently proved fatal. SWB victims were often strong swimmers in competitive squads, exactly the sort to push themselves too far, to challenge one another. It occurred more often in males than in females.

Though Georgia had not been involved, I thought I might have a quiet word with her when she was finished, ideally out of earshot of Molly. She might be able to use her influence to caution her male friends against such stunts.

However, when the time came she declined my offer of refreshment and issued one of her own: 'My mum said to say you should come for lunch on Sunday, if you're free.'

'That's very kind of her. I'm sure we'd love to,' I told her. 'Where do you live?'

'On The Rise. Our house is called La Madrague.'

I restrained myself from crying out, I *knew* it would be The Rise. I *knew* it would be a house that had a name and not a number – let alone, like ours, a letter.

Behind me, Molly had emerged from her bedroom and I saw Georgia send her a look of ironic sympathy. She asked her if she wanted to walk to the high street together.

'Go, darling,' I urged. 'You said you needed a new protractor.'

Molly shot me a poisonous look.

'That's hilarious,' Georgia said. 'I would have thought you'd have, like, a ton of maths equipment in this house.'

'These things get lost,' Ed said.

'No way. It's so super-tidy here,' Georgia said, eyeing the immaculate piles of papers and mugs on coasters on the coffee table before sending another sympathetic glance Molly's way. 'You could win an award or something.'

'I know, I'm not even kidding,' Molly said. 'I don't need a protractor anyway. But I do need a lip balm.'

'Hey, I'll show you the one I just bought from Elm Trader,' Georgia said. 'It's guava and lychee.'

Lip balm was practically a currency in its own right for this generation. Accounts of olden-days-style scrimping and saving for a single roll-on gloss having been met in the past with condescension, I didn't offer one now.

Since Molly was there, I had no opportunity to raise the issue of breath-holding games, though I admit it's possible that, excited by the invitation – the two invitations – I might not have remembered even if she'd been absent. Instead, I shared my findings with Ed when the girls had left.

'Shallow-water blackout? I don't think we need worry about that,' he said, and here came the expression I'd grown used to seeing in such discussions: exaggeratedly co-operative, not a million miles from patronizing. 'She's not going to drown on dry land, is she?'

'Not Molly,' I said, 'the other kids. People Georgia knows. You know what the pack mentality's like. They urge each other on.'

'Don't get neurotic about it, Nat. They've all got parents of their own.' He wasn't normally so explicit, but he'd had more than his fill of pack mentalities in term time, perhaps. Remembering Gayle's comment about my dismissiveness, I made a point of agreeing.

As we lapsed into silence, I found myself recalling Molly's comment about *Lord of the Flies*, and for the second time in recent days I thought with a shudder of my old friend Mel.

Of the sound of our laughter over still, dark water.

Stoneborough, August 1985

My grandparents' village of Stoneborough had a population of 490. It had woods, a recreation ground, and a newsagent's with stale chocolate and uncertain opening hours. The bus service to Southampton operated twice a day except on Sundays, when it didn't operate at all.

It was a backwater if ever there was one: my father's words, not mine. The first time we visited after I'd heard the term, I'd actually expected to find streets of rivers, like in the flooded villages I'd glimpsed on the television news and later understood to be in Bangladesh. Then I realized he meant it was boring, which made it the perfect place to send a girl who'd received a warning from her school about disruptive behaviour and whose parents had finally twigged that discussing a child as if she were hard of hearing might be a contributing factor to those behavioural troubles. Warring parents who wanted her out of the way so they could war more freely. Sort out a few things on their own, as they put it.

'It's only for a month,' Mum told me. 'You'll make friends.'

'I don't want friends,' I said.

'Everyone wants friends, Nat.'

And I remember the hug she gave me – close and long and a little desperate, as if I were an evacuee whose destination was a question of pot luck and who might never return. She didn't ever hug me like that again – I wouldn't allow her to because when I came back I was shadowy and uncommunicative, a person with secrets to guard.

'Apparently, at this time of year you can swim in the pond in the woods,' she said. 'All the kids do, Gran says.'

Automatically I touched my right eyebrow. I didn't like swimming, at least not with other children. The water would slick back my long fringe and expose my horrible birthmark.

'Will it be safe to swim in that pond?' my father queried, and I knew he wasn't really concerned but was just looking to find fault in any idea that happened to be my mother's.

'Oh, for God's sake, go with her and be a lifeguard, if you're that worried,' Mum snapped, and I watched the fury flare and catch as he searched for the last word.

'On your head be it,' he said.

I met Mel on my second day in the village. It was raining and I was bored and angry; I thought I might throw one of my grandparents' heavy glass photo frames through a window just to make something happen. When

I watched television I had the hot, combustible feeling that it – or I – might explode into a thousand pieces.

'There's a nice girl about your age in the house on the corner,' Gran said. 'Cheryl's youngest. Why don't you go and introduce yourself?'

Mel was a year older than me. She was stout and defensive-looking, with very shiny dark-red hair and a left incisor that had grown over the next tooth along. Her most marked feature, however, was the central one, her nose: upturned and flattened, it was as if she'd been slammed face first into a door. It made me think of Boxer dogs, but I soon learned the local kids preferred an even crueller likeness – to a pig.

'What's that red smudge on your face?' she asked me.

'A birthmark.'

'It's really big.'

'Thanks for the newsflash. So, what's there to do around here?'

'Nothing,' Mel said. 'It's fucking boring.'

The thrill I felt at the swearword was the first pleasurable sensation I'd experienced in days.

'We normally go to the pond, but it's been raining.'

'I heard about the pond,' I said. 'You're allowed to swim in it, are you?'

She scoffed. 'Who cares if you're *allowed*? We'll go tomorrow, see who's there. I'll call on you in the morning.'

Not a proposal, but a plan.

Not a friend, but a partner in crime.

11

Monday, 31 August, 3 a.m.

Exhaustion drags at my eyelids, seals them shut, and at once an unsettling psychedelia of images begins to flicker: black figures silhouetted on night-grey brick; stricken faces caught in the neon-green glow of an emergency exit sign; blue light from the ambulances swirling in the street. Paramedics in fluorescent jackets questioning weeping parents; a police officer with a humid sheen of sweat on his face, standing with Liam and Matt, making notes, looking our way.

How am I going to explain the missing minutes?

My eyes snap open, all my reflexes suspended until Molly is found to be where she should be, in her bed, sound asleep. Her breathing is audible, as if she's consciously controlling its rhythm, as if she's not disposing of last night's events so much as reliving them. How many hundreds of times – thousands – have I seen her sleeping face? But only this time do I feel I know her dreams. I wish I could divert from her to me all the terror of the fall, leave her with only the sweet relief of rescue.

I cross the room and sit on the side of her bed, taking her hand and laying it on mine, a touch without pressure. Her cheeks bear stains of mascara and I have the urge to wipe them clean, restore her innocence, but I resist. I don't want to wake her. Her rest has never been more precious.

My arms ache from more than tiredness and I know there must be marks under my sleeves.

Back in my seat, I spare a glance for Ed, wary of more insinuations about misdeeds, and am brought up short. I have rarely seen him look so ill, as if he was the one pulled from the water. His skin gleams grey, as it does after he's eaten shellfish.

We're bruised and broken, all three of us.

'Go to bed if you like,' I tell him, and whatever he thinks of me, whatever he suspects, the tenderness in my voice is not manufactured. 'I'll stay up. One of us should keep our strength for tomorrow.' Strength for the fallout, for word from the hospital. 'I'll phone for news in the morning,' I add, but when I look at him again his eyes have hardened. 'What?'

'You know what.' His voice is cold. 'As far as I'm concerned, I don't care if I never see that couple again.'

Couple, not family: is he conscious of the distinction? 'Oh, Ed. Whatever you think of the Channings, they don't deserve this. No one does.'

He accepts this – not to do so would be to have no soul.

'But I think you're right,' I say. 'We should stop seeing them. All of us, all of them. Nothing matters now except Molly.'

Ed frowns, suspecting a bluff, even an outright untruth. It is clear that he no longer trusts my word – when did that happen? Was it when I stopped caring about his?

'Easier said than done,' he says. 'Is it even going to be our call? How do we know what happened to Georgia won't turn them crazy?'

He doesn't know the half of it, but the half is enough to bring emotion to his voice as he adds, 'If she . . . if she doesn't make it, who is Lara going to blame then, Nat?'

And the honest answer is, I don't know. I can't speak for Lara Channing. I've seen her more than anyone else these last weeks: we've become very close very quickly.

And yet I haven't got a clue who she is.

I 2

Though right about the street, I'd been wrong about the house. I'd assumed the Channings were in one of the detached Edwardian villas that formed Elm Hill's millionaires' row, but in fact they were in one of the only pair of thirties houses on the southern side of the park. Not suburban semis, you understand, but the curved white kind you see in Agatha Christie films, with a glamorous top-floor sun terrace from which one guest might send another to his death. *Evil on The Rise*, perhaps. I said this to Ed as we lingered by the gate, adding that I hoped it would not be one of our family who got murdered today.

'If it is, let it be me,' he said glumly, for the expedition combined two behaviours of which he was most deeply suspicious: spontaneity, which he associated with exposure to the risk of humiliation, and social climbing, which he thought best confined to TV sitcom. It hadn't helped that I'd Googled 'La Madrague' before we left and found it was the same name as Brigitte Bardot's house in Saint-Tropez.

'Who does she think she is?' he said.

'She thinks she's your new client,' I replied.

'A *madrague* is a trap, isn't it? For catching tuna.'

'Very sinister,' I said, but mildly because, like Gayle, he had every right to expect me to mock such pretensions as readily as he did. That was what people like us did about people like them.

The truth was, however, that I appeared to be breaking rank; I appeared to be prepared to make an exception. As we stood in front of the stainless-steel nameplate on the pristine white wall directly opposite the steps to the lido, I struggled to recall a time in recent years when I'd felt more exhilarated. Whatever this lunch invitation was – and I was quite certain it was enviable, it was exclusive, it was an opportunity to embrace my declared summer's mission to 'live' – it was not the usual way we spent our Sundays.

'Come on,' I said to Ed and Molly, and I stepped on to the footpath of grey pebbles that ran alongside flower-beds filled with the stiff, hardy shrubs of a windswept coastline. In the drive there was an old Jag and a new Mini Cooper, both parked askew as if by the drunk or distracted, all the more breathtaking for the presence a couple of feet away of one of those sculptures of implausibly self-balancing stones. As we knocked at the door, eyes screwed to the violent collision of midday sun with pure white walls, wild laughter rained down on us from the terrace.

Then the door opened and Miles Channing stood before us. He was clothed in black linen, the colour contriving – or accentuating – a blank, depthless quality in his dark eyes. 'Hello?' His voice was polite but uninviting, his mind obviously on some other interrupted activity.

I smiled at him, noting at closer quarters the brand of corporate ex-pat surface glamour I'd seen at a distance in my classroom. Though he had not yet smiled, I knew that when he did it would be to reveal artificially brightened American teeth. 'Miles, isn't it? Hello again, I'm not sure if you remember me? Natalie Steele.'

'Oh, yes.' He regarded me a little bleakly, not acknowledging the other two at all. In any case, I knew that both would be looking away, appalled by our host's making no attempt to conceal the fact that he had no idea who we were.

Counter-intuitively I felt emboldened, keen to show I had the necessary social aplomb to meet this challenge. 'Georgia invited us for lunch . . . But perhaps we got the wrong day? It wouldn't be the first time we'd got muddled up.' It *would*, I sensed Ed thinking; it was unheard of. 'Should we make a graceful retreat and never speak of it again?' I added wryly.

'Nat,' Ed began, but he had no need to go on because suddenly there was Lara at Miles's shoulder, dressed in something silky and midnight blue, admonishing her husband while welcoming us with open arms. 'Miles, it's the Steeles! What *are* you doing barring them entry like this? You're making them feel like Jehovah's Witnesses – or, worse, those people who sell boxes of organic chard.'

I laughed. Even Ed managed a smile. Molly downgraded her position from shamed-to-the-point-of-suicidal to standard mortified. Miles stepped aside, apologizing in smooth, neutral tones. 'Please, come in. I was just on my way to get more wine . . .'

As he withdrew down a ground-floor corridor, Lara embraced us in turn and directed us to a circular staircase to her left. 'Sorry about Miles,' she said unapologetically, 'but he's not quite in the land of the living yet. Heavy night last night, but nothing the hair of a pack of wolves won't solve. Right, we're on the terrace, as you can probably hear. Follow me!'

Such was the immediate dazzle of shiny surfaces, I could not at first register anything but her bare feet as I tailed them up the stairs, the faint grey dusting on her smooth soles. By the first-floor landing, however, I had recovered sufficiently to admire the enclosed spiral of polished wood, the wrought-iron banisters and marble treads; the glimpses through half-open bedroom doors of gleaming walnut headboards and grass-deep rugs, of pale paintings with sinuous, unknowable subjects. At the top we reached a spectacular set of double doors with a design depicting Diana hunting, and these Lara shouldered apart to lead the way into a vast room.

Entering, we Steeles halted, as if caught in searchlights: the sun streamed in from both flanks, causing us to shield our eyes. Adjusting, I saw that we were in an extraordinarily beautiful sitting room, the colour scheme black, white and petrol blue. Of the details, my eyes picked out a central conical light fitting, a large lacquered coffee table heaped with books, a pair of fan-shaped velvet-covered armchairs, a fireplace of chrome or nickel or something else shiny. A perfect balance of materials that reflected and fabrics that absorbed. Beyond, the open-plan kitchen was a showroom of soot-black appliances, marble worktops and sparkling glassware.

'Lara, this is wonderful!' I exclaimed, and such were the acoustics of the enormous room that my voice filled it, crashing crudely back at me.

'Don't shout, Mum,' Molly hissed, and Lara eased her pain by putting an arm around her waist to guide her deeper into the space.

Now that she was standing still, I could see that the blue garment she was wearing was a silk kaftan, with silver embroidery at the neck and cuffs: it looked like something from a rooftop party in Marrakech in the sixties.

'So what do you think, Molly?' she asked, both hands on Molly's waist as if she were about to spin her.

'It's cool how the living room is up here at the top,' Molly said shyly.

'I'm so glad you like it.' Lara beamed. 'You know, some people say they couldn't possibly live in an upside-down house.'

Only people who have no idea how it feels not to have *any* house, I thought, but barely critically because I already knew that to mix successfully with the Channings was to overlook their carelessness of their own privilege. I already knew that I was going to be able to make this compromise. Ed, who had yet to speak, I was not so sure of.

As Lara called for drinks – I imagined a half-naked manservant appearing through a hidden door – I became aware of music, a voice I didn't recognize: an old recording of a woman singing of love and grief, the kind of music that made you abandon all earthly protest and surrender to the melancholy of the human condition. (Hard to believe I hadn't had any alcohol yet.) Then, at a sudden shout of laughter from the terrace, I felt nerves: I'd expected just our two families. This was something more.

'It's not remotely formal,' Lara said, guessing my thoughts. 'Just a little Sunday gathering of the godless.'

'Mum! How do you know they're not perfectly godly and just came from church?' Georgia stepped forward from the kitchen to greet us, a jug of something pink in her hand. She was dressed in denim cut-offs and a cheesecloth blouse similar to one my mother had worn in the seventies and therefore, presumably, prized vintage. Her hair was pinned from her face, her skin flawless, a fabric fresh from the bolt. I knew Molly would be raising a hand to the crop of spots on her chin, regretting perhaps her decision to wear a sundress, though to my eye she had never looked prettier.

'Oh, bugger, you're not happy-clappies?' Lara said. 'Have I offended you?' She spoke in the tone of one who can no longer remember a time when she was not forgiven her trespasses.

'It's all right, we're not churchgoers,' Ed said, with the slightly wary formality that told me he, for one, had not forgotten the professional relationship between our hosts and us.

'Pleased to hear it,' Miles said, appearing beside us with armfuls of wine bottles. They must have a cellar, I thought. His mien was quite altered now, relaxed and personable and ready to entertain – or, at least, be entertained. I had a sense that those unguarded moments at the door were exceptional, a glimpse we might never be given again.

'We're having Negronis,' Lara said, and she reached for two cocktail glasses, positioning them for her daughter to pour from the jug. 'Interested?'

Ed and I were not cocktail aficionados. This one tasted like pure gin, its effect instant and burning. Pink lemonade was produced for Molly. The same glasses were in use for the children's drinks as the adults' and I couldn't help noticing how easy it might be for one to be mistaken for the other.

'Right, come and meet the gang . . .' Lara ushered us towards the open terrace doors. 'Angie and Stephen are here. Ange is dying to see you again, Natalie.'

Given that we'd met only once and for five minutes, this was an extravagant claim and I thought momentarily of Gayle's remark about overfamiliarity.

Though the sitting room was larger than the entire square footage of our flat, a full-width swathe of the top floor had been sacrificed to the sun terrace. Broad enough to seat a dozen people, it was an exotically dressed room in its own right, with a sofa, a hanging chair and several other lounging options. The floor was scattered with kilims and there were potted bays, hydrangeas and tropical plants I couldn't name. Neither could I tell if the entrancing scent of vanilla and freesias was coming from the greenery or from one of the guests.

Angie drew the eye first, prone as she was on a steel spider's web of a sun lounger and dressed in blood-orange Capri pants and a revealing silk vest. Those unsettling pale eyes were safely hidden by sunglasses and my attention was drawn instead to her slightly downturned smile, which lent her the sardonic air of an Austen wit. Her limbs, however, were pure twenty-first century: sharp and slender and conspicuously exercised to the point of looking as if the fluids had been drained from them.

Her husband, Stephen, was one of those heavy-set men with a bashed-up face whose youth had likely been misspent on the rugby field. He was gung-ho in his handling of their two teenage children, one of whom, Josh, I recognized as the boy from Georgia's lido group; he eyed me with polite blankness, clearly not remembering me. The girl, a classmate of Georgia's, was named Eve and had a fitting self-consciousness. As quick to colour as she was to please, she was in Georgia's thrall, I saw; acolyte rather than deputy. To my delight, the group accepted Molly willingly and immediately disappeared.

The other guests were a gay couple in their late thirties, Douglas and Andrew, owners of the adjoining house, who sat hip to hip on the hanging chair. One had eyes the vivid green of a budgerigar and a jutting bony nose, the other smoother, more forgettable features.

'Come and check out the view, Natalie,' Stephen said, seeing me hover. 'Don't look so scared – I'm not going to push you off.'

'I should hope not.' Remembering my melodramatic thoughts on arrival, I joined him at the railing and exclaimed in pleasure. In all my years in the area I had never had the privilege of such a view: the low-slung structure of the lido in the foreground – we were not quite high enough to see the water, but close enough to hear the squeals – and, beyond, the green mounds and folds of the park, then the brick-brown parallel lines of the nineteenth-century homes off the high street, predictably dubbed The Toast-rack. Hidden from sight at the outer edge, on the site of the former municipal dump, was Rushbrook Primary, the employer that had brought Ed and me to the area years ago. It had never seemed so remote from me as it did now. Feeling a surge of elation, I lowered myself on to a pouffe patterned with the face of Frida Kahlo.

'This is amazing,' I said, to the neighbours in the hanging chair. 'You must have the same terrace next door.'

'Same size, but Lara's is nicer,' Douglas said, adding, 'Bitch.'

'Don't listen to a word those two say,' Lara said sweetly. 'We only invite them to these things because we feel we have to. It's either that or risk having them call the police to complain of a disturbance.'

As both men hooted, I could see Ed eyeing them as exotic creatures, imagining they must be in musical theatre, and I wanted to laugh when they gave their professions as anaesthetist and solicitor.

Further small-talk revealed that Angie and Stephen had followed Lara and Miles to Elm Hill from Battersea, where all offspring continued to attend Westbridge. They referred to the Channings as pioneers, as if no one had set foot in the postcode before, and to Lara as a Glenda Jackson figure on account of her campaigning zeal (I could imagine Gayle's response to *that*). 'The lido was a big draw,' Angie explained, 'because of Josh's swimming. He trains with his club down in Surrey, but it's good to have somewhere so close for him to go every day. We bought the house before it was public knowledge that the pool was reopening, but Lara had tipped us off.'

'Insider trading – is that allowed in property?' Andrew asked.

'Who cares what's *allowed*?' Lara said, and the phrasing reminded me of Mel, whose unwelcome cameo I dismissed from my mind's eye at once.

Upright now in her web, Angie began listing the many training sessions and expeditions required for Josh's swim team and complaining about 'bloody diving trips' to the Caribbean with the school, information that pre-dictably offended Ed's sense of social equality.

'Compulsory, are they?' he mocked. 'The trips to the Caribbean? I wasn't aware there was a GCSE in scuba diving.'

'Not GCSEs, just the various PADI certifications,' Angie said, smartly choosing not to acknowledge the sarcasm. I tried to transmit to Ed that if he didn't lighten up soon we'd be queuing to push him over that railing. At least he was draining his Negroni: that could only help.

'Does Lara still act?' I asked Douglas and Andrew.

'Twenty-four hours a day, darling,' Douglas said, 'but not professionally any more.' He called out to interrupt the tête-à-tête our hostess was having with Stephen: 'What d'you call yourself these days, La? A roving ambassador for the aquatic arts? No, that's to do with fish, probably. A humanitarian?'

'I have many hats,' 'La' said, and her hand went to her head as if expecting to find one there. Eyes wide with surprise, she forked startlingly long plum-coloured fin-gernails through sun-fired hair.

'Not as many as you have pairs of shoes,' Douglas drawled, which of course drew everyone's attention to Lara's feet, bare, fine-boned, presumably highly flexible after her years of synchronized swimming; I wondered if anyone else was imagining them as I was, emerging from the water with the upper arches stretched flat and the toes pointed skywards.

The voice drifting from inside was a new one, both soulful and charged, over what sounded like the trombone. 'Who is this singing?' I asked Angie.

'Bessie Smith,' said Georgia, who had reappeared for waitressing duties. I couldn't imagine many other fifteen-year-olds knowing that.

'Not the same Bessie of Yorkshire pudding fame?' Douglas led another gale of laughter and below, in the street, a pair of passing faces turned in surprise.

I wondered what the temperature was up here in the golden glare of the sun; it felt like several degrees above that at ground level.

'Can we get Molly to help with drinks?' I offered, even though Ed and I did not approve of children serving alcohol. 'Or can I?'

'No, no,' Lara said. 'Georgia likes doing it. And Marthe is here somewhere. Talking of which, we *will* eat soon, I haven't forgotten . . .'

So vague was this promise that it was a surprise half an hour later when a lunch of roast chicken and summer salads was served by a cheerful soul I gathered to be Everett's nanny, though the boy himself was at a friend's for the day. The teens joined us for food, clustered on a rug as if at a picnic, Molly in a straw hat borrowed from the Channings that made me think of Lucy Honeychurch in *A Room with a View*. It jolted me to see her like that, as a stranger might.

Lara had squeezed next to Ed on a rocking loveseat. 'How did you and Natalie meet?' she asked him. 'I'm dying to know. Was it at *teacher training*?' This she enunciated comically, as if it were some vaguely rude foreign term, which set off more cackling from Douglas and Andrew, and caused Miles and Stephen, who'd been talking together, to fall silent. As Ed set aside his plate to reply, Molly lowered the brim of her hat in horror.

'Actually, we were undergraduates,' he began.

'Beware a story that starts with those words,' Andrew said, but Lara shushed him and urged Ed to continue.

I held my breath slightly. My husband was a chronicler rather than a raconteur, not one to let a good story get in the way of the facts. I hoped he would at least be brief.

'We met at a house party. We were the only sober ones there. The whole thing had been taken over by this crazy fast set –'

'"Fast set"? Was it the nineteen twenties, then?' Angie cut in, giggling.

'Sounds marvellous,' Lara said.

'I'm afraid it wasn't our scene at all,' Ed said. 'You could say we bonded over our condemnation.'

'Stop, Dad,' Molly pleaded, and Eve placed a consoling hand on her shoulder.

'Condemnation?' Stephen said, in his bold, bombastic way. 'That's a bit strong, what were they doing? Speedballing?'

'I don't know what that is,' Ed said, 'but I guess it was standard student debauchery.'

Two things struck me: one, he sounded a little pomp-ous; two, this must be how I normally spoke too.

'Oh, wow, louche behaviour,' Lara said, curling her legs against Ed and enjoying herself immensely. 'I hope today isn't bringing back bad memories for you both. So you got together at this student bacchanal, did you? Who made the first move?'

I decided to wrap this up. 'To cut a long story short, some guy insulted me and Ed shot him down and rescued me.' But the crude finality of my tone didn't deter anyone: they clamoured to know both the nature of the rude remark and just how Ed had responded. I drained my glass. 'He asked me what was wrong with my face and Ed told him to shut up. He said why should he shut up, to give him one good reason, and that was when Ed quoted Abraham Lincoln.'

Molly groaned and placed her palms over her face. Georgia and Eve giggled. The three made a picturesque tableau.

'Abraham Lincoln?' Angie's brows were raised so high they were visible above the top of her sunglasses. 'This is getting surreal.'

'What was the quote?' Lara demanded, fingers pawing Ed's arm. 'I *love* a quote.'

Ed cleared his throat, though thankfully did not attempt an accent: "''Tis better to be silent and be thought a fool than to speak and remove all doubt.'''

'Ooh, I like that,' Lara said. 'I'm going to use it myself at the next opportunity. Girls, could you get that into a philosophy paper or something?'

Georgia and Eve exchanged pitying looks. It was reassuring to see that even Lara suffered the condescension of her youngers.

'I don't understand,' said Douglas. 'What did he mean about your face, Natalie? It looks perfectly all right to me.'

'And he *is* the only one of us who's a medical doctor,' Angie pointed out, chuckling.

'It's my birthmark,' I said. 'It was hot at this party and my make-up must have melted. I'm like the Phantom of the Opera under my foundation.'

'You're not, Mum,' Molly protested.

'She's exaggerating,' Ed confirmed.

'Well, I am a bit.' Looking up, I saw that Stephen was watching with an interest that was faintly cruel. I had the sense that he might be one of those people drawn to others' frailties.

Through all of this Miles had been silent. My eye had strayed to him often during the afternoon; though not loud or insistent in his speech like Stephen, he had the power to draw your gaze and hold it. Compared to the rest of us, who were animated or agitated or drunkenly unsteady, he sat quite composed, swivelling his left ankle sporadically as if easing an ache, an old injury perhaps. A question about his job had drawn an indescribably dull answer that confirmed my snap judgement that what he brought to the table was material in nature. The Channings were, I assessed, the classic Daddy's rich/Momma's good-looking union, she the prize, he the winner. Cordial though he was (that blank welcome notwithstanding), he lacked Lara's ability to lubricate the dry spells in a conversation and, with her by his side doing the talking, had had no reason to develop the skill.

As the conversation moved on, I escaped to the bathroom – an assemblage of black marble and stainless steel that might have graced the suite of a transatlantic liner – where I studied myself in the mirror. I could see at the edges of my make-up a rare drunken flush; the skin at my neckline and on my bare arms burned hot too. Had Ed and I really just shared that story? I had a terrifying and pleasurable feeling that when I re-emerged I might say anything.

Passing back through the sitting room, I lingered by a wall of art, mostly full-colour photographs of swimming pools. There was the famous one of Faye Dunaway the morning after the Oscars, newspapers scattered at her feet, and another of two blonde women lying by a pool, hazy purple mountains in the background.

'Slim Aarons.' Lara had appeared by my side, close enough for me to feel the heat of her skin, though she was not flushed like me. 'He's my all-time favourite. He understood about pools and how they make people feel. You know how he described his job? "Photographing attractive people doing attractive things in attractive places". See? I told you I like quotes.'

'That's fun,' I said. And however rarified her status, her lifestyle, it seemed to me that Lara was in fact very inclusive. She made you feel like *you* were one of the attractive people and Elm Hill one of the attractive places, that just by being with her you were doing an attractive thing.

Our eyes locked. 'Lara, I haven't had a chance to thank you for recommending the hypnotherapist. Molly's had two sessions already and says it's really useful.'

'Oh, I'm so pleased.'

'Not that I have any idea what they've actually done,' I added. 'She won't tell me a thing about it.'

'Well, from what I gather it's about the power of suggestion. Like brainwashing.' She said this as though brainwashing were the most marvellous thing, something to which we should all aspire to be subjected. 'So when the fear or the temptation itches, the suggestion overrides it.'

I giggled, not an appropriate response when musing on my daughter's chronic psychological difficulties and the very opposite of the one I'd experienced in Bryony Foster's waiting room. Clearly, I was not quite in control of myself, but if Lara noticed, she didn't mind. I peered at a framed photograph of a girl in a blue tracksuit, recognized my hostess in a teenage shot. She held a trophy, but for a girl posing in triumph there was an odd sense of sorrow in her expression that stirred some memory in me. 'Have we met before?' I blurted. 'I mean before this summer?'

'Not that I know of.' Her gaze followed mine to the photograph. 'Not unless you were on the south-east synchro circuit or in showbiz or at one of the kids' schools.'

I admitted I was not.

'I often get that,' she said, shrugging. 'People think they know me from their childhood. Or they come up to me in Waitrose and ask if I used to be a BBC weather girl. But you get used to the double-takes.'

'I've had a few of those,' I told her. 'At least yours are because people *like* how you look.'

There must have been unintended self-pity in my voice because Lara seized my hand, brought her face so close that I could feel her breath on my cheek. 'You don't actually care about some old *blemish*, do you?'

I blinked, not yet used to her abrupt displays of fervour. 'Not now, no. But I used to.' It was strange: I'd gone months without giving my birthmark a thought, and here I was, drawing attention to it twice in the space of an hour. What would a psychologist say? That I was casting myself as Beast to Lara's Beauty, perhaps. 'Now I bare all quite happily,' I added lightheartedly.

'Talking of which, let's get some more sun!' Lara declared, dropping my hand. To my astonishment, she wrenched her kaftan over her head to reveal a black swimsuit with plunging lines. Her skin was the glossy caramel the media had taught us to desire above all other hues. 'Come on, Natalie, don't look so appalled, join me!'

I gaped. 'Oh, no, I'm not wearing swim stuff, just ordinary underwear.'

'Anything goes here, darling.' And, flinging the kaftan on to the nearest chair, she took my hand once more and led me back out to the terrace. The teenagers had scattered and the adults made no comment about her having stripped, Angie absently removing her vest to reveal a bikini top. Seated, I pulled up my skirt an inch or two. As if in response to the bared skin, the sun grew hotter; it seemed to me to be almost at the point of eruption.

During my absence, Ed had once again become the centre of attention, Douglas and Andrew in particular seeming very struck by him. I imagined Lara telling them before our arrival, 'Just you wait, boys. He's *so* like Alain.'

If 'Alain' had considered views on the shockingly erratic grading of GCSEs.

'I'm fascinated by those big comprehensives like All Saints,' Andrew was saying. 'Is it like on that TV series? Do the kids *really* speak to the teachers like that?'

'And are they always having sex with each other?' Douglas asked. 'If you believe what they say in the papers, it's *Lolita* in every classroom.'

Sozzled as he was, Ed was quick to object to this remark. 'That depends which papers you read. Believe it or not, the idea is not to have an affair with your pupils, but to teach them your subject and get them through their exams.'

I hoped Ed wouldn't mention Craig's trials: Gayle (not to mention Craig himself) would be mortified.

'What about you, Georgia?' Douglas teased, and I saw that she was back, wine bottle in hand. 'Any hot guys on the staff at Westbridge?'

Georgia burst out laughing, a sound that somehow incorporated both knowingness and innocence. In my drunkenness I wanted to gush admiration for her good humour, her sweetness, her poise.

'Dougie, you *know* I would have told you already if there were,' Lara said. 'But there aren't, are there, darling? Not since Mr Roddick left,' she added, winking at Angie.

'Ooh, Mr Roddick, I like the sound of him,' Douglas said, and the laughter this provoked would have befitted Monty Python at the London Palladium, not least from me. When the others stopped, I found that I was still laughing. I had not been so drunk since Christmas. Why was I being so uninhibited today? I wondered a little wildly if the cocktails had absinthe in them or maybe that poppy-seed tea I'd read about in an article on the dangers of adolescent drinking.

'Does she always take this long, Ed?' Stephen said, the cue for more gaiety, resulting in Lara dropping her glass over the railing. There was a brief shocked silence at the tiny musical shattering below and then laughter rocked the terrace once more. Marthe was sent down to pick up the pieces.

Fearful perhaps that the party had lapsed into a more dangerously hedonistic phase, Ed suggested a Steele family departure and though I longed to stay I also knew it was in my best interests to quit while I was ahead. As we waited for Molly to reappear, Stephen treated the group to a joke about synchronized swimmers.

'I bet you've heard that before, have you?' I asked Lara.

'Oh, darling, I've heard them *all* before,' she said, in the same tone of delighted indulgence she'd bestowed on Everett at the pool. There was something undeniably adult, however, about the way her palm lingered on Ed's back as she accompanied us to the door.

I was glad Ed didn't get it into his head to repeat Stephen's joke to Molly as we walked home. I was confident she wouldn't have found it at all funny: *If one synchronized swimmer drowns, do all the rest have to drown too?*

It goes without saying that I Googled the Channings' house the moment we got back to Kingsley Drive. They'd bought it two years ago for £2 million and it had no doubt doubled in value since then. After a little research, I found the photo Lara and I had looked at together: 'Poolside Glamor' by Slim Aarons. The house in the picture was in Palm Springs, the subjects not models but society ladies at a drinks party. 'When you photograph a lot of women, you get to know things,' Aarons famously once said, which pretty much brought me up to speed on him.

A Negroni was one part gin, one part Campari and one part vermouth. James Bond made one for himself in *Thunderball* and had not, I imagined, quoted Abraham Lincoln as he drank it.

Without knowing surnames I couldn't examine the professional credentials of Douglas, Andrew or Stephen, but I found Miles Channing easily enough. He was chief risk officer at Enfield Baines Morrow, a global provider of insurance products. He looked extremely self-important in his photograph, a corporate warrior *par excellence*, the match of any form of adversity, act of God or otherwise.

Company motto: *Risks you never knew existed*.

None of this I shared with Ed. Though, in the end, he'd thoroughly enjoyed himself at La Madrague, I knew he would make a point of not being interested.

13

Monday, 31 August, 6 a.m.

Dawn seeps comfortingly around the edges of the blinds, soft and innocent and healing. My eyes go to the clock on the bedroom wall, strategically placed for a sleepy school-girl to see from her pillow. How many thousands of times have I called to her from the kitchen, 'You need to hurry'; 'You're running late'; '*Now*, Molly!'? Those were our dramas then, the threat of a missed bus, a late registration.

We didn't know we were born.

Ed is no longer in the room. Guessing he must have taken me up on my offer and gone to bed, I sink with relief into the sofa and the back of my head meets the wall, hard against my skull. I'm aware of tenderness on my right cheekbone, but don't go to the mirror to check for bruising: to do so would be to acknowledge the horror of how it was earned. Then I hear the flush of the toilet, the pull of the light cord. Ed's footsteps across the hallway have purpose.

I rise and meet him outside the door so our voices won't disturb Molly.

'I just found this in the bin.' He's holding the balled-up dress. 'Why have you thrown it away? It probably cost a fortune.'

I snatch it from him. 'I must have put it in there by mistake. I meant to put it in the laundry basket,' I say, but it's too late, his brain is alighting on details he noticed earlier.

'Before,' he says, 'when we came back, it looked like it was torn.'

I can tell he wants to take it back and check for damage, for clues. I watch him weigh up the consequences of seizing it from me: accusations, an argument, all the denials or disclosures he thinks he wants to hear. I ball the fabric tighter, press it to me. 'That must have been from the chaos of the accident.'

'Come on,' he says, 'it was like that when you found us – not just the dress, your hair, everything. You'd been with *him*, hadn't you?'

'Who?'

He grows angry. 'How many candidates are there?'

Knowing better than to allow myself to be provoked, I strain to neutralize my tone. 'If you must know, I was going to get in the pool. I must have torn the dress as I was getting changed.'

The admission horrifies him, as I would expect it to, but it is not without precedent and he believes me.

'I must have been drunker than I thought.'

Surprise, surprise, he's thinking. 'Did you even have your swimming stuff?'

'No, it wasn't planned. I borrowed a swimsuit from Lara. She keeps spare kit behind the counter in the café.'

'For just such law-breaking opportunities, eh?' He grimaces. 'Where were you getting changed?' He is focused on the logistics of my misdemeanour; the teacher investigating the pupil's crime.

'In one of the huts.' I swallow, my throat dry and painful. 'But as soon as I realized something was wrong I came straight out to find you. I hadn't even strapped my shoes on.'

He frowns. The chronology of the evening has not yet cleared in his mind. 'I was thinking,' he says, a new touch of determination to his tone, 'won't they have security cameras? You know, around the pool and by the exits.'

'I don't know,' I lie.

'If they do, there might be something useful in the footage.'

Something useful for understanding Molly's actions, I wonder, or for understanding mine? I hate myself for the thought.

As I hasten past him to find a new hiding place for the dress, somewhere I might never find it myself, the voice I hear belongs to Gayle:

You'd think, as a maths teacher, he of all people could put two and two together.

142

14

'I think this is my favourite colour,' I said to Gayle, squinting as citrus-fresh morning sun bounced off the surface of the water. 'Swimming-pool blue.'

Saying it, I felt the now-familiar sting of betrayal: how could I take such pleasure in the very thing that caused the person most precious to me to experience primal terror?

There'd been by now a third hypnotherapy session and still no initiative by Molly to venture here again. At Bryony's suggestion, I neither hid nor flaunted my own daily swims: 'The more relaxed you are around the subject the better,' she said, echoing every one of her predecessors. The fact was – and this never stopped being hard to hear – Molly's terror was directly associated with me. She might have begun to cast me in the role of tedious authority figure, there to be challenged and mocked, but if I'd learned anything from the years of therapy it was that I was her primary role model and what I did, what I said, mattered.

'I think *my* favourite colour is that almost-black brown of really good chocolate fudge cake,' Gayle said, and it was clear already that if either of us was going to flag in this fitness regime it would be her. It was she who had pulled us over for a rest just a couple of lengths into our swim. Feet pedalling, we clung to the rail at the deep end, not far from where her younger daughter Harriet and a friend lay coiled on their towels, like snakes sleeping in the sun. Gayle's other daughter, Alice, was there too, with an assortment of friends, as were Izzy and Rosie and others from Molly's school. Sometimes, at the lido, it felt as if there were only one girl missing.

'They're not coming into the water?' I asked Gayle, nodding towards Harriet and her friend.

'Oh, Nat, they're not here to *swim*.' She regarded me with amused indulgence. 'If only I could go back in time and be as lovely and unsuspecting as you.'

I smiled. 'Go on then, tell me what their real agenda is.'

'Not what. *Who*.'

I followed her gaze to the lifeguard, the one called Matt, who was not on patrol this morning but occupied in stacking equipment in a large crate near the emergency exit. By now I understood that the staff were rotated scrupulously, watching eyes kept fresh. (They were required to wear sunglasses to combat the glare.) 'One of them likes him?'

'Both, I'm afraid. He's the hottie of the season, I understand. May the best girl win.'

Provided Georgia Channing wasn't interested, I thought.

It was an odd thing, but I had not told Gayle about the lunch at the Channings'. Had we met on the Monday, I rationalized, I would have done so without thinking, but we didn't meet until the Tuesday, by which time weekend activities were not foremost in our minds; then, today, it seemed peculiar to mention it when I hadn't before. Which was insane, because I would have loved to have shared the details of the party with her: Miles's not expecting us; men sitting hip to hip in a hanging chair and laughing like loons; a glass dropped over the rail; near-naked women tanning themselves. Maybe I was worried she would be envious or, more likely, scornful or, just as likely, amazed that I was not.

I noticed that Lara's preferred table was occupied today by a trio of twenty-something homeworkers absorbed in their laptops. They'd fitted little sun visors over their screens.

Harriet and her friend watched through half-closed eyes as Matt came out of a storage room and spoke into a walkie-talkie, the sort the police would use. It was an eye-catching combination, I had to admit, that decent, responsible demeanour and the eroticism of a half-naked young man.

'So do you think you'll stay on at Elm Hill Prep?' Gayle asked me.

'Yes, of course.' Then, sensing the significance in her silence: 'What? You thought my conscience would be too painful to bear and I'd go running back to

Rushbrook? They're just kids, Gayle, same as all the others. They're not criminals because their parents are paying for their education. I'm not sure we'd do any different if we had the spare cash.'

Under water, Gayle's feet kicked in protest and, seeing her stout white legs, distorted unflatteringly by perspective, I thought of Lara's slender limbs soaked golden in the sun. 'That's not what Ed thinks,' she said.

'No, but it's what *I* think. And Ed hasn't got a leg to stand on now he's tutoring. He's not discovering geniuses in the ghettos, you know. They're mostly from private schools.'

'So you said. Georgia Channing *et al.*'

Which made me remember Craig's remark, *Et tu, Brute*, and I thought, *How ridiculous they are*. Trust us to have as our closest friends two of a dying breed who genuinely believed teachers in independent schools were the pampered enemy, when repeatedly studies showed the hours and even the pay in the two sectors were so close as to be splitting hairs. I understood now at least one reason why I'd concealed the Channings' lunch from her: she'd brand it a bid for advancement inspired by my defection to the private sector. 'Ed says it's just as tiring as his All Saints classes,' I said.

'I'm sure it is, but that's not the point, is it?'

A swimmer approached, her head surfacing between us, mouth sucking air, and I recognized my neighbour from the ground-floor flat. She and her boyfriend were younger than Ed and I and we'd never established a friendship with them as we had with Sarah. Why not? Why had we aligned ourselves with the older, not the younger? I smiled and she turned, dipped below the surface, pushed away.

'So what *is* the point?' I said.

Gayle pouted. 'That it's unfair for only a tiny minority of children to have access to one-on-one tuition in the first place.'

'Of course it's unfair, but almost everything is in this city, this *life*, so let's not waste our energy on futile indignation. Besides, there's more than one way to skin a cat.' And I felt quite proud of myself standing up to her like this. Compromised though my old self's principles might have become, they were my principles to compromise, not hers or Ed's or anyone else's. 'Talent rises in the end,' I added.

Gayle raised an eyebrow. 'Are you sure you don't mean shit?'

Friday, 31 July

It was another two days before I saw Lara again. Gayle having taken Harriet and Alice to their grandparents for the weekend, I was at the lido alone, enjoying the tightening sensation of water drying on hot skin, when I became aware of a fall in volume as people turned to watch someone swimming.

I looked too. It was the first time I had seen her in the water. She moved in a sleek and frictionless way, almost as if luxuriating in a flush of current, the water guiding, not resisting. When she climbed out, her hair was smooth on her skull and down her spine and she was breathing visibly, torso rising and falling. I could see the girl in her, the teenage athlete from the photograph, and again I experienced *déjà vu*, that sense of prior connection.

I followed her to her VIP table on the terrace, feeling slightly shy in doing so, as if I'd misunderstood our lunch together or even imagined it and an approach now might be unwelcome. 'Hi, Lara.'

'Natalie, what a lovely surprise!' She kissed me on both cheeks, her skin warm and moist, and patted the seat next to her. It was the first time we'd been alone together and some nameless impulse caused me to glance about and see if anyone had noticed. I spotted the mother of a child from my EHP class a few tables away ('We're not happy about this *at all*,' she'd told me at parents' evening on establishing that Elsa, nine, was not at the top table for literacy). I couldn't help feeling a little smug at her expression when she saw just who I was with and I directed a cool smile her way before turning my full attention to Lara.

'Thank you again for the lunch on Sunday. It was wonderful.' The sky was white today, sunglasses redundant, and there was a new starkness to our eye contact. 'Such a treat to spend time in your beautiful house. If I lived there, I don't think I would ever leave.'

Lara laughed. 'You say that but, honestly, the best thing about it is how close it is to here.' She stretched her fingers towards the pool as if expecting to be able to dip them in the water. 'I can't believe I used to get in the car every day and drive all the way to the Harbour Club.'

Every day, I thought. The Harbour Club (later I would Google its membership fees and find the matter too delicate for general publication). It was a likeable trait, I reminded myself, to want to eschew the superior luxury of a private club in favour of a public facility, not to mention to have helped campaign for its existence.

'I'm amazed you haven't built a pool of your own,' I said. 'You have space in your garden, don't you?' Through the upper rear window of La Madrague I'd seen a perfect square of formal French garden, with a generously proportioned lawn beyond.

'Actually, I would have liked to, but Miles wasn't so keen. I suppose that's why I threw myself into the lido – in all senses of the word.' She flicked the ends of her wet hair and laughed, lighthearted again. 'He's not a water-baby like the kids and me, though he *is* a water sign. But the weird one, Scorpio. The strategist. Jealous and vengeful.'

'Right.' Not even Lara was going to be able to interest me in horoscopes.

'I've noticed you're here almost as much as I am, Natalie. I'm impressed. It's not so long ago you thought it wasn't going to be possible, because of Molly.'

'It still isn't,' I said, 'at least not as a family. But I hope it will be, one day.' My ear caught a familiar shower of laughter: Georgia, here with Eve and Josh in their regular spot. Lying with their heads together, they rolled on to their stomachs, a muddle of bent knees and elbows.

Lara followed my gaze. 'It *will* be possible, and not "one day", *soon*. Trust me.'

I do trust you, I thought. *I don't know why, but I do.* 'Anyway, with Ed at home to keep an eye on Molly, I can come on my own.'

She regarded me approvingly. 'Have you always swum? Did you swim as a child?'

'A bit. Nothing like you, but there was one summer when I swam pretty much every day. It wasn't a proper pool, just a pond in the woods, but it was quite big and deep in the middle. We'd spend hours in it, till our skin wrinkled.' I wondered why I was telling her this, when I spoke of it so rarely, so warily. 'It would probably be banned, these days, considered too dangerous for kids to swim in.'

'Where was that? I don't think I've asked you where you grew up?'

'I grew up in Surrey, not far from Guildford, but the bathing pond was in a village in Hampshire called Stoneborough. That's where my grandparents lived. I was banished there one summer when my parents weren't getting on.' To my horror, I felt a strong confessional impulse, an urge to disclose not the sanitized version that Molly – and, to an extent, Ed – had been fed, but the true, indigestible one. Then, seeing a flicker of recognition in her face: 'You know the village?'

'I know Guildford.' Lara rolled her eyes. 'For my sins, I was once in a play at the theatre there. It had terrible reviews. I shudder to remember it.' A brief frown gave way to wickedness as her eyes found the vivid cluster of poolside manager Ethan and two of his male staff. 'I do like the cut of those yellow vests, don't you?'

In fact, the sight reminded me of something more serious. 'Lara, I was wondering if you know if anyone has ever spoken to the kids about shallow-water blackout?'

Her smile faded: perhaps she was dismayed by the notion that a person might wilfully kill the mood like this. Nonetheless, she resigned herself to my lecture, gamely composing her features into something close to interest.

'I was reading up on it. It can happen when someone is deliberately holding his breath; they call it static apnoea, or just swimming under water for a couple of strokes too long. You can pass out without any warning, you see. And some people deliberately hyperventilate first, which artificially lowers the level of carbon dioxide in the blood and fools the body into thinking it doesn't need oxygen. Which makes it even more dangerous because it stops your brain thinking you need to take a breath. More of a teenage thing, I read, it can be a problem in competitive squads.' I stopped at last, hearing the teacher in my voice.

Lara squeezed a tube of sunscreen on to the back of her hand, using her skin as a palette as she applied the lotion to her face in luxurious, circular movements. 'Natalie, you're talking to a woman who used to swim lengths under water with her legs only. I know all about the risks of breath-holding exercises. Lung busters, they call them.' She smiled, pinched her nostrils with her fingers. 'The nose clip helped, mind you. But seriously, Ange said Josh's club had a big talk about SWB last year after a couple of deaths in the States that were all over the press.'

The phrasing was a little casual, as if the lives lost could be spared easily enough, but then this was Lara. She wanted to know about attractive people doing attractive things, and dying by accident was not attractive.

'It's nothing to worry about,' she said, 'take it from me. Drills are all strictly controlled by the coach and no one trains alone now. That's when accidents tend to happen, when someone's stayed on their own after practice. They're more exhausted than they realize.'

'What about when there isn't a coach? When it's just a regular swimming pool, like here?'

'There are always other professionals – just look at the staff ratio here. I went to one of the lifeguards' briefings before this place opened and I can assure you it was all terribly serious. They scan continuously. If someone is seen motionless under water even for a second or two, they go straight in.'

'But how can they always see?' I persisted. 'It's so crowded all the time.'

'They're trained to see. They keep their eye on anyone behaving unusually.' As if understanding were dawning at last, Lara put down her sunscreen and reached for my hand. Hers was warm and greasy, white lotion caught under the nails. 'I know it must be hard for you with Molly. Believe me, I of all people understand. I mean, *my* mother was only a stage mother, she had nothing medical to worry about, not like *your* situation, but even so, I do get it.'

I blinked. A stage mother? She thought I was wildly overprotective, clearly. Maybe she was even wondering which had come first, the chicken or the egg, Molly's phobia or my hypersensitivity. Maybe she was wondering if the wife of her daughter's new tutor had a screw loose.

'You're right,' I said. 'The lifeguards seem excellent. I chatted a while ago to the one called Matt . . .'

'Ooh, good choice. I've slightly got a crush on him,' she said, her girlish, confiding tone signifying that our serious talk was at an end. 'Don't tell Georgia, though, will you? Lusting after the same boy as your daughter, honestly, it would be quite – what's the word? – unseemly.'

'Yes.' I couldn't help wondering what Ed or Gayle would say to *that*.

When I said I needed to head home, she decided to leave too, tucking her arm into mine and steering me on to the path leading to The Rise, the wrong direction for me. Did she know where I lived? Did she assume that anyone worth knowing lived on this, the more desirable, side of the park?

'I go the other way,' I said, finally.

'I know.' Her arm tightened, clasping me to her side with an endearing possessiveness. 'Kingsley Drive.'

Of course, she must have made it her business to know where her daughter went for her maths tuition. Georgia cycled over, as I recalled.

'How long does it take you to walk from here?' she asked.

'About twenty minutes. It's a nice wander, through the park, then under the railway bridge and along the high street.'

'You have to cross the high street, do you?'

'Yes, we're one of the roads just off the north side.' It amused me that she obviously hadn't set foot across the divide herself. 'You should come over some time and have a drink. You'd be very welcome.'

I was instinctively vague, however, for when I pictured Miles and her turning into Kingsley Drive, with its hotchpotch of thirties semis and postwar buildings, finding themselves at the door of our downright ugly eighties building, when I imagined them entering the dreary common parts and traipsing up the stairs with bemused expressions, wondering if the building might be ex-council, well, it seemed not so much shameful as fantastical.

'Sure.' Equally non-committal, Lara released me. 'Now, that reminds me. We wondered if you guys would like to come tomorrow evening for a movie.'

'A movie?' Did she mean a trip together to the Picture House?

At the sight of my face, she said, 'Of course, you haven't seen our new screening room, have you? It's pretty cool. Our little treat to ourselves when we were doing up the house.' (As if the rest of it were utilitarian and joyless.) 'Say you'll come, it'll just be a few of the gang. A kind of celebration of our new local treasure.'

Preposterously, for a second I thought she meant me and I blushed, but of course she meant the lido.

'It will be *La Piscine*, in case you hadn't guessed.'

'I'll have to check we're free,' I said, knowing we had only a provisional plan to drop in on Sarah for an early-evening drink. Two invitations to the Channings' in seven days – how exciting to find ourselves in a social flurry after all these years. And there could be no objection from Ed this time, surely: he'd ended up having a lovely time at the lunch.

Breaking my own pointless embargo, I texted Gayle as I walked home: *Guess who's invited Ed and me over tomorrow? The Local Celeb.* When reporting on it afterwards, I would incorporate details from the first visit, thus solving the problem of my previous secrecy.

Gayle's response – *You don't mean Lara Channing? Why would she do that?* – hurt my feelings a little, though I was not so deluded as to fail to recognize it as a reasonable question. For while no one would question my having been charmed by her, why *she* should have taken a shine to *me* was less plain. It couldn't simply be to keep her daughter's tutor sweet: she was paying Ed very well and presumably paid many different people for their services without inviting them to a private screening in their home. Had she made some sort of project of me, then, her compassion stirred by that story about my birth-mark? Might I expect a makeover (I was the first to admit that I needed one)? Or was it Molly she pitied? 'I'm determined to get her in the water,' she'd said. Was the befriending of Ed and me part of that larger altruistic aim?

Perhaps it was simpler: she just happened to like us – *me*. I imagined her saying to Angie, 'I know I said I wouldn't take on any new friends, goodness knows I don't have the slots, but there's something about Natalie, don't you think?'

And Angie would say, 'I know what you mean –'

Stop, I told myself, before I could script the whole conversation. There was such a thing, after all, as making a fool of yourself in your own head.

15

'Do you think we should bring Molly?' I asked Ed.

This being an evening at the Channings', there was a certain vagueness regarding arrangements. Not so long ago this would have vexed me, not least on account of the corners I'd have to cut with household chores to accommodate the impromptu date, but it seemed this was a learning curve I was scaling with enthusiasm. To hell with the chores.

'I'm sure she's welcome,' I added, 'but it might be a late night. I could ask Sarah if she can help out? We'll be there beforehand anyway so she'd probably be happy to babysit if Molls stays up there.'

But Molly bristled at both the term and the suggestion. 'No, I want to come. Anyway, Georgia's expecting me to be there.'

It was news to me that the girls were directly in touch, though it was in no way surprising since the march of social media meant that, in spite of our most scrupulous parental blocks and spot checks, our daughter was in contact not only with complete strangers but also, in some cases, their pets. She had not had older friends

157

before and I had mixed feelings about the development. On the one hand, older girls were a risk, what with all the inappropriate activities they might introduce to a younger child; on the other, they could be a good influence, a boost to self-confidence. And let's not forget this was no ordinary girl: this was the daughter of Lara Channing. There'd be kudos for Molly if she socialized with Georgia and her friends (even if the word itself was no doubt disused and mocked).

'Great,' I said. 'We'll all go.'

'Are we having dinner there?' Ed said.

'I don't know. Lara didn't say.'

'Can't you phone her and ask?'

'It's just a movie, so probably not dinner. Maybe there'll be popcorn. We'll feed Molly just in case.'

'*Feed* me? I'm not Inky!' Molly protested.

I sighed. 'I meant we'll lovingly prepare you a balanced snack so you're sufficiently nourished.'

'*I*'ll need to be sufficiently nourished as well,' Ed said, digging his heels in.

The two of them were driving me up the wall. 'Why's everyone fussing about food?' And then I felt guilty for snapping, for allowing the excitement of a second invitation to the Channings' to eclipse my domestic responsibilities. 'Molly will make a cheese omelette for you both,' I told Ed, which I knew would please him since we were of one mind that Molly needed to expand her culinary repertoire beyond a bowl of Shreddies and Marmite on toast.

With that, I retreated to the bedroom to shower and change. It was oppressively humid again, the gentle slap of door on jamb the only clue that air was stealing through the open windows, and my make-up was melting even as I applied it. I dressed in a lucky find from the charity shop on the high street: a paisley print hip-length kaftan in black, purple and green that had washed and ironed beautifully. It was two sizes too small but the style was loose enough for it not to matter. I liked to think my denim skirt slid more easily over my hips thanks to the swimming, though there was no denying the way the waistband cut into my skin when I sat down.

'Off to Woodstock, are you?' Ed said, when I emerged.

'Very funny. You look gorgeous,' I told Molly, who wore a tiger-print top with the shorts and tights combo favoured by her age group even in a heatwave. But compliments from mothers had little value these days, and she raised her eyebrows at me as if questioning a joke in poor taste.

'Right, let's go up.' I gestured to the detritus from their snack. 'Leave this mess, we'll clean up in the morning.'

'Oh, wow,' Molly said. 'Did you *actually* just say, "Leave this mess"? Is this, like, a *miracle* or something?'

'Only one drink,' I warned Ed. 'It's already six thirty, we don't have long.'

But this was one instruction too many and he frowned in resistance. 'Calm down with the military precision,

Nat. We can be a bit late leaving Sarah's. She's been in the diary a lot longer than this thing at the Channings'.'

To my dismay, he *had* objected to the date – or at least been lukewarm.

'But I thought you had fun at the lunch?' I said.

'Sure,' he said. 'It was fine for a one-off.'

'Well, at the very least we would have had to invite them back,' I pointed out.

'Hmm, maybe with Craig and Gayle?'

'Maybe.' How could he not see what a disastrous match *that* would be? Lara with her flippant remarks about attractive teenagers and Gayle with her determination to disapprove.

At Sarah's, there was happy commotion as Inky, having not seen Molly for some time, leaped like a yo-yo to lick her face before drawing her to the floor to wrestle. Though it meant I had to mop up a spilled drink, the routine heartened me: the day Molly stopped mucking about with Inky – on account of her hair, perhaps – was the day I'd really know she'd outgrown us.

Amid talk of our taking the dog on our approaching holiday in the New Forest, my phone pinged and I saw it was a text from Lara: *Just mixing the first Martinis. See you soonest!* And I found myself going to the window, as if La Madrague were visible from it and not a mile and a half away on the other side of Elm Hill. Sarah's armchair remained angled towards the junction with the high street – and I thought how lonely it looked, that single seat, compared to the collection on the Channings' terrace. Sarah, like my mother, had divorced in the years following her children leaving home.

Through the glass, the heat of the evening sun seemed to swell, not recede, the leaves on the trees powder-dry, utterly still.

'Nat?'

I looked up to find Ed and Sarah expectant of an answer to a question I'd missed. I returned to my seat. 'Sorry?'

'I was just saying to Ed how well you're looking,' she said. 'You've been swimming, he says.'

'Yes, I've been to the lido a few times. I'd forgotten how much I love the water.' I was careful not to be seen to exchange glances with Ed for Molly was acutely sensitive to a ploy. It was all very well Bryony advising me not to make a big deal of my own swimming, but it sometimes felt that not making a big deal *was* the big deal.

'Maybe we can all go together when I'm mobile again,' Sarah said to Molly, and I knew Ed would be in silent agreement that it was ideal for the suggestion to have come from her.

Not that Molly responded to it. Surfacing at last from games with Inky, she joined her father on the sofa. 'Shall I top up your drinks?' she offered.

Like Georgia, I thought, and as she poured the wine Ed, to his credit, did not lecture her on the evils of handling alcohol.

'Is there a plan yet for your birthday trip?' Sarah asked us.

My birthday was at the end of August and it was a tradition to celebrate it on the bank-holiday weekend with a couple of nights away. It struck me how horribly predictable we were when our neighbours knew what we were doing weeks before we did. 'I haven't checked which day it falls on,' I said, in an act of small defiance. I did know, of course. It was the day of Lara's pool party, the Last Day of Summer.

'It's a Sunday,' Ed said, adding to Sarah, 'I have a few ideas, yes.'

He chatted on, oblivious to the time, until at last I felt I had no choice but to get to my feet mid-conversation. 'Sorry to love you and leave you,' I told Sarah, 'but we're expected somewhere for dinner.'

'A barbecue?' she asked, and the thought of Miles Channing tending chicken thighs over smoking coals made me chuckle.

'We don't even know if it *is* dinner,' Molly told her. 'Mum hasn't got a clue.'

'I'm sure Mum has a perfectly good clue,' Sarah said. 'Where are you off to?'

'It's Lara Channing's place,' I said, 'just on the other side of the park.'

'You mean that actress we talked about?'

'Yes.' Again, I couldn't help being gratified by the astonished reaction. It seemed a lifetime since I'd flipped through Sarah's magazine and made those ignorant comments about Lara; I rather pitied the old me. 'Ed's tutoring her daughter and we've got to know the family a bit.'

'That's why Mum's wearing that weird top,' Molly said. 'She's trying to look cool.'

When do they learn tact? I'd asked Gayle not long ago, but untypically she'd had no answer ready, had just pulled the same hopeless face she'd worn when I'd wondered about wet towels left on the bathroom floor or snacks discarded in the foot well of the car. 'I'm not sure they ever do,' she'd said eventually.

Arrival at La Madrague felt different in the evening. Though it was still light, a trail of copper lanterns burned along the pathway, lending the place a seductive, adult air. This, in spite of the appearance at the door of Everett, still in clothes dusty from the park or garden, a sprig of turf attached to the toe of his trainer. 'Molly!' he said, as if she were there on her own.

'Evening, Everett,' Ed said, and I guessed he was thinking, as I admit I was, that at his age he should probably have been in bed by now, or at least bathed and in his pyjamas. As the boy scampered off to alert an adult, I sensed Ed's impatience.

'Sorry we had to abandon your debate with Sarah about the new slip road,' I said, but it sounded sarcastic when I'd meant only to be humorous and, unsurprisingly, it failed to raise a smile. No matter: I was confident that Lara, as last time, would work her magic on her reluctant guest.

We assembled once more on the terrace, Angie and Stephen comprising the rest of the 'gang', along with their children and dog, a miniature greyhound named Choo. We were serenaded by what I already thought of as the Channings' signature music, all creeping piano chords and crackling, moan-like vocals. In the soft evening light, the greens of the park swarmed like a billion butterflies and I felt immediately connected, powered by light and colour.

'Hard liquor coming your way,' Lara said, as she and Georgia distributed the promised Martinis. They were both dressed in white and I thought once more of those pictures of famous actresses and models posing with their daughters. How did it make you feel, when you were adored for your beauty, to watch yourself wither as the other bloomed? How much fun was that? Conversely, to remain always in the other's shadow, even at your youthful peak, how did *that* feel?

Better to be ordinary, perhaps.

'I hope you're paying your daughter for her waitressing service,' Stephen said to Miles. 'Does she work for tips?'

There was a lascivious undertone to his comment, exacerbated presumably by the very alcohol the girl dispensed, but Miles did not react. His composure was not only enviable but also a little mysterious. I had decided by now that, of this group, Stephen was not my favourite. There was something about him that made me nervous.

It was pleasing that Lara and Angie complimented me on my new top. When Georgia gave it a second – and a third – glance, I really knew it must pass muster.

The Channing home cinema, on the ground floor, was quite an indulgence. The screen was almost as large as the smaller ones in our local multiplex, the seating comprising three tiers of red-velvet sofas, and there was a gleaming wheel of a drinks trolley, presumably an art-deco original, with a thicket of bottles and a tray of polished crystal. There was even a little cloakroom wallpapered with vintage maps of Hollywood.

As Miles took care of technical requirements, Lara called over her shoulder and up the stairs to the children: 'Are you guys coming for the movie?'

Ed objected before I could, though I would not have physically raised a palm, as he did, in the manner of a lollipop lady. 'Not Molly, if you don't mind, Lara.'

She halted, stricken. 'Goodness, I didn't think! Does she not like to see swimming pools on screen?'

As a matter of fact, she could tolerate it well enough, but that, I knew, was not Ed's primary concern. Earlier, I'd seen him look up *La Piscine* for just this purpose.

'The film's a certificate fifteen, Lara,' he told her, 'and it looks like it could be quite adult. She's only thirteen.'

'And Everett will need keeping company,' I added, before Ed could imply that our hostess planned to expose her own eight-year-old to sexual themes.

'Quite right, Edward!' And Lara clutched his arm with delight, as if it were a rare treat to be in the presence of such a law-abiding creature. 'Georgia, you take the younger ones back up to watch, I don't know, *Freaky Friday*.'

With this, she drew Ed to the front-row sofa and placed him between Angie and herself. More to my amusement than concern, she proceeded to swing her legs across him to rest her feet on Angie's lap.

'Isn't this just heaven?' Angie said, as Ed shrank visibly from the contact. 'Choo and I like to pretend we're on a private plane when we're in here.' She settled the dog next to Lara's feet, the wriggling toes attracting an immediate licking. Ed's hands went to his glasses to remove and wipe them with his shirt-tails, something he did when uncertain. But there was nothing I could do to help him: he was out of my jurisdiction, a child strapped into a theme-park ride more thrilling than any he'd braved before.

I took one end of the middle row and Miles, when he was ready, chose the opposite end of the sofa behind. I presumed that Stephen, in the loo and the last to settle, would join his good friend, but to my surprise he opted for me, sitting very close, almost but not quite touching. Having smirked at Ed's plight, I was immediately discomfited, unable to concentrate properly on the opening credits of the film. Then a close-up of Alain Delon appeared and my attention was riveted, for there *was* a likeness to Ed. It was not in facial feature so much as general physicality, a slightness, an elegance. Ed, however, did not stare at people as if he didn't know whether to seduce or kill them.

In front, the women were exclaiming at the resemblance. 'Look what you could be doing instead of teaching!' Lara cried. 'You're wasted on our children, Mr Steele.'

'She's right, sir.' Angie laughed.

Alain, Edward, sir: there was no end to their pet names for him and, far from being threatened by this, I felt the new girl's delight in having her lunchbox treats accepted as tribute by the popular crowd.

'You *so* could be a nineteen-sixties matinée idol,' Angie added, 'not toiling in some south London school in special measures.'

'All Saints is not in special measures,' Ed protested. 'And, anyway, I can't act to save my life, so your theory's dead in the water.'

I had an absurd vision then of Lara offering him lessons, of the two of them performing together in some am-dram production staged on the lido sundeck. *A Streetcar Named Desire*, perhaps.

'Shush, you lot,' Stephen was telling them, and I felt his breath on my skin. Had he inched my way a fraction? I decided I might casually relocate to the sofa behind after a bathroom break.

The movie played on, Delon and Schneider soon joined by Jane Birkin and an actor I didn't know. Miles rose to mix and distribute more of those lethal Martinis. I was learning that at La Madrague glasses brimmed no matter how quickly you sipped from them; it was like *The Magic Porridge Pot*. (Water was not served.) At last I lost myself in the sun-drenched visuals, the careless, brittle dialogue, the sexual tension between the four characters so excruciatingly real we might have been voyeurs watching through the hedgerows.

It was only when the action turned sinister that I became aware of my own environment again and found I was now the only female in the room, Lara and Angie having slipped out without my noticing. To check on Everett, I guessed, for how easy it was to forget the children in this deluxe adult cocoon (I knew better than to embarrass Molly by actively supervising her). Ed, marooned in the centre of the sofa, had been left with Choo on his lap, the little thing alert for the return of his mistress. Was it as hard for him to watch the scenes unfolding as it was for me? To watch a man drown another? Was he remembering, too, how casually permissive Lara had been about the children joining us?

Beside me Stephen shifted, his thigh touching mine, and I felt suddenly overcome by unease, by the sense that variables were at play in this room – many of them new and alien – that removed the outcome from my control.

'Ed,' I murmured, but he didn't turn. Instead, Stephen did, his breath on my cheek once more, and I sensed rather than saw the smile on his lips. That was when my mind took a peculiar turn: I began to feel an awful fear that I was in danger – and that he was the reason. Turning wildly to the door in the hope of seeing Lara or Angie come through it, my eye met Miles's and his gaze lowered from my face to my shoulders, their psychedelic swirls spot-lit by sudden daylight from the screen. His expression was quite fascinated, as if I were a specimen presented for clinical observation. Now, with both men unnerving me, I sprang to my feet and fled to the cloakroom, my breath strained and dry. Focusing on the whir of the fan overhead, the faint thuds from two floors above, I ran the cold tap over my wrists and counted to twenty, silently intoning the names on the old map in front of me: Sunset Boulevard, Plaza Hotel ... Why was I experiencing this irrational turn? Was there some ingredient in the drinks that had caused me to hallucinate (and hadn't I had a similar suspicion during the lunch party)? Or was it the unexpected sight of watching a drowning, albeit acted, make-believe? I'd have done well to do my homework, as Ed had; I could have prepared myself.

Recovered, a little sheepish, I returned to my seat and tried to forget the episode. Lara and Angie were back on either side of Ed. Stephen, wedged now into the far corner of our sofa, acknowledged neither my frantic flight nor my slinking return. Behind me, Miles had sunk deeper into his sofa, eyes on his phone, fingers engaged in discreet messaging.

Afterwards, we climbed to the terrace. Below, the park was in darkness, only the railings and near wall of the lido lit by the streetlights on The Rise – you could just make out the silver lettering at the entrance. The temperature had scarcely dipped, the scent of freesias – or was it jasmine? – full and heady. We were quiet at first, steeped in that half-present mood of film-goers withdrawing from a powerful netherland.

'Well, that was an interesting love triangle,' Ed said, as if starting a discussion with his class. He sounded sober; I guessed he had found a way to evade those relentless refills. I should have done the same, perhaps.

'I think it works because they were real-life partners years earlier,' Lara told him, and after my odd reaction to the men her earnestness was comforting. 'Alain and Romy. They were the love of each other's lives and had that tension, that knowledge. Your body doesn't forget, does it?'

Ed nodded, from politeness as much as recognition.

'And then the daughter,' Angie sighed. (You'd never have guessed she had missed half the film.) 'What a terrible act of revenge, seducing a man's daughter.'

'You can hardly blame him when the daughter's Jane Birkin,' Stephen said. 'Eh, Ed?'

'She was very beautiful,' he agreed, with a trace of reluctance. 'Though not a child. In her twenties then, I would guess.'

'But playing a teenager,' Miles said, and his gaze raked Ed's person as if alert to small clues unknowable to others.

It struck me that the two men had not accepted Ed and me as willingly as their wives, and that this might have contributed to my earlier agitation. Perhaps it bothered them to see Lara and Angie paying Ed so much attention.

'I read that Delon can't watch that film any more,' Lara said. 'His co-stars, the director, they're all dead. It's like the thing was doomed.'

'Well, it *was* forty-five years ago,' Miles said, in his cool, phlegmatic way. 'None of us lives for ever.'

'What did *you* think, Natalie?' Lara asked, noticing my silence.

'I found it unsettling,' I admitted. 'It made me a bit scared.'

'Scared?' Stephen mocked. 'You must be of a very nervous disposition, then.'

'Stephen,' Angie warned, but I laughed off the remark, not looking at him.

'Maybe I am. I can see why you love it, Lara. A swimming pool is a great stage. It's such a symbol of pleasure, yet you can never escape the potential for danger.' Again, I could think only of Molly.

'Did I tell you I thought we could do some open-air cinema over the road next summer?' Lara spoke of the lido as if it were an extension of her own property. 'This would be a perfect one to screen.'

'You've got to be kidding! It's a terrible choice,' Stephen told her. 'It's like choosing *Alive* for your inflight entertainment.'

'Why? Just because someone drowns? Come on.' She scoffed at the idea that someone might not be able to separate art from life. 'No one's going to drown over the road. Not with our crack team of lifeguards. Wouldn't you say, Georgia?'

That was when I realized Georgia was sitting in the hanging chair; to do so without it swaying even a fraction seemed to me a rare feat. Had she been there before we arrived or had I missed her joining us?

'What?' she said to her mother, not so much insolent as indifferent, before answering with a sigh a question that hadn't been asked: 'They're all fine. Everett's asleep, the others are still watching the movie.'

'*Freaky Friday*?'

'No. They wanted *Mermaid*.'

'*Mermaid on Mulberry Street*?' Lara, momentarily startled, began laughing. 'Oh, you haven't put them through that ordeal, have you?'

'They're enjoying it,' Georgia said, quite matter-of-fact. 'Kids like a bit of old-school.'

'How awful to be described as old-school,' Lara said, and I couldn't tell if she was offended or just affecting to be. In any case, she'd lost her daughter's attention because Georgia was staring at me, a dawning clarity on her face.

'Mum, I've just realized!'

Lara reached theatrically for her daughter's hand, squeezing the tips of her fingers between her own. 'What? That your parents are dreadful lushes who should be reported to Social Services?'

'No, I realized *that* a long time ago.' Georgia smirked and, to my discomfort, her gaze returned to me. 'No, I mean Natalie's top. Isn't it from that bag you threw out?'

There was a bewildered silence as everyone turned to look at me and then Lara's laughter rang out again. 'I think you might be right, darling. And it wasn't thrown out, it was *donated*.'

'I did buy it from the charity shop on the high street,' I said, annoyed with myself for flushing. I'd thought myself loosely inspired by my new friend, but now it looked like I was stalking her for her bin liners of old clothes. Well, it explained Miles's fascinated attention, if not Stephen's.

'What an extraordinary coincidence,' Angie said.

'Not at all. We obviously have the same excellent taste,' Lara said easily. I knew then that she must have recognized the garment the moment she saw me, and I felt sure she would have made no comment had Georgia not brought it up. That was kind, I thought. Far from being the vain creature supposed by Gayle, and perhaps others who didn't know her, she was in fact very sensitive to people's feelings.

Below, a car pulled up. 'Our taxi's here,' Ed told me. 'I thought it was a bit late for Molly to walk.'

I hadn't realized he'd ordered one, but had no choice but to follow. I was relieved that Stephen was once more using the bathroom and I was able to avoid saying goodbye to him.

'What did you think of the film?' I asked Molly in the taxi. 'Was Lara good in it?'

'Yeah, it was fun. She was fine.'

Fun, fine: high praise from that age group. The heightened colour in her face did not escape my notice: the evening had meant something to her.

'I've seen photos from it,' I said. 'Lara's more glamorous now, if you ask me.'

'She's not glamorous,' Ed said, 'she's just rich.'

'Oh, come on,' I protested, 'that's unfair. Glamour is about confidence and experience. Wasn't it Marilyn

Monroe who said it can't be manufactured?' Then, having reached the level of intoxication at which such things got muddled: 'Or was it the other way around?'

'All glamour is manufactured,' Ed said. 'It's dependent on products of one sort or another. Haven't you noticed that no one ever thinks a homeless person is glamorous, however good their bone structure?' He was being a little humourless, I thought. 'Anyway, we're far too old to have our heads turned by someone like Lara Channing. Don't tell me you actually believe all that stuff?'

'What stuff?' As the car sped along the curve of the park towards the high street, I felt quite nauseous.

'The whole bohemian set-up. The impression they like to give that their lives are so free-spirited and spontaneous. You must see that it's all being funded by a City job – and City jobs are the opposite of free-spirited, believe me.'

'Maybe. Well, personally, I find Miles quite enigmatic,' I said.

'In my experience, enigmatic usually just means dull,' Ed said, and I frowned at him, not appreciating his negative stance, especially in front of Molly.

Evidently she agreed. 'That's really rude, Dad. You were just his guest.' Which succeeded in silencing him where I had failed.

Once home, Molly safely in her bedroom, I suggested a nightcap in the kitchen. The blind was up, the lights on, and our figures reflected in the black window. All I could see was the patterned top, once worn by Lara. My skin tingled with fresh embarrassment, yet I knew I wasn't going to throw it away.

'That wasn't like you,' I said to Ed, 'slagging off other parents in front of Molly. Clients, as well.'

'It wasn't like you not to agree,' he said.

'What do you mean? Of course I don't agree, I think they're a great group.' I did not confess my reservations about Stephen, but he was already on Ed's mind for other reasons, it transpired.

'Stephen's obviously some sort of cokehead. They were all at it, in case you didn't notice.'

At least he hadn't said *that* in front of Molly. 'What makes you think that?'

He rolled his eyes. 'Those constant trips to the bathroom, for one thing. It wasn't a problem with weak bladders.'

I shrugged. 'They're private citizens. It's none of our business.'

'It's not a question of privacy, Nat, is it? Cocaine is a class-A drug and it's just as illegal in the home as it is anywhere else. Their children were there. *Our* daughter was a couple of rooms away.'

'Look,' I said, 'even if you're right, which I'm not convinced you are, *we* don't take drugs and we have to trust we've brought Molly up not to be interested.' I was pleased with this response: for a mother prone to overprotectiveness, for a woman who liked a certain degree of control over her environment, it sounded sanguine, commonsensical, the sort of thing Gayle might say.

'Well, mixing with households like the Channings' would not appear to be the way forward,' Ed said, tutting with fresh disapproval. 'I worry for those kids' welfare. The constant partying. Lara said it herself, didn't she? That remark about Social Services.'

'That was a joke, Ed.'

'Apart from anything else,' he said, continuing over me, 'we're educators. We can't be seen to be involved in this kind of, I don't know, libertine behaviour.'

'Educators? Libertine?' I heard the scorn in my own laughter. 'Do you realize how sanctimonious you sound? And why do we have to be defined so completely by our profession, anyway? Why do we have to be these sensible, dutiful people who always, *always* have to do the right thing?'

An approaching car threw sudden light through the window, illuminating Ed's indignant face. There were sounds of parking, then the sudden absence of engine noise, a silence for his verdict. Of course, I knew him well enough not to expect an answer, only a question of his own.

'Why are you so keen to get in with that group?' he asked. 'It's as if they've appeared out of nowhere and now they're the only people you want to see.'

'They didn't appear out of nowhere, Lara and Miles have lived in Elm Hill for two years. And they've invited us to their house twice, that's all.'

'Twice in the space of a week.' His mouth remained open for some seconds before he remembered to close it. I wondered what he'd left unsaid and if it might be the very question I'd asked myself, the one that Gayle had posed so baldly: *why?* Why was Lara actively drawing us into her social circle, when her husband was at best disinterested?

Then it came to me, with a clarity that made me marvel both at my own stupidity and the delicious irony of it: it was Ed. He was the reason. Not because he was Georgia's tutor but because Lara liked the way he looked. Its origins were in her fixation with Alain Delon, on full view that evening.

We obviously have the same excellent taste . . .

Did Ed realize this? Was that why he was backing off so categorically, citing drug abuse when he had no genuine evidence? Had there been an overture of some sort on the front-row sofa?

'Did something else happen tonight?' I asked. 'Something you're not telling me?'

He stared at me, the question catching him off guard. What was curious was how unafraid of his answer I was, how flattered by my own suspicions. It was certainly not the response I would have expected of myself, and I was rocked by a surge of exhilaration at my own permissiveness, fleeting though it doubtless was.

'Nothing happened.' His gaze lowered to my top and I knew he must be remembering that moment of exposure before we left. *Is that* really *her cast-off you're wearing? I knew it wasn't your style.* But Ed didn't say things like that, he didn't *think* things like that. And if he could have read my thoughts he would have had every right to be disgusted.

He stood to leave the room, snapped off the kitchen lights even though I was still sitting there.

'You're out of your depth, Nat,' he said.

16

Monday, 31 August, 7 a.m.

Text alerts startle me, an abrupt succession of them, like something coming to life inside my handbag. I scramble to silence my phone, though in her bed Molly sleeps undisturbed, her arms thrown above her head on the pillow, quite still. Ed, too, is slumbering, chin sinking, eyes closed.

Georgia, I think: there must be news. And my pulse drums in my wrists, giving me a queasy feeling as I scroll through the messages of concern and support from Angie, Douglas, Sarah and others.

There's nothing about Georgia, nothing from Lara. But that is to be expected.

I select Angie's message and reply: *Fine here. Is Josh OK?*

She must have had her phone in her hand because she answers within seconds: *Exhausted but also fine.*

Have you had any word from the hospital? Robbed of breath, I wait for her response.

Not yet. We're praying.

The godless are praying: that is how bad it is.

Phone in hand, I fetch the laptop from the kitchen. Chances are the ceaseless, sleepless internet might know something Angie does not. Sure enough, there's a new message up on the lido website:

Monday, 31 August

The pool, café and other facilities will be closed today owing to unforeseen circumstances. Pre-paid bookings for classes and events will be refunded in full. Please check back later today for information about our reopening times. We apologize for any inconvenience this closure may cause.

Liam Rudd, Manager

Unforeseen circumstances: I want to vomit.

'Ed?'

He's like a guard dog, instantly awake, reflexes sharp. 'Is she –'

'She's fine. Look at this.' I point out that Liam posted the message only ten minutes ago. 'So he must be back up there already.'

'He probably didn't go home.' Ed springs to his feet. 'I'll ring him – he might have heard something.'

Presently I hear murmurs from the kitchen. When they peter out, I join him, feeling again that sense of not recognizing the space I have occupied for more than ten years. He is sitting at the table in the dark, the blinds still drawn, and I wait in the doorway for his attention.

'He's been up all night, sounds knackered. The poolside manager's just arrived.'

'Did you find out about the CCTV?' My voice rings with fear; we both hear it.

'They have a digital system, cameras in several places. He's just checking the files now. He's going to call me back.'

'If he finds anything.'

'Yes.' He is watching me oddly. 'One thing he said that was weird: in one of the changing huts, they found towels and a change of clothes.'

'Left by someone during the day?'

'No, the cabins were checked and cleared before the party.' A pause. 'I told him I thought they might be yours, from your little jaunt.'

'Maybe.' It feels like the safest thing to say.

But not right, plainly, because now he looks displeased. 'Except he said there were two sets. One male, one female. So not you and Lara then?'

'No.' I've walked straight into his trap. All I can do is pretend I haven't noticed.

'He's expecting the police back any minute,' Ed says.

'I still don't see why they need to be involved.'

'Because it's a serious accident, that's why.' He frowns. 'It might even be fatal.'

'Don't say that,' I plead, and I reach for the light switch, as if brightness will improve the tone of this exchange.

'One of us needs to. Georgia might die, Nat.'

And though his voice is untainted, I see it in his eyes, in the fraction of a second after the light snaps on, before he recognizes and obscures it: a spark of ferocity that tells me our daughter's ordeal is not his only source of terror.

17

Monday, 3 August – four weeks earlier

I'll never forget the day, even if I never know why it should have been that particular one. Who knows how to deconstruct the alchemy of a breakthrough?

In this case, it included puberty hormones and hypnotherapy (there'd been by then three sessions, each declared 'excellent' by Bryony and confirmed as 'fine' by her patient). Perhaps it also owed something to the new order of a mother whose swimming kit was a fixture on the laundry rack, the routine talk of the new pool and the vibrant scene it had attracted. Or it might have been to do with the heatwave. It was August by then, the sticky core of the school holidays, and we'd grown complacent about the temperature, the smell of sunbaked concrete and grilled greenery, the rogue ice cube pooling on the kitchen counter. Every morning, we plucked the lightest-weight clothes from our wardrobes without first checking the sky.

It could have been all of those factors or none. All I knew was that after nearly a dozen years there was progress and that it came, just as Bryony had predicted, from Molly herself – and in stark rejection of me.

'What shall we do today?' I asked her that Monday morning. 'I'm meeting Gayle for a swim at eleven but this afternoon I'm all yours. We could borrow Inky and go on an adventure?'

Molly grimaced. *Go on an adventure*: it was a call to action for a younger child, yet more shameful evidence – as if there were not enough already – that I was woefully out of touch, that she'd outgrown my area of expertise.

'I want to go to the lido,' she said and, just like some old cartoon character, I felt my heart bounce against my chest like a rubber ball. It was the first time in at least a decade that Molly had expressed a desire to travel towards water and not away from it, but the years of practice in hiding my reactions – let alone overreactions – meant I didn't gasp or cheer or weep at this declaration but said, in the very steady tones of the clinically sedated, 'You want to come with me when I meet Gayle?'

'No, not with you.' Molly shook her head, as if to free herself of the very notion. 'On my own.'

'On your own?'

'I mean with friends.'

'Which friends?' She had, of course, long had the freedom to meet local friends and hang out unattended, but this was different for obvious reasons. This was not the high street or a shopping mall.

'Georgia and Eve and some of their friends from Westbridge.'

'Okay.' Impressed though I was by Georgia, I was not ready to ignore altogether the picture I had of her at the lido with Josh and his mates, the swim-team swagger and – if Matt were right – taste for the incautious. Would they be there too? 'They're a lot older than you, Molls. What about asking Izzy?' Long-term friend and local, Izzy was *au fait* with Molly's history and could be trusted not to get carried away.

'She's on holiday, I told you.' Molly was growing cross. 'God, I can't believe you're stopping me doing the exact thing you've been trying to force me to do all my life. That's *so* messed up.'

I hesitated. I was the villain here and this was a quandary of the most critical order. I needed to think reasonably and act gently. 'I'm not stopping you, of course I'm not. What time were you thinking of meeting?'

'About twelve.'

'Right.' I remembered Bryony's advice: 'They don't like to feel they're being observed.' If I brief the lifeguard on her limitations, I thought, I'll be able to back off next time. *Next time* . . . How fast hope finds its feet. 'How about I sit in the café and read?' I suggested. 'I won't be watching, but I'll be there in case you change your mind.'

'I won't change my mind.'

I must have looked doubtful because she demanded, with sudden belligerence, 'Are you me?'

I was taken aback. 'What do you mean? Of course I'm not you.'

'Then you don't know how I feel, do you?'

'Tell me then,' I said. 'I want to know.'

'I've already told you. I want to go on my own. I don't need you.'

'The words every mother longs to hear. I'm pleased you plan to go, Molly, but this isn't negotiable. I need to be there, just to keep an eye from a distance.'

'Why?'

'Because you can't swim.'

And she glared at me as if that were my fault too.

In thirty-two-degree heat, the largest crowd to date had assembled poolside, as near as prone people could get to starting a riot, and I wondered how rigidly the staff were upholding regulations on capacity. Though it was the kind of restless crush in which you could hide in plain sight, Georgia's preferred spot was on the raised section of the sundeck, which meant I could see the group from the scrap of stone Gayle had colonized for us about 20 metres away. Josh and a younger boy appeared to be the only males in attendance, flat on their backs with earphones in: I could hardly object to that. As Molly picked her way over, I used the opportunity to corner Ethan and have a discreet word. He promised to pay special attention and to make sure the rest of the team was briefed.

When I next looked, there she was, stripped to the pristine navy swimsuit bought for her last abortive set of lessons, the girl who two years ago had become so hysterical in the queue for a water ride at Thorpe Park that she'd had to be led away and made to breathe into a paper bag; the girl who the year before had cried so hard at the suggestion of a boat trip on the Serpentine that her swollen face had taken twenty-four hours to shrink back to normal.

'Breakthrough' wasn't a big enough word for something so almighty, as Gayle's exclamations confirmed.

'Oh, my God, she really is here, isn't she? In a swimsuit! I couldn't believe it when I got your message.'

'I know. I can't believe it either.' Aware that I was shaking, I sat on my hands. 'She hasn't set foot in the place since June and that was under sufferance.'

'How did it happen?' As Gayle prepared her hair for submersion, I saw crinkly silver threads spring from the rest to form a light metallic fuzz in the sun. The skin on her throat was puckered. 'Is it the hypnotherapy?'

'I think it must be, at least partly.'

Not that Molly was in the water, don't get me wrong, but she was closer to it than she'd willingly been since before she could speak in proper sentences. She was watching the others slip in and out without getting distressed. She was subjecting herself to splashes and drips. She was, if I was not mistaken, laughing, laughing at something one of the others had yelled to Ethan, who was receiving quite a heckling from the group and doing a good job of ignoring the jokers to concentrate on the packed pool.

'You know what I think?' Gayle said.

'What?'

'She must like one of the boys. Does she?'

'Not that I know of,' I said.

Gayle chuckled. 'If I ever write a parenting manual, that will be the title: *Not That I Know Of*.'

'Funny.' But this was different, I thought. I knew everything there was to know about Molly's long history of aquaphobia. I'd been with her every step of the way and I didn't think for a moment that this sudden leap was a case of a lovelorn teenager tailing some crush. But Gayle was certainly closer to the truth than I'd been, because the driving force *was* this new circle of friends. Peer pressure had never worked in the past – Molly had turned down invitations to pool parties many times over the years – but Georgia's was an older, cooler group than any who'd brought influence to bear in the past.

'It must be the arrogant muscly one,' Gayle suggested. 'Josh, is it?'

But I was too agitated to gossip. 'Do you mind if we drop the subject? I'm worried if I over-analyse it I'll break the spell.' Because that was how it felt, unreal, like an enchantment.

'Of course,' she said. 'Shall we swim?'

'You go in. I might give it a miss, just this once.'

In an instant Gayle's motivation vanished. 'I'm not sure it's actually possible to swim in that moshpit.'

It was true that the pool was more human flesh than water. I couldn't imagine how the lifeguards could possibly see the bottom of it with this crowd density. Even where there was an unoccupied patch the surface was opaque with bright light. And there were no underwater cameras, I'd learned from my chat with Ethan, which meant all safety relied on direct human observation, on a team of youngsters, some teenagers themselves. What a day to choose, Molly!

'Shall I get us a coffee? How long's the queue at the kiosk?' Gayle scanned the rest of the crowd. 'Oh, look, there's your illustrious new friend. I suppose you'll want to go and say hello.'

So intent was my surveillance of the teenagers that I hadn't thought to check for Lara, but there she was at her VIP table on the edge of the café terrace. Choo was on her lap, which meant Angie couldn't be far away. It struck me that going over to thank her for Saturday night would be an excellent exercise in taking my eyes – my mind – off Molly, if only for a minute or two. No disrespect to Gayle, but if anyone could distract me, it was Lara. 'Maybe we'll stop by quickly on our way to get the coffees,' I said. 'Come and meet her properly.'

At our approach, Lara pushed aside the magazine she'd been reading, but not before I – and presumably Gayle too – had seen the article, a profile of herself complete with a still from the mermaid film, silver tail and all.

'I think I prefer your outfit today,' I teased. Indeed, her black bikini and headscarf of a vintage pink and orange print recalled Jackie Kennedy kicking back in Capri. Her sunglasses today were tortoiseshell Chanel.

I'd never in my life been interested in fashion, but somehow Lara made you want to know the details of how it was done.

'Natalie,' she purred. 'Look who it is, Choo-choo!'

'Hello.' I touched his ear. He was like a fawn, eyes watching for Angie as Lara idly scratched his throat. His coat was satiny cool in spite of the heat.

'I was just about to tell Gayle what fun it was on Saturday night,' I said, though truthfully the situation with Molly had excused any such need. 'We went over to Lara's to watch a film,' I explained.

Gayle smiled weakly.

'And she left *far* too early.' Lara sent me a wicked look. 'You *so* don't want to know what we got up to after you'd gone.'

Actually, I did, but rather hoped she wouldn't tell me in case Gayle reported it to Ed.

'I don't think we've met,' Lara said to Gayle.

'Yes, you have,' I reminded her. 'Out by the entrance a few weeks ago. We were walking my neighbour's dog and you told us about the party.'

At this her beam grew wider. 'It's sold out already! Did I tell you that? And as soon as we announce the band, I guarantee we'll have to start a waiting list.' In her urgent, conspiratorial way she spoke of the acclaimed east London jazz band she'd persuaded to play for a much-reduced appearance fee. 'I had to cook the books a bit, ditch the security guard and one of the bar staff, but it'll be worth it for these guys. They are *sublime.*'

'Brilliant, Lara,' I congratulated her. 'I hadn't realized you were so involved in the organization of it.'

'Oh, you know me, I like a project. But listen, darling, *far* more important than that, I assume you're seeing what I'm seeing?' She gestured in the direction of our daughters, and I needed no second invitation to peer once more at the group. They'd tired of baiting Ethan, and Molly and Eve were now on their knees, as if in prayer, in front of a phone Georgia was holding out. You wouldn't have picked Molly out as different from Eve or anyone else. It was both alarming and intoxicating to think of her as one of this circle, the rest of whom were not only phobia-free but also supremely self-confident. Membership was doubtless widely coveted.

'I told you, Natalie, hypnotherapy reaches the parts other therapies don't. I've decided to get Bryony on to Miles's smoking – not that I've told *him* yet, so don't say anything, will you? He'll resist, naturally.' She let rip with her ringing laughter and when Choo glanced up, surprised, she bent her head to kiss his nose.

A month ago I would have argued that a child's long-standing phobia was an entirely separate matter from a grown man's self-indulgent addiction, but that would have been churlish in the face of evidence that something – *finally* – was working and I had Lara to thank for it.

'It's still a bit of a mystery to me, the process of it,' I said. 'It feels like such a risk, going under. I know it's different for kids, more like having a daydream, but isn't there a regressive element? I worry what Bryony might stir up in Molly, you know, other stuff.'

'Ooh, what other stuff is there? Stuff between you and Alain?' Lara looked at me with mischievous interest, her glass raised to her lips.

'Oh, nothing in particular.' My flushed cheeks told otherwise. 'I mean, not that we don't argue sometimes.' I didn't add that the last row had been about her and her suspected drug-taking.

'Of course you argue,' Lara said. 'You're a married couple. But I imagine it's all very respectful. Not like Miles and me. I threw a shoe at his head the other day. Given the heel on it, he was lucky not to lose an eye.'

As I giggled, Lara looked beyond me and I was startled to remember Gayle was still standing there. Hearing myself through a third party's ears, I had an image of her telling Craig, 'You should have seen Nat with that Channing woman. So sycophantic. All over her like a rash.'

Having said that, there was a directness to the way she was regarding Lara that made me see that *I* was less her object of contempt than Lara herself.

'You threw a shoe?' she said. 'Golly.'

Lara couldn't know that Gayle only ever said 'golly' to poke fun, but the deliberate limpness of the tone and damningly faint smile were unambiguous enough for her to pause in petting Choo and push her sunglasses into her hair, exposing eyes narrowed in confusion.

Resistance to her charms was presumably a rarity in her experience. Ridiculously, this made me feel protective of her and I rushed to make amends. 'All I know is this is a day to remember: Molly Steele hanging out at the pool like a normal kid. I can't thank you enough, Lara.'

'Oh, don't mention it. You're the one who took a chance on Bryony.'

'Only because you magicked up an appointment for us.'

As if to signal that she could bear to witness this mutual-admiration society no longer, Gayle told me she'd get our coffees and meet me back at our base on the other side of the terrace.

'Sit for a bit,' Lara suggested to me, nudging the second seat, presumably vacated by Angie, with her foot. 'Here, take Choo a sec, will you? He's making me hot. Angie's just nipped back to her house to fetch something for Eve.' She made no further reference to Gayle, as if she had never been there, and I felt the downward pull of guilt as I obeyed.

'Just for a couple of minutes.' Choo adjusted himself on my lap, paws poking my bare skin before he settled. My hands cupped his shoulders and head to support his weight. It was like holding a baby. 'Are dogs allowed in here?' I asked.

'Not in the pool area, no, but in the café it's at the discretion of the management.' Lara chuckled. 'Isn't that one of the most comforting lines in the English language? So listen, now Molly's one of the gang, you'll be able to come to the party, won't you? I'm so chuffed.' It was as if the original problem were solved and the matter of our attendance at the event the crucial new issue. She had a childlike approach to problems that was tempting to share.

I laughed. 'I thought you just said it was sold out?'

'It is, but I've kept tickets back for the Circle of Trust. I have to have *some* perks.'

The Circle of Trust. I felt a thrill deep inside me. 'Actually, it's my birthday that weekend and we normally go away.'

Lara's posture straightened, the smile stretching from ear to ear once more. 'It's your birthday? That's *perfect*. I'll give you the tickets as a gift. How about that? You can have a staycation.'

In the face of such persuasion (and generosity, for the tickets, I remembered, were not cheap), I didn't have the heart – or the mind – to object.

'By the way,' Lara added, 'I had an update from Alain earlier.'

'Ed?' Oh dear, I hoped he'd kept his more judgemental opinions about her lifestyle to himself. 'Did he phone you?'

'Emailed. We're very pleased with the progress Georgia's making with her maths. I'm sure it will make all the difference to her grades when term starts.'

'I'm so glad it's working out. I'm sure Ed told you this is a fairly new venture for him.'

'He did. Here's to new ventures.' She held my eye and inhaled deeply, her chest swelling. 'Where *is* Angie? She must have been waylaid. What a bore, I need to pick up Everett from his friend's – Marthe's got a doctor's appointment. Can I leave Choo with you till she comes back?'

'Of course.'

In fact, Angie was another twenty minutes and by the time I returned to Gayle, she was packing up her things to leave. 'I'm so sorry,' I told her. 'I couldn't get away.'

'I'm sure you couldn't,' she said.

'I have to stay till Molly's ready.' I had not been aware, in the hour or so that we'd been there, of Molly once looking my way.

'Who's "Alain"?' Gayle asked.

'Oh, that's Ed. Lara thinks he looks like Alain Delon.'

'The old French actor? Is she for real? Who references someone like that in the year 2015? In *Elm Hill*?'

'She's eccentric, it's not a crime. And he *is* a screen legend,' I added.

Gayle regarded me not so much with annoyance as satisfaction that some dark, long-standing suspicion had at last been confirmed. 'The way she was looking at you, Nat . . . What kind of a twisted thing have you got going with that woman?'

'Don't be crazy,' I said, but I felt a distinct pleasurable charge at her words, powerful enough to cause me to flush.

'By the way, your coffee's cold,' Gayle said.

At home, I reported to Ed my conversation with Lara about the tutoring. 'She really cares about the grades,' I said. 'You wouldn't expect that, would you, from some-one so cool and relaxed?'

Ed chuckled. 'Oh, believe me, that type cares more than anyone, hence the tutoring. You're drinking very quickly.'

'Am I?' In the spirit of celebration, I'd poured myself a glass of rosé. Ed, upholding our term-time rule of drinking only at weekends, had declined to join me. 'What do you mean, she cares more?'

'For the same reason those families are known as the Noblesse,' he said. Gayle must have told him that. How predictable that they'd joined forces in disapproval. 'They feel entitled to the best, and that includes their children's exam results. If Georgia doesn't get ten A-stars next summer, they'll probably . . .' To my astonishment, he was growing a little emotional.

'Probably what?' I prompted.

'I don't know. Sell her into slavery or something.'

'Well, they could get quite a price for her,' I said. 'She's a beauty, all right.'

'Who's a beauty?' Molly appeared suddenly, silently, in the doorway. She must have picked up that disconcert-ing habit from her new friend.

'You,' I said, instinctively reaching to pull her to me in a hug before remembering that wasn't allowed now, that I had to wait for her to offer herself. I hugged her any-way. 'You, of course. What an amazing day, eh? You should be so proud of the progress you made.'

Now I was the one becoming emotional. They say that with your children you care as much as if their triumphs and disasters are happening to you, but that's not true. You care more.

'*Mum*,' Molly protested, extricating herself from my clutch. 'Why do you always have to overreact?'

That red-letter outing to the lido was followed by a second, and a third, and again I insisted on being present on the sidelines. Though Molly made no contact with the water, on one occasion she approached the edge to sit with Eve, their heads bent together over a phone. Focused as I was on Molly's body language, it was a few minutes before I realized what the girls must be doing: timing the laps of those in the water, chiefly Josh, Georgia and a male friend whose name I didn't know but who, judging by his quicksilver flip turns, must have been a teammate of Josh's. The lanes being busy, there was obviously no space for a head-to-head race and the youngsters seemed to have commandeered a lane between them.

Well, there was no rule against racing.

Of course, I'd made it my business some time ago to study the list of activities that *were* prohibited poolside, and I revisited it again when waiting for Molly to join me to walk home. It was reassuringly thorough: no running, diving, ducking, fighting, pushing; no wearing of snorkels or flippers, no throwing of balls . . .

'Makes it look like you can't have any fun at all, doesn't it?' said a jovial male voice at my shoulder. I turned to find Matt, just arrived for a shift, judging by the laundered-cotton smell of his lifeguard's vest. Though he radiated youth and rude health from every pore, it was his eyes that struck me: clear and trusting, with none of the muscle memory of pain.

'No, I think it's an excellent list,' I said. I couldn't tell if he remembered me from our previous conversation or related me to the girl with aquaphobia. I resisted the temptation to repeat the briefing I'd given his manager.

'Which one is it you're worried about?' he asked.

'I was thinking about the ducking,' I said truthfully.

'Hmm, not always easy to spot, but don't worry, we're on to it. Ducking is actually a form of bullying,' he added. 'It can be very upsetting for the victim.'

'I agree.'

When he moved on, I was alarmed to find myself gulping for air, forgetting for one ghastly moment that he had spoken to me as to an adult, a member of the community. A fellow enforcer of decency, not a perpetrator.

Stoneborough, August 1985

When Mel said she was bored, it meant something was going to happen. Like stealing cigarettes from her brother or – in one sting that owed more to luck than judgement – a whole packet from the newsagent's, spoils that we would take to the pond to flaunt in front of the other kids. Like sneaking into the building site on the new estate and looking for something to loosen or break or hide. Like stripping the boys of their shorts and spinning the thieved garment on our fingers the way a martial artist twirs a staff.

Soon this last prank was our favourite. Fast, simple, as old as the hills, it never varied: we'd select our victim carelessly at the end of the day, picking off the weakest in the confidence that the pack would keep on running, then bringing him down by the side of the pond or a few feet into the woods before tearing off his swimming trunks and hiding them in the bushes (local sales of boys' swimming kit must have rocketed that summer: it was not unusual to see a twelve-year-old in shorts too big or too small, borrowed from a family member). Afterwards, we'd sit and watch his naked arse flash off in search of cover.

The main impediment to success was laughter. If we started laughing too early it made us too weak to finish the job and might even land us a blow, like the split lip Mel got one time from a little bastard called Colin. 'Stop making me laugh,' she'd cry, as one of our victims proved exceptionally wriggly. 'Sit on him, Nat! I can't get the fucking things off him!'

'I'm going to wet myself,' I'd heave. It was just so funny, the sight of those righteous, powerless faces — and all the funnier when they thought they were about to get peed on.

At first it was interesting to see under their shorts, the varying stages of male development, but after a while boys were just boys — there were more intriguing things happening under our own clothes – and their protests, their insults, all sounded the same.

'Piggy! Pock-face!'

'Snout-nose! Stain-head!'

'Freaks! Ugly Sisters!'

'Everybody hates you!'

'Yeah, yeah,' we'd say, and afterwards we'd link arms to double our defences, sometimes striding all the way home intertwined.

Did we do what we did because they hated us so much or did they hate us so much because we did it?

Either way it didn't matter to us. As far as we were concerned the boys were complicit: why else did they keep coming back for more? It was only a matter of time before we grew bored and looked around for someone better to torture.

A girl, ideally.

18

Saturday, 8 August

And so the impossible became the inevitable. After her Saturday tutoring session, Georgia announced that she was 'stealing' Molly for the afternoon and offered the frighteningly vague promise that 'If we go to the lido, I'll make sure she's okay.'

'I've got everything I need,' Molly pitched in, equally casual. 'You know, sun lotion and all that.' Not you, was the message.

'But . . .'

'Leave it,' Ed warned me in an undertone. 'I had a quick word with Georgia just now and I'm confident she'll take good care of her.'

So they'd discussed it, without my input.

'She knows Molly can't swim,' he said, 'and she'll make sure she doesn't go in the water.'

I wasn't convinced this was a strong enough 'word', but by now the front door was closing, the girls already laughingly on their way. I had a sense of watching myself, powerless and appalled, of recognizing just too late that I'd witnessed an abduction.

'Anyway, you've briefed the staff, haven't you?' Ed said. Whatever his misgivings about Lara, they clearly did not extend to Georgia. 'Molls just times their laps for them,' he added.

'I know, I told you that before, with Eve. The others race. Georgia and Josh and some of his swimming buddies.'

'Exactly. You know Josh is some sort of regional champion?'

'Yes.' I didn't remind Ed of his sarcasm when Angie had detailed the young prodigy's efforts. 'So you really think we can trust Georgia? This is *in loco parentis*, Ed. What if Molly suddenly decides she wants to stop timing laps and get into the water? Even the shallow end is quite deep, and total chaos with all the younger kids jumping in and out, pulling each other under.' My intestines knotted at the thought of Molly being lost from sight in the mêlée, the lifeguard squinting in vain at the rippling surface, and me, where? At home, outmanoeuvred.

'They've all done life-saving courses, from what I gather,' Ed said, 'and Georgia's taken kids from the Greendale to the swimming pool as part of a community-service initiative at Westbridge. Some of them have never been in a pool in their lives, she said.'

The Greendale was a shelter for victims of domestic abuse and their children. 'I didn't know she did that,' I conceded. 'That's impressive.'

'To be honest, I think she hides her light under a bushel a bit, what with the other big personalities in the family.'

Miles being laconic by anyone's standards and Everett relatively unknown to us, he could only referring to Lara.

His student arrived then, and I spent the next hour divided between my laptop research into the health and safety guidelines for lidos and my phone, alert for breaking news of a terrible tragedy or, at least, for Molly's tearful summons. To stop myself phoning to check on her, I replayed the exchange I'd had with Bryony Foster on the phone the previous day, when I'd called to consult her discreetly on Molly's quantum leap and had, in passing, asked if it was normal for parents to be sidelined in the way we'd been.

The answer was yes. 'All this time she's been on the outside looking in,' Bryony said. 'If she needs to push you to the outside a little bit in order to feel like *she's* getting in, well, it might be worth the short-term sacrifice. This sort of thing is not an exact science and I know it might feel counter-intuitive, but it's going to be fine, trust me.'

It's not an exact science because it's not a science, I imagined Gayle saying, but then I remembered Lara's expression when I'd raised the issue of shallow-water blackout, that flicker of scepticism, as if Molly's lack of progress all these years might have had something to do with my mollycoddling (the pun had not passed me by). Not for the first time it struck me that there might very well be people – my own mother, perhaps – who suspected the original episode had been all in my mind, the ensuing drama some sort of drawn-out Munchausen syndrome by proxy.

No, I had no choice but to try to do as Bryony and Lara advised, and as Ed was already succeeding in doing: trust.

The student left and another arrived. After that, Ed started making noises about packing for the holiday. 'D'you think you might be able to start on it?' he said, and I couldn't confess I was too keyed up to tackle the task. When, by four thirty, Molly had still failed to make contact, I phoned, only to find that the group had left the lido and decamped to Georgia's house. I volunteered to drive over to pick her up.

'She's lost the use of her legs, has she?' was Ed's only remark, but I could tell he thought I'd done well to last as long as I had. 'Don't be long,' he added. 'There's masses to do.'

At La Madrague, the terrace was the usual sunlit, hedonistic scene and, once I'd reassured myself of Molly's survival ('Uh, yeah, I'm *fine*' – this uttered with the breathtakingly dismissive gall of a true revisionist), I surrendered to it with relief. Angie was there, sharing a bottle of rosé with Lara, Choo circling their chairs and snapping at insects. He approached me, tail swinging, recognizing me now.

'Just one more, ladies,' Lara said. 'Miles is taking me to Claridges for our anniversary and I ought to make an effort of some sort.'

'Yes, your standard vagrant chic won't wash there,' Angie said, with characteristic irony. 'We can't let you disgrace yourself in public *again*.'

'How many years have you been married?' I asked Lara.

'Oh, I forget. It was before Georgia – terribly conventional of us.'

'Well, you know the date and that's what counts,' Angie said, giggling. 'I wonder if Stephen knows ours?'

Ed knew ours, of that I was certain, though here and now the fact did not present itself as one to admire.

'Where's *Alain* this afternoon?' Lara asked me, and I thought briefly of Gayle; what with the new complications of accompanying Molly to the lido, we had not been able to co-ordinate our own swims since Monday.

'*Alain* is packing for *les vacances*.' The ice-cold wine, combined with the relief that Molly's excursion had been a success, had produced an elation I'd rarely felt before. 'We head off tomorrow.'

'I forgot you were going away as well,' she said, in flattering dejection. 'Angie goes to Italy on Monday. That's a bore.'

The Channings, I knew, were not going on holiday until after the bank holiday, Westbridge's start of term being later than the local schools', which allowed them to bypass the August bun fight.

'La?' Miles was at the terrace doors, frowning mildly in his wife's direction, presumably on account of her lateness in preparing for their date. Unheeded by her (of the three of us, I alone looked up), he appeared for a moment a little lost. It occurred to me that, for all the time I'd spent thinking about the Channings to date, I had not asked him a fraction of the questions I had his wife and the little personal information I did know had come from her (or the internet) – his age (two years younger than Ed and me), his Kent childhood, his relatively early marriage and young fatherhood. Seeing him in the shadows, perplexed and diminished, I understood suddenly Ed's assertion that he was not enigmatic, just dull. An ordinary man with the trappings of wealth and glamour, the reflected glory of a dazzling wife. Imagine if he lived at Kingsley Drive, if he wore Ed's or Craig's clothes and not his own, a small man in a small house doing a small job. Married to a small woman.

Not an epiphany to share as the first and only drink inevitably became a second.

'Claridges,' I said, after Lara drifted indoors after him, leaving Angie and me alone. 'I'd love to go there. It must be so nice to have such a besotted husband. I bet Miles would do anything for her, don't you?'

Angie lifted her sunglasses and looked at me as if trying to gauge my intended degree of sarcasm. 'Do you really think so?'

'Well, yes. I do.'

As her pale eyebrows rose, she let the glasses drop back on to the bridge of her nose. I had never known a group so committed to their use of sunglasses as theatrical props. 'How funny. I see it as the other way around. *She'd* do anything for *him*.' She chuckled. Everything she discussed was an amusement to her, which made her very easy company. 'He's obviously never asked you to do anything for him. If he had, you'd know what I mean. I shouldn't be saying this, but La and Miles, they're both, you know . . .' When I failed to respond, she lowered both her chin and her voice: 'They may be celebrating their anniversary, but they're not always as observant as they might be about their marriage vows. They have an agreement.' Her chin was up again, voice back to normal: 'You didn't hear that from me.'

I tried not to show how taken aback I was. If this was true then neither Ed nor I had gained a correct impression of Miles. As for Lara, well, I had to admit, it was easier to believe. 'I read a piece in the *Guardian* about open marriages. It suits the man better than the wife, as a rule.'

'There's a surprise.' Angie laughed. 'It doesn't help that men continue to be found attractive long after we've been retired from the game. Isn't that a demoralizing thought?' She paused for a deep medicinal swallow of wine. 'Sometimes I think this could be my last year of having anyone want to sleep with me. I should make the most of it.'

'Hmm.' In light of my own peculiar responses to her husband, I felt it best not to comment on their marriage. A thought struck: what had Lara said at the pool after our movie night? *You don't want to know what we got up to . . .* Did that mean Lara and Stephen, Miles and Angie? Wife-swapping? My face burned.

'Do *you* feel that?' Angie said, peering at me.

I hesitated. My better judgement distorted as it was by sun, alcohol, maternal relief, it was tempting to confide that Ed and I had let the sexual side of things lapse a little in recent years. It was nothing uncommon but, in this company, seemed shameful, something to mark me as predictable. Less desirable. Lara – and Angie too perhaps – enjoyed extramarital adventures while I barely enjoyed marital ones. When a cool breeze from the park touched my hot skin, it seemed to me it contained the faint threat of summer's end, an elemental reminder of approaching old age. No wonder people rushed to seize the day, I thought, to act on the horrible knowledge that nothing lasted for ever. I promised myself there and then that something needed to change, that this group had right what I was getting wrong.

'I do a bit,' I admitted, finally. 'I've definitely been feeling older lately. It keeps hitting me, not how I feel physically, but more how other people treat me. I wondered if it was to do with having a daughter growing up.' Off balance, I asked Angie a question I had not intended to ask: 'What you just said . . . about Lara.' I lowered my voice. 'Do you think she has her eye on anyone in particular?'

The sunglasses came up again and I saw Angie's eyes widen with new interest.

'I don't mean Stephen,' I blundered, 'obviously.'

She cocked her head, smiling. 'Are you asking me if I think you should be worried about *your* husband?'

'No. Yes.' I saw that she looked rather impressed by this answer.

'I would say no,' she said. 'Don't waste your energy. Because if that's what La wants, then that's what she'll try to get, and there'll be nothing you can do about it.'

'Wow.' I wasn't sure what to make of either the opinion or the utterly matter-of-fact delivery of it.

'She and Miles have that in common. They go for what they want. They're heat-seeking missiles.' Angie paused, reflecting. 'But it's never anything personal.'

Returning with Molly to Kingsley Drive, I was aware straight away of a dangerous calm. In the hallway, two large holdalls, so plump with Steele possessions that they strained their fastenings, sat accusingly alongside a bag from Sarah containing items for Inky.

Ed was in the kitchen, prodding a wooden spoon at a dish of bolognese sauce. At the sight of me he said nothing, did not return my greeting, but turned on the gas under a pan of steaming water and began feeding handfuls of spaghetti into it with a pointedness that spoke volumes. It was only then that I realized how late it was, almost eight thirty. How had I let that happen? I had left to collect Molly before five. Miles and Lara would be in their taxi headed for Claridges.

It was my turn to cook.

'No issues with the lido outing,' I said in a regular tone.

'I told you there wouldn't be.' His eyes were reluctant to make contact, his tone bitten down, familiar signs of short-term sulking; if I avoided making any provocative remarks, he'd be fine in about an hour. I felt a rush of tenderness for him, for his being so transparent to me, so legible. There was something to be said for knowing what you were dealing with.

Only when satisfied that every last strand of his spaghetti was submerged did Ed turn to face me. 'What on earth took you so long? We're going on holiday in the morning, or have you forgotten?'

'Of course I haven't. Sorry, the time just flew. Thank you for packing for us. And for cooking – I feel like I haven't done it for ages.'

'You haven't.'

I resisted the urge to pour myself a glass of wine. 'Shall I grate the Parmesan?'

'Already done.'

The table was laid too, water poured. Seeing no way in which I could help, I took a seat. 'I'm really looking forward to getting away.'

'So am I.' There was a sullen pull of breath. I saw I'd underestimated his mood and what it would take to improve it. 'To be honest, I think it might do you good to have a break from your new crowd.'

'Do me good?' I echoed. 'And what d'you mean, *my* crowd? They're yours as much as mine.'

'I would dispute that,' he said, tone grim. 'For me, they're clients first and foremost.'

I would dispute that, first and foremost: pompous, Ed-in-a-mood phrases. *First and foremost*, we were teachers, role models in a society full of drug-users and big personalities. *First and foremost*, we were topping up our pension. That initial affection soured somewhat: how had I not noticed before what a killjoy he could be? Was it because – oh, goodness – was it because I had been one too?

A feeling of disobedience overcame me, an urge to shock him as if he were parent and not partner. 'D'you know what Angie just told me? The Channings sleep with other people. Miles and Lara, that is. I obviously don't mean Georgia.'

Having been about to extract a string of spaghetti with a pair of tongs, Ed's arm halted. Steam flew up, enveloping his fist, but he did not flinch.

'So watch out, "Alain". You know how much she likes you, eh?' It was naughty to tease but, really, he needed to lighten up.

But when he turned, his expression was as righteous as I'd ever seen it. 'You're not suggesting what I think you're suggesting?' In his fist the lid was poised like a cymbal and I imagined him crashing it against his own head – or mine. 'This isn't the Bloomsbury Set, whatever Lara likes to think. Quite apart from the fact that there's something totally fucked up about that mother-daughter relationship, I'm not interested in being unfaithful to you. I'm sorry if that disappoints you.'

There was a catch in his voice that both squeezed my heart and, faintly, despicably, stirred disenchantment in me. Couldn't he at least *imagine* illicit impulses, have a little fun joking about them, even if he – neither of us – had any intention of acting on them?

'I wasn't saying *that*,' I said. 'I was just gossiping, that's all. And hang on a minute, there's nothing fucked up about Lara and Georgia. They have a fantastic relationship.'

'You really think so?'

'Why wouldn't I? Or do you mean what you said about her being tough on grades?'

'I'm not talking about grades. Open your eyes, Nat. The only time they spend together is when Georgia is acting as a maid for her. Serving drinks, babysitting her brother –'

'Helping your daughter with her crippling phobia,' I interrupted. 'She's doing that because Lara asked her to, I bet she is. You know how they stick to their peer groups at that age – someone like Georgia Channing isn't going to befriend someone like Molly for no reason.'

Ed was silent.

'We of all people know how dangerous it is to presume we know what's going on in someone else's family,' I continued. 'Georgia strikes me as a very self-possessed individual and nobody's fool. If she wasn't, then we wouldn't have let her take Molly to the pool today, would we? Come on, you said it yourself – don't you remember?'

'Said what?'

'That she's the real deal. She's special.'

Ed turned off the heat, put on oven gloves to drain the pasta over the sink. 'Can we drop the subject, please, and get on with the hundred things we need to do before tomorrow? Call Molls, will you? This is almost ready.'

As his voice was engulfed by the sudden roar of the extractor fan, I stuck my head around the open door, only to find Molly just feet away in the hallway. She'd showered and was in pyjamas, her hair dripping on to a towel twisted around her neck, and it no longer felt a pipe dream to imagine her damp from a swim, not a shower. I hoped she had not been there long enough to overhear our discussion.

'Dinner's ready,' I told her.

'I ate something at Georgia's,' she said.

'Then eat something here as well.' I stepped towards her, spoke in a conspiratorial tone: 'Blame me, not Dad. I shouldn't have kept us out so late.'

The younger Molly would have fallen into line, wanted to please her father, but this new version just rolled her eyes. 'I can't help it if I'm not hungry,' she said flatly, before walking, straight-backed and undaunted, into the kitchen. 'I'll tell him myself.'

19

Monday, 31 August, 7.30 a.m.

SOUTH LONDON FORUM

Accident at Elm Hill Lido
A local girl is in critical condition at Trinity Hospital following an accident last night at a party at the newly opened Elm Hill Lido. A second girl and a boy were treated at the scene. It is believed that one of the girls, a non-swimmer, fell accidentally and that her friends got into difficulties rescuing her.

'A non-swimmer,' I say, showing the first online report to Ed. 'That's all she is to the rest of the world.' How we've planned and coaxed and agonized over the years in a bid to remove that 'non' from her label, to return her to the state of innocence lost that day in the paddling pool. 'When you think about it, it's amazing that we survived over a decade without something like this happening.'

Ed nods.

As Molly sleeps on, her physical, if not her emotional, strength silently reassembling, I read the comments below the report:

Angel78: Just walked past the lido a minute ago and the police are there.

R_robinson: I hope it doesn't get closed down so soon after it opened!

Angel78: I just pray those kids are OK. What a terrible thing to happen. Where were the parents when all of this was going on?

My fingers are moving across the keyboard independent of rational thought and, focusing, I find I'm looking at visitor times for the critical-care ward at Trinity. At once I know what I must do.

'If you think you're OK on your own for half an hour,' I tell Ed, 'I might head up to the hospital and check on Georgia. Visiting hours start at eight.'

'You've got to be joking,' he objects, and I avoid searching his face for anything but the broadest response. 'You can't leave Molls now!'

'Just for half an hour. She didn't fall asleep until after midnight. I'll be back before she wakes up.'

Inevitably, suspicion returns: 'Where are you *really* going? Are you seriously leaving your daughter who almost died just for the chance to see *him*?'

'That's not it, Ed. Don't go barking up the wrong tree again.'

But the barking is already in full voice: 'You *were* with him, weren't you? In the changing hut. I know you were.'

'I was with Lara. I'm sure she would confirm that.' But I flush and he sees my guilt.

213

'I had a feeling, you know,' he says. 'Right from the beginning. You and him.'

That stuns me into silence.

'The way he looked at you. And me, in a way. Like he was relishing the challenge of it.'

I shake my head, feel the soreness on the side of my face. 'You're wasting your time thinking like this. Please, just trust me.'

He watches, silently hostile, as I kiss Molly's hot cheek, adjust the sheet a little, thank God again that she's here and not in the place I'm about to go to. She coughs again and I wait for her to resettle before I leave the room.

Locating my jacket in the hallway, I hear Ed muttering to himself and when I return to the bedroom door, his face is filled with an anguish close to heartbreak. 'What, Ed?'

At the sound of my voice, he starts, fails to hide his agitation. 'I was just thinking, thinking I can't believe I cancelled Paris for last night.'

'Paris?' I stand there arrested, bewildered. 'What do you mean?'

'I had a weekend in Paris planned for your birthday. I hoped it might help . . .' The thought, the hope, disintegrates on his lips and his tone hardens. 'But you were so keen on this bloody pool party I cancelled it.'

'I wish I'd known.'

'Would you have come?'

'Of course I would.'

And as I leave, I think how there are times when life unfolds tidily in precisely the sequence of events you'd like and expect, the right words said to the right person at the right moment.

And then there are times when it unravels in a way you know is wrong and was never meant to be. A way that has the power to destroy everything.

20

Monday, 10 August — three weeks earlier

Given Molly's recent advances, the arrival of our holiday appeared to represent unfortunate timing. It was also the first and, it would transpire, only week of the summer in which it rained: daily, hourly, by the second, a relentless pulse that maddened the blood. Ironic, then, that Ed and I had, as we always did, selected a location a safe distance from water: from our small stone cottage in a hamlet accessed by a muddy lane, there could be no accidental stumbling upon coast, lake or waterpark.

Instead we caught up on reading and TV and plundered the chest of board games provided by the owners. Somehow Molly's childhood had passed without a game of Cluedo and it was this that proved her favourite.

'I'm not sure about this new board,' said Ed, of the latest-edition visuals.

'What's new about it?' Molly asked.

'The original one had a billiard room, not a spa, and you went to the cellar to make your accusation, not to a swimming pool. Why would you make an accusation in a swimming pool?'

'Why would you make one in a cellar?' I said.

'It's a question of self-preservation,' Ed said. 'If you're in a pool, you're barely clothed, a hopeless condition for fleeing in the event of conflict.'

'Well, in a cellar, you could be trapped. That's no good for fleeing either.'

'You're not arguing, are you?' Molly said, and Ed and I looked at each other with consternation.

'Of course not,' I said. 'Just having fun.'

'I'll see if I can track down the original board and you'll see what we mean,' Ed told her.

'Mum and Gran might have one in Stoneborough,' I said. 'They're not known for updating their entertainment offering.'

'I'm not even kidding,' Molly said.

Her question notwithstanding, the mood was far easier that week than I'd expected, or deserved, frankly, given the tensions that had preceded the trip. I was ashamed of taunting Ed with the Channings' alleged open marriage – what had I been thinking? It had served no purpose whatsoever – and grateful that he had been able to set it aside, if not forgive me wholesale. Neither of us wanted to ruin this holiday for Molly.

Though she had been the keenest of all of us to bring Inky, predictably she now refused to come on the rain-splashed dog walks. Last summer we would have overruled her and insisted she join in, but now we said fine, we respected her wishes.

'It *seems* like she's being lazy,' Ed said, as we trudged through cool, wet woods, the morning sky as dim as twilight. The ground was so sodden it tried to glue us to it, our wellingtons making obscene sucking sounds each time our feet pulled them up. 'But actually it's a really big thing to be left alone in an unfamiliar place at this age. It's good for her psychologically.'

'If she was our third or fourth child we wouldn't even be having this conversation,' I agreed, suspecting that we were having it anyway because, historically, discussion of Molly had united us like nothing else. Of course I was mindful of the ongoing need to stop obsessing (I couldn't shake that stage-mother comment of Lara's), but building bridges with Ed superseded that. 'She's craving independence,' I added. 'Look at the lido situation – amazing! When we get back to London, should we organize swimming lessons, d'you think?'

'No,' Ed said. 'She'd say if she wanted that. Also, don't you think the fact that we *haven't* tried to organize anything has been a part of what's worked? Like that business of the tour.'

On the drive down, news of a further leap had been announced. Full of bright ideas, as those with a guilty conscience often are, I had proposed once more a behind-the-scenes tour of the lido with Liam, only for Molly to respond that she had already arranged it for her return and that Georgia would be accompanying her. This she reported with an offhandedness that indicated pride, and I guessed it had been Georgia's enthusiasm for the scheme that had prompted the approach – not to Liam, but to Matt – in the first place.

'So what are these secret plans for my birthday you told Sarah about?' I asked Ed now.

'Be patient,' he said, and it was a relief to hear the old twinkle of affection in his tone.

Encouraged, I said, 'It's just that I like the sound of this pool party.'

'What pool party?'

'You know, the one at the lido, the night of my birthday. Lara's involved – it's a nineteen-sixties Riviera theme.'

Ed pulled a face, as if he knew what bacchanalian depravities *that* would involve.

'Only if you fancy it,' I said hastily. 'But she wants to give us tickets as a gift. Molly too. It's very generous of her.'

He conceded this. 'Would Molls want to go to something like that?'

'It's not a swimming party. The pool itself will be closed. I think it could be fun.'

'We'll decide nearer the time,' Ed said, which was code for no. 'I thought maybe we could do something active, like walk the South Downs Way.'

Given his earlier secrecy, this was certainly a red herring, but the truth would not be so different, not so different from *this*, a fern-scented waterlogged English forest that was not without its charms. I was aware of the conflict more than once that week: the cosy appeal of the familiar versus the hunger I'd felt for change – revolution, even – when talking days ago to Angie.

Ed brought us to a halt on the edge of a mud bath where several paths crossed. Rocks and vegetation were disappearing under rainfall. 'Where on earth are we?' he said, frowning.

'On the sea bed?' Waiting at his side as he pulled a map from his anorak pocket, I was speared without warning by nostalgia for a different wood, a drier day, the dusty tangle of branches and the smell of pond water drying on burned skin. We'd be going to Stoneborough at the end of the week, my first visit of the year and one of sufficiently few for me to be able to recall each individually. Was that why I'd been so besieged by thoughts of the place recently? Or was it the swimming? That and the sweet exhilaration of making new friends had combined this summer to stir sensory memories of *that* one and it seemed I could regulate neither their frequency nor their effect.

Behind the drone of the downpour, I suddenly fancied I could hear those jazz piano chords Lara liked so much, those plaintive strings. Then, from across the years, another kind of music, sung by young voices in a twang not quite comic enough to stop it sounding sinister.

'Are we lost?' I asked Ed and my tone was almost hopeful.

'I think we might be.' He looked through the trees at the swollen clouds, just in time for a large drip to break like an egg on his upturned face.

*

As if to illustrate my point about Georgia Channing being special, Ed revealed that she was the only student with whom he had agreed to stay in contact during his week away. A brief session on FaceTime had been arranged in lieu of their regular Wednesday slot.

As they were finishing, Lara appeared on screen beside her daughter. She was in a primrose-coloured sweater, that imperfect smile brightening the visuals like a change in settings.

'Hi, guys! Don't you dare tell me about your amazing weather because it's *abysmal* in London.'

'Same here,' I said, over Molly's shoulder. Clearly she'd forgotten we were less than a hundred miles away, still in England.

'I've just been swimming and I was *literally* the only one in the pool.'

'You still went in, even in the rain?'

'Yes, but it was in my top ten worst swims, *really* grisly. The sky was so low, I was practically breathing in cloud. I'm surprised I didn't choke to death.'

I imagined the sensation of swimming through the rain, the thousands of drops drumming the surface of the water like hammerheads on soft metal, and for a moment I wished I'd been there to brave the assault with her. 'It'll clear soon, Lara. The forecast is better for next week.'

'I bloody hope so or I'm going to have to raid the Pharm good and proper.'

'Oh, Mum, don't be so outrageous,' Georgia said good-naturedly.

'You *know* I need the sun, darling.'

'Yes, it's a very reptilian trait.'

Lara feigned giving her a shove. 'I prefer to think of myself as a tropical plant.'

'Deadly nightshade?' Georgia said and, after a blurred bobbing of heads, the screen cleared and I saw mother and daughter were hugging and laughing together. I laid a hand on Molly's shoulder and felt a stiffening of muscle under the soft fabric of her fleece. As soon as the call ended, she disappeared to her room.

'Not so fucked-up after all, eh?' I said to Ed, but not provocatively because it was nice to be friends again.

He shrugged. 'What's the farm? Some posh spa, I suppose?'

I told him I didn't know, even though I did and it was perfectly harmless – the Pharm was Lara's nickname for her medicine cabinet. But given Ed's earlier suspicions of cocaine abuse it seemed inadvisable to fan the flames.

When Molly reappeared, her hair was in a high ponytail, long strands at the front falling into her face. It didn't take Cluedo wizardry for me to figure out when and where I'd seen the style: Georgia, the FaceTime call from La Madrague, maths textbooks on her knees.

Later in the week, in an immaculately chosen private moment that doubtless rankled with her as much as any ill-chosen public one, I sought Molly out in her bedroom. She was in front of the mirror, her expression both self-critical and reflective, her lips slicked with a luscious pink no one but her parents would see. I paused in the doorway, not wanting to break her spell. No sense in pointing out that she – and all girls her age – looked a hundred times better bare-faced, that they didn't know how beautiful they were.

'Bored?' I asked, and when her eyes flicked towards me, that candid, receptive gaze so characteristic of her was replaced almost at once with an opaqueness that excluded me. For all I could tell, she was thinking profound and conflicting thoughts or she was thinking nothing at all.

'Aren't you?' she said, shrugging.

It was as if every day she came up with a new way to avoid giving information (in fact, answering a question by asking one of your own was pure Ed). I responded conversationally, invoking the only piece of advice all parents and teachers seemed to agree on: keep the lines of communication open. 'Not so much bored as soggy. I didn't think we'd need our wellies and raincoats inside.' This was a reference to the many leaks that had made themselves known in the upstairs rooms.

Still the rain lashed, the windows squares of smudged grey beyond which the world had been liquidized.

'Molls?'

'Yes.'

'I'm so pleased things are starting to happen – you know, with the hypnotherapy and the trips with Georgia to the lido.'

No reply.

'We understand you want to do it alone, or not with Dad and me involved, but I just wanted to say that you can always talk to me, you know that, right? Not just the pool stuff, anything. Even if it's embarrassing or awkward or something you think might make me angry, I'll always listen. I'll always be on your side.'

'I know.' Another quick glance, another good intention annihilated by teenage distaste.

'Okay.' I wasn't sure whether she was only saying what I wanted to hear. While it helped to draw on my own feelings and behaviour at the same age, there was no family precedent for how I should respond; I had never been given such overt reassurance by my own mother. If I had, might I have behaved less deplorably? Was I even now, in some dysfunctional way, blaming her?

'Mum, can I have the laptop next week, when I stay at Grandma's?'

'Sure,' I agreed. 'Let me just check I have everything I might need before you take it.' Not that I intended doing anything work-related; there'd been moments these last few weeks, whole days, when I'd forgotten teaching altogether.

Downstairs, transferring a couple of documents from hard drive to memory stick, I had a quick glance at Molly's desktop. Though I told myself it was a routine parental check, I knew full well that my eyes were alert for anything phobia-related – all right, not 'anything': one thing in particular.

A journal. Bryony had told me about it when I'd phoned for advice the previous week: in their very first session, she'd recommended Molly keep one to record her feelings about the new pool, in particular about the occasion she'd gone there with me. Of course there'd since been expeditions involving Georgia too – in fact, so much had happened since Molly had last seen Bryony that I wondered how they would fit the hypnotherapy itself into their next half-hour appointment.

At first I'd assumed the journal would, if it existed at all, be the traditional kind, handwritten entries in a note-book, but Ed had reminded me that this age group wouldn't dust down an ink pen if their lives depended on it. 'Not that it matters either way,' he'd added. 'A diary is private, end of story. None of our business.'

'Of course.'

And now here it was, a Word file sitting just above the Trash icon, as if it might at any time find itself nudged into oblivion: 'MS Journal'.

Don't click, I warned myself.

I clicked. The file was locked. Which both served me right and allowed me to pretend I'd never committed the infraction in the first place.

I was about to shut down when another Word file caught my eye: 'NOP'. What did that stand for? Some teenage acronym, like GTG or BFN? (Traditionally, Gayle had translated them for me.)

I opened this one without trouble and found my answer in the heading: 'Normal Operating Plan'. It was an excerpt from a lido staff document, perhaps shared by Matt in advance of the girls' tour:

Elm Hill Lido Normal Operating Plan
Awareness of risks

a. Youth and inexperience. Pay particular attention to those who appear nervous or afraid. Never forget that the life expectancy of a drowning non-swimmer is measured in seconds, not minutes.
b. Alcohol and drugs taken before swimming. Persons who appear intoxicated must be excluded.
c. Unclear pool water, preventing casualties from being seen.
d. Unauthorized access to pool intended to be out of use. Managers must assess effective measures to prevent access. These may include physical barriers and staff supervision.
e. Absence of pool attendants in an emergency.

I read point (a) a second time, before closing the lid and leaving the laptop on the kitchen table for Molly to reclaim.

21

Sunday, 16 August

We did not pass Mel's house as we drove into the village, but even so I buried my face in the hydrangea on my lap until Ed had parked the car at my grandmother's door.

I'd been back to Stoneborough numerous times, of course, since *that* summer – flat refusal would only have roused suspicion – for many years careful to keep myself indoors and out of sight. Later, on the rare excursions to the shop or village green with a young Molly, I'd taken refuge in the camouflage of motherhood, though by then the community had developed and those who'd been children in the 1980s and hadn't fled to the city were unrecognizable from their young selves. As for Mel, a chance remark of my grandmother's had let me know she'd left the village for Southampton in her early twenties. Her mother, Cheryl, was still there, though unlikely to be able to identify a girl she'd scarcely laid eyes on at the time.

Why, then, did I still feel the need to hide? Paranoia, I told myself. How could it be anything more after thirty years? And yet it was hardly less stressful than having something real to fear.

'What an enormous plant!' my mother exclaimed at the door. 'You're far too generous,' she added with genuine reproach. I'd heard of mothers who could see no wrong in their grown-up daughters, but mine, alas, had not.

'It's only a hydrangea,' I said.

'But in a *very* nice pot. It looks hand-thrown.'

'Hand-thrown?' Ed echoed. 'Wouldn't that mean it was smashed to pieces?'

'Ha-ha, Edward. Have you two won the pools or something?'

'What's the pools?' Molly asked, wearing the same mistrustful look that I could only hope had skipped a generation.

'Football scores,' Ed told her. 'It was a gambling game that people used to play before the Lottery.'

'Still do,' said my mother. 'The woman in Boots' brother's friend just split a million with two others. That's worth having.'

'Three hundred and thirty-three thousand, three hundred and thirty-three pounds, thirty-three and a third pence,' Molly said, before Ed could ask.

'I don't suppose they argued about the penny,' said my grandmother, from the room beyond.

'Granny, hello!' I called. 'Can we come in and sit down?' We were still in the hallway, but conversation – or confrontation – with my mother tended to begin the moment the door opened. Already there was an odd disconnect between my own grudging conduct and the willing banter of everyone else.

Once the door was closed behind us, I unclenched a little. We unloaded Molly's bags and arranged ourselves in the sitting room, where there was, as always, the faint smell of cats, in spite of there being none in residence. Perhaps they wandered in unnoticed by the chattering women and helped themselves to nibbles, like the ones Mum now distributed with drinks.

'Wotsits,' Ed said, 'king of the extruded snack,' and I could tell he was wondering about Molly's nutrition during the forthcoming week.

'Nice and easy on nonagenarian gums, eh?' my mother said, from her drinks cabinet by the window. 'Do you know what a nonagenarian is, Molly?'

Molly looked hopeful of a rude punch line but I could have told her to expect a straight definition.

My mother had moved here on retirement four years ago, my grandfather having died not long before and my grandmother, then in her late eighties, not able to live alone. Ed and I had always regarded this as an act of duty to be admired, celebrated. If and when the time came, we hoped that we, and Molly after us, could be counted on to fulfil the same familial duty. Nothing in his manner suggested any change of position on this. I, however, was aware almost on arrival of a brand-new emotion in my own response, an unwelcome, guttural one that I could only imagine had been exacerbated by general nerves: revulsion. Because my grandmother looked – not to put too fine a point on it – decrepit. Her eyes were glassy and remote, as if peering at us from inside a jar, and her skin fell from the bone like oversized clothing. The idea of my mother nursing her struck me as not so much heroic as perverse; I didn't want to be responsible for someone in this condition any more than I wanted to foist it on my own daughter.

'Thank you,' I said, accepting a tepid gin and tonic with weak fingers. What was wrong with me? Was this another manifestation of the crisis I'd experienced on meeting Georgia for the first time or, in a smaller way, the conviction I'd felt talking to Angie that I owed it to myself to seize life while I still had the muscular strength to do it? Looking to Molly for reassurance, I saw that she was regarding her great-grandmother in exactly the way she always did, with respect and wonder, rather as she would marvel at the longevity of a giant tortoise. She made no connection between her own flesh and that of her aged relative's. Between us, drinks distributed, sat the interim model that was my mother, aged seventy, sprightly enough, and single by choice since divorcing my father almost two decades ago. (In the end, they had waited for me to leave home, an ill-conceived act of selflessness if ever there was one.)

I thought of that sense I'd once had that the men had been eliminated from society and eyed Ed with gratitude and unexpected desire.

Catching my eye, he frowned his 'All right?' frown and I nodded, swallowing a damp Wotsit.

'So have you got all your textbooks with you?' Mum asked Molly. 'What will we test you on this time?'

'Nothing,' Molly said. 'I didn't bring any schoolwork.'

My mother and grandmother exchanged a look of astonishment.

'She had a few bits and pieces at the beginning of the holidays, but now she's mostly just hanging out with chums,' I said. 'She doesn't have any studies to do while she's here, not unless she wants to.'

'I don't,' Molly confirmed.

'Has something happened?' my mother said, looking from Ed to me. 'Normally the poor girl doesn't have a minute to herself. Why's she suddenly been let off the leash?'

'I wouldn't call her a poor girl,' I said, '*or* on a leash. Molly's older now, Mum, she's thirteen. She can decide how she wants to spend her free time.'

I didn't point out that, with his roster of private students, Ed had neglected the extracurricular enrichment of his daughter's state education this summer; when the first tranche of maths had been exhausted, he had not had time to set the next. Meanwhile, distracted by the lido, by new friends, I had been cutting her slack of my own. The week without us in Stoneborough had been Ed's idea, proposed in the spring when we'd planned the main holidays. At the time, I'd suspected he was concerned about my tendency to restrict her freedoms, thought Molly and I needed time apart. But that had been before Bryony, before Georgia. Before Lara. Such thoughts were unappealing, like remembering how it felt to be penniless after you'd struck gold.

'Can I help with lunch in any way?' I offered. The fact that neither hostess needed to be in the kitchen foretold of some one-pot affair that Molly would be sure to reject. I noticed there were extra place settings at the table, but did not draw attention to the miscount. I thought again of the missing men.

'No, all done,' my mother said. 'We made the casserole the day before yesterday. I hope the potatoes haven't gone liquid.'

I didn't look at Molly. All I could hope for was that there was no offal involved.

'By the way, Natty, we have a surprise for you. Don't we, Mum?' My mother became animated, almost gleeful. 'I was in the shop yesterday and I happened to overhear her talking, so I threw caution to the wind and asked her outright.'

There was a silence. 'Asked who what?' I said at last.

'If she was your old friend Mel, of course,' Mum said.

I had the sensation of being poised at the top of a tall slide, an inch from tipping, my arms only just able to withhold my bodyweight from the plunge.

'And she was! She's been up all week visiting her mum while the damp's sorted out in her flat.'

My eye fell again on those extra place settings. 'Mum, you didn't?'

'Invite her for lunch? Of course I did.'

Now I was plummeting, friction burns on my legs and elbows.

'Cheryl can't come – she works in a pub in Eastleigh at weekends – but she's bringing her grandson instead.'

'Cheryl's grandson?'

'Mel's. She's got four, she told me. The little boy hasn't inherited her nose, which is a mercy.'

'Why, what's wrong with it?' Molly said, then, remembering my stories, 'Oh, Snout-nose.'

'What a thing to say,' Mum said, frowning.

'You should be ashamed of yourself, Molly,' Ed said. 'I hope you won't say that in front of Snout-nose herself.'

As father and daughter giggled, I looked helplessly at them. Ed wouldn't be joking like this if he knew the truth. You have to face your fear, I told Molly (or at least I had until one therapist deemed it an unhelpful mantra), but I'd never faced my own and now I was going to have to, with five minutes' notice. I was going to the gallows without being allowed a last prayer.

It had not been easy to restrain myself, but over the years I had not once asked my grandmother for news of Mel or her family and she did not have the kind of personality to tittle-tattle unprompted. That one mention of Mel having relocated had been all she'd given and all I'd needed. My mother was a different matter: it would not have taken her long to penetrate the Stoneborough network, to acquire the intelligence needed to identify strangers from a moment's eavesdropping.

'Are you all right?' Ed asked me. 'You don't look too well.'

'I'm fine, just a bit thrown. No one likes a blast from the past.'

My mother was incredulous. 'I thought blasts from the past were exactly what people liked. All this Facepaging.'

Molly and Ed giggled again. What was suffocating terror to me was high comedy to them. I was on my own.

The doorbell rang. 'I'll get it,' Ed offered.

I didn't know her when she entered the room, a small boy in her wake: she did not resemble her younger self at all. She was heftier, close to obese, and her hair, which I'd remembered as having the colour and shine of young conkers, was black and charred-looking, like the remains of a bonfire. And yet my face burned, my ears filled with the whine of tiny insects, my heart banged harder still. How did the brain do this, provoke the fight-or-flight response to danger long lapsed?

'Hello again, Mel,' Mum said, with a merriment she had not shown at *our* arrival.

'We've got you some chocolates,' Mel said in reply, gripping a box of Cadbury's Heroes like an award, and it was her voice – the twang of its accent perfectly suited to the throwaway tone – followed by the rebellious bark of her laughter that made me know her.

My first lucid thought: did she remember the circumstances of our parting? Of course she did. How could she not? A better question was whether or not she despised me for it. But she was here, wasn't she, her eye contact perfectly guileless? The flatness of her nose was not so noticeable: it had been an unnecessarily cruel fixation.

'Nasty Nat!' she said, and when Molly gasped, she smiled warmly at her.

My heart rate steadied. How could I imagine I was in danger? She had never harmed me, she had *favoured* me. What I was feeling was the result of the same loose wiring that had caused that episode with Stephen in the screening room, linked perhaps to the intermittent midlife crisis. This was not a woman with a grudge, but one with soft spots – and adult responsibilities.

The boy was about Everett's age and rather bold, judging by his opening remark: 'Where's your birthmark? Nan says it's as big as a fried egg. That's unless you've had it lasered.'

'I haven't,' I told him. Long experience in speaking with children of his age calmed me. 'It's hidden under my make-up.'

'We used to call them angel's kisses,' said my grandmother.

Not around here, I thought, but I smiled gratefully at her.

'How many kids have you got, Mel?' Ed asked.

'Three. All grown-up. Rio's my oldest daughter Justine's second boy.'

I supposed being a grandmother in your mid-forties was not so unusual. At Elm Hill Prep the mothers were still producing their own babies at that age, but at Rushbrook there'd been a smattering of Mels.

'What's for lunch, Nan?' Rio asked.

'It's a corned-beef hotpot,' said my mother, and the boy's dismay mirrored Molly's. I knew I wouldn't have been able to eat even if it had been a Michelin-starred feast.

'He won't eat that,' Mel said, matter-of-fact. 'Fussy eaters, the lot of them.'

'To be fair, I don't think kids today are familiar with corned beef,' Ed said, and I thought of the class discussion about ersatz foods, the paste sandwiches and rock cakes at the D-Day party that had remained largely untouched by children who knew how to roll their own sushi.

'Are you still called Mean Mel?' Molly asked the guest, when we were finally called to the table. She was considerably more engaged than she had been at any time in the preceding week, Cluedo included.

'Not often,' Mel said, cracking a grin that exposed undersized teeth. And though I'd not given it a thought in thirty years, the sight now of one of the central incisors overlapping its neighbour was as familiar to me as my own eye colour. I felt a lurch inside me, not so much of remorse as loss. I blinked. Now that the adrenalin had drained, so had lucidity of thought, and I was finding it a strain to connect to this experience fully.

'You're not mean, Nan!' Rio protested loyally. He was a sweet thing, really.

I wondered if Mel had taken him to the pond to swim and was about to ask when she winked at him, answering, 'Depends who you listen to, love.'

At this, my mother's antennae twitched. 'Does he know about . . .?' As she allowed the question to fade delicately, I froze, petrified. Did *Mum* know, then? But the unspoken intelligence was new to me too, it emerged, for no sooner had Rio finished not eating and been allowed to slide from the table to play on his DS than Mel was confiding to us that in her twenties she'd served six months in an open prison.

'Blackmail,' she said baldly, which made me gulp. 'I'm not proud, but there we are.'

There we are, she kept saying. Yes, I was inside, but there we are. Dean and me split up, but there we are. One of my daughters hasn't been to visit in nearly a year, but there we are. Nat and I were feral bullies one summer, but *there we are*.

She didn't say that, of course. She didn't mention our shared summer at all, in fact, keener to describe her daughter's travels in Thailand and a recent coup in obtaining studio audience tickets for the forthcoming series of *The X Factor*.

'How long are you staying at your mum's?' I asked. I could feel a distinct tingle of unease, the beginnings of panic, and it wasn't hard to identify its source: I didn't want to leave Molly in Stoneborough if Mel was there. Blithe she may have become, but I didn't trust her.

'Just till tonight. I have to work tomorrow. But Rio's staying another week. The whole block's got damp, it's a nightmare.'

The tingle subsided.

'Maybe Molly and Rio can play,' my mother suggested, and Molly looked aghast at the idea.

'Molly doesn't really "play" any more,' I said.

'They could go down to the shop together then,' Mum modified.

Molly pulled a noncommittal face, addressing Mel: 'Mum told me how you used to steal cans of Coke from Mr Moron's and when you opened them they exploded all over your clothes because you'd been running.'

'Another vintage anecdote,' Ed said, winking at Molly. 'I assume that wasn't Mr Moron's real name?'

'No, Morton. He's long gone,' said my mother.

I was staring at Mel by now, mesmerized by the planes of her face, the light and shade cast by her chewing muscles, the familiar and unfamiliar messages her eyes sent. 'We were horrible to him, weren't we, Mel?'

'I don't remember him.' She sighed. 'We were so bored that summer. Like *every* summer. Nothing to do in Stoneborough. No offence, Mrs Waters.'

'None taken,' my grandmother said. 'It's precisely because there's nothing to do that we like it so much.'

As fear gave way to disbelief, I turned my frowning face from Mel to my grandmother and back again. What did she mean, nothing to do? Three decades I'd been haunted by that summer. It was impossible to accept her perfunctory dismissal of it.

Ed, at least, sensed the source of my disquiet. 'I think "Nasty Nat" has rather sentimentalized her summer of delinquency,' he said, smiling at Mel. 'Your reign of terror over the neighbourhood boys?' Even the little he knew he had reassessed, I saw, likely thinking that Mel's prison sentence made our juvenile misdemeanours pale into insignificance.

'I have *not* sentimentalized it,' I said, struggling to manage my distress.

Soon after, I engineered a moment alone with Mel when she was in the garden, smoking. We must have stood here together before, I supposed, possibly shared one of the cigarettes stolen from her parents and brother.

'How's Nick?' I said. 'Do you remember how he was supposed to be looking after us while your mum went to work, but he just got on the bus to Southampton every day to see that girl?'

Mel chuckled. 'He's still the same lazy bastard.'

I held her eye, aware of the neediness that must be so evident in my own. 'Do you think we look different now, Mel?'

She sniggered. 'It would be a bit fucking weird if we didn't.'

But she understood, as her next comment showed: 'Didn't you want to have a skin graft or whatever?'

The birthmark, she meant.

'I don't mind it so much now,' I said. 'It's faded a lot. Anyway, these things are a part of us, aren't they? I wouldn't want Molly to think you should have to fix your imperfections and be the same as everyone else.' I thought of Lara's smile, the surprise of the gaps between

239

her teeth, little breaches of her beauty. 'But it wasn't very nice when we were her age, I admit. All the name-calling, remember?'

Mel drew on her cigarette. 'Do you think your mum is going to open the Heroes? I told Rio she would.'

'I don't know.' It wasn't only frustration I felt at this obtuseness – or evasion – it was also sorrow. Once she'd been my leader, but now she was left behind, and not just by me, I guessed. Lara's face flashed a second time: she was a different kind of leader, a saviour from ordinariness, from myself. What would Mel make of *her*? The thought made me glow with secret pride. How far I had come, how well things had turned out for me, if *she* was my friend now.

It was time to be direct, I decided. Who knew if I would see Mel again? I might never have another chance at exorcism. 'You know, I always wondered what happened to that girl.'

'What girl?' As she drew on the cigarette, deep grooves appeared around the edge of her upper lip. 'Oh, the blonde cow. What did we call her again?'

'Nessie.' And just like that, with those two syllables, my heart was a drum again, battered with steel-capped sticks by some hyperactive demon.

'That's right!' Mel exclaimed, with delighted laughter, exactly as if she'd not given the subject a thought in years. I couldn't tell if she was acting; I couldn't read her at all.

'Do you remember my gran thought it was short for Vanessa? She thought she must be one of our friends.

"Do you want to invite Nessie for tea?" she used to ask me.' My voice caught. 'Maybe I should have done that. Maybe we would have been friends.'

Stubbing out the cigarette in a flowerbed, Mel whistled. 'God, Nat, you really hold on to this shit, don't you?'

'I suppose I do.' I was pleased that she lit a second cigarette, was prepared to talk on. 'I still feel bad about it, Mel. She didn't do anything to hurt us – she didn't say a word to offend us. What we did, it was evil.'

'Don't be mental, Nat. We were kids.'

We stared at each other.

'The family left, didn't they?' I said. 'Do you know where they went? Sometimes I feel like I should get in touch, try to explain.'

But she was utterly lacking in remorse. 'Seriously, if that's the worst thing you've ever done, then you must have been living like a nun all these years.'

'It's not just Nessie,' I said. 'I felt awful for leaving you in the lurch. I've never been able to tell you that.'

Her lips parted, her surprise genuine, and I realized then that she'd not seen it as I had. She'd seen it only as the way she was used to people behaving towards her, the same way she expected them to behave towards her in the future. It was wretched and there was nothing I could do to make amends. I knew for certain I would not see her again.

No sooner had Mel and Rio left than Ed began making noises about traffic on the M3.

'What do you have planned while Molly's with us?' Mum asked, and all at once the week stretched ahead of me like a stroll through the Promised Land. Ed would be working, but I would be free.

'Swimming at the new lido, a few drinks things,' I said.

'Well, quite the *bon vivant*. You'll have to keep an eye on her, Ed.'

To my horror, I blushed.

We said goodbye to Molly. It was bittersweet to know that I was sadder about the separation than she was. It was another thread broken. But that was right and natural, I knew. The threads were the dissolving kind – you couldn't find the ends to fuse them again, you had to let them go.

Driving home, I was overcome with a relief so heavy it was almost a sense of reprieve, even reward. It was nothing to do with having left my beloved daughter, of course. It was to do with Mel, her casual dismissal of our wickedness, her absence of hard feelings towards me. She didn't care, it wasn't a big deal. If I took her lead as unquestioningly as I had at the time, I'd live the rest of my life guilt free.

I stared through the windscreen at the thickening red string of brake lights ahead as the motorway curved towards London. Soon the evening would fade and we'd be dazzled by headlights. I reached to touch Ed's hand, resting between us on the gearstick.

'What?' he said, glancing across.

'Oh, you know, just seeing Mel, it made me think, there but for the grace of God . . .'

'Come on,' he scoffed. 'You shared a few japes when you were Molly's age, that's all. I don't know why you're so hung up on it. It couldn't be more obvious that you have nothing in common.'

'It was a lot more than japes, Ed.'

'What are you saying?' He inhaled sharply, for effect, I sensed. His mood was playful. 'Not that you and Snout-nose –'

'Don't call her that.'

He glanced again. 'Did you two share some sort of an "awakening"?'

'Don't get excited, nothing like that.' But I squirmed. 'Do you think . . .?' I began.

'What?'

'Molls'll be all right, won't she? Without us.'

'Of course she will. If last week's anything to go by, she won't set foot outside the house.'

'I hope she gets *some* fresh air.'

I tried to picture Molly swaggering around with a Mel of her own, being urged to climb scaffolding and roam the woods like a savage. For all her pleas for freedom, would she like that level of permissiveness? After all, the lack of that freedom was probably what saved her from being mocked for her condition. Back then aquaphobia would have been mistaken for cowardice, a fault more despised than an unfortunate birthmark. She'd have been the one getting her swimsuit pulled off by Mean Mel and me.

Or worse.

The thought made me shudder.

'Listen,' Ed said, 'I was thinking, about your pool party.'

'Oh, yes?'

'Since you're so keen on it, let's go. We can have a little birthday celebration there, can't we?'

I was overcome by delight. 'What made you change your mind?'

'I just want you to have what you want. It's *your* birthday, not mine. We'll make sure Gayle and Craig and Sarah are going too.'

'We'll only go if Molls is happy with the idea,' I promised. 'I would never leave her out.'

'Of course not.'

I watched him watch the road, make his lane changes in precise and considered manoeuvres, keep the correct distance from the vehicles ahead; he could have been a driving instructor. We would have sex later, I recognized the aligning stars: the empty flat, the rapprochement of the holiday, the mood of the drive. And, in my case, the sense of release from a long dread, an ordeal sprung without warning and somehow survived.

Ed had been right about one thing: the summer of 1985, I'd sentimentalized it — or, more accurately, demonized it. I'd fixed it in my mind quite differently from how the other players had.

I'd not remembered it as a game at all.

She was Mel's and my *bête noire*, though I wasn't entirely sure how to pronounce that and, in any case, the truth was that we were hers – a beast with two heads.

She came from the new estate by the woods, where we hung out sometimes on the building site of half-complete houses and where the finished articles, like hers, seemed to us millionaires' ranches from American TV shows. In truth, that would have been enough to win our interest had she not been so pretty where we were plain, so popular where we were feared. She was also the best swimmer. The way she held herself in concentration before plunging into a dive, only to emerge seconds later with an expression of unselfconscious joy on her face, pieces of broken light spraying behind her: it both fascinated and infuriated me. The boys, usually chortling, called her the Nymph and competed over who would go out with her.

We called her Nessie, short for Loch Ness Monster.

The first time I remember seeing her at the pond she was with her mother and that in itself was something to be despised because this was a place for kids, not adults, everyone knew that.

'She's got no other protection,' said Mel. Most of the kids had siblings, Mel and I each other, but Nessie's sister was away for the summer at some watersports camp. (They were evidently an aquatic clan.)

245

The sole adult voice rang out repeatedly that afternoon: 'Come out of the sun, darling'; 'That was a better dive!'; 'Careful out there in the middle. Your feet could get caught on roots.'

She was one of those neurotic mums who saw danger lurking everywhere, who made such a big deal about being Nessie's mother it was as if she thought she *was* Nessie. (When my own mother phoned from home, I refused to speak to her.)

'Show-off,' Mel said loudly.

'Slag,' I agreed. Though neither of us looked in Nessie's direction, everyone who knew us would guess who we meant because it was common knowledge we had it in for her.

'Who are those girls?' Nessie's mother asked. 'Are they your friends?'

'In your dreams,' Mel drawled, under her breath. That was one of our lines that summer: *In your dreams*. We never said it to each other: it was as if we understood at some elemental level that the other would not dare have dreams of her own.

'You know what?' Mel said. 'We should do her some time.' She meant ambush, strip, humiliate.

'Who – Nessie? Seriously?'

A decorum of sorts prevailed in our dealings with the group. A boy could be stripped and insulted and left to wriggle his way home, but his hands could cover all there was to cover and he'd usually come back the next day. (In Stoneborough that summer, there was nowhere else to go.)

246

A girl was different. We hadn't done a girl before.

'Actually, forget it,' Mel said, lighting a cigarette stolen from her father and sending smoke in Nessie's mother's direction, challenging her to tell us off for it. When she passed it to me, the end was damp from her mouth. 'We need something better for her.'

Better as in worse.

22

Monday, 31 August, 8 a.m.

I push open the main doors of our building, moving blindly, by memory, and almost crash into someone arriving. It is only when she says my name that I focus: Gayle.

'I didn't expect to see you,' she blurts, and it takes her a moment to recover herself. Her eyes are prominent and raw, her neck blotched with a rash. The last time we stood face to face like this, I wondered if we would ever speak again. 'I heard about last night. I'm so sorry.'

Automatically wary, I listen for the bitter edge to her voice, but cannot find it. 'Thank you.'

'How is she?'

'She's all right,' I say, 'thank God.' *Thank God*: I hear it in a different place, another time, and feel a rush of shame so intense it threatens to knock me off balance. I can't deal with this now. I make off down the path towards the car, but of course she follows.

'Wait, Nat! What happened exactly? Is it true she fell in and the Channing girl went in to rescue her?'

My fingers on the car door handle feel icy. It's early, but I sense the air temperature will stay low all day – it's as if the season has turned overnight. 'She has a name,' I say. 'It's Georgia.'

'Of course, sorry. What I mean is, wasn't there a guard on duty?' There's a touch of familiar indignation in her voice now. 'That place isn't safe, if you ask me.'

'It wasn't their fault,' I tell her. The ferocity of emotion in her eyes is too intense to engage with for more than a second or two. 'The kids weren't supposed to be anywhere near the water. It was all roped off.' And I remember then: Lara used the security budget to help pay for the band. 'I don't mean to be rude,' I add, 'but I can't really talk. I need to get somewhere.'

'Right.' She's puzzled: why would I be going somewhere that will take me away from Molly?

'But Ed is upstairs with Molls if you want to see them?'

'No, I don't want to bother him. I wasn't going to come up, I just wanted to deliver this.'

I notice now the item under her arm, a small cream tote patterned with roses. 'Is that Molly's bag?'

'Yes. Alice brought it home last night. She said she found it unclaimed after . . . after you'd left, and Liam said it was Okay to look after it for you. Her phone's in there. I thought she might want it today. She'll be getting messages from her friends.'

'Thank you, she'll be pleased.' I stand by the car, stranded and awkward.

'What happened to your face?' she says. 'You look like you're getting a bruise.'

'I don't know.' I shrug. 'I must have knocked it last night in all the chaos.'

'We'll talk when everything's back to normal,' she says, gauging my mood, pledging her support and saying the right thing in one fell swoop. That, I suppose, is what a true friend does, and I feel a second, hotter, gush of shame, a yearning for some breath-sucking velocity that might transport me back in time and let me do better what I have done so badly.

In the car, I sift through Molly's bag on the passenger seat: lip balm, keys with a starfish key-ring, a notebook. Her phone in its lilac-coloured case, low on power, probably only good for another hour or two. The passcode doesn't work; she must have changed it. Hardly a crime – it's natural to want privacy, to keep secrets. That makes me remember her journal on the laptop. Might the police ask for access to her devices, if and when they come knocking? If Georgia were to . . . to not make it, a diary or email exchange might cast light on the girls' state of mind.

Well, whatever helps their investigation, I think. Georgia is the victim, but Molly is hardly anything less. She has nothing to hide.

I return the phone to the bag and start the car. I have no doubt I'm still over the limit. Margaritas last night, Lord knows how many, very little food, no sleep. I could easily cause an accident. It's the kind of thing you read about in the papers: one poor decision leads to another, blunder begets disaster.

And I would be able to say exactly how mine began, too: with Lara's voice, the private, grainy seductions of it; with Lara's eyes, dark with kohl and glittering with caprice.

I thought she chose me because I was special, but it turns out I was only special because she chose me. And if that still matters to me even the smallest of jots then I am a terrible, terrible woman.

23

Monday, 17 August — two weeks earlier

'Thank *God* you're back!' Resplendent in a metallic-grey silk playsuit no mortal had the right to carry off, hair ablaze with gold in the high sun, Lara leaned on the balustrade with one foot poised on the lower rail as if she might at any moment spring up and jump. Below, sunlight struck off the silver lettering at the lido entrance and rinsed the brickwork clean. The building was ringed by its queue, a double string of figures in bright clothing and sunglasses, while more customers arrived on bikes, carrying the light with them in little flashes. In the distance stood the pearlescent cluster of skyscrapers of the City, our own Manhattan.

Though I could see London, I could smell only countryside, the lush, loamy fragrance of the horse-chestnut trees, the rich earthiness of the park after a week of rainfall.

As a sudden eruption of laughter caught on the breeze, Lara turned to me with a lavish, almost ardent look. 'You're obviously some sort of solar deity, Natalie. It rained every day last week and now look at it!'

She reached to grasp my hand and I responded like any willing audience to the star turn: riveted, motionless, all disbelief happily suspended.

'*Promise* you'll never leave us again.'

I promised. No matter that it had rained *everywhere* the previous week, washing out my own family holiday. Lara wasn't interested in *that*. The glass of champagne in her hand was her second since my arrival thirty minutes ago.

'Good. For a moment there last week, I thought it wasn't going to be the perfect summer after all. I was really quite cross.'

I felt a flush of pleasure that this was as special a time for her as it was for me.

The music she was playing today was the Byrds.

Miles was working from home that afternoon, a rarity, I gathered, though I assumed he was senior enough in the company hierarchy to do as he pleased. I was aware of him inside, circling the living room, talking into his phone in presidential tones, on one occasion exclaiming in exasperation. After an hour or so, he joined us on the terrace for a cigarette (Lara's plan for Bryony's intervention had not yet been implemented, evidently). It was the first time I'd been with the Channings since that discussion with Angie, and then Ed, about their alleged infidelities, and I couldn't prevent a certain heightened interest in the dynamic between the two of them.

'What's wrong?' Lara asked him, that restless foot back on the rail.

'Oh, just the usual screw-ups,' he said.

'Well, at least you know you're indispensable.' She lifted her foot rather spectacularly to the upper rail, stretching the hamstrings with no apparent discomfort.

'Hardly,' Miles said. He held his cigarette in a careful, almost precious, way. 'They happen whether I'm there or not. Watch yourself on that railing, La. We don't want our nice white pebbles getting bloodstained.' And the way he looked at her was suddenly different, surprising, the way you would look at someone you didn't know at all, almost as if he were deciding whether he could trust her. That was her allure, I thought. Her spontaneity. It kept us all guessing, even her own husband. I remembered Angie's angle: that *she*'d do anything for *him*. She knew the couple far better than I did yet I couldn't help thinking she'd got it wrong. That I, the newcomer, knew better.

'Have you noticed,' Lara said, 'that in film and TV, no one smokes any more? Or if they do, it's only to signify villainy. James Dean, Steve McQueen, Delon, of course: they smoked and they were the heroes.'

'Anti-heroes, don't you think?' I said, recalling Delon's character's actions in the only film of his I'd seen: strong arms denying his enemy air, forcing the other man's lungs to fill with water. 'And didn't everyone smoke in the sixties? Heroes, villains . . .'

'Small children, farmyard animals,' Miles said, smirking. When he exhaled, his facial muscles froze in a kind of grim rapture.

'My point is that now it's *only* the villains,' Lara said, holding his eye.

'What are you trying to say about me?' There was a note of challenge in his tone. 'Or is this just more of your GCSE media studies gibberish?'

Offended, I opened my mouth to protest, but of course Lara could defend herself.

'Don't be tedious, Miles,' she said, and sighed, half amused, half exasperated. (I imagined using those words, that tone, with Ed. *Don't be tedious, Ed.* It would be satisfying, for sure.) She finished her champagne and, noticing my empty glass, demanded, 'Do we need a new bottle?'

'What you "need" is a job,' Miles said.

'I have one, remember?' She held his eye before adding, 'Being me *is* a job,' and as she drifted past us towards the kitchen I laughed, both at the remark and Miles's indulgently defeated expression.

In his wife's fragrant wake, he turned his attention to me. 'I hear you're joining us for the bank-holiday party?'

'Yes, I hope so.'

'And it's your birthday that day?'

'It is.'

'Good.'

Flattered that he knew – and approved – I had an odd sensation, like pins and needles in my lungs, that he was going to say something important. But then Lara reappeared and he looked away, grinding out his cigarette in a glass saucer. I watched as he used his fingertips to tidy the ash from the edges of the saucer into the centre circle, a curiously fastidious act. I imagined those ashy fingers touching Lara's skin after I'd gone. In her fist, the champagne bottle foamed, eager to spill into our glasses. Miles took the tumbler she offered – I wasn't sure if it was whisky or brandy but in any case it was decadent for a homeworker mid-afternoon on a Monday.

It took effort to remember my own working week, the daily structure: assembly, maths, break, literacy, lunch; in the afternoon, something creative, the making of a collage depicting London during the Blitz, perhaps. Fire-red skies and ruined buildings. I had not forgotten my stated aim at the beginning of the summer break to forget being a teacher and live like a civilian, but this rarified version surely exceeded the greatest of expectations. Drinking champagne with a couple from a social stratum normally well beyond my powers of access, sitting with a heart-stopping view across London – and getting so used to it that I was mesmerized instead by the sun-fired hair of my hostess. My mood soared higher.

But when Miles's office rang and he retreated to his study on the ground floor, I found Lara's spirits had, conversely, dipped somewhat. She plucked idly at one of her photography books, a Slim Aarons collection of swimming pools on the French Riviera, in the California desert, on the Florida coast. Her favourite was California, she said. She showed me a picture of a modernist house in a seared landscape, a pool of untroubled blue: 'Don't you wish you could reproduce that feeling?'

When she closed the book with a little gesture of defeat, I longed to make it better. 'What – of living in Palm Springs? I don't think that's possible here. Even with my return, the sun isn't hot enough.'

She barely registered the reference. Having declared herself delighted by my attendance, she now had the air of keeping her chin up under house arrest, rather like Molly in the rain-pummelled cottage in the New Forest. Miles's mockery had hurt her feelings after all, perhaps, and I longed to let her know I was on her side.

'I went there once, you know.' She leaned on her elbow, steering the branch of a potted oleander from her hair. 'To LA. To try to "make it". I had an agent there.'

'What happened?'

'Nothing. That was the problem. I wasn't special. They didn't like my teeth, kept saying I should fix them. But I like flaws. They're the interesting bits. Who wants to be "fixed"?'

'I completely agree. I was just saying that to someone yesterday, in fact.' I couldn't believe it was only twenty-four hours since I'd been in the same room as Mel. She was a mythical creature now, had no place in this sphere, not even in my thoughts.

'And my voice,' Lara said. 'They said it was too husky, like I had a throat condition.'

'Your voice is wonderful,' I said.

'That's sweet of you.' She shrugged. 'So I came back. I met Miles. I suppose I just gave up. I thought being twenty-two lasted a lifetime. I thought I'd have a hundred more chances.'

'Well, at least you tried,' I said. 'That's more than most.'

But they sounded such mundane platitudes and had no useful effect. I tried to express some of the passion I truly felt: 'You've done things other people can only dream of, Lara. Look at your life here.' I gestured to the park, the glowing grass, the threads of pathway that gleamed like metal. 'Seriously. What could be better than this? It's our green and pleasant land right on your doorstep.'

'Oh, that. Blake. "Bring me my arrows of desire".' She surprised me sometimes with her sudden quotations, though she was an actress, of course, and it was natural she should have a memory for them. She tore off her sunglasses and I saw that her eyes were full of melancholy. The shock of it made my heart hammer.

'Are you all right, Lara? Is it Miles, what he said about – ?'

'God, no, Miles is fine. I'm just feeling a bit . . .'

If not prepared to criticize her husband, she might, I thought, talk more about her acting career, those dreams of Hollywood that didn't get off the ground, but what she confessed was rather closer to my own realm of neurosis: 'Georgia will be leaving home soon. It makes me sad, that's all.'

'Georgia?' I laughed in surprise. 'She hasn't even done her GCSEs yet. She's still got three years left at school.' Molly had five, but I'd be lying if I said I hadn't considered how I was going to feel when she left, especially this week when I was without her. Our family reduced by a third, our life would flatten, darken. As the younger's world opened, so the elders' would shrink, a natural process but not necessarily a welcome one. Perhaps Ed and I would drift apart and I would, in time and without fanfare, enter the Stoneborough house for abandoned females. 'Plus you've got Everett,' I pointed out. 'It's a long time before you have to worry about being alone. I'll be an empty-nester before you.'

'That's true.' She smiled at me, grateful, fond. 'I'm just being silly. We all have our sad days, don't we?'

'We do.'

'I miss Angie when she's away. But my sister Iona is arriving tomorrow. She'll cheer me up.'

I agreed that her sister would, though not without a pang of dismay that, in spite of her earlier pronouncement, I had not proved equal to the job.

'Shall we swim together this week, Natalie?'

My spirits leaped. 'You won't be going with Iona?'

Lara's normally expressive eyes were suddenly opaque. 'Oh, she doesn't swim.'

'Then I'd be happy to step in.'

'Tomorrow at three?'

'I'll be there.' And I strolled home across the park with the exhilaration of an unexpected promotion.

Mindful of the sourness of the night before we went to the New Forest, I was careful to get dinner started at a reasonable hour, only to find I had forgotten another duty: Inky's early-evening walk.

'Sarah counts on us, Nat,' Ed said. 'What was so important that you decided to blow her out like that?'

259

One day back and already I was disappointing him. And lying too, apparently: 'I bumped into Gayle and got chatting, that's all. But it's not a big deal, I'll take him out now, it's still light.'

'It's fine. I did it myself,' Ed said. 'But you will be able to do the afternoon walk for the rest of the week, won't you? I'm chocker.'

'Yes, yes, don't worry.' I didn't need reminding that I was the one on holiday, not him.

'Don't leave it too late, because Sarah has her evening routine. They've reduced her painkillers and she's in quite a bit of discomfort. She said she's going to bed earlier than usual.'

'Poor thing. Leave it with me.' Of course, I'd just agreed to meet Lara at the lido the next day at three, which was about the same time I'd called around today – and yet I'd only been able to leave when I had because she'd grown uncharacteristically glum. How was I going to fit Inky in?

Naturally, it was out of the question that I should cancel my plans with Lara for the sake of an old friend in chronic pain.

It's easy to see, in retrospect, where my instincts went awry.

Tuesday, 18 August

She was not glum. She was a woman who had never known a moment's glumness in her life. 'Don't get me wrong, Natalie,' she giggled, 'he's an absolute angel, but is he *ever* going to stop yapping?'

Inky, making his lido café debut, was too stimulated by the shrieking and yelling, by the ceaseless slap and thump of bare feet on stone, to do anything but bark.

I could understand his awe. Alone with Lara at the VIP table on the terrace, her special guest and chosen companion, her substitute Angie, I was exactly like a teenager falling in love for the first time. My head had not only been turned, it was spinning.

Lara scooped Inky into her arms and babied him, blowing gently into his face to calm him. Her fingernails today were cranberry, her sunglasses nude Stella McCartney cat-eyes.

'You'll make up the numbers, won't you, darling?' she said, sing-song and silly, 'while Choo-choo's away? Stop us being lonesome?'

Inky watched, silent at last.

Of course, the idea of Lara as some neglected, unfulfilled figure was preposterous even before you took into account the constant stream of courtiers to our table that week. I'd thought I knew everyone in Elm Hill but plainly I knew none of those Lara had collected in her brief tenure, not only the rich high-maintenance women and successful, driven men, but also receptionists, shopgirls, litter-pickers. Occasionally, she invited someone to join us for a glass, and that person would look at me, talk to me, as if I must be worth knowing too.

'You'll miss La when she's off on holiday, I expect?' said a man called David, a neighbour on The Rise. 'Do you two swim together every day?'

'For now, yes, but I'll be back at school in a couple of weeks.'

'What do you mean,' he said, '"back at school"?'

'I'm a teacher,' I told him. 'I teach at Elm Hill Prep.'

'A teacher?' He was astonished. 'I thought you were one of La's ladies who loaf.'

'Sadly not,' I said, smiling. 'The loafing has just been a summer job.'

If only it could go on, I thought. If only it could be the lido's opening season, the hottest summer in ten years, the year I met Lara, for ever.

David moved on. The lifeguards rotated and it was Matt's turn to climb the rungs of the chair nearest our table.

'*That*'s better,' said Lara, lowering her sunglasses for a full-glare vista.

A second guard took his perch at the far end, another youngster wearing flashy gold aviators. Not so long ago I would have assessed him purely for signs of former professional acquaintance, but now . . . when in Rome. 'Look how well he handles that flotation aid,' I said, in a wicked undertone.

Lara cackled, delighted. 'We can only hope he's left full-time education – just think of your place in the Establishment,' she teased. 'Actually, they have to be eighteen to apply, so you're off the hook. Oh, bless Inky, he's falling asleep.' She ruffled his curly ears, then, as R&B came over the pool's sound system, she was on her feet and passing him back to me. 'I just need to go and have a word with Reception . . .'

When she came back, they were playing 'Heatwave' by Marilyn Monroe, which made me remember that ridiculous conversation with Ed when he'd said that no one ever thinks a homeless person is glamorous.

I watched, giggling, as she lip-synced and angled her face in coquettish Monroe poses, finishing with a little kick in the air, a flourish of her foot.

'I suppose I ought to get back to Iona.' I said I'd only be an hour and it's been, God, what, *three*? Why don't you come and meet her, Natalie? Inky too, of course.'

After the event, I wished that this had been one invitation of Lara's I hadn't accepted, for the encounter marred an otherwise idyllic stretch. Unsure of Inky's reliability in so expensively furbished a house, I left him in the shade at the front door before going up to the sitting room alone, Lara having diverted into her bedroom to take off her damp clothes. But Iona hardly glanced at me when I walked through the Diana doors. Sprawled on one of the petrol-blue sofas, she was playing with Everett, his blond head bent over a scattering of dice on the coffee table; only when he was dispatched to the freezer for a victor's ice lolly did she favour me with her attention.

'He's been teaching me how to play Perudo.' She spoke in the lazy tones of a cut-glass accent deliberately scuffed. 'Honestly, it's the most I've achieved in about six months.'

So she had Lara's flippant manner if not her beauty. Though her face bore traces of Markham heritage in its fine-boned nose and oversized eyes, the arrangement, head-on, was askew, a face with a touch of the Cubist to it. She was fleshier, with none of Lara's mercurial elegance, and I would have put money on her having been one of those girls whose attractiveness had peaked in her early teenage years before she could make use of it, which made it the cruellest of gifts.

'You're Natalie, are you? La said she might bring you back. Where is she?'

'Just changing downstairs,' I said. There was a sense of reckoning about the way this woman was looking at me and I hesitated to join her on the sofa without a direct invitation. Instead I hovered, unsure whether to offer her a drink or to wait to be offered. 'You didn't fancy a dip in our new lido?' I asked cheerfully.

'You've got to be kidding.' Iona looked at me with barely concealed displeasure. It wasn't only her physical form that was heavier: where Lara's personality ran a gentle finger down your arm, hers threatened to shake you till your teeth rattled.

'I don't understand,' I said.

'You're talking to someone who finds the Red Sea too cold,' Lara said, joining us in her fluffy robe, and within moments she'd uncorked the inevitable bottle of bubbly. 'She never used to be like this, Natalie. She used to be amazing in the water. But now she's a scaredy-cat, just like Mary-Lou.'

Iona's voice grew shrill in playful retaliation. 'Yeah, right, Amanda. Olympic wannabe.'

'Who are Mary-Lou and Amanda?' I asked. 'Old synchro teammates?'

'Teammates? They're characters in *Malory Towers*.' Iona said this as if she should really not have to explain something so blindingly obvious. I could see she must have been the know-it-all Alfie Mellor of her own school (I often thought how easily we announced our childhood selves and how rare it was to come across truly convincing reinvention).

She went on: 'Mary-Lou's scared of swimming in the rock pool and Gwendoline Mary holds her under to give her a fright. And Amanda swims out to sea and almost drowns, so she misses the Olympics because of an injury. Just like our little nymph here.'

'I see.' I wasn't sure if it was the stories of near drowning – old habits died hard and I was used to people censoring themselves in Steele company, I suppose – or the nymph reference, but I felt myself startle.

Noticing my confusion, Lara laughed. 'You must think we're nuts, Natalie. I need to explain that we had a summer when we were little when we read all the books and went around speaking like the characters. Mum was completely fooled – she thought they were our real friends.' Everett had reappeared bearing an ice lolly shaped like a dagger and Lara pulled him on to her lap.

'At first it was quite piggy-hoolier talking like them, but then it became rather smashing,' Iona said.

'What's piggy-hoolier?' I asked.

'Don't you remember the Mamzelles?' Lara cried. 'It was how they pronounced "peculiar".' As if finding himself bombarded with a foreign language, Everett slipped from her grip and disappeared downstairs. The sisters hooted. 'Oh, Iona, we're clearing the room. I don't think anyone else gets it but us!'

'Everyone gets it,' Iona said, in her scathing way. 'Otherwise those books wouldn't have sold zillions of copies, would they? Maybe it's because Natalie's a teacher. That's what you are these days, aren't you? Old Enid's frowned upon by the PC crowd, isn't she?' It was not quite an accusation, rather an exposure of mediocrity, and I knew that by becoming riled I would only be falling into her trap. I was bewildered too by that 'these days': she spoke as if she'd met me before. I satisfied myself with a faint raising of the eyebrows.

'Natalie isn't PC,' Lara objected. 'She doesn't even work in a state school. Didn't Molly read *Malory Towers*, darling?'

'No, she wasn't really interested in stories set in schools.' This struck me only now as odd; normally young children enjoyed any connection with the professions of their parents.

'Are you OK?' Lara asked.

'I've just got a bit of a headache. It must be the heat.'

Iona held up a palm, terminating a remark already made. 'Never blame the sun,' she chastised. 'We need to keep on its good side or it won't come out again.'

She appeared to share Lara's rather pagan veneration of the sun. I was not enjoying her company.

'Go and grab something from the Pharm,' Lara suggested. 'That'll sort it out.'

'I'd forgotten you call it that,' Iona said. 'Promise me it's kept under lock and key, safe from underage fingers, La?'

Lara rolled her eyes. 'No, I leave it open. I want nothing more than to have my offspring and their friends die of an accidental overdose of Valium. The code is my birthday, Natalie.'

'Wow, we won't need an Enigma machine for that,' Iona sneered, and Lara flapped a hand in her direction. Iona seized it to begin some sort of play fight, calling out, 'Beast!' and 'Smelly!' and I left the room to the yelping sounds of puppies.

Arriving in the main bathroom, I thought how Lara had rightly assumed I knew the date of her birthday. What else did she assume? Was this how all friendships worked between those with Wikipedia pages and those without? Tapping in the combination and releasing the lock, I was taken aback by the sight in front of me. It was as if someone had robbed a hospital: pots of prescription medication three or four deep, as well as over-the-counter items from the UK and other countries. Don't get me wrong, there were no bags of cocaine (at least, not that I identified); if Ed had been right in his suspicion of street drugs then they were certainly not stored here.

Street drugs: I sounded like my mother.

I helped myself to two Nurofen and carefully closed the cabinet door.

Upstairs the sisters had moved outdoors, the chatter continuing ceaselessly in voices raised over the rush-hour car engines of returning residents and arriving evening swimmers. Walking barefoot across the sitting room towards the kitchen for a glass of water, I thought I heard my name mentioned and out of instinct rather than guile I kept the water flow light and soundless so I could listen.

'They really haven't got a clue?' Iona said.

'No, and you're the only one I've told.'

'You guys are crazy. I don't know how you get away with this stuff.'

'I can't help it if other people aren't as inventive as we are.'

'*Inventive?* What kind of a euphemism is that?'

There followed a scramble of giggling and snort-ing, one sister indistinguishable from the other. It was impossible not to call to mind Angie's hints of an open marriage, and when I finally turned off the tap and stepped out into the evening light, I knew I was blushing.

Seeing me, Iona said: 'Natalie, can you believe it? This slut hasn't got any underwear on.'

My mouth opened.

'She means because I took off my swimsuit,' Lara drawled, unruffled. 'I didn't want to sit on a damp gusset. I really don't think Nat's interested, Iona.'

'Oh, I don't know,' Iona said, and the giggling resumed. What an unpleasant woman she was.

Below, Inky had begun to bark and at the next interruption from Everett I made my excuses and prepared to leave. 'I'll leave you to enjoy your evening,' I said, with clumsy formality, and it seemed to me that Iona made it clear in the tone of her goodbye that she didn't expect to see me again.

'It's the Land of Do As You Please here, isn't it, Natalie? Remember what happened there, eh?' This was the last thing she said to me.

'Iona, you're being very weird today!' Lara protested, but weakly because she was drunk and giggling. I knew I had no right, but I couldn't help feeling betrayed.

In spite of myself, I looked up the reference as soon as I'd delivered Inky to Sarah and got home. It was Blyton, of course, from *The Faraway Tree*. (Who was this woman who could make *The Faraway Tree* sinister and threatening? She was surely suffering from some sort of arrested development.) The children didn't enjoy their time in the Land of Do As You Please, where they drove a runaway train.

Breakneck was exciting for only so long, seemed to be the message.

24

Wednesday, 19 August

The next morning, I lacked the mojo I'd grown accustomed to feeling on waking and experienced instead a disappointing throwback dullness that made it hard to raise my bones at all. I didn't like to dwell on what had caused it, but as I shuffled to the kitchen for coffee, I considered giving the lido a miss that day. No firm plan had been made with Lara, so I wouldn't be letting her down.

To cheer myself up, I phoned Molly. Mobile signal being uncertain at the Stoneborough house, I'd been calling her there on the landline, trying not to feel hurt on the occasions she chose not to come to the phone but have her news relayed through an elder. When she did, she released few snippets. Great-grandma's glasses had fallen off her nose into the trifle. The custard in said trifle hadn't set properly and Molly didn't want to eat it. ('You know I can't eat anything sloppy.') It was too hot. Her bedroom smelt weird. Also, she hadn't been able to WhatsApp her friends because the house was the only place in the western hemisphere without WiFi.

'Have you seen Rio again?' I asked.

'We saw him with his great-gran yesterday. Grandma says there isn't a great-granddad, not because he's dead but because he's a deadbeat.'

'I see, how witty. Well, he used to be around, in the old days.' I had a memory then of Mel's father, a muscle-bound pit bull of a man, arguing in the street with another kid's mother. Not Nessie's — I would have remembered if it was hers. Someone else's, one of the boys'. 'Your daughter is a hooligan,' she'd shouted, 'and so is her horrible friend.' And Mel's dad had shoved her and sworn at her. Mel and I had taken pleasure in being called hooligans.

'Don't get involved,' I said, glad to be out of earshot of Ed, who was in his study prepping for his eleven o'clock.

'Get involved in what?' Molly asked.

'Just them. That family. You know, if they approach you . . .'

'Why? What're they going to do to me? Drag me into the woods and tear my clothes off? He's, like, eight years old, Mum! That's messed up.'

At the sound of her snickering, I sighed. 'Even when I'm being mocked, it's lovely to hear your voice. We miss you, Molls.'

'Actually, I did go to the woods yesterday,' she said unexpectedly, 'with Grandma. She showed me the pond where you and Mel used to go.'

'Oh.' Immediately, I cursed my mother. I had briefed her minutely on Molly's recent progress and my thoughts for avoiding any relapse, yet she'd apparently decided it a good idea to lead her straight to a body of dark water hemmed in on all sides by tall trees. 'I hope you were all right, sweetie?'

'I was fine,' Molly said, her tone a little shorter. 'The water's drained now.'

'Is it?' There was a pause as I asked silent forgiveness of my mother. (Would Molly do this one day, always assume the mistake was mine? Perhaps I'd never know, not if both accusation and apology, like so many of mine, went unvoiced.) 'Well, I'm impressed she managed to get you out for a walk,' I said. The pond was a good couple of miles from the house.

'I thought I might be able to get a signal on my phone,' Molly said. 'But it was still rubbish.'

'In the middle of the woods? That's a surprise.' That made me smile. 'Can you imagine a whole summer, a whole childhood without technology? Only a landline nailed to the wall that you had to ask permission to use. That's all *we* had.'

'I'd rather be dead,' Molly said.

As I hung up, the sound of the intercom rang out, presumably Ed's student arriving. It was one of his older ones, attending without a parent, and I decided to keep out of sight. Though I was out of my pyjamas, you'd be hard pushed to know it since I'd traded them for sloppy leggings and a T-shirt and hadn't yet cleaned my teeth or brushed my hair.

'It's Lara,' Ed called. 'She's on her way up.'

'For you?'

'No, you.'

And before I could make any attempt to improve my appearance, he was opening the door and exchanging pleasantries with her. I smoothed my fringe over my birthmark from nervous memory as much as anything else: Lara had seen it before; she didn't care.

'So this is where the mysteries of quadratic equations are laid bare,' she teased Ed, and I thought how incongruous that throaty speakeasy drawl sounded in this sober and orderly space.

'Lara,' I said, emerging, 'what a lovely surprise. You must excuse my bag-lady scruffiness. I'm not exactly up yet.'

'Bag-lady scruffiness is what I aspire to,' she said gamely, though she wore on this insignificant weekday a beautiful burnt-orange crêpe maxi dress with a piped keyhole neckline, the type of garment I had little chance of carrying off at a wedding.

I led her into the living room. It was the first time she'd been in our flat and, having mentally rehearsed the event several times, I succeeded in keeping at bay my natural feelings of shame. It was a perfectly nice place to live and there was nothing to be gained from comparisons with the palatial glamour of La Madrague.

Of course, I'd not allowed for the fact that she conferred glamour on all that met her eye, all that bore her weight. The IKEA armchair with sheepskin throw became suddenly exotic, a reindeer skin worthy of the set of *Doctor Zhivago*; a bare foot rested on the corner of the coffee table announced to the world that this was *the* place for feet to rest. The filtered light caught the folds of her dress and made me think of celestial drapery in Renaissance painting.

Crazy. Even so, when I brought in coffee I was pleased to be able to offer costly chocolates from the last of my EHP end-of-year gift stocks.

In my absence, Lara had been casting her own eye about the room. 'I had no idea you were such a neat freak,' she said. 'Look at your shelves – are those books colour co-ordinated?'

'Better than in alphabetical order,' I joked. I considered blaming Ed for the obsessive-compulsive vibe, even wondered if, had I been given warning of her visit, I might have faked dishevelment. At least she knew to attribute the tidiness to one of us and hadn't assumed we had a cleaner. 'You have to stay on top of things in a small flat. And Molly's not here to create chaos.'

'Mmm. Prestat, my favourite.' Her attention turned to the chocolates, she chose the one wrapped in gold foil, unsheathing and eating it quickly, before announcing, '*Please* can we tackle the elephant in the room before it breathes all our oxygen.'

'I don't think an elephant would fit in here,' I said, adding, 'but I'm not sure what you mean?'

'Seriously? Yesterday at my place?'

'Oh, your sister.'

Lara's gaze grew filmy and tender. 'She was a horrible old witch to you, wasn't she?'

I hesitated. 'I thought she was very entertaining.'

'Really?'

'Really.'

Now it was she who paused. 'So you didn't hear what she said when we were on the terrace? When you came up from the bathroom?'

If she meant that inappropriate inference about Lara's underwear, I was not about to acknowledge it.

'She was being a bit outspoken about Miles and me. She has firm opinions about our marriage, let's put it that way.'

'Well,' I said, 'we all know what they say about opinions, don't we?'

Lara beamed. 'I'm so glad. I was worried we might have put you off.'

'Put me off what?'

'Off me.'

Our eyes locked. A gaze of this length was an intimacy I shared with few, if any, beyond Ed and Molly.

'No,' I said simply. 'I haven't been put off.'

'Oh, good.' She sighed, stretched, selected another chocolate. 'I always feel slightly depressed after a visit by Iona. That's probably why I'm eating all your chocs.'

'Go ahead.' I remembered Sarah and I had laughed about Lara liking to gorge on pralines, and considered making a thing of finding one for her, then thought it might seem like the behaviour of a stalker. 'It must be difficult, your being so close and her living so far away.'

'Oh, I don't mind about that,' Lara said. 'I meant because she's so young and pretty. She makes me feel like a has-been.'

I was flabbergasted. Lara was not one to fish for compliments so this had to be a genuine perception of sororal rank. 'I didn't realize she was younger. She doesn't look it. And, no disrespect, she seems like a lovely person, but you are far more attractive, Lara.'

'Bless you, Natalie.'

And I did feel blessed. Blessed to have her to myself for the rest of the week, Iona being off with an old friend for the day, I learned, and due to leave for her home on the Devon coast early the following morning.

Angie would not be back from Italy until Friday.

'Are we swimming today?' I asked.

'I certainly hope so,' Lara said, adding, with an extravagant air, 'To swim is to survive.'

'Who said that?' I thought it was another of her quotations.

'I did.' She chuckled. 'Do you think people will quote me when I'm dead?'

'Oh, without a doubt,' I said.

Stoneborough, August 1985

It was Mel's idea, of course, our moonlit swim. She released the idea into the wild one afternoon, like a baby shark into a mangrove, and by the time we headed home for tea it had chased down every life form in its path. One o'clock was deemed safe: even the night owls among the village's parents would be in a deep sleep by then (my own grandparents turned in at ten; Mel's parents, drinkers, were less reliable).

About twenty of us assembled at the mouth of the footpath, including former victims of our strip-and-run prank. There'd be none of that tonight, however, for there was an unspoken agreement that we'd stick together, look out for each other, all return home in the same clothes we'd arrived in. Tonight, the joke was on the adults, not on each other.

The trudge through the woods was creepier than anticipated, the light from our torches little more than pinholes in the claustrophobic blackness, our breathing louder than our footsteps. 'Zombies,' someone groaned, and 'Werewolves', which caused squeals among the girls. One of the boys mimicked the banjo music from *Deliverance* (it was a badge of honour to have seen the film, with its adult rating).

But our legs knew the way, delivering us dependably to the clearing and the welcoming silver gleam of moonlight. There were relieved giggles as our eyes adjusted and we began undressing. The straps on my swimming costume had twisted and Mel straightened them for me, her fingers continuing to move on my skin after the adjustments were made.

'Hang on a minute.' Her ears picked out a voice she didn't care for. 'Who invited that cow?'

'Not me,' I said quickly.

'She wasn't supposed to know about it. Who told her?'

Nessie pretended not to hear, but continued to slip out of her clothes. She was one of the first to slide into the water, slighter in the pale light, her blonde hair ghostly. As Mel and I waded in after her, the water colder and silkier at night, I watched as she disappeared from view, swallow-diving in that sudden nerveless way of hers. There was a sensation of dread like fingernails clawing inside me; you couldn't see the bottom in daylight either, but somehow it bothered me far more now in the darkness.

At last she resurfaced, an elegant eruption, hair flying in a liquid arc, her upper body heaving, the boys staring.

Mel said loudly, 'Shame she didn't stay under. No one would have noticed. Then they'd find her body in a year's time, all rancid and rotting. Like when crocs pull you under and store you till you're soft enough to chew.'

On the way back to the village, Nessie stuck close to the boys, which displeased us. Not that Mel and I were interested in boys, not in that way, but it didn't mean we wanted them to ally with another girl against us.

'If anyone breathes a word about this, the hillbilly inbreds will come and get you,' Mel debriefed the group before we parted, and as that twanging sound effect started up once more, I knew she'd be giving Nessie the evil eye.

And I turned away slightly for fear of her eye falling on me next. I knew just how it would look: soft and relenting at first, then a little more complex, seeking of me something more than loyalty.

25

The morning is empty and expectant, the traffic lanes bank-holiday clear. I park on yellow lines opposite the hospital's emergency bays, where a lone police car idles, windows down, its driver smoking a cigarette.

The hospital has opened a new wing since I was last here, a curved, glossy structure, the lines of which distort as you walk under a glass canopy to the entrance. Inside, the atrium foyer is empty, like an evacuated hotel, the reception desk unmanned, the check-in monitors unused. The only sign of life is at the Patient Transport desk, where a driver directs me to the third floor.

I pass signs for Breast Radiology, Rheumatology, Neurology, doors to a thousand nightmares past and future, before taking the lift towards the one that the Channings are living in the present. The school-age artworks, no different from those on the walls of my classroom at Elm Hill Prep, are a reminder that Georgia is, in law and in medicine, still a child.

The doors to the unit are locked and I ring and wait, watch through a narrow glass panel as preoccupied staff move between further sets of secure doors. I can already hear Lara's voice telling me everything's fine; I can already hear her tone of relief, taste the sweet perspective it brings. 'Nothing else matters,' she'll say, or I'll say, or we'll both say, our words bumping together. The most important words will be unspoken, but there'll be smiles, tearful ones. Does Miles agree? I'll ask her, as I asked before in better times.

Does he?

At last a nurse approaches, nudges open the door a fraction.

'I've come to see how Georgia Channing is,' I say.

'I'm afraid it's not possible to see her.' She begins to tell me about bank-holiday visitor arrangements; they differ from those shown online, and only immediate family are permitted this morning.

'I know I can't go in,' I say. 'I just wanted to find out how she is.'

'I'm not in a position to tell you that.' Nor, evidently, is she willing to make eye contact and that is, in a way, more of a shock than the safeguarding of information. In recent weeks, a constant at Lara's side, I've been visible, worthy of attention, and I've grown used to it. How quickly I've forgotten that people are not always friendly – or, at least, they're selective in their friendliness.

'I'm a good friend of Lara's,' I say softly, and there it is, the magic word, almost certainly the last time I'll be able to use it; the nurse raises her eyes to mine, says she'll go and check.

I watch as she approaches the next set of doors, which open at the touch of her security pass, and just as they swing closed I catch a glimpse of something identified by my brain as precious: bold colour, viridian, the fabric of Lara's dress. The lurch this causes is sharp, an organic tug back to last night, to when I thought I knew differently. I blink and the green has gone, but already the doors are reopening and I see a sliver of bedside equipment, enough to visualize the full picture of monitors and tubes and probes, the artificial supplies and suctions of a body that cannot run itself.

The nurse is back, the crack through which she chooses to speak even narrower than before. 'Mrs Channing asks that you leave.' Eye contact has been withdrawn once more.

'I understand,' I say, and inside me there is the sensation of collapse. 'Please give the family my best wishes.'

She hardly acknowledges this and as I say my goodbyes to a closed door I can't blame her. Wishes have no place in here, only ECG machines and ventilators and the precise administration of intravenous fluids.

Wishes are no better than superstition, or maybe witchcraft.

26

Ed's face wore an expression midway between appeal and glower. 'More drinks with the Channings? Really, Nat? You've been with Lara every day this week. Isn't that enough?'

'Keep your hair on,' I said easily. 'It's just a glass of wine. And it's not at the Channings', it's at Angie and Stephen's. They're just back from Liguria this afternoon.'

'I'm delighted for them.' He sighed. 'I thought we might go to the Picture House with Craig and Gayle.'

'But I've already said yes,' I told him.

Glower began to eclipse appeal. 'You've always already said yes. How about getting my take on it *before*, not after? And who sees their friends constantly like this at our age? The same day they come back from holiday? Seriously, Nat, you know what I think about that group.'

Here we go again, I thought. It was clear by now that my friendship with Lara and her circle was developing in spite of Ed's wishes, if not at his expense. He had decided on his position after the night of *La Piscine* and it was one of polite closed-heartedness. It was as if,

282

having tried a free sample of a new product, he'd strengthened his preference for the brand he already used. Why I was not flattered by this declaration of satisfaction with the status quo — more than flattered, moved to tears — Heaven only knows, but instead I was determined to challenge it.

Sheer decency meant he would honour the commitment I had made, though not without staking a complicating claim of his own and arranging to meet Gayle and Craig at the Vineyard after their film had finished. 'Gayle says she hasn't seen you since before our holiday,' he reported. 'I thought you said you ran into her the other day.'

'We've texted,' I said vaguely. Displaying precisely the behaviour I counselled my daughter — and pupils — against, I appeared to have sidelined a loyal long-standing friend in favour of a glittering untried one. Indeed, the texts we'd exchanged had left me feeling guilty on more than one level. *Ed told me about your birthday plan*, Gayle wrote. *Tried to get tickets for pool party but it's sold out. Sorry.*

Of course, *Ed told me* meant that she was less sorry that the party was sold out than she would have been if I had been the one to invite her. Or thought to arrange tickets at the same time that I'd arranged my own.

I scrambled to make amends: *Let me see if Lara can help.* I would have enjoyed being able to fix things for her, but when I asked Lara, she told me that even she had no more spares, a response I did not question. *You're right*, I texted Gayle. *But she can put you at the top of the waiting list?*

When her response came, I could hear the scornful laugh that accompanied it: *Don't worry, it's not the be-all.* Then: *Surprised Molls good with plan tbh.*

I couldn't help reading the rebuke in that, not least because I had yet to consult Molly on the matter. *Let's have a drink another night instead,* I texted, finally.

Gayle did not reply. I cared, just as I cared that I was no longer swimming with her in the mornings but with Lara in the afternoons, but I admit I didn't care as much as I should have.

As for Molly, though I would have preferred to ask her about the pool party face to face, Gayle's comment weighed heavily on me and I decided it couldn't wait.

'Listen, darling,' I said, when I next called, 'Dad and I thought the three of us might go to this party at the lido for the night of my birthday. Would you be Okay with that? I've checked with Lara and the pool itself will be closed. They'll just be using the café and the sundeck as a venue.'

'Sure,' Molly said.

'I think you'll enjoy it. There'll be a barbecue and a jazz band.'

'Yeah, Georgia said. She told me all about it.'

'Great.'

It had been so straightforward that I was momentarily lost for words. Was I to gather that I had Georgia to thank for this easy acquiescence?

At this rate I'd soon need to send the girl flowers.

*

Angie's house was on Steadman Avenue, one of the roads running south off The Rise, a relatively modest Edwardian semi from the street but opulent and mon-eyed inside, with one of those glass and granite kitchen extensions that cost more than the entire Steele pension fund. The garden, where we assembled for drinks around a rattan table, had been landscaped with minimalist severity; it was not clear if the vegetation was the photo-synthesizing real thing or simply top-grade counterfeit.

The cocktail *du jour* was the Aperol Spritz.

'Welcome back to shore, babe.' Lara toasted Angie as if she'd returned from sailing the *Cutty Sark*, not people-watching from a hotel terrace in Portofino. 'If it weren't for Natalie, I swear I would have expired in your absence.'

'You mean your beautiful children aren't enough to sustain you?' Angie laughed. At her feet, Choo was sav-aging what looked like a snorkel, still frantic with excitement at being reunited with his mistress.

'God, no,' Lara said. 'Are yours? I don't go along with those weird people who say children are more interest-ing than adults.'

'I've never heard anyone say that,' Angie said.

'But *honestly*, darling, we've been *bereft*. Haven't we, Miles?'

'Oh, quite distraught,' Miles agreed, in his sardonic way.

'You're a bad liar, mate,' said Stephen, tanned and well fed from Italy. Though he had welcomed Ed and me with faultless bonhomie, I couldn't help being relieved when he'd taken a seat on the far side of the table from me.

The kids wandered out to graze on our bar snacks, inoffensively remote as ever. Georgia, long-legged in fraying cut-off shorts, a pink vest and a trilby, was every inch the girl who routinely shunned model-agency scouts. The sight of her cheered Ed, at least, giving him the opportunity to emphasize a point about co-sines, which, when Lara listened in and contrived to understand, taxed her acting skills more sorely than any challenge I'd seen her face to date.

'How's Molly?' Angie asked me, when the youngsters had drifted off again. Here, the kids chose the soundtrack, and as she spoke, some R&B star shrieked his parallel narrative. 'Eve hasn't been able to get hold of her all week.'

'Her mobile signal's been a bit dodgy in Stoneborough,' I said, pleased on Molly's behalf that she'd been missed by the older girls. 'I was just telling her the other day how it was when I spent a few weeks down there in the eighties. Just a landline that you had to get permission to use. You'd have thought I was talking about the *eighteen* eighties the way she reacted. Gayle says she has pupils at Rushbrook who literally don't know what a fixed-line phone is.'

'Remind me, is Gayle the one whose daughter likes Georgia's new boyfriend?' Angie asked.

'I'm not sure who her girls are interested in at the moment,' I said. As Ed had pointed out, it was a while since she and I had had a conversation of any length. I would ask her tonight, I thought. 'Who's Georgia's new boyfriend?'

'Matt, of course,' Lara said. 'I thought I'd bored you enough this week with tales of my rampant sexual jealousy, Natalie.'

I chose not to catch Ed's eye, this being exactly the sort of comment he would stockpile in evidence against Lara. (He'd probably have something to say about the three-year age gap between Matt and Georgia too.)

'Well, I saw him first,' she continued, giggling. 'No one can dispute that. I was there for a meeting the day they interviewed the lifeguards.'

'Spare us your tales of the casting couch,' Stephen said.

'You shot yourself in the foot hiring him,' Angie told her. 'Your own daughter is the least of it: the moment that place opened, he was public property. You'd have been better getting him to do your gardening.'

Lara was delighted. 'You're right, I could have been Lady Chatterley! What's that great quote: "We fucked a flame into being"?'

As the group fell about, I felt Ed wince.

'You can just imagine the hormonal tensions, can't you?' Angie said. 'Near-naked teenagers in the best shape of their lives, boys at their sexual peak.'

'It's certainly a formative time,' Stephen said, 'and not one I'd want to revisit.'

'None of us would,' I agreed. I was becoming aware that I was trying too hard with Stephen. I was the dog who'd singled out the human in the group the most indifferent to me. 'It's so lovely and peaceful on this side of the park, isn't it?' It was all too easy to imagine us Steeles in a house like this, living the life of the one-percenters. ('Isn't that a gang of motorcycling outlaws?' Ed asked, when I later made the mistake of sharing the thought.)

'Compared to during the day, it is,' Angie agreed. 'But you get used to the screams.'

'And that's just the Channings' sex life, boom-boom,' Stephen said.

Miles gave a tolerant roll of the eyes. The two men were seated side by side, complementary characters. Stephen was animated, a crude alpha commentator, Miles self-contained, an observer. It seemed to me that what they shared was an understanding that it was the women who counted in this group; I could hardly say the same for my husband.

'I *love* the lido noise,' Lara said. 'All that excitement in the air. It feels primal.'

On cue came the sound of a fox, its cry like some diabolical instrument; it was impossible to know if we were hearing agony or ecstasy.

'Without the crowds, it's like there isn't a pool there at all,' I said. 'You probably don't, remember the days when the skateboarders used to break in. And the illicit raves.'

'We didn't live here when they had the raves,' Angie said, 'but the neighbours say it was a nightmare.'

'I imagine it was,' Ed said.

'Not your thing at all,' Lara told him, teasing. '*I* would have gone over and joined them,' she declared. 'I would have made you all come with me.'

I thought of what Molly had said about the Stoneborough pond having been drained. Did kids still congregate there? Or did they sit in their bedrooms alone with their technology? What was Molly plugged into right now? What was she negotiating to watch on television? I used to know the answers, but now I didn't. She was becoming a stranger. 'Don't fight independence,' Gayle always advised. 'It's a natural process. Besides, what's the alternative? A daughter in her twenties or thirties who can't cross the road or boil a kettle on her own?'

Yes, I thought, taking another mouthful of Aperol. There was something to be said for Lara's and Angie's more hands-off approach to parenting. With a twinge of guilt that was becoming familiar, I corrected myself: what I'd meant to think was that there was something to be said for *Gayle's* advice.

'Nat . . .' Ed was on his feet, reminding me that we needed to depart to meet Gayle and Craig. Though night had fallen, the sky growing inky, I sensed he was moving us along a little more promptly than was necessary.

'You go on your own,' I said. 'I've just started this drink. I'll join you in a little while.'

He looked hard at me. 'You should come. I'm sure they'd love to see you.'

'I know. I'll be there.'

There was a pause. He wouldn't make a scene, we both knew that; even if the Channings had not been his clients, he would have kept up appearances.

As he left, a fox, a skinny young thing, ran along the beam-narrow brick wall at the end of the garden, startling me.

'I've just had a thought,' Lara said suddenly.

'What?' we all said.

'Ooh,' she said, and she radiated that special energy of hers, edgier than mischief, too guileless to be criminal. 'It's a bit naughty.'

Amid groans from the men, Angie and I clamoured to hear it.

'*I know the alarm code*,' she said. 'For the lido.'

'You don't mean . . .?' Angie said.

'Don't tell her what she *doesn't* mean,' Stephen said. 'It only gives her more ideas.'

Out of the corner of my eye I saw Miles's raised eyebrows, his amusement at both his wife's implied misconduct and his own tolerance of it. Ed had never looked at me in that way, not once.

Lara gave Stephen a playful slap. 'I'm just saying, if a bunch of kids had the nerve to break in, then surely we do.'

'There wasn't any water in it when they did,' Stephen pointed out.

'So we won't need our skateboards, will we?' she shot back.

'You're a monster, La,' Angie said. 'Someone should take you into custody for your own safety.'

Even for Lara this was bold. I was thrilled by that boldness, thrilled by Miles's lack of censure, thrilled, too, that Ed had left, for he would have made it his business to shut this down and, in the event of failure, would likely have phoned the police.

'Lucky Ed's gone home,' I heard myself say, blithe, treacherous.

'We'll have to work on him,' Lara said kindly. 'Some nuts are harder to crack, but the summer's not over yet.' With that, she was on her feet, Ed forgotten. 'Let's go!'

'What about the kids?' I said.

'We'll leave Milena in charge.' And it seemed that a matter of seconds later the au pair had been briefed, towels bundled into a bag, and we adults were strolling across The Rise towards the park entrance.

This might be the most important summer of my life, I thought, drunk enough to mistake arrogance for significance, weak enough not to realize it at the time. The most important *night*.

Stephen and Miles were bantering about how the group might best be hoisted over the locked gate without injury, when it was discovered that it had been left open.

'What about security cameras?' I said, and we all halted, bumping into one another and giggling. I like to think now that a part of me was paying tribute to Ed, or at least remembering that I had a respectable job to lose, but I suspect the reality was I just wanted to belong, to be a vocal participant in this escapade.

'The pool lights won't be on,' Lara said, 'so it'll be too dark for the cameras to catch our faces.'

'She's got a point, though,' Angie said. 'What about when we go in through the door? There'll surely be a camera on the entrance and I'm pretty sure Reception has some sort of night light.'

'Oh, for goodness' sake, girls, it's not a jewel heist,' Lara said. 'I'll have a word with Liam tomorrow and get him to delete the evidence.'

'Will he agree?' I asked.

'People don't turn Lara down,' Miles said, and smiled at my immediate acceptance – and therefore demonstration – of the point.

We're playing by different rules, I thought foolishly. *We're living life faster, higher, more memorably.*

We entered in fact through the staff door to the side of the main entrance, Lara concentrating comically hard as she disabled the alarm. And then we were in, past the café loos and through the unalarmed door to the pool terrace. The only light was the green security panel above the emergency doors, the rest of the site a palette of blacks. The water was smooth, its dimensions ambiguous, like a secret lake.

When it became apparent that Angie had not packed swimwear, I imagined we would keep on our underwear, but in a matter of moments Lara, Angie and Stephen were naked, hardly bothering to cover themselves with their hands as they dropped into the water with stifled cries.

Exhilarated, I did the same, at once breathless from the cold. Unlit, the water was a sublime unknown and my sense of the distance to the edge imprecise. My blood raced in my veins and I was a child again, imagining myself in the middle of an ocean at the mercy of deadly currents or silent submarine ambushes. The same unseen that frightened my daughter excited me. It always had.

'Isn't it the most gorgeous sensation in the whole world?' Lara was gliding up beside me and treading water.

'The swimming or the breaking in?'

'Both. I'm so glad you came with us, Natalie.'

'So am I,' I said. 'What an adventure.'

'Have you ever done anything like this before?'

I had an unpleasant involuntary memory of her sister teasing and belittling me for my unexciting ways. 'I've swum in the middle of the night, but not, you know, skinny-dipping.'

'Was that in those woods you told me about? In Stoneborough? I remember what you said that time about feeling free.'

'Yes.' I was overjoyed that she remembered details like this. It was as if she instinctively recognized the experiences that had shaped me. 'We didn't have to break in, of course, but we had to break out of our homes.'

Her face came closer, hair sleek, cheekbones and brow sharp. 'I bet you were the leader, weren't you?'

'Deputy, in fact. To a girl who's since been jailed.' I spoke with a heedlessness that was only half affected.

'Goodness,' Lara chuckled. 'So you were led astray by a delinquent then?'

'Let's just say I was open to suggestion.'

'I've noticed.'

As she began to circle me in that smooth way of hers that hardly rippled the surface, I grew freshly aware of our bare skin under the water. If our feet or hands or knees or elbows made contact, would it be different knowing the rest of us was naked?

'Tell me more, Natalie. Who was this jailbird accomplice of yours?'

'She was a girl from the village. I didn't really know her. It was more a friendship of convenience. We didn't keep in touch afterwards.' Though it was still only a matter of days since I'd been reunited with Mel, the occasion already felt deep in the past, its purpose served, on its way to being expunged from the record. At the centre of her turning circle, I clumsily trod water, straining to track her moving face. 'But that summer, when she and I were together it was like there were no rules. No one to tell us no. I don't think I've ever had that since.'

Delighted as I was with Lara's response to the persona I'd adopted during this little speech, I was unprepared for the wild, seditious thoughts that came next: Ed was the kind who would have told us no. If he had stayed this evening, I wouldn't be here now: I wouldn't have been allowed. Was that how it was going to be from now on? A succession of nos to every one of my yeses? We admitted ourselves that our relationship had been built – partly, at least – on a shared system of disapproval, a belief that we were right and others were wrong. But it only worked, didn't it, if we agreed?

At last Lara stopped moving and hovered in front of me. Under water her hand reached for mine, lacing our fingers together. 'I think you must be a water-baby like me,' she said.

There was a hammering at my pulse points. 'I think I must be.'

'You know, I always think that if Heaven falls, I'd like to be swimming.'

'If Heaven falls? You don't mean . . .?'

'Not the desperate, struggling kind of drowning,' she said, 'just being swallowed by the water in a peaceful way.'

'Oh.' I was suddenly uncertain, for, inevitably, Molly had sprung to mind. *The water will swallow me.* But Molly was safe in her bed in Stoneborough, I assured myself. She need never know about this Elm Hill adventure. Lara's fingers still gripped mine, her face close, inches away, eyes darker than all the blacks around us, pulling me into them. As a swell surprised us, splashing my face, she let go of my hand and rose with the water in perfect synchronicity, minutely attuned to ebb and flow. Beyond, at the nearest edge, I caught movement, a slow stride, and realized it was Miles. He was still dressed.

'Isn't he coming in?' I asked Lara.

'Oh, he doesn't do pools.'

'But he *can* swim?'

'He can, but he doesn't.'

'Like your sister,' I said, thinking how interesting it was that two of the people closest to her had rejected the great passion of her life. Not her children, though. And not me. 'But they *could* swim, if they had to? Not being able to, like Molly, that's the dangerous thing.'

'I can tell you're still really worried about her, aren't you?' Lara said, and to my disappointment she paddled slightly away from me. 'I think you should stop. Things will happen as they're supposed to. Divine justice. Karma.'

These were the sort of remarks I would normally dismiss as hogwash, but that night, spellbound, they sounded like the answer to everything.

As she swam off to join Angie and Stephen, I climbed out to use the staff toilet by the kitchen. Alone, inside, the sense of trespass was much greater; I imagined my towelled figure being caught on CCTV, studied by Liam and his team in the morning. Tipsy enough to be more tickled than appalled by the thought, I was giggling when I emerged, only to find Miles waiting in the narrow corridor that led back to the café.

'You gave me a shock,' I said.

'Hello, Natalie,' he said, and it was the entirely normal tone and volume that made it so disquieting, as if there were nothing odd, nothing illicit, about our being in a locked building in the middle of the night. I, by contrast, was keenly aware that I was half naked, damp and unkempt, while he was fully clothed, wholly composed.

'Is everything okay?' I asked, a tactful way of asking him to move aside.

'Couldn't be better.'

Still he did not move. My choice was to remain motionless in front of him or to navigate past, back to the wall and breath held. I chose the latter, but as I edged past he took a step to trap me tighter, as good as pressing me to the wall. Confused, embarrassed, I eased myself the rest of the way, my bare skin making contact with his clothing and dragging slightly against the fabric. Only when this excruciating manoeuvre was complete did he turn from me quite leisurely and enter the lavatory, the door closing soundlessly behind him.

I hurried across the terrace to where the other three were now dressing.

'Clothes on,' Angie hissed, passing me my dress. 'We thought we'd better quit while we're ahead.'

When Miles returned he made no mention of our peculiar interaction, so neither did I.

'I should think about getting home,' I said.

'Come back to ours and we'll order a cab for you,' Lara said.

At La Madrague, Angie and Stephen peeled off for Steadman Avenue and Lara settled me with a drink in a ground-floor room I took to be Miles's study. When Miles excused himself, I assumed for the night, Lara followed him upstairs to find her phone to call the taxi.

Perhaps it was the cosy decor, the chocolate leather furniture, crammed bookshelves and wool rugs, but it felt several degrees warmer in the room than outside and I rose to open the only window, a little porthole overlooking the drive. As I did, traces of conversation between the Channings drifted into earshot from above.

'Couldn't be more perfect . . .' (Lara.)

'. . . too drunk . . .' (Miles.)

'. . . *always* too drunk.' (Lara, louder.)

The voices receded. Another eavesdropped tail-end of a conversation: I was making a habit of it. I thought of that complaint of Lara's about her sister's opinions on her ménage – *I can't help it if other people aren't as inventive as we are* – and of the oddness with Miles just now, his immovable, unfriendly body against mine. Then I had a new thought, a fuzzily cautious one: had Lara gone to the Pharm? Was she going to offer me cocaine or some other drug? Should I agree? Should I do it, just once? What would Ed and Gayle and Craig say about *that*?

When Lara reappeared, her glass still in hand, she clinked it against mine and said, 'I've got a confession to make.'

'Sounds dangerous,' I said, smiling.

'I didn't order your cab.'

'Why not?'

She looked unblinkingly at me. 'Because I thought you might want to stay over.'

I caught my breath, electrified.

'The kids are sleeping at Angie's, Marthe's at her boyfriend's, so we'll have the house to ourselves.'

'But I only live a few minutes away,' I said, throat dry, already doubting that I had interpreted this correctly.

'I know that,' Lara said, and continued to look hard at me, a faint curve to her lips. There was no ambiguity now, or at least little enough.

And I thought, just as I had about the drugs, *Should I?* Should I allow myself to feel feelings just like she felt them? Reckless, euphoric feelings that denied the advancing years, years in which I'd done so little against the grain it was pitiful.

'Lara,' I said. 'I'm not sure if –'

Her murmurs shushed me as a kiss on the corner of my mouth shocked me into stillness. 'Miles will explain. He's just coming down now . . .'

Miles. Until that moment I had not understood of myself what I now did: if anything were to happen, if any line were to be crossed, I was not interested in crossing it in *his* direction.

From above there came the sound of a door closing, then slow footsteps on the polished staircase.

I sprang to my feet and put the glass down. 'Thank you, La. I don't know what to say, but I really had better go. Ed will be wondering what's happened to me – he'll be phoning and getting worried. And it doesn't matter about the cab, I can easily walk.'

Trembling, every pore of me alive with nerves and confusion, I slipped into the passageway and towards the front door, just in time to meet Miles at the foot of the stairs.

'Natalie,' he said, and it seemed to me that his tone had a trace of appetite to it.

I stammered a goodbye.

'Don't rush off!' Lara protested, behind me.

And the two of them stood in the open doorway, watching as I scurried across the pebbles. When I turned, waving awkwardly, Lara blew me a kiss, her other hand on Miles's arm as he swung away. I could not see their expressions, but I imagined them as beautifully impassive, roused at most to mild surprise.

I made my way at speed down The Rise, past the grand houses, towards the main road. Though yellow light still glowed behind some of the windows, they'd been closed to the night and not a human sound leaked from them. As I walked, there came across the treetops the scream of a police siren and, for an anxious moment, I thought it was coming towards me. But then I realized it was in fact getting fainter and was soon lost altogether.

Saturday, 22 August

By the time I emerged from bed in the morning Ed was already in his office, so I took him a cup of tea and sat in the spot reserved for his students.

'Don't ask me to do any algebra,' I said. 'My brain isn't working yet.' Neither was my voice, which was painfully rough, as if damaged from smoking crack. I hadn't yet decided how much I was going to divulge about the previous night, so I asked after Craig and Gayle. 'I'm sorry I wasn't there. I did swing by the Vineyard at about midnight, but you'd left.'

In truth, the walk in the dark had been more intimidating than I'd expected, and when I'd found the Vineyard closing, I'd been glad to continue straight home.

'They were fine,' Ed said. 'Disappointed to miss you, though. They've invited us for dinner on Wednesday, so it would be great if you could make yourself available.'

'Of course I will.'

'You look terrible, by the way. Hangover, I assume?'

I gave a weak smile. 'Were you on the peppermint tea yourself, then?'

'It's not a competition,' Ed said mildly. 'We're all old enough these days to feel the extra glass.'

'Speak for yourself,' I said, though my throbbing head told me he'd made a good point.

'So how was the rest of the night with the Borgias? Did you have an orgy with any courtesans or spike any drinks with arsenic?'

Though I knew full well humour was his way of showing forgiveness, my hangover made me defensive. 'It was great, actually. We went swimming.'

Clear skies clouded. 'You did *what*? Where?'

'We broke into the lido and we swam in the dark.'

I hadn't intended confessing, but it was worth it – almost – to see his disbelief, his astonishment at what I might be capable of. 'No you didn't,' he said.

'We did. It was completely wild.'

In retrospect, I see that this was the tipping point, the conversation during which I tipped from seeking his approval of my new friendship to toying with his disapproval of it; to keeping details secret, details like what had been insinuated – was it too bold to say proposed? – in those final few minutes with the Channings.

'It was just a bit of fun,' I said, shrugging.

'It was just a bit of breaking and entering.' Outrage coursed from him in almost visible waves.

'Not really. Lara's practically one of the staff there. She knew the alarm code.'

'I bet she did, but I don't suppose she was authorized to use it. Imagine if Health and Safety . . .' He tailed off, hearing himself, changing direction. 'I can't believe you'd do that when you were all so drunk. You of all people know how dangerous it is to go in the water under the influence. It's a suicide mission.'

'We were fine, Ed, no one died. You're always telling me I need to stop obsessing about safety.'

'I didn't mean you should go to the other extreme! Where were their kids while all of this was going on? Please tell me you didn't take them with you on this crime spree?'

Crime spree, suicide mission, it was all so puritanical, and I remembered now the illicit thought about not spending the rest of my life with a man who always said

no. The instinct I'd had about it being the most important evening of my life, maybe that had been true. I
pressed my lips together, not trusting the words that
might escape, the truths.

Lara and Miles want me. *Me.*

'Georgia is one of my students, Nat,' Ed said.

'Well, you can rest easy because she wasn't there. The
kids stayed at the house with Angie's au pair. They were
all asleep by the time we left.' I tried to recall if I had
actually seen Milena, but it was a moot point: Josh,
Georgia and Eve were all of a reasonable age to be left
in charge of younger children. 'Don't look like that.
They're all perfectly responsible parents.'

'They're perfectly responsible *children*, I'll grant you
that.'

'Come on, Ed, not this again.' I might have been
remaking myself as a rebel without a cause, but he was a
conformist with too many causes to count and that,
surely, was worse.

In tighter control of himself now, Ed looked at me
with a teacherly tolerance so exaggerated it left me in
no doubt of his true intolerance. 'I don't have time for
this debate. I've got Georgia arriving any minute now.'

'Then you'll see for yourself she's quite unharmed.
I'm going back to bed,' I said, as if in agreement.

And it seemed to me that there was the faintest trace
of admiration in the way he looked at me as I left the
room, a woman he no longer recognized. A woman who
no longer quite recognized herself.

27

I walk back to the lift with the dazed eyes and unsteady gait of a victim emerging from an explosion. The floor beneath my feet feels uneven, the walls warped. Mrs Channing asks that I leave. Lara wants me to go. Did I really expect anything different?

Then, like a supernatural phenomenon, her voice reaches my ear.

'Natalie! What the hell are you doing here?'

I have heard it like this only once before, severe and accusing, and grievous though it is, I feel hope stir. She has changed her mind and come out to see me. *She doesn't hate me.*

I turn to find her six feet from me. Everything in her face is strained and tightened; those smiles, so freely given, so sure of their effect, no longer have any place here. The magnificent green dress is wilted, the sculpted hair in near collapse. 'Lara, I didn't mean –'

She interrupts: 'It's not Molly, is it? Tell me she's not here as well!'

'No, no, she's at home with Ed, she's fine. I'm sorry, I didn't mean to disturb you, I just wanted . . .' I'm stammering. What *do* I "just want"? *She* is who I want to see, but *he* is who I need to see. 'I just wanted to find out how Georgia is.'

Her face sags, nude lips tremble. 'She's alive, she's, oh, I don't know. They've told us that because she was unconscious when she arrived, she's less likely to . . .' Her voice falls away, broken.

I know better than anyone how the sentence ends. 'That's just a statistic,' I say. I wish I could comfort her physically, but we're as estranged as two people at touching distance can be and I keep my arms pressed to my sides. 'There are always exceptions, the lucky ones. She'll be one of those.'

In response, she leans against the wall, her face now in profile to me.

'Are there enough staff on duty?' I ask. 'It's so quiet downstairs, I was worried there might not be.'

She nods, a desolate, exhausted dip of the head that stays low, as if her hair is too heavy for her. 'They've been great. The consultant came straight in. Donglas rang him and he just got up in the middle of the night and came. Thank God he wasn't away for the bank holiday.'

It doesn't surprise me that strings have been pulled for her, but it seems to surprise her. She is, understandably, not herself.

'Lara, we're so sorry. I mean, if Georgia was in the water to help Molly in some way . . .'

She turns, interrupts me, smothering a touch of belligerence: '"In some way"? I can't think of any other reason she was in there, can you?'

I can't. However I've skirted it these last hours, I cannot deny it now: Molly is the reason Georgia is here. There was an incident involving a non-swimmer in the water in the dark; she could only have been a liability, lashing in all directions, wild enough to pull stronger swimmers under. I think of the burden of her soaking dress. I imagine the weight of her fear.

'Well, we're grateful.' It's inadequate, insulting. It would have been better to say nothing at all. It would have been better not to come.

'I have to go back in,' Lara says, and she takes a step backwards.

'Of course. Please give Georgia our love when she's strong enough to get messages.'

She is silent but there is assent in her silence, an acknowledgement of optimism.

I'm already walking away when I sense rather than hear footsteps behind me. Turning, I get quite a fright to see her so close to me, her eyes livid with feeling.

'Natalie?'

'Yes?' And there is a moment of preternatural clarity when I not only hear what she says before she says it, but also have my answer ready. Oh, Lara. When darkness fell, I didn't see it for what it was. In my blindness, you continued to glitter; in my ears, your murmurs still seduced.

'I thought you might have understood?' she says, and though she makes it sound like a question, she doesn't wait for a reply.

28

Sunday, 23 August — eight days earlier

The deep end was as restless as the ocean, water leaping at me from all sides. The wind, low and swirling and full of the threat of September, made my ears ache.

Dipping sleekly under the lane divider into the free area, Lara gestured for my attention. 'Let's take a break,' she called. 'We need to chat.'

'Thank God. I can hardly move,' I gasped, my lungs pumping and straining. She'd already begun swimming when I'd arrived and this was our first chance for conversation. 'I blame Friday,' I added, low-voiced and conspiratorial. 'Isn't it surreal to think we were right here in the middle of the night?'

I'd done my very best to resist obsession since then, not to overthink what had been intended by a taxi not ordered and Miles's footsteps on the stairs as he came to 'explain'; or by a hand grasping mine under water and lips that lingered on the corner of my mouth. I'd reminded myself over and over that this was Lara and such overtures might be everything or nothing. Nothing, I'd judged, when I'd received her breezy text proposing a swim this morning.

I followed her up the ladder to where she was settling herself at the water's edge, calves dangling into the pool. Her golden skin shone, her hair dripped down her face and neck, over her collarbone. I could feel her breath, laughably untroubled considering the dozens of lengths she'd just completed, lapping me several times.

'No Angie today?' I asked. 'I thought she'd be keen to get back in the groove after Italy.'

'Actually, I asked her not to come,' Lara said. 'I wanted you to myself.'

Such was my vanity, I actually tipped back my head to the sun as if anointed.

Lara, however, grew uncharacteristically solemn. 'I promised Miles I wouldn't say anything . . .' As two women approached and began setting up camp a few feet from us, she lowered her voice; this in itself was odd, for normally Lara didn't care who heard her views. She expected people to listen in, to pay attention. 'But I didn't want to keep secrets from you.'

'Oh.' I could feel the creeping sensation of shyness – as well as the beginnings of alarm. Having not allowed myself to obsess, I had also not properly considered what on earth I would do if nothing turned out to be everything. If I had to ask myself, Who am I really and what do I want? 'About Friday, you mean? I hope I didn't offend you by rushing off like that, I wasn't –'

'No,' she broke in, frowning. Again, it was unusual of her to be so impatient. 'It's not that. This is about Georgia.'

This was the second time Lara had admitted to being troubled and the second she'd cited Georgia as the cause. I began to shiver as the wind chilled my damp skin. 'What's wrong? Problems with Matt? He is a little older, but you've presumably discussed the implications with her.'

This warranted no more than a brief, querying look. 'Occasionally I check her social media,' Lara said. 'Email and texts, as well.'

'Really?' She was the last person I would have expected to confess this: liberal and permissive, she was often seen laughing at Choo's Twitter account, managed by Eve, or jokingly requesting Georgia share photos of Matt and his colleagues in their lifeguards' uniforms. She would have been astonished to see us sit Molly down, as we had done not so long ago, for a family viewing of the latest police child-protection video. (As for what she would make of my having tried to open my daughter's journal, perhaps she'd be more sympathetic than I might have guessed.)

Seeing my surprise, she added, 'I don't mean I read all the messages and posts, I'm not a glutton for punishment.' There was a chuckle here, but even that was abbreviated, almost curt. 'I just scroll through the contacts and followers, see who she's been chatting with. Just in case.'

'I think that's very wise,' I said earnestly. It would be pleasing to be able to report this conscientious parenting to Ed. 'Ed and I try to keep up to date with Molly's passwords. Our view is that if there's something worth hiding, then there's something worth finding.'

Of course the truth was that if there was something worth hiding then these half-child half-adult creatures would stop at nothing to hide it, and if we thought we had the faintest chance of outwitting them we were fooling ourselves. Their skills at subterfuge were superior, their self-absorption more complete.

'Anyway,' Lara said, 'yesterday I noticed something that worried me.'

'Oh, Lara.' I reached to pat her arm in sympathy. 'Tell me. Maybe I can help?'

She held my eye – she was rare in not letting her gaze drift upwards to the birthmark – and then, very gently, she brushed my hand from her arm and placed her own hand where mine had been. There was something in the gesture that turned me cold. 'I noticed she had an awful lot of messages from Ed,' she said finally.

I blinked, once, twice. 'From Ed? Well, of course. They're presumably about scheduling their sessions. Or links to revision sites and so on.'

There was just the barest trace of pain in her eyes, too obscure to name, before she looked down. 'Maybe, yes. I just thought there were an awful lot. Some were from when you were away, which struck me as inappropriate.'

Never before had I heard Lara use this word as a negative. As far as she was concerned, inappropriate was a hoot, a cue for applause.

'I know there was a FaceTime session,' I said, battling my confusion. 'I was in the room when he took the call from her. You and I spoke afterwards, remember? You'd been here, swimming in the rain.'

'I don't mean that. These were emails, a whole string of them. Georgia doesn't normally bother with email. She does Instagram and WhatsApp, all that stuff. This felt secret. The email address was different from the one he uses when he sends me an update or an invoice.'

'Secret?' I faltered, my chest tightening. If she was suggesting what I thought she was suggesting, then I had to shut this down directly. It went without saying that I trusted Ed implicitly and knew him to be beyond reproach, in thought as well as action, but I couldn't vouch for Georgia and the vagaries of the teenage psyche. Who knew what nonsense she and her friends had been exchanging on the subject of her 'old but hot' maths tutor? In my experience, the most attractive girls were the very ones interested in the challenge of gaining adult attention, their peers having proved all too easy to win. If I'd had to guess, I'd have said that, buoyed by her success with the older Matt, Georgia had perhaps made some regrettable comment about Ed that Lara had stumbled upon, prompting this investigation. Yes, it was a predictable enough suspicion (and one I might have anticipated had I not been so focused on Molly and, I admit, myself).

Most crucially, if Craig's experience had taught me anything it was that parents – *people* – had only to hear the word 'smoke' and they were already warming their hands on the fire. God, teenage girls were a liability; it was a miracle society survived them.

'Let's start at the beginning.' I spoke with the firm-not-forceful tones of a teacher that, in the past six weeks, I'd almost forgotten I possessed. 'Ed always communicates by email or phone with his students. Texts are too easily missed and there's often detailed information to give, or attachments. I have no idea how many accounts he uses, but I do know he's highly organized and I wouldn't be surprised if he runs his admin from one account and pupil liaison from another. You say the correspondence felt "secret": in terms of the content, did you actually read the emails?'

'No,' she admitted.

'Well, you should – if only for peace of mind. Come on, let's go back now and read them together and you'll see there's nothing whatsoever for you to be worried about. It's not an invasion of privacy if it's correspondence with a teacher. I'm sure Ed wouldn't mind us looking. All teachers know communication with pupils needs to be transparent.'

Lara sighed, as much the sigh of a thwarted child as an anxious parent. This sort of confrontation didn't come naturally to her, I guessed. 'She's out with Eve, she'll have her phone with her.'

'If it's email then you can access it on her laptop or whatever device she uses. Do you know the password?'

'There's no point. She'll have deleted them by now.'

'Why would she have done that?' I knew from Ed's and Craig's stories of confiscated phones that young people (all of us for that matter) were less efficient in deleting sent emails than received ones, and lengthy exchanges could be revisited easily. 'Lara, have you talked to Georgia about this?'

'Not yet. I was hoping . . . I was hoping I wouldn't have to.'

Again she exhaled heavily, tiring of this, and I saw that I was going to have to press her to be explicit. 'Are you asking *me* to raise this with Ed? If so, I honestly think he might take offence. He's absolutely scrupulous about teacher–pupil boundaries. He doesn't even approve of our socializing, to be honest.'

I didn't add that Lara had personally blurred the relationship to a level that could surely be construed as more troubling than anything Georgia might have done. *I bet the girls love him*: that had been one of the first things she'd said to me. She was, after all, a woman who was blithely lustful of her daughter's eighteen-year-old boyfriend.

'Forget it,' Lara said, abruptly, decisively. 'I shouldn't have said anything. As you say, I'm sure it's completely innocent.'

'Of course it's innocent. Seriously, if I thought for a moment Ed had crossed the line with a pupil, any pupil, believe me, we wouldn't be having this conversation. I would be at home spitting blood.'

Saying this, I was struck by what was fundamentally unnatural about this conversation: *she* was not spitting blood. Yes, *I* knew this was nonsense, scarcely worth my rousing any but routine defences on Ed's behalf, but if she really believed there had been any impropriety between Georgia and a teacher in his forties, shouldn't she be on his doorstep demanding answers? Wouldn't Miles be at her side, ready to punch his lights out?

Inexplicably, through some rogue neurotic impulse, an image of Stephen sprang to mind.

'Look, I ought to get back,' I said. Cold now, I was also feeling the beginnings of nausea, not because of any doubt I had about my husband, but for the dawning knowledge that my friendship with Lara was now at risk. 'Molly will be home in a few hours and I don't want to be out when she arrives.'

As I struggled to my feet, I felt her fingers lock around my ankle. Then, when I pitched slightly, her other hand rested briefly on my calf to steady me. Her eyes were fierce with pleading. 'Listen, you won't say anything to Ed, will you? Don't give this another thought, I'm just being paranoid, stressed out about the party next weekend.'

I couldn't see what possible connection there might be.

'This doesn't change a thing between us,' she continued. 'See you tomorrow as usual? We'll have lunch here, shall we?'

'I'm not sure what my movements will be,' I said truthfully. 'It depends what Molly wants to do.'

At this, Lara became more animated still, as if I'd hit upon some inspired solution to save the day. She released my ankle and sprang to her feet. 'Bring her with you – I'd love to see her again. Let's see if we can't get her in the water this time!'

She was almost wild; I didn't recognize her.

'Text me, Natalie, promise?'

As I moved away, I saw people watching with interest, including the two women stretched out near by. They didn't know me but, like most, they either knew who Lara was or were naturally attracted to her. They wondered who had inspired such entreaties; it was not the dynamic they would have expected, the beauty begging the disfigured. And, to my shame, I enjoyed that confounding of preconceptions.

Given the food for thought I carried away with me, I enjoyed it more than I should have, just as I did the memory of her fingers on my ankle.

Arriving home, I was calmed both by the gleaming cleanliness of the place (part in atonement for Friday's antics and part in preparation for Molly's return, I'd spent the previous afternoon deep-cleaning) and by immediate evidence of the professionalism I'd just been defending in my husband. For sitting in his office cell, producing invoices, was a man who gave sixty or seventy hours a week to his job in term time and who was applying the same dedication to his tutoring. All these weeks that I'd been indulging myself, he had not once complained that he was working when he could have been relaxing: he was utterly committed to the new venture. It was inconceivable that he would jeopardize it with even the smallest ambiguity.

I showered, then joined him in the living room, where he'd adjourned with his laptop. I was determined to do as Lara had insisted and keep the matter to myself. The problem was – and it's hard to admit it even now – I continued to be agitated, not by the threat to Ed's reputation so much as the one to my relationship with Lara. We might have parted with her publicly begging me to agree that nothing had changed between us, but the very fact that Lara Channing was begging meant something was seriously amiss.

'Are you all right?' Ed asked.

'Fine.' And in that single syllable I knew I was going to allow Iona's runaway train to derail. I could feel my hands slipping from the wheel, my feet rolling from under me. 'How is it going with Georgia since we've been back from holiday?'

In spite of the abruptness of the question, he answered willingly. 'It's going perfectly well. We had a good session yesterday.' Then, at my silence: 'What?'

'Nothing,' I said.

'Nat, just spit it out.'

'Just, well, you don't think . . .?'

He looked up properly, fingers motionless on the keyboard. 'I don't "just, well" think what, exactly?'

'That maybe she might be getting a little too fond of you? Developing a bit of a crush.'

Ed stared at me, irritated. 'What on earth makes you think that? We get on well, of course we do, but I find that that's slightly more constructive than encouraging students to hate me. Better for business, too.'

I consciously relaxed, meaning my body language to show how casual my remarks were, how expectant I was that he should dismiss them out of hand. 'I don't mean you would ever do anything, of course you wouldn't. I just mean her. Maybe she's not the innocent we think she is.'

Faint colour stained Ed's cheeks. 'Whether or not she's "innocent", whatever that means, is not my concern, is it? I teach her maths, not morals. End of story.'

But his tone was anything but terminal. Sensing the magnitude of my mistake, I blundered instead towards generalization. 'I'm just saying, with girls of that age, the ones who come on their own, maybe we should make sure I'm here at the same time? Just to be on the safe side? You can't be too careful – we know that from poor Craig's ordeal.'

Ed set aside the laptop. 'Why would you bring that up? Craig was the victim of a malicious campaign.' As the words formed, there it was, the sudden flush of comprehension that seemed to make his eyes change colour. *Now* he exploded. 'This has come from *her*, hasn't it? You've just seen her at the pool and she put this idea into your head? Interfering witch.'

'Ed!' Instantly I was ambushed by an instinct to defend Lara from his accusations, not him from hers – what was the matter with me? Even as I engaged in it I recognized my behaviour as both disloyal and self-sabotaging. 'Ed, don't get this out of proportion. All she said was she'd noticed Georgia had had a lot of emails from you, including when we were on holiday. She wondered if that was the normal amount between a tutor and his pupil and I said it was. Don't worry, she hadn't actually read them.'

He flushed deeper still, enraged. 'You say that like there was something to read! And you're prepared to cover it up like some complicit political wife. Like *she* no doubt would for Miles.'

My head pounded. 'No, I don't. If I thought that, then don't you think I'd be confronting you myself? Obviously, I knew it was nonsense.'

'So you agreed to have a quiet word with me, did you? Aren't you insulted on my behalf? Doesn't it make you wary of this woman?' He laughed, bitter, scornful. 'No, of course it doesn't, not when you're a desperate acolyte.'

As I gaped, he startled me by picking up his phone and flinging it on to the sofa seat next to mine. It bounced against my leg and I put out a hand to stop it falling to the floor. 'I haven't deleted any emails or texts for weeks. Read any you like. Go on! All the sent ones are still there too. Feel free to show the police.'

To my horror, he reached next for his laptop. 'If you throw that at me as well,' I said, 'I swear I'll leave and not come back.'

'Where will you go?' he demanded. 'To the Channings'? Do you *really* think they'd have you? The wife of a sex pest?'

By now, the scene had gathered a combative heat that was unprecedented between us and no less distressing because I had commanded it myself from perfect tranquillity and order. 'Calm down,' I said. 'Of course I'm not going to read your private messages.'

'Not private. Professional.' His tone was as black as his expression.

'Yes.' I laid the phone on the coffee table, face down, as if that were an illustration of my honour.

'Do you want to know what I think?' Ed said.

'You've already told me, haven't you?'

'I think she's fucking toxic, your great mate Lara. I think she's pathologically jealous of Georgia and is trying to damage a perfectly healthy and productive teacher–pupil relationship. She's using you to help her.'

'She's not.' Oddly, it was this, more than anything, that cut the deepest: that I should be being used, not loved for myself. 'She had a brief concern and she aired it discreetly. If you must know, she begged me not to mention it to you.'

'I bet she did. She's stirring trouble for her own entertainment. This is probably what she does for a hobby while Miles plays golf.'

'He doesn't play golf.'

'Was she pissed? At the pool?'

'Of course she wasn't. It's the middle of the day.'

'So what? They probably start on the booze the minute they wake up.'

We're too drunk. We're always too drunk.

I suppressed an involuntary impulse of dread or lust or something equally violent. 'This is a mistake, yes, we can agree on that, but don't forget all the lovely things she's done for us. Think how she's helped Molly.'

He made a contemptuous sound. 'It's Georgia who's helped Molly, and before you say it again, I don't believe for a moment that Lara ordered her to. All *she* did was recommend a therapist and anyone could have done that.'

'It was more than that,' I protested. 'She even rang Bryony in advance.'

Ed's exasperation flared once more. 'That's how she operates, don't you see? She does favours, puts herself at the centre of things. Like the lido. The way you describe her, she's like some mobster running her front-of-house from there, controlling guest lists, keeping everyone quiet with cocktails, leading midnight break-ins.'

I burst into laughter. 'What are you talking about? That's not remotely how I describe her! And she spent two years on the restoration campaign, which is hardly a quick favour. It must have been pretty tedious and was probably unpaid as well.'

'She doesn't need the money. She just fancied having a pool across the road from her house and had nothing better to do with her time. It's all power play.'

'It's good works, Ed, and friendship.'

'A funny kind of friendship. But maybe that's what you prefer, these days. Over the people who genuinely care about you.'

He meant Gayle, of course. This conversation was an out-and-out disaster. Only a physical withdrawal was going to stem this flow of hateful comments and I got to my feet to leave the room. 'Look, please don't blame Lara, blame me. It wasn't even an allegation. I should never have said anything.'

'The point is, I would *expect* you to say something,' Ed said. 'You're my wife. At least, I *thought* you were.'

'*What?*'

'Mum?'

We both started at the sound of our daughter's voice, the sight of her moving from hallway to open living-room doorway, her face appalled.

'Molls, you're early! I didn't hear you come in.' I hurried to hug her, but her arms remained by her sides.

'Because you were shouting,' she said coolly. And she looked first at her father and then at me, as if to say we had deliberately ruined her homecoming.

Behind her, my mother appeared. 'You do know that everyone on this floor can hear you going at it hammer and tongs? Honestly, Nat, you'll have people complaining you're lowering the tone.'

With Herculean effort, I ignored this remark.

'Hello,' Ed said blandly. 'Come and sit down. Tell us all about your week away, Molls.'

'Nothing to tell,' Molly said. 'I'm going to my room.'

'Don't be so rude,' Ed began, but I stopped him.

'Leave her. I'll put the kettle on.'

'That poor girl,' my mother said, tailing me into the kitchen. 'What a way to see your parents after being away from them for a week.'

I had an image then of the first time I'd seen her and my father after my summer in Stoneborough. She'd been in the kitchen getting lunch ready and he'd gone over and kissed her. The joy of seeing them affectionate and peaceful again, it had felt like all I needed in the world. There was no lunch waiting for Molly, but I would set about rectifying that right away. I would make one of her favourite snacks, hot sausage sandwiches with grilled tomatoes.

'She won't eat those,' my mother said, watching me pluck the packet from the fridge. 'She says she's on a diet.'

I stopped in my tracks. 'She doesn't need to diet. I hoped she didn't know what a diet was.'

'Well, she certainly does.'

The heat of the row with Ed still visible on my skin, I warned myself not to create another family crisis out of a passing remark. As I put the sausages back into the fridge, I tried to recall the last meal I'd shared with Molly. She'd not eaten the corned-beef hotpot, but that was evidence of sanity not disorder, surely. In the New Forest, she'd eaten normally, but I hadn't thought to pay special attention. Before that, I could hardly remember, mealtimes, domesticity in general, having been downgraded, only the more exciting times distinct in my mind.

'I take it your week alone hasn't gone too well?' my mother asked, and when I looked at her I couldn't reconcile her with the woman in the kitchen who'd kissed my father and welcomed me home. When had she stopped being on my side?

'You sound as if you want it to have gone badly,' I said, my voice tremulous.

'Don't be ridiculous,' Mum said.

But after the day's difficulties with Lara and Ed, I couldn't face another argument. 'It's been great, actually. You just caught us at a tricky time. Let's have a cup of tea.'

'Before I forget, your friend Mel popped by before she went back to Southampton.' She was not one to let ill feeling get in the way of gossip.

'Did she?' Molly hadn't mentioned that when we'd spoken on the phone.

'She said to give you a message about your old friend – Vanessa, is it?'

'Nessie,' I said cautiously.

'That's it. She said she asked her mum about her and Cheryl said the family's not in the village any more. They moved away years ago.'

'Oh. I wonder where to.'

'According to Mel, London. They're probably just around the corner.' Mum raised the blind and peered from the kitchen window. Foxes had been at the bins and left an unsightly scattering of rubbish across the road. 'If you ask me, they must be mad,' she said.

29

Tuesday, 25 August

The next few days were miserable. Lara phoned several times but, too wretched and uncertain to know what to say, I rejected each call.

While refusing to utter another word on the subject, Ed simmered almost audibly. As for Molly, I couldn't tell if she was still unsettled by the homecoming row or had simply developed a taste for greater independence, but either way she demanded she be allowed to go alone to her Tuesday hypnotherapy session, which had been rescheduled from evening to morning.

'I'm thirteen. It's not a big deal. I go to Oxford Circus with Izzy all the time, so what's the difference?'

'This is a medical appointment, not a shopping trip,' I said. 'I have to come with you in case there's anything Bryony needs to discuss afterwards. Besides, this is a big week. You haven't seen her since before we went to the New Forest and you've got a lot of brilliant progress to report.'

'It's not "brilliant", Mum.'

'*I* think it is.'

Even without looking at me she was able to convey how little she rated my opinion. 'I'm still a freak,' she muttered.

'Don't say that,' I protested. 'You're a fantastic, brave girl.'

She allowed a brief touch of my hand on her arm, her eyes bright with the honesty of her response, but then she blinked and they'd clouded again. During the journey into the West End, she was mutinous, glaring as if she hated me.

'I've lost control of her,' I told Sarah that evening. Though Molly and I had visited together after Inky's walk, she'd left within minutes to fetch her phone. 'God forbid she be separated from that thing for half an hour. I'm convinced it's why she's withdrawn from us — it supplies all her needs. Perhaps it might cook her meals for her too. Actually, she's saying she wants to cook for herself from now on. Where will it end, Sarah? A legal bid for emancipation?'

Sarah laughed. 'I think that's an overreaction. Don't forget, she's just been away from you for a week. Trust me, I'm sure it's all perfectly natural.'

Trust me: they all said it. They all meant it, too. Seeing Sarah was like catching up with common sense, bracing and soothing in one. Like Gayle, she'd been neglected in recent weeks.

'So long as she's confiding in *someone*,' Sarah added.

'I'm not sure she is.'

'What about the friend who's here all the time?'

'Izzy?'

'No, the other one. Blonde, very pretty. Comes on her bike.'

'Oh, you mean Georgia, Lara's daughter. You must have seen her when she comes for her tutoring with Ed.' I wondered if Georgia would turn up to her session the next day, the first since the 'delicate' matter had been raised. For Molly's sake, I hoped she would. To my knowledge, the two had made no plans to meet since Molly's return from Stoneborough – but what did I know?

Nothing.

'Have you seen the glamorous Lara lately?' Sarah asked, and the question produced an ache of grief I wasn't prepared for.

'Not in the last couple of days. I haven't been swimming,' I said. 'That's where I usually see her, but I've been a bit busy.'

'Well, her daughter's certainly inherited her looks, hasn't she? And she's so elegant, the way she moves. Quite balletic.'

'I know. I always think she's like a pixie compared to Molls and the other girls. Though Molls does have the misfortune of having a walrus for a mother,' I added, eyebrows raised.

Sarah smiled. 'Hardly. You're the picture of health these days, Nat.'

Just then Molly reappeared with her precious phone.

'You weren't supposed to hear me call myself a walrus,' I told her drily, taking no offence when she failed to

326

protest at the comparison as Sarah had done. I left the two of them to chat while I put together something for Sarah's dinner.

Bless her. Whatever she said to Molly must have penetrated the teenage self-absorption more effectively than any of my own efforts because when we returned downstairs she followed me into the kitchen and asked if she could help make the vegetable lasagne for supper.

'Everything all right, sweetie?' I said, as we stood at the chopping board together.

'Fine.' And she looked not so much abashed as grateful.

'Think of everything your mother does for you,' I imagined Sarah saying to her, but, no, Sarah was not as overt as that.

Perhaps Molly simply wanted to check how much fat I was putting into the lasagne.

Wednesday, 26 August

Inevitably, there was apprehension before Georgia's session the next day, apprehension that had to be concealed from Molly, which meant an additional tension.

'Do not say a word,' Ed warned me. 'I have no intention of dignifying Lara's ridiculous paranoia with a response.'

Georgia arrived on time, looking and behaving exactly as she always did; either her parents had not shared their concerns with her or she was an even better actress than Lara. Afterwards, she chatted with Molly and me in the usual way, saying she'd arranged to meet Eve and Josh at the lido and did Molly want to come too.

'Sure,' Molly said. 'That'd be cool.'

It seemed to me there was something artificial about Molly's manner and I couldn't help recalling that comment she'd made about being a freak. This would be her first outing near water since before the holiday and it would be quite understandable if she were especially nervous. Divining my fretting, Molly shot me a warning look.

'Ed?' I said. 'Are you okay with this?'

'*Mum!*'

'Yup, fine by me,' Ed said. Either he remained genuinely convinced of Georgia's good influence – and quality of guardianship – or he had a point to make to me. I had a horrible feeling we might have entered a marital war of attrition.

It was like sitting with leeches on me after the girls had gone. No doubt exacerbated by the new misunderstanding with the Channings, my anxiety exceeded all previous levels and I managed little more than an hour before mobilizing, not specifying to Ed my destination, though admittedly the grabbing of a recyclable shopping bag might have given the (mistaken) impression it was the local Sainsbury's.

Walking through the park, I resisted the urge to tear across the grass like a lunatic but proceeded at a deliberately sedate pace, forcing myself to notice the mother and her toddler twins resting in the shade, the black Lab eating dandelions, the shorn grass that filled the air with the rich scent of sap. From the distance came the sound of a whistle, long, warbling, the kind you hear at carnivals, which reminded me that it would soon be the bank-holiday weekend, the Notting Hill Carnival and other summer's end celebrations. In Elm Hill, there'd be not a carnival but a pool party. Would we still go? It seemed unlikely that Ed would want to; was it so abhorrent that I did? How would things stand by Sunday? Would I have seen Lara by then? Was she, and not Molly, the reason I was attracted to the lido this afternoon as iron is to lodestone?

If nothing else, such soul-searching sustained me to the end of the main path. As I neared the building, I was struck by the absence of the shouts and squeals I was used to hearing on approach and, peeking through the turnstile at the eastern end, I was confronted by the unprecedented sight of virtually every bather on his or her feet, like crowds on a football terrace. Was some sort of an event taking place? I imagined Georgia and Josh in one of their head-to-heads, Lara having persuaded the mob to clear the pool and pick a side to cheer. But there was no cheering, no laughing, only the murmur of low voices, the uncertainty that comes of unscheduled inter-ruption. Through a gap I glimpsed the pool itself: empty of swimmers, untouched even at its edges, the water was quite still, almost as if it were in disgrace. Now I could see that everyone had turned not to the pool itself but to a spot out of my sightline on the far side.

Something had happened.

I called through the bars, to anyone who would listen, 'What's going on?', and was shocked by how my voice sounded, a trapped animal's, frantic with fear.

'They've just cleared the pool,' said a woman, exiting through the turnstile.

I scuttled aside to let her pass. 'Why?'

'The lifeguard had to go in and fish someone out. I think they've called an ambulance and –'

An *ambulance*? She was still speaking as I turned rudely from her and broke into a sprint, reaching the main entrance short of breath and wild-eyed, pushing past the queue to gatecrash a conversation taking place at the front desk. Apparently the admission of newcomers had been suspended.

'I need to go in,' I cried. 'It's my daughter!'

'Natalie, hello.' One of the reception staff who knew me as Lara's friend gestured for a colleague to let me pass. 'But, wait a second, you –'

I didn't hear the rest as I barrelled through the barriers and into the pool area. Even among the forest of people, it wasn't hard to identify the focus of attention, a gathering of crouched lifeguards around a prone female figure. As I neared, I glimpsed a portion of a navy swimsuit, a section of white leg. I felt vomit fill my mouth, swallowed painfully.

Molly, I thought, *Molly*. It had happened just as I knew it would. Tired of being a 'freak', she must have followed Georgia into the water. The shock, the sheer unfamiliarity, of being immersed would have disorientated her, only for her to find that the floor had vanished beneath her feet. I *knew* I should have gone with her. I *knew* my instinct had been the right one, however retrograde. Ed had been wrong, *wrong* to think we could trust Georgia...

A woman of my age was among those tending Molly, a woman I recognized, and my hijacked brain was slow to make the connections.

'Gayle,' I said, in that same wild tone, 'is it her?' And as my old friend's head turned at the sound of my cry, a space opened and enabled me to see the girl fully. Her feet were raised on the lap of a lifeguard sitting beside her – Matt, soaked from head to toe – and he was arranging towels and a foil blanket over her legs. Her swimsuit was in fact dark purple and the style asymmetrical, with a single shoulder strap stitched with love-hearts. Her face, turned from the water and visible to me now, was not Molly's but Harriet's.

Thank God.

Gayle sprang to her feet, took a step towards me. '*What* did you say?'

There was a moment of terror, a moment of knowledge that something horrendous had been committed and it would not be forgiven.

'Did you say, "Thank God"?' Gayle placed her face close to mine in tear-stained challenge, and I could smell the hot odour of anger on her skin. Behind her, uncomprehending glances were cast my way before attention returned to Harriet. One of the guards was checking her vital signs, while Matt, calm, grave, dripping, continued to adjust the coverings. 'Thank God my daughter's had an accident?' Gayle pressed. 'Might have drowned?'

At last I took command of myself. 'No, no, of course not. I meant thank God she's fine. Because she is, isn't she?' Indeed, the way Harriet was murmuring to Matt and the others at her side, her distress appeared minimal, closer, in fact, to embarrassment.

But Gayle was not to be mollified so easily. 'That's not what you meant at all.' Her voice was a furious hiss.

I reached to touch her. 'Please, what happened? Is she hurt?'

She swatted my fingers from her forearm and ignored my question. 'You thought it was Molly, didn't you?' And she laughed, a nasty, abrasive laugh I'd never before heard her utter. 'It's not all about her, you know. There *are* other children in the world, other parents. Parents who care about their children just as much as you do about yours. An astonishing idea, eh?'

All around us faces stared, ears strained, as it became evident there was a second scene to be witnessed. Matt and Harriet looked our way too, with the same slanting expressions of concern.

'Gayle, please, just tell me what's going on. Tell me if I can help.' But, met only with hostility, I appealed to one of the staff, the young man about whom, just last week, I'd made lascivious remarks to impress Lara. 'Can I do anything to help?'

'Would you mind stepping back, please,' he said, 'while we follow procedure? We'll be reopening the pool shortly.'

By now Gayle had turned from me and rejoined her daughter. I shuffled backwards before meeting the resistance of the crowd and stood quite frozen, not knowing what to do or say or think, not daring to do or say or think anything at all. My eyes began to leak: tears of anxiety for Harriet or of personal shame, I didn't know. *Other parents, other children*: Gayle's words burned.

I said her name again and she didn't react. I felt the withdrawal of others' attention, a collective shift from me, a shunning. As I heard the pool manager explain to Gayle that an ambulance was not required after all but that she should take Harriet herself to Accident and Emergency 'just in case', I started to sob.

Then I felt a hand on my arm, the caress of a thumb over my skin. Lara, I thought. She'll make it all right. That weird conversation, that rift, will be meaningless now. This will restore perspective.

'Come with me,' Angie said. 'You look like you might need a drink.'

I turned, mouth open, brain reactivating. Not Lara, Angie. 'Have you seen Molly?' I cried. 'Do you know where the girls are?'

She put an arm around my waist. 'I've just sent them all to my place. Let's go and find them. They're just a couple of minutes ahead of us.'

'Is Lara with them?'

'No, she's at a meeting in town.'

I followed her through the throng – it parted only sluggishly, for Angie had not the same effect as Lara – to the queue for the turnstile.

'Are you all right?' she asked.

'I don't know.'

'You've had a shock, that's all. No one was hurt.'

'I feel terrible,' I told her. 'Gayle . . . Did you hear what she said to me?'

Though I couldn't see Angie's eyes through her sunglasses, I caught the flicker of an averted gaze. 'She'll understand. Of course Molly would be your first thought. How could she not be?'

I almost wailed. So *she* thought I'd meant 'Thank God not Molly,' too. 'I didn't mean it like that,' I insisted. 'I didn't know what I was saying. I *love* Harriet.'

'I'm sure you do, darling. Don't get upset.' Her voice was both soothing and hollow, not solace enough and yet the only salvation on offer.

As we passed through the turnstile, I felt like a different person from the one who'd stormed the barriers ten minutes ago. Even the scent of the cut grass had turned, tinged now with rot.

Angie led me through the park gate and across The Rise to her house on Steadman Avenue. The swept path and immaculately pruned roses compounded my sense of unreality, as if I were being led into an illusion of a suburban house, a trick done with mirrors. In the hallway she called up to the floor above, 'Girls? Are you there? Come down a moment, will you?'

Reluctant footsteps on the stairs produced first Eve, then Georgia – both damp-haired – and next Molly, bone dry. All three appeared unperturbed.

'Are you okay?' I asked, the fist-sized knot in my stomach loosening a little.

'Yes, thanks,' Molly said. The other two only shrugged.

'Harriet's going to be all right,' I reassured them, and saw Georgia and Eve exchange an inscrutable private look. 'Molly and Harriet know each other quite well,' I explained to them, with sudden heat. 'I thought she might be worried.' I had the sense that these remarks, or perhaps the display of passion that had accompanied them, embarrassed Molly so I said no more. She was safe – they *all* were, including Harriet – and that was what mattered. I would contact Gayle later and make things right.

'Phone your mum,' Angie instructed Georgia, 'in case she's heard something and is worried about you.'

'Sure,' Georgia said, in an obedient, humouring way. It was clear that the girls had already turned their attention to more important things.

'Come in here,' Angie said, ushering me into the sitting room at the front of the house, 'where we can have some peace.'

By the time I'd taken a seat in one of a pair of tub armchairs by the fireplace, Angie had delivered two glasses of something potent and repulsive that it took me a moment to identify as grappa. There was no immediate effect so I took another large gulp. Now details came into focus: a zebra-print rug, a row of potted orchids on the mantelpiece. After initial enthusiasm, Choo resettled on a sheepskin throw.

Angie perched settled next to me, wordless as a counsellor. Distant sounds through the open window brought the news that normal business had resumed at the lido.

'Did you actually see what happened?' I said.

'No, I was in the café on my phone when I heard the whistle and I saw the lifeguards go around clearing the water. I thought there must be some technical thing, or something in the water. They clear it, you know, if there's vomit, that sort of thing. But then they shouted, "Lifeguard going in," and the next thing you know Matt is in the water helping someone out. But it was only a false alarm. The kind of alarm we like.' Even so, Angie continued to look vexed, as if the worst part of the story was still to come.

'What? What are you not telling me?'

'I don't know if I should say. It's just gossip.'

'Seriously,' I pleaded, 'I need to know everything. When I get home I'll call Gayle. She'll want to know any information I can give her.' She won't speak to me, I thought, swallowing. Not yet, maybe not ever.

'Well, don't tell her *this*,' Angie said, rolling her pale eyes.

'What?'

At last she spilled: 'The girls think Harriet faked being in trouble in the water. If so, then that was a very dangerous thing to do, not to mention totally disruptive.'

I was taken aback. 'But why would she do that?'

Angie's attitude was markedly less easy-going than usual: she was, in her own way, shaken. 'Well, to get her knight in shining armour to jump in and save her, apparently.'

I remembered now the casual gossip about Georgia's boyfriend and Harriet's interest in him. 'You mean Matt?'

'Got it in one. The incident happened right where he was patrolling. It was quite a coincidence.'

'That doesn't sound like Harriet at all,' I said doubtfully.

'Does anything *ever* sound like the child we think we know?' Angie said. 'Honestly?'

I thought of Gayle's joke about writing a book called *Not That I Know Of.* Poor Gayle. She'd been there on site with Harriet yet it hadn't been enough. These girls of ours, their thoughts were their own, their impulses, their mistakes.

'As if we haven't got enough worries,' Angie sighed as she trickled the last of the grappa into our glasses. 'Oh dear, Stephen will have a go at me for finishing this. He's convinced I'm on the slippery slope to rehab. Like *he's* a pure vessel, eh?'

I sipped the alcohol, disconcerted by the mention of her husband. 'Angie,' I blurted, 'I wanted to ask you about him. Have I . . . have I done anything to offend him?'

She looked astonished. 'Stephen? Of course not. What makes you say that?'

'Oh, nothing.' I shook my head, at last learning my lesson about cutting short these potentially damaging conversations. 'I'm sure I just imagined it.'

The readiness – more than that, the air of know-ing – with which Angie accepted this made me suspect that she might have taken part in some past discussion about my state of mind, presumably with Lara, and I felt suddenly victimized. Fine, so I'd been unusually vigilant about poolside safety, and fine, I'd lost my mind slightly regarding Stephen – it wasn't as if I'd got the measure of Miles either, for that matter – but I wasn't the one spinning this nonsense about Harriet or fabricating a flirtation between Georgia and a middle-aged man. Maybe Ed was right: this group *was* trouble.

'I should take Molly home,' I said, getting to my feet.

'Of course. Let's go and tell her to shake a leg,' Angie agreed, and when she hugged Molly and pressed biscuits on her before leaving, I felt guilty for those previous uncharitable thoughts. What was wrong with me, sec-ond-guessing my friends when they were only trying to support me? If I continued like this, I'd have none left.

'Thank you for everything this afternoon,' I told Angie. 'I needed . . . well, I needed a friend.'

'You're very welcome.' At the door, she kissed me on the cheek. 'Where've you been this week, anyway? I haven't seen you since our fun and games last Friday. Nothing's wrong, is it?'

'No.'

'It's not to do with La, is it? Not that silly business about Ed? You really mustn't worry. I'm sure he's quite safe from her clutches.'

I couldn't quite stifle my gasp, startled by her casual reference, but then I saw she meant Lara's attentions, not Georgia's, and must be referring to our conversation at La Madrague about the Channings' marital indiscretions. One thing about this afternoon: it had put the ambiguity of the events of late Friday night into perspective. *Not that*, Lara had said as if it were trivia, just another jape with the gang. Miles's and her peccadilloes, either individual or shared, were none of my concern.

'Seriously, Lara's one of the good guys,' Angie said. 'You can take my word for it.'

30

Monday, 31 August, 9.15 a.m.

In the hospital atrium, I stop to buy a takeaway coffee, drawn as much by the cheer and energy at the counter as by any need for refreshment. They're soothing, the stock mundanities between the server and the customer – 'Drew the short straw, did you?' 'Every time, love, every time. Sugar with that?' – and the discordant roar and sputter of the coffee machine.

I decide on green tea. It comes too hot to drink.

I thought you might have understood . . . Don't think about what that means: nothing matters now except the girl up there in Critical Care and the staff working to bring her back to her family.

I sit at an empty table to phone Ed. As I dial, I cradle Molly's phone in my other hand, as if it connects me to her just by touch.

Ed answers at once, no greeting, only the question 'How is she?' and the sound of his voice, the urgent dread in it, undoes a catch in me and I have to breathe deeply before I can reply.

'I don't really know. I saw Lara, but I didn't get much information. She was very upset.'

'That's understandable.'

'It's serious, though, Ed. I don't think Georgia's regained consciousness and the longer it goes on . . .' I tail off, unable to articulate the rest of the thought.

'Where are you? In the car?'

'No, still in the hospital. I stopped to pick up a drink. I felt, just, overwhelmed.'

'You've been awake all night – you need to come home and rest,' he says, and I search for the tenderness in his tone but cannot find it. I cannot find it.

My eyes refill, colours swim, the passive expressions of those around me distort into anguish. I blink and a woman comes into focus, blue overalls, a stethoscope and security pass around her neck; a man in green, AMBULANCE spelled out on his back in yellow.

'Has Molly woken up yet?' I ask.

'No. I've come into the kitchen so I don't disturb her.'

'Tell her I'll be back very soon with breakfast. I'll stop by La Tasse and get her favourite croissants, the almond ones.'

'Look, I need to go,' Ed says. 'I've just missed a call from Liam.'

'Wait, one thing: Molly's pin doesn't work on her phone. Do you know if she changed it?'

'What are you using?'

'One nine oh nine.' Inky's birthday. Every year she makes him peanut-butter biscuits, says they're his favourite, though the truth is he likes all biscuits the same.

'She changed it from that a few weeks ago, don't you remember? It's oh three oh eight now. Try that.'

Maybe they told me or maybe I haven't been around to be told. I hang up, key in the digits. Is 0308, as the previous one was, a memorable date? What happened on 3 August?

I'm in. I scroll through the most recent images: nothing from the party, which seems odd, but dozens of pictures of the lido in daylight hours, dating from the preceding days. Faces and legs are cut off, the subject a door or a light, sometimes out of focus as if the phone had slipped as her finger tapped the screen. Then, in perfect clarity, Georgia, in the pool, teeth bared in a theatrical growl, tiny white straps on suntanned skin. The thought of this radiant creature having been rendered inert, inanimate, by the very water she is pictured in: it breaks my heart. It would break any heart.

I open WhatsApp and scan for Georgia's name. There's a group called 'Water-babies' involving her, Josh and Eve, a long thread of messages dating from weeks ago and continuing till yesterday. Words jump out – 'Pussy', 'Champ', 'Result!' – and there are numbers, 2/05, 2/36, 1/57, 2/58, inexplicable to me, as are many of the emojis and acronyms. Some I recognize (PIR: parent in room; CTN: can't talk now), others are no more than gibberish. PB: who knows what that might be in this new foreign language. Parental bitching? When I was at school, it meant 'personal best'. Your fastest cross-country score, your longest jump.

When I was at school . . . I stopped doing sports after that Stoneborough summer. Remorse, dread, cowardice: one or all had diminished me and I spent my free time instead in the school library. Indoor spaces, solitary pursuits: these were safe and I had a greater chance of controlling them. But before I'd been active. Gregarious and full of life. I'd been in groups and teams and gaggles.

If the start of the summer feels far gone then the earlier part of my childhood is so remote as to have been built on air. Will I feel like this when Molly is grown and gone? Will all the crisis and drama of the last twenty-four hours seem as if it was dreamed up by a fantasist?

My tea is cooler, drinkable now. It tastes bitter, woody, bracing.

As I close the screen, the last thing I see is: *3/01? F*cking amazing!*

Friday, 28 August – three days earlier

I see now that I wasn't thinking straight that weekend. Maybe I hadn't been thinking straight since the beginning, since that luminous Saturday morning in July when I took my seat at the lido café and came face to face with our bewitching new lake of ultramarine. Since I'd begun seeing Elm Hill in spangled, crackly cine-film vision, as if it were old Hollywood, its trees not elms but palms or cypresses, its people golden and decadent, subject only to the laws of their own making. Since I'd worshipped at the altar of La Madrague and believed myself to be, like its residents, closer to the sun than other people.

It was going to be as hard to remove myself from the fantasy as it had been easy to be seduced by it.

But remove myself was what Ed expected me to do, evidently.

'I'm going to give the Channings notice on the tutoring,' he told me on Friday morning, even before I'd got up. Though he came bearing coffee, he stood at my bedside ready to do battle. This was how it was now and I can't say I didn't feel sorrow: when he announced news that was important to him, he counted not on support but on strife. It was as if the New Forest holiday had never happened, or the previous ninety-nine per cent of our marriage, for that matter.

'Oh, Ed, I wouldn't do anything too hasty. Apart from anything else, they're a really influential family.'

'Exactly. I can't risk rumours circulating. I need to nip this in the bud. The timing's good because they're about to go on holiday and by the time they get back term will have started and everyone will be crazy busy. I'll let them know in writing and it will get lost in the general excitement.'

He was like a civil servant burying scandal in news of a war.

'Fine,' I said, 'whatever you think is right.' Though I hadn't seen Lara for five days, his reminder that she would soon be departing for a holiday disheartened me.

Pleasantly surprised, Ed sat on the bed, his manner more conciliatory. 'Before you ask, I don't mind Molly still being friends with Georgia and the others. I can't deny they've been a good influence.'

'You can't stop friendships,' I agreed. 'If they want to be together, they'll be together, whatever we say.' Indeed, Molly had seen Georgia again the previous day for their lido tour with Matt and declared plans for today too. They were becoming inseparable.

'But the adults,' Ed said. He paused and I saw the absolutism in his eyes. 'I'd rather we stopped seeing them altogether.'

My rejection of this was both instant and wholesale. Yes, I had paused communication of my own accord, but the idea of being forbidden Lara's company perman-ently was unthinkable – and the notion of being told to do it by my husband untenable. 'The problem is, Ed, like I just said, you can't stop friendships. I can't just cut people out like that, and even if I could I wouldn't. This isn't Saudi Arabia. We vote, we drive, we choose our own friends.'

'I see.' He stood up again, and there was a sense beyond his immediate physical withdrawal that he was disconnecting from me – and also that he had antici-pated having to do so. 'Well, it goes without saying that we can't go to the pool party on Sunday. *I* can't, anyway,' he corrected himself. 'Not being a Saudi female, you must decide for yourself.'

'Thank you, I will.' Though on the surface quite unruf-fled, I was profoundly disturbed by this exchange. 'Seriously, Ed, I think you should keep an open mind about the Channings. The way you're feeling, it's not even their fault. It's mine.'

He scowled. 'What is it with this woman? She's even got other people blaming themselves for her crimes!'

'There *are* no crimes,' I protested.

'Not on my part, there aren't. I can't speak for the rest of you.' And he left the room.

Devastating though this was in one way, in another it was constructive, providing as it did the catalyst I'd needed to break my paralysis and act. When Lara phoned again and left a voicemail suggesting I drop by her place 'any time, any time at all', I replied by text saying I would call around that afternoon. I had a mission: far from sharing Ed's determination to cut off relations, I planned to erase the issue that had fractured those relations and continue just as we had been. I would enlist her help. Perhaps if she were to apologize to him or appeal to him directly, we might even be able to change his mind. He was not a tyrant; his decision was not irrevocable.

Hope made me naïve. Something else – I couldn't name it yet – made me careless.

First, before I saw Lara, I needed to make my peace with Gayle. I still had *some* sense of priorities.

Wednesday's planned dinner had been abandoned, of course, Craig having phoned Ed to cancel after returning from the hospital, where Harriet had had her lungs checked. They had been found undamaged. He'd evidently made no reference to my part in the aftermath of her accident, which was no small mercy since I honestly didn't think I could bear disapproval from Ed on a whole new subject. Neither Ed nor I brought up the parallel with Molly, who'd had the same examination in a different A & E department all those years ago.

Gayle had rejected several calls from me, just as I had Lara's, so I cheated now by ringing her from Ed's phone.

'Oh. Nat.' Her tone was neutral, with just a touch of distaste.

'I know you don't want to hear from me,' I began, 'but I just needed to make sure Harriet's all right. Ed says she had the all-clear from Trinity?'

'She's absolutely fine. It was all a storm in a teacup – she's not even sure how it happened.'

'I thought maybe she collided with another swimmer? It can get very crowded in the afternoons –'

'I know,' Gayle interrupted, an edge to her voice. 'I do swim there myself, hence being on the scene when it happened.'

I knew what she meant by this and rushed to address it. 'We should co-ordinate our times again, like we used to?'

Before I'd ditched her for Lara. It served me right that she continued as if I'd not made the offer: 'To answer your question, she doesn't remember any collision with anyone else, just being under water and becoming a bit disorientated.'

'Was she holding her breath? It could have been that thing Matt told us about. Shallow-water blackout?'

'Not everything has to be some dramatic medical event, Nat,' she said, sighing. 'Far more likely it was the effects of the sun. Who knows with girls, hormones running riot like they do? Anyway, she didn't lose con-sciousness. She would have surfaced by herself if Matt hadn't spotted her, but she was under just a bit longer than they like. Better to be on the safe side.'

'Absolutely.' I was encouraged by this flow of infor-mation. Realistically, I'd expected to be hung up on. 'So there aren't any after effects?' I was not sure what was driving my persistence, genuine concern or the desire to disprove that accusation: *There* are *other children in the world . . . parents who care about their children just as much as you do about yours.*

'Like I said, she's fine.' Gayle was growing impatient. 'Was there anything else?'

'No, yes . . .' I had rehearsed my line and it was time to deliver it. 'It's just, I'm sorry if you thought I said "Thank God".'

She snorted. 'For Heaven's sake, you know I can't bear those passive-aggressive apologies. There's no "if you thought" about it! You *did*. There were witnesses. Can't you just say sorry and be done with it?'

'I'm sorry. I really am. And I'm sorry the focus always seems to be on Molly.'

'Not "seems", Nat, *is*.'

'Yes. I hadn't realized. I've allowed her phobia to dominate, but I'm trying my best to stop that. I'm sorry.'

Gayle sighed again. I was becoming tedious. 'I have to go. Have a good day on Sunday and enjoy the Noblesse pool party. Is Ed still going?'

I was a little taken aback by the question, since Gayle didn't know about Lara's implications of wrongdoing or Ed's decision to sever ties. He'd confided in her and Craig his more general objections, clearly: our division over the Channings was now an established fact.

'Of course,' I lied. 'We all are.'

She gave an odd little chuckle.

'What?'

'It just strikes me that you'd think, as a maths teacher, he of all people could put two and two together.'

'About what?' I asked, confused.

'Nothing, Nat. Just . . . happy birthday.'

I didn't know what she was talking about. And though her birthday wishes were grimly given, I thought I detected an undercurrent of relent, a nail-hold on the cliff-face of our friendship, and I accepted them with eagerness.

I couldn't keep away, it was as simple as that. The truth – and I was perhaps the last to acknowledge it – was that if any Steele was in thrall to a Channing it was not Ed to Georgia, or even Molly to Georgia, but me to Lara. Arriving at La Madrague at five o'clock, I was sent by a departing Marthe up to the terrace; she was, she said, about to collect Everett from his friend's. Georgia, I happened to know, was in Starbucks on the high street with Molly and Eve. The house was silent, no music, no chatter, none of the usual Lara effects. I entered the living room and crossed the parquet stealthily, as if I had no business being there. At the doors to the terrace, I lingered, thinking at first it was as deserted as the rest of the house and that Marthe had mistaken Lara's whereabouts. Then I saw her, in the hanging egg chair, which had been turned from its usual inward-facing position towards the park; she was quite lost in her thoughts. To my surprise she was smoking, a veil of grey filling the egg, and as she exhaled she let her head fall backwards in a pose of tragic abandon. It was clear that she'd been subject to one of her low moods: her expression was that of the forgotten wife, the dismissed mother, the ageing beauty. I hoped her gloom was not to do with Georgia and Ed.

I felt suddenly unequal to the task ahead and was on the verge of turning and leaving when she stirred, called my name. 'You're here! How wonderful. As you can see I've fallen into a decline and it's all your fault.'

At once my ears burned and roared and strained for more. 'I told you I was coming.'

'But I didn't know if you meant it. Are we friends again?' she asked, eyes huge, expression vulnerable and childlike. 'Say we are.'

She was irresistible. 'Of course we are. We never weren't,' I said.

She slithered from the chair to hug me. Her scent was cedarwood and cigarette smoke. Wine was fetched and we drank it side by side overlooking the lido. It seemed to me – maybe I imagined this – that for the first time I could glimpse a triangle of blue.

'Just so you know,' I said, 'I spoke to Ed about what we discussed and we're a hundred per cent sure you have nothing to worry about. He's happy to talk it through if you'd like to, put your minds at ease.'

I was lying, saying things I thought she'd like to hear. Now his letter giving notice on their arrangement would cause even more of a stir.

Before I could commit further treason, Lara reached to put a finger to my lips, slender and cool with a coral blade of nail. 'Darling, I told you there was no need to raise it with him.'

'I know, but when you're a teacher, especially a male one, you have to be vigilant. A friend of ours had a horrible time with a false allegation.'

'No allegation has been made. You need to learn when to ignore me,' she said, and she smiled with the blend of graciousness and gratitude that passes between the admirer and the admired. The rightful order had been restored and it was a relief to us both.

'What about Miles?' I said.

'What about him?'

'Does he agree the whole thing can be forgotten?'

'Of course he does.' There was a suspicion that we were talking at cross-purposes, but I had no desire to delve. As with Gayle, I had prepared lines to deliver.

'The thing is, I think it's best if we don't come to the party on Sunday. It just removes the possibility of any awkwardness and I know you have a long waiting list for tickets so it isn't as if they'll go to waste. Someone will be thrilled to get lucky. Maybe Gayle.' Yes, I thought, that would be poetic justice: with Lara's agreement, I'd offer her our tickets.

'I heard what happened with her,' Lara said, pouting sympathy. 'The way she shouted at you, you poor thing.'

'I deserved it,' I said. 'I'm just pleased she's still speaking to me.'

'I know *that* feeling,' Lara said sweetly.

'So I hope you understand? About the party?'

'Of course I do. But before you decide . . .'

'What?'

'Come with me. I have something I want to show you. Bring your glass.'

Bearing both her own glass and the bottle, she led me to the floor below, to the master bedroom at the front. I had not been in it before. A room more spacious than the two bedrooms in Kingsley Drive combined, it was directly below the terrace, with an elongated horizontal window overlooking The Rise. A run of mirrored palazzo doors, like a wall of folded silver, bisected the space; the central two were open, giving on to an en suite of grey marble and polished nickel, clusters of scent bottles and lipsticks on the glass shelves.

Was this where she and Miles would have brought me on Saturday night had I stayed? I erased the notion. Hadn't I already decided that I'd been mistaken or deluded, that subsequent events had overtaken it and that, in any case, Lara had not given it a second thought?

She directed me to the little white sofa at the foot of the bed and, to my surprise, threw herself at my feet, her free hand wrapping itself around my left calf, as it had at the lido when we'd last parted. This time, however, the fingers did not lock rigid, but moved, caressed, rose to my knee and rested just above, only the thumb now in motion, somehow both idle and deliberate. At once all bodily sensations were condensed into that small area of skin. I swallowed more wine, failing to moisten a suddenly dry throat.

'What did you want to show me?' I asked.

'Oh, yes!' As she jumped up, the withdrawal of touch was as unwelcome as an application of pain. 'I found a dress I thought might suit you. For Sunday.'

'But I told you, I'm not going to —'

'Wait till you see it before you decide.' She slid open lacquered wardrobe doors and found what she wanted. It was a long column of rose-print with a halterneck and a smocked waist, clearly a costly designer item.

'It's beautiful,' I said, putting down my glass to touch the fabric with both hands. It was silk, erotically soft.

Lara smiled. 'Try it on, go on, where's the harm?'

I realized she intended staying in the room while I undressed so I moved discreetly into the en suite, though it seemed prudish to seal the doors behind me and the many mirrors and reflective surfaces made modesty impossible.

I slipped the dress over my head. It stuck.

'I'll do it.' Lara was behind me, her fingers tugging, and the dress slid down an inch or two. 'You can't wear that bra with this neckline, you'll need a strapless one, if at all.' She unhooked my bra and brushed the straps from my shoulders, then when it fell to the floor, she slid the dress over me, running her knuckles over the fabric to smooth it. Her body was so close to mine, our body heat overlapped, doubled, and though covered now in the dress, I felt more naked than before, more naked than when we'd been in the pool together. In the mirror, my cheeks fired as I struggled to master a maelstrom of colliding words: . . . *just gossip* . . . *the Land of Do As You*

Please . . . I have a confession to make . . . Miles said I shouldn't say anything . . . What about him? . . . Come with me . . .

Her face was at my right shoulder, our hair touching, our breath flowing in parallel. Her hands remained on the fabric, fingers moving idly, deliberately, on my stomach, ribs, the underside of my breasts. I felt both wild, enemy fear and the confidence to overcome it.

'La . . .' I turned my head towards her face. Her mouth was at my ear, fingers moving slowly, possessively, over me.

'You like that?'

I spoke without thinking or caring. 'Yes.' I wanted more. My head pushed, mouth seeking hers.

'Marthe,' she murmured, her voice thickened. 'She'll be back soon with Everett.'

'Of course.' But I couldn't leave it in this teasing, unexplored way. 'When?'

'At the party.'

'At the party? But . . . How?' This was an empty house. That would be a teeming throng, how could it work? 'What about tomorrow?'

'Tomorrow will be crazy,' Lara said. 'Miles will be here, and the kids. We'll be packing for the holiday. But at the party we can get lost for a little while. No one will notice who's there and who's missing . . .'

At the windows sheer drapes billowed, the breath of the real world outside. Then came the sound of footsteps on the pebble path, a boy's cry rising in excitement. Everett.

'Take the dress home,' Lara said, her voice still hushed, secretive.

'I can't.'

'Yes, you can.' The same fingers that had smoothed it down began puckering it, pulling it up again. 'You will wear it, won't you? To the party.' She ran a finger over my skin a final time. 'You have to come now, don't you?'

'Yes,' I said.

Stoneborough, August 1985

At the pond, when we were tired from swimming, all the kids would sit together in a loose crescent at the water's edge or lie in a ring with our heads meeting like daisy petals and we'd play truth or dare. Which was really just truth. Which was actually insult, because none of the questions were designed to elicit answers that flattered or praised.

Who here would you *least* like to kiss?

Who would you save *last* from a burning building?

Whose pants do you reckon are the smelliest? (Cue laughter and concealed gulps of fear, followed by the inevitable citing of the latest boy to have been yanked out of the group for a family holiday or, as happened once or twice, to be kept out of Mel's and my path.)

'If you had to choose one person to have plastic surgery, who would it be?' That was one I would remember because I knew I must be a contender. Beside me, Mel's pull of breath was discernible only to me: she'd expect to be in the firing line too. Then again, as the more feared of the two of us, she also had the better chance of evasion.

Two of the boys made jokes about a third's penis size.

'Come on, you're not allowed to bottle it,' Mel said, her tone bitter, for it was Nessie's question. It was as if she was willing Nessie to pick her just so she could punish her for it.

Nessie hesitated. This was a question she would have preferred to go to someone else, safe in the knowledge that she would have been the last to be named. Instead, she was required to deliver pain.

'Otherwise you're never allowed back here again,' Mel said.

'You'll be *shunned*,' I added, ever the spineless henchman.

Nessie's worried eyes moved from face to face, until, two from where the ring returned to her, it flickered, briefly, tellingly, on me, on my forehead and the raspberry stain there. She never smiled, I thought, or at least never anywhere near me. Even when she spoke, her lips hardly parted. 'I choose myself,' she said at last, her voice very small. 'I'd change my ears. I hate them.'

'Liar,' we began, but the others were clamouring to hear more from her – 'Why, what's wrong with them?' – and she was showing them the way her ears were positioned a smidgeon less flat to her skull than they might have been.

'My brother says they look like shells,' she said unconvincingly.

Mel and I swore in disapproval when this prattle was judged valid and the game moved on.

'She thinks she's it,' we told each other as we walked home.

'She thinks she's better than us.'

'It's that bloody hair. Like in *Splash*.'

'She must bleach it. Slag.'

There was a gathering energy to our hostility, a reaching towards something previously unvoiced. Our footsteps became more certain, matched, an army of two. Sure enough, by the time we reached Mel's door, she had an idea of how we might teach Nessie a lesson.

'Brilliant,' I said, and we stood face to face, hands joined.

We would have to bide our time, of course, and secure our weapon: a pair of scissors from the kitchen drawer, which I placed with my swimming kit in the backpack I used for days at the pond. When my grandmother missed them, I told her I'd borrowed them for a collage I was making as a souvenir of my special summer with her and Grandpa, and her eyes shone for a moment with sentimental tears.

32

Sunday, 30 August

It may be a false memory, but it seems to me there was melancholy in the air on the day of the party, that hovering sense of cusp, of the season deepening from gold to bronze and curling at the edges. There was a mood of . . . well, if not anticlimax, then a kind of foreseen grief.

At the party we would touch again and my blood would sing in my veins, my skin would shiver on the muscle. What she and I had started would continue and, whatever it was going to be, I wanted it. I wanted it enough to manipulate my husband, to bend his will by any means necessary.

'I have to go to the party,' I told Ed. '*You* don't have to, I completely understand, but I promised I'd help out and I'm not in the habit of letting people down at the last minute.'

Had it not been my birthday, a day to be counted on for the suspension of hostilities in any civilized home, I would not have got away with that last pronouncement. Gayle, Craig, Sarah, Ed himself: there were countless recent examples to be cited of my having let people down.

'Besides, Molly's really keen to go. Remember, we're the Channings' guests, Ed, and she has no reason to think anything's changed. She won't want to disappoint Georgia and Eve.'

It was shameless to use our daughter like this. Unforgivable.

And effective. It was agreed that Molly and I would go to the party as planned while Ed stayed at home and brooded.

But when I was getting ready, trouble flared afresh.

'I haven't seen that before,' he said of the rose-print dress, which, admittedly, a household pet would have noticed had more chic than my usual attire. I was nothing short of entranced by how the fabric fell, the way it kissed my skin without clinging, the touch of Lara in its fine weave. Lightly tanned and toned from all the swimming, I hadn't looked this good in many years and, against my better judgement, that felt important.

'When did you get it?' Ed asked, and then, 'It looks very expensive. How much did it cost?'

'It cost nothing,' I said.

There was a dangerous pause, a gathering of rancour. 'Don't tell me: *she* lent you it. When?'

'Ages ago,' I lied.

'Are you even the same size? It's probably not supposed to be that skimpy. And your shoulders are going to get cold – it's almost September, you know.'

I thought about the compliments Miles must surely pay Lara when she dressed for a party, or Stephen Angie, or even Craig Gayle, and I thought, too, of that spiteful comment of Ed's that I was a desperate acolyte. Enough was enough. 'You think I'm best kept covered up?' I snapped. 'Not as svelte as some of your year elevens?'

There was an ugly silence. I was as shocked as he was and immediately apologetic. 'I'm sorry. I shouldn't have said that.' Yes, I'd been provoked, but it didn't take a psychologist to spot that I was deflecting my own feelings of guilty anticipation; in making Ed the villain, I was willing him to be deserving of betrayal.

He was staring at me in something close to horror. 'You say these things and I don't recognize the person who's speaking any more.'

Neither did I. But whoever she was I wanted to be her – this evening, if not for ever. The truth was, I could not think beyond tonight.

From the next-door bedroom came sounds of drawers sliding open and thumping shut. Had Molly heard the exchange? Yet another argument between Mum and Dad. I knew all too well the feeling of being the child of parents who rowed, the turning off of the television or radio only to expose the bitter voices you hadn't known were being smothered. The feeling that peace would never last long enough or go deep enough to reach your soul. Hadn't I vowed Molly wouldn't have to feel it too?

'She's destroying us,' Ed said.

'No, *you* are,' I replied, 'because you keep overreacting.' And of all the things I said that summer, this was the most unjust.

I became aware then of Molly outside the door, of that prickle of energy her presence caused in me. 'Molly's here,' I said brightly. 'Doesn't she look wonderful?'

If she'd heard any of our row, she gave no indication of having an opinion on the matter. 'I said I'd meet Georgia at seven,' she said. 'Can we go?'

As we left the building, I said, 'I'm sorry about all the arguing lately. It's nothing to worry about, honestly.'

She looked ahead in the vacant way I knew meant she would rather walk on hot coals than talk about it.

'It's completely normal. I think it must be amplified because we're in a small flat. I promise it will stop. After tonight. We'll be back to school in a few days' time and everything will be back to normal.'

'Thanks for reminding me,' she said.

Beside me, her stride was short to the point of reluctant, and as we reached the lights on the high street I took her arm to stop her crossing. 'Are you sure you want us to go to this party? Because we don't have to. I mean it.'

Did I – *did I* – give her adequate time to reply? Certainly there was enough time for me to notice that her face was flushed the most lovely pink, making a mockery of the unnatural hues of the make-up she wore, the clogging black fingers of mascara. The dress she'd chosen, fitted on top and full-skirted, accentuated her new curves.

'No, I want to come,' she said. She seemed nervous but determined, and I was proud of her. Then, more matter-of-fact than anxious: 'Dad isn't very happy, is he?'

And I had a rush of memory, of saying those very words to my grandmother towards the end of my summer in Stoneborough. I hadn't had any communication with my father during my stay and the new school year was about to start, my family status uncertain. Gran had replied, 'If we didn't feel unhappy some of the time, we wouldn't know how to recognize happy', a life philosophy I had not forgotten.

'Maybe not today,' I told Molly. 'But things change.'

I'd lost track of whom Lara had co-opted for the job of set designer, but whoever it was had done her proud. Strings of variously sized paper lanterns criss-crossed the café terrace in a solar system of blues; potted palms and sand-coloured beanbags were scattered in a chill-out zone to one side of the sundeck; on the whitewashed brick wall opposite the bar, classic pool scenes flickered (when we arrived, Dustin Hoffman was gliding under water in *The Graduate*, but it was only a matter of time before Alain Delon would saunter in and steal the show). Outside, a barbecue smoked; inside, frozen blue margaritas were served with pink straws and watermelon garnish.

The band would be playing outdoors on the far side of the sundeck, their backs to the pool, which was, as promised, strictly decorative. Hundreds of pastel-hued helium balloons bobbed over the water, and I smiled to imagine Lara charming the lifeguards into tying string after string to the lane dividers.

Noting the abundance of rope barriers and 'No Access' signs, I thought of how, as recently as two months ago – had I by some miracle been able to persuade Molly here – I wouldn't have been standing sucking a blue margarita on arrival, but sweeping the site for hazards as one might for a daredevil toddler. I wouldn't have let her out of my sight. I would have experienced the whole event as if the phobia were my own, tracking her like one of those surveillance cameras with a motion-sensitive lens.

This was so different as to feel surreal, like being in someone else's family, living someone else's life. Watching her slip away in search of her friends, seeing her pop up in the queue for the barbecue, as if a deathly peril did not lurk a splash away: it was what I'd always wished for – and I was not about to complain of being abandoned.

Besides, there were plenty of people to talk to. Of the throng at the bar, I recognized the mainstays of Lara's set: Angie and Stephen, of course, as well as Andrew and Douglas, David, the neighbour who'd taken me for an inveterate loafer, and his wife Suki. No Gayle, Craig or Harriet, but Alice was there with a group of her friends and I made a point of catching up with her first.

'How's Harriet? She had quite a scare the other day.'

Alice, already tipsy, was reassuringly friendly. 'Hmm, still feeling a bit sheepish. She hasn't been back here since.'

'She shouldn't be sheepish,' I protested, and the girls, whose jug of cocktail was drained to the ice, joked that this was a tongue twister. As we chatted, all I could think was how very young and smooth their faces were; how big multi-generational gatherings only emphasized the exquisiteness of youth, the unintended reproach of it. Alice mentioned that her parents were at the Vineyard and I told her I would try to drop in on my way back, if it were not too late for Molly.

Though Molly was in cahoots with Georgia and Josh, I could see no Eve.

'She's running a temperature,' Angie told me, 'so we made her stay at home with Milena.'

'I bet she was cross about missing this.'

'Oh, livid, but if she's got some virus we can't let her infect the whole neighbourhood. She's run down, needs to recharge before term starts.'

'Don't we all.' I studied more closely her pink gingham dress and wide hairband. 'Are you Brigitte Bardot, Ange?'

'I am! I would have come barefoot but I thought I might get trampled on when the band starts. Stephen is, I don't know, generically summery. He's already rumpling, look.'

In a white linen suit, Stephen's solid physique looked cumbersome, unmanageable. It seemed impossible that he had torn off his clothes so recently and plunged naked into the water.

All at once, fingers hooked my waist, compliments crooned in my ear: 'What a sexy dress! Couldn't have picked a nicer one myself.'

'Lara!' She looked extraordinary even by her stand-ards, sheathed in a green-and-yellow maxi dress, her hair fixed smooth and high in that sixties way, eyes huge and spellbinding, mouth the exact pink of the watermelon garnish. 'You look astonishing,' I said.

She pouted. 'Miles says I hover between costume and homage. I'm not sure if it was meant as a compliment, but you know what? That's how I've chosen to interpret it.'

I couldn't help but contrast this with Ed's charmless comments – and my own ugly response.

Lara lowered her voice, the syllables tickling the skin on my neck: 'So, you came on your own, then?'

'Yes. Well, with Molly.'

'Good. I hoped you would. I'll get Georgia to keep her occupied.'

At that moment Georgia, in a sunflower-yellow cro-cheted beach dress, was locked in a kiss with a very conspicuously off-duty Matt, while Josh and Molly were fixated on their respective phone screens. At least poor Harriet wasn't there to witness it.

Lara's voice became more public again: 'Miles, look! Natalie's here, and she's on her own. We'll need to look after her.'

Miles stepped forward, tanned and dissolute-looking in a pale suit, so similar in style to Stephen's I wondered if they might have co-ordinated in Rat Pack costumes or some Riviera equivalent.

I kissed him hello, at once feeling the nervous energy but unable to tell whether it was mine or his – mine, most likely. It was the first time I'd seen him since our encounter there the previous weekend, but much had occurred in the intervening days, not least Lara's shared – and retracted – concerns about Ed. Had he dispensed with the issue so easily? It certainly appeared so. The only problem was the one I'd caused by escalating it with Ed.

'Isn't the pool beautiful tonight?' I said.

Miles gave a half-nod. 'Hmm, balloons.' He spoke as if he'd never seen anything so absurd in his life.

'La says you don't like to swim. I hadn't realized.'

He narrowed his eyes, whether in acknowledgement or denial I couldn't tell. It was another detail Lara had dismissed without a care but, expert that I was, I sensed something deeper than idiosyncrasy. 'Did something happen when you were little? Like with Molly?'

As compassion flooded me, his gaze lit with sudden interest. 'All this summer and you only ask now? Why, I wonder?'

His tone was good-natured, ponderous rather than critical, and I couldn't begin to fathom what he meant by the question. It didn't help that I now caught Stephen's eye, had the impression he had been staring, and allowed myself to become flustered.

'I'm sorry. I didn't mean to be nosy. It's none of my business. Lots of people don't swim.'

'There doesn't always have to be a reason,' Miles said, as if in agreement, and it made me think of Gayle's comment that not everything had to be a dramatic medical event.

'You're right.' I considered telling him how grateful I was that, with the help of his daughter, mine was conquering a lifelong phobia, that with the help of his wife, I was conquering neuroses of my own, but I decided against it. The truth was, I did not know what to say to Miles and was not sure I ever would.

As my gaze strayed over his shoulder, my smile froze on my face.

'Something wrong?' he asked.

'Yes. Would you just excuse me for a minute, Miles? I need to check on Molly . . .'

To my horror, she was standing, quite alone, in the last place I would have expected to see her: in the prohibited zone, at the main-entrance end of the pool, barely a metre from the edge. Her back to the water, she began taking slow measured steps towards the emergency doors at the rear of Reception. The main entrance was closed this evening, a side door in use for the party, so at least she would not be seen and reprimanded, but that was hardly my first concern. Abandoning Miles, I hurried to the edge of the sundeck and leaned over the rail, waving wildly.

'What are you doing over there?' I yelled. 'Come away!'

Turning by the fire doors, she caught sight of me and at once made her way towards me, walking close to the wall at the cautious pace of a cat entering unfamiliar territory. 'Don't shout,' she admonished, and as she approached, her eyes radiated fury.

'The pool area's off limits,' I said at normal volume. 'You know that.' I could hear the slight shake in my voice. 'You mustn't go out there again, understand? There's no one on duty.'

'Fine. Sorry.'

We both caught our breath. 'It's OK,' I said, instinct telling me to leave the matter there. 'Come and hang out with me for a bit.' She ducked under the railing and hovered expectantly beside me, as if waiting for me to pitch for her custom.

'Look, isn't it pretty inside from out here?' I tried, and we looked through the window together, my hand on her waist. The whole interior was bathed in ultramarine from the film footage, the light striking off the guests' drinks and phones, off their silver fingernails and studded ears and bared teeth. With Molly safely by my side, I was filled with sudden wonder that this glamorous, rarefied spectacle could be happening in Elm Hill and that we were a part of it.

Turning to seek similar emotions in her response, I saw instead pure relief.

'Here's Dad!' Her voice lifted and then she was darting past me into the bar.

'Dad?' I was slow to react, thinking initially that she'd just said the first thing that popped into her head in order to give me the slip. But, astonishingly, she was right: there was Ed, chatting to Liam, passing him some folded banknotes. A conflicting chain of thoughts ensued: he was here, he hadn't given up on me, thank

God! Or was he here not for me but to confront the Channings? And, whatever his reason, how was his attendance going to affect my access to Lara?

I waited a few minutes before collecting a fresh margarita from the bar and sidling up, Molly having already greeted him and gone. 'I'm so glad you decided to come,' I said.

He turned with the scarcest of smiles, as if we were not husband and wife, or even friends. 'Nat, hello. I thought you'd be busy helping out?'

'Oh, I've done my bit,' I said vaguely.

'In that case, can I have a quick word?'

He ushered me to the quietest corner of the deck, not far from the spot where I'd just hailed Molly, next to an open window. On the far side, Angie and Stephen chatted with David, Suki and another couple, while Lara talked to two men whose civilian clothes placed them with the band. Miles was nearest us, having drifted indoors with a woman I half recognized from my lido afternoons with Lara; his grip on his drink was crushing, as if the glass might crack, and I had a queasy premonition of sliced flesh, of blood dripping to the floor. I was aware of nerves and that they were connected with him, with the danger of his looking up and spotting Ed, deciding to come over and face him down about Georgia.

'I've been thinking,' Ed said.

'Oh, yes?'

'I know this isn't the best time, I know it's your birthday and you just want to enjoy the party, but I have to say it.'

'Say what?'

'No more.' As I reacted with a look of query, he snapped, 'Stop pretending you don't speak English, I'm serious about this.'

'About *what*?'

'You said I can't tell you who you should and shouldn't spend your time with, and I'm not going to do that. But I'm making a request. And I'm saying that your choices will have consequences.'

'What on earth do you mean, "consequences"?' I demanded. 'You're speaking to me as if I'm a pupil you're threatening with detention.'

Ed's expression was as severe as I'd ever seen it. 'I'm saying what needs to be said. If you choose to carry on with this group, then I don't know if I'll be able to carry on with us.'

'With us?' I waited for my heart to skid, but it did not. It did not. For a moment I feared I might not experience any emotion at all, but then exasperation reared: 'Have you gone completely mad? We've been married for sixteen years, we have a daughter! We're a family.'

'I know that, which is why it shouldn't be hard for you to choose.'

I paused, allowed the clamour of other people's conversation to separate us. I couldn't deal with this, not tonight. I needed to find a response that would please both of us, that would act as a placeholder. 'I would never put you in that position,' I said finally.

'I would never put *you* in the position of having to put me in this position,' Ed said.

'Of course not, because you never do anything wrong, do you?'

You never stand in front of a mirror with a friend's hands on your body, her lips at your neck.

'We're agreed then?' he demanded. 'After this party, it's over?'

I glared at him, reacting correctly at last. I was frightened and indignant and impotent. 'It doesn't seem like I have a choice, does it?'

He stepped away from me, the subject closed. 'I'm going in to get a drink. I don't think you need one, do you?' It was less an offer than a judgement: I was drinking too much. It was not appropriate, not for an *educator*.

'Ed?'

He turned, his expression not open, but not closed either.

'Why were you giving Liam money just now?'

Now it slammed shut. 'What – you think I'm buying drugs now, as well?'

I gasped. 'I didn't say that!'

'You didn't need to. It was for your cake, Nat. Your fucking surprise birthday cake.'

Shamefaced, fuming, I sucked at my straw, felt a chute of icy liquid hurtle down my throat, suppressed the reflex to splutter. Through the window I noticed Molly at a nearby table, on her own again, fiddling with her phone. I hurried inside, crouched beside her. 'What is it, darling? Why aren't you with your friends?'

She looked faintly hostile and I knew I had not been forgiven for calling her away from the water as I had. Only now did I understand she'd been testing herself, taking the kind of leap of faith that had to be taken alone, and I'd blundered in, crying out, like the overprotective mother I was.

'Mum?'

'Yes?'

'Can we . . .?' And she paused, eyes unsettled.

'What? You want to leave already? The band hasn't come on yet.' And I heard it just as she did, perhaps a split second before, the unguarded impatience, the touch of petulance that said, I *knew* this would happen. I *knew* you would ruin it for me.

'It's OK,' Molly said. 'It doesn't matter.'

Over her shoulder Josh was gesturing, trying to get her attention.

'No, it does matter, sweetheart.' My tone was on track, and my instincts too. 'Listen, I'm sorry I shouted like a fishwife earlier. I was just concerned. This is all new to me too. We'll talk properly in the morning, all right? I'll be all yours.'

'All right.'

'Do you want to come with me and chat to some of my friends?'

She said something then, in a mumble, not meant for me to hear.

'What did you say?'

She looked at me, defiance in her eyes, chin high: 'I said, none of your friends are here.'

Though I was taken aback, I didn't allow my smile to waver. 'That's a bit rude, darling. They're new friends, same as yours. I think Josh wants to talk to you, by the way.'

And Lara wanted to talk to me. No sooner had Molly joined Josh than she was by my side.

'After the band, I'll come and find you,' she said.

'Ed's here,' I told her. 'And he's very cross with me.'

'Oh dear. Should I recruit someone to keep him occupied?'

She probably meant Miles, or else Angie or Stephen, but putting Ed together with any of the group was not one of the better ideas I'd heard that evening.

'No, it's fine,' I said. 'I'll make sure I'm alone.'

'I look forward to it,' she said.

33

Sunday, 30 August

The jazz quintet was all that Lara had promised, a swing-ing and throbbing and keening musical brew, its hypnotic fixed point an almost motionless female singer with snaking raven hair and sultry, trembling vocals. As the evening darkened, the intimacy between her and her audience deepened.

I watched with Ed. My feelings for the man by my side, the man with whom I'd fused genes to create a little family and with whom bodily contact continued to be made as the crowd on the terrace stirred and shifted with each change of tempo – well, those feelings underwent several stages. First, I consciously refused to give headspace to his ultimatum; next, having failed in the first, I was deluged by resentment of his self-righteousness (not helped by the evident ease with which he was now enjoying the music – at *Lara's* invitation, at *Lara's* expense); then came remorse, the veracious, irrevocable knowledge that he was the vic-tim here and not I. *I* had forced *him* into a corner, not the other way around. Last, as a break in the crowd in front allowed a glimpse of green-and-yellow print, the sight of Lara swaying to the music, I forgot he was there at all.

When the band finished and the stage lights dimmed, there was a general retreat indoors to the bar and I supposed he must have headed in too. I didn't follow. As for Molly, one second she was in a tight scrum with Georgia and Josh, and the next the trio had vanished. I guessed I had at least twenty minutes before she thought to find me again. Lara was side-stage congratulating the musicians, but I was too shy to join her, moving instead to the far edge of the sun-deck, the point at which 'our' table would normally be situated. The underwater lights had come on, creating pretty clouds of neon blue below the gently bobbing heads of the balloons. I thought of the same water last weekend, ink-black and concealing, and was moved by the different human moods it was able to reflect – or dictate.

Then Lara was beside me, our bare shoulders bumping. 'Weren't they fantastic?'

'They were. Do you need to see them off?' There was an injection of hunger in my tone and she responded with a brush on the back of my hand with hers.

'Already done, they're packing up now. They have to scoot straight off to a second gig. Liam and the guys are helping them with their gear.'

Of course. I smiled at the image of Lara helping lug amplifiers into the back of a scruffy van. How had she ever washed ashore here, in Elm Hill? How lucky we all were. How lucky I was.

'So, can I borrow you for a moment?' she said.

'Yes . . . Just . . .' Having been sure, I was suddenly jittery. My brain flashed to Molly, the irritability I'd betrayed when I'd thought she wanted to leave. I would make it up to her; after tonight, I would refocus, reprioritize. 'Where are the kids, do you know? I've lost track of them.'

'The teens were last seen demanding mocktails from the bar staff, poor sods. Everett's with David and Suki and their kids. Don't worry, they won't miss us.'

Would Ed? I thought. Would Miles?

She was leading me now past the chill-out zone to the narrow gap between railing and wall, unhooking the security rope and pulling me through before reattaching it. 'We're being a bit naughty, going off limits . . .' And that step into prohibited territory stirred my blood like a criminal's. Seizing my hand, she pulled me around the perimeter towards the changing huts on the opposite side. The darkness was thicker at the edges, cloaking us as we came to a halt by the hut closest to the turnstile; the door was yellow, tinged green with the blue light from the pool. At the far end, the main entrance appeared more distant than the 60 or 70 metres I knew it to be, the floating field of balloons between. 'Come in,' Lara whispered. 'Quick, before anyone sees us.'

It was lightless when she closed the door behind us and for a moment utterly silent.

'Lara? You are in here as well, aren't you?'

'Of course.'

The space was tiny, the air extremely warm. Unable to see her, I giggled, groping for the nearest surface. My fingers touched the back wall, my knee the edge of the seat, and then I found smooth partitions to either side, which meant she had to be leaning against the closed door. Feeling her soft, humid breath, I was reminded of her standing close behind me in her bathroom at La Madrague, her fingers smoothing the fabric of the dress, and I responded with a groan. My desire was swelling, growing uncontrollable, and I pressed myself against her, my mouth searching for hers, greedy for her touch, for those fingers to graze and probe. 'Oh, La –'

'Don't call me that,' she said, her voice very low pitched, almost a growl, and she moved her face from mine. 'I know you have before, but not again.'

She thrust me from her. Overbalancing, I made heavy contact with one of the sides and righted myself.

'Why?' In the dark, my cheeks flamed. Did she wish me to use her full name, as she did mine? To leave the playful single syllable for Douglas and Andrew and the others? 'Why?' I repeated. I wanted to hear her say it, say I was special, but her voice, when it came again, was different. It had a flatness to it, a deathly lack of inflection: 'You have no idea, do you?'

'No idea about what?' I said.

'About what you did.'

I felt the blood slow in my veins and with it came the beginning of lightheadedness. 'What I did? What do you mean?' Self-preservation – hope – made me dense, limiting my mind's reach to those sources of confusion closest to the surface: did she mean what had happened in her bedroom? Had I overstepped the mark, misinterpreted that encounter, or the promise of this? Or did she mean my having mentioned the Georgia concern to Ed when she had explicitly asked me not to? Had it had repercussions I was unaware of? Had Ed confronted her privately and upset her? That was surely it. How automatic it was, my blaming of Ed, how traitorous. He was no longer my mate but my scapegoat.

'Years ago, Natalie,' Lara said, and her voice was gentler now, laced with a new emotion: sorrow. 'Years ago.'

Two words that got my blood moving again, that might even have changed the direction of its flow in my veins. Two words and all my fancies, all my vanities, were exposed. Because I did have an idea, of course I did. I think I'd had it all along.

Stoneborough, August 1985

The occasion arose in the nick of time: not only was I due to be collected from my grandparents and returned home the very next day, but there had also been a break in the weather, a spell of rain that had put paid to any last woodland adventures. Without access to the pond, Mel and I had stopped talking about our Nessie plot, had all but given up, distracted in any case by the tension between the two of us, the future of our friendship, whatever it had been, whatever it might become. It seemed to me that planning our persecution of Nessie had been virtually as satisfying as doing it.

Then, on my last full day in the village, the heavens cleared and we all converged on the pond for what would undoubtedly be the final swim of the summer.

Nessie was there, of course, for everyone else the star turn, and as if responding to our telepathic will she stayed in the water longer than usual. Time after time she sank into the invisible depths, twisting and tumbling and rolling, before exploding into view in that trademark way of hers. Most often, she would surface in the spots touched by the last of the sun, as if caught in her own mission to shatter liquid into glitter. By the time she waded out, the group had thinned and there were few enough left for Mel to be able to order them to scarper and be obeyed. Which left only the three of us.

She was still towelling herself dry when we pounced. As planned, I pinned her down, face to the ground, while Mel set about her hair with the scissors. The blades were blunt, not at all fit for the task, and the sound was obscene, the sawing of something fibrous and alive. Mel cut it really short, too; right to the scalp.

Nessie screamed and wriggled so much it was her own fault when her ear got nicked. 'You're mental,' she sobbed, her cheek greasy with blood. 'There's something wrong with you two.'

'Shut your face, bitch.'

Mel spat on her then, a sticky blob that sat on her bare skin between her shoulder blades.

'Everyone hates you!' Nessie cried. 'Everyone. All the boys –'

'I *said*, shut your fucking face!'

I started thinking how weird it felt to hold a girl down like this against her will. We'd done it so many times with the boys, but this was different. There was none of our usual suppressed laughter: this time we were hard-nosed, iron-handed, like trained officers taking part in a raid. Her response was not predictable, either, for I could feel strength in her fear, not the futile lashing out I was used to, a gathering of spirit rather than an ebbing of it. I had the horrible premonition that she was about to rear up, like she did in the water, to somehow double, triple in strength and defeat us, the way good always defeats evil.

Almost as if I'd determined it, there was a sudden scramble and she was slithering free, her bare feet sliding backwards in the mud as she tried to launch herself forwards. Without her long hair, she was like a boy, narrow and sinewy, a Mowgli figure.

'Nat, you idiot!' At once Mel grabbed at her calves and brought her back down, finding time to shoot me a bad-tempered glare.

'Sorry,' I said, redoubling my grip.

'My mum will call the police,' Nessie screamed, in breathless gasps, as the final strands were sliced from her scalp.

'What – to tell them her daughter's a slag?' I said.

'No one's going to tell anyone anything,' Mel said, her voice a blade's edge, sharper than the tool in her hands. Her blood was up now. Nessie had landed with her head closer to the water's edge than before, which gave Mel an idea. 'Hold her under, Nat.'

'What?'

'I've got her arms and legs. You hold her head under.' She meant under the water. 'You don't –?'

'Just do it before the bitch gets away again!'

And I did. I held her head under. The water was shallow at the edge and the strain of keeping her face down, her head steady, made my muscles ache. I gripped her hair to get tighter control, thinking about how her long hair used to pour from her skull to her elbows when she surfaced, how hard it was now to get even a short handful.

'How long for?' I asked Mel, panting with exertion.

'Keep going. Count to twenty.'

I counted quickly, cheating. Then I began to fear I'd lost sense of fast and slow and correcting that added further seconds. I wondered how long Nessie could hold her breath – she sometimes dived for what seemed like minutes – and that took us forward by another ten seconds or so. Then, just as I was about to ask Mel again, Nessie went quite still, her neck devoid of tension, and I slackened my grip in a reflex of terror. *Move*, I willed her, please move, but her head remained weightless in the water.

We've killed her, I thought.

'Fucking played dead,' Mel said. 'Oldest trick in the book. Let's get out of here.'

By the pond's edge Nessie's hair lay in long muddy rags and we kicked it into the water, like the leftovers of a disappointing snack. The scissors, we lobbed into the pond, right into the deepest part. We didn't even wait to watch the ripples.

Sunday, 30 August 2015

'Did you change your name?' I whispered. In the darkness of the hut my vision was sharpening and I could make out the faint gleam of light particles clinging to the curved bones of her face.

'What?' Her voice was curt, impatient. 'Why would I change my name?'

'You weren't called Lara,' I said. 'I know I would have remembered that. What were you called? Did you use your middle name or something?'

'What *are* you talking about?'

'You're the girl.' My emotions were too unruly to control and the muscles in my face were spasming. I thought I could feel my birthmark pulsing but I knew I must be imagining it. 'You're Nessie. That's what we called you. Did you even know that?' And it came to me then that her real name had been Leah or Leanne, something like that. It had been exotic then, and considered pretentious on the part of her parents. *My stage mother.*

Years I'd waited to be found and punished and now, just as I'd learned to let it go, it had happened.

'You used to practise at the pond,' I said, my voice trembling.

'Practise what, darling?' Though her tone was flinty and sarcastic, I felt her fingers touch my face quite tenderly, finding the spot above my eyebrow and smoothing it with the pad of her thumb. Thanks to this mark, this identifying stain, she had recognized me on the very first day.

Lara was Nessie.

'Your synchro, I suppose. All the turns and dives, it was lovely to watch.' My voice sounded dreamy, disembodied. 'I know I didn't say it at the time, but that's what I thought. You were beautiful.'

Her mouth came close to my ear, startling me. 'I think you must have a defective memory, Nat. My name is Lara and always has been. But I suppose guilt does strange things to your mind. And lust, of course.'

Even with the distraction of her lips so close to my face, I knew she wasn't answering in the way she should be: she was speaking lines from a different script. And yet it was what she said, not I, that rang true: of course she'd always been Lara – her name was in the public record; before Channing she'd been Markham. She'd been a competitor from a young age. It was not feasible that Nessie could have been involved in something as uncommon – and ripe for mockery – as synchronized swimming and been able to hide it from the other kids. That was why I had denied the instinct before I could name it: it was false. Meeting Lara, being with her, it had been a true déjà vu, not a second intersection of our fortunes. And it had been caused, as she'd judged in an instant, by guilt.

But if she wasn't Nessie, then what *did* she think I'd done years ago?

It struck me then that I might be so drunk I had concocted the last few minutes, imagined her whispered comments in some guilty delusion brought on by the recent reunion with Mel and compounded by the stress of my escalating conflict with Ed. I was a believer in the power of hypnotherapy, after all, a fearer of the human mind.

But no, this was real, because she was continuing to talk to me in the same uncaring way, her fingers rough in my hair. 'Don't you agree, Natalie, guilt messes with your brain? Sends you slightly mad?'

I was suddenly very afraid of her. 'I want to go back to the party,' I said, reaching to find the door handle. 'Please let me out.'

'Oh no you don't. You'll stay where you are.' She blocked my way.

I knew she was stronger, I knew I wouldn't fight. I let out a sob, too fast to catch, and at once felt fingers on my face again, touching the tears.

'I'm sorry, Natalie.' She was gentler again, almost tender, disorientating me. 'In a funny way, I *am* sorry. It could have been fun. I hope you believe that.'

'La . . .'

Her voice hardened once more. 'I *said* don't call me that. Only my family do, and my real friends.'

And at last a fingernail hooked at a thread of memory: there had been a sister. Nessie had had an older sister who'd been a sporting prodigy, away at a residential camp while her sister was left to contend with the village bullies. If that camp had been a training programme for genuine hopefuls, a regional or national squad perhaps, Lara might have been the absent one, the one who returned at the end of the summer to find her sister terrorized and broken.

A younger sister whose beauty had peaked at an early age . . .

The first knock was so faint I hardly registered it, but Lara reacted before the second one came, manoeuvring me deep into the corner, the edge of the seat cutting painfully into my legs. 'Don't even *think* about trying to leave.'

'Iona,' I said simply. 'Nessie was Iona, wasn't she?'

34

My tea is finished but I'm thirsty, so thirsty. Captivated by the display of water bottles in the chiller cabinet, backlit and glowing like elixirs or medicines, I decide to buy one to drink in the car. It will not heal me but it will restore me for now.

By the time I've taken one and turned to face the room again, there's a new presence in the small, cheerful space, an alteration in the atmosphere, as if the morning has only now chosen to reveal itself.

And yet everything looks the same.

I join the queue to pay. At home, my family awaits: my duty, my love, my meaning, everything. Molly's phone is still in my hand, its screen displaying those messages shared with a girl upstairs fighting for her life. *2/36, 1/57, 2/58 . . .* An idea sparks: the numbers are timings, perhaps, from those sprint races at the lido, the role that helped her overcome her terror of the water's edge. My pulse quickens as a tangle of thoughts begins its unravelling, but before I settle on any single one my eye is caught by a familiar mannerism: an ankle rotating, a well-shod foot circling one way and then the other, as if to ease an ache in the joint. Above, a pale trouser leg, creased and discoloured. I hear a trace of a voice giving thanks, then the man turns, a coffee in each hand.

He sees me. He waits for my gaze to rise to meet his.

For a few moments I can't breathe. I put the water bottle down on the nearest table and step away from the queue, but my legs don't work as they should and I stumble.

When I look again he is directly in front of me, feet planted solidly, takeout coffees clutched like twin grenades.

Him.

35

Sunday, 30 August – eleven hours earlier

'What *are* you talking about?' Lara snapped. 'Iona's got nothing to do with this. You really have lost your mind, haven't you?'

'But –'

There was the sound of a bolt sliding from its casing, a sudden release of heat, then the re-sealing of the door. Now there was a third person in the hut. I would have known him by senses other than sight, the quiet tension of him, an energy separate from heat or odour.

'Hello, Nat,' Miles said.

'Thank God!' I cried. 'Do you know what's going on here?' There was the lilt of appeal in my voice, a note of umbrage, as if Lara had failed me, mistaken me, and now Miles must adjudicate and – quickly, please – free me.

But he did not answer.

'Miles? Is this to do with Iona? Tell me!'

'Forget Iona,' Lara said. 'You're deluded. So shut up, please.'

Now I became properly aware of the temperature, uncomfortably, unnaturally high. There were three of us in a confined space and I was conscious of every breath,

389

thermal, thick with tequila. Blood roared in my ears as I felt the beginnings of claustrophobia.

At last Miles spoke, his tone as remote and agreeable as it had been when we'd spoken earlier in the evening. 'Take your clothes off.'

'*What?*'

'I'll do it,' Lara said, and now I felt what, moments ago, I had longed for, her hands on my clothes, my body, undressing me.

But it was a rough, careless disrobing and it was at his command, not mine. I sucked in my breath, too stunned to protest. My cognition was already blurred by her denial of Nessie and now here was Miles acting on some other unconnected agenda. My brain turned full circle: this must be something sexual, not the rendezvous I had wanted but a more complicated one, one that did not require my consent. I felt the drilling sensation of fear. 'Guys, please, stop. I'm not interested –'

Miles laughed and it was not the urbane, sardonic laugh I knew, but an utterance of raw hostility. 'You don't seriously think we want to fuck you, do you? Look at yourself, you dumb bitch.'

I gasped, turned my face in humiliation. My jaw made contact with a wrist bone and the sharp pain it caused was a distraction, almost a mercy.

'Is her dress off?'

'It's not *hers*,' Lara muttered, as if it revolted her to find me in it, as if the pleasure of her gift of it had never been experienced. I could feel liquid bubbling in my stomach.

The dress was at my feet and now Lara's hands were on my skin, long nails scraping my back as she unhooked my bra. Again, I strained for clarity, finding one last solution: this was a misunderstanding. They'd misunderstood about Ed and now they'd misunderstood about me. Someone was smearing us, poisoning minds against us. I was filled with moral urgency, the need to clear my name, be my right self in their eyes. To go back to what we had been twenty minutes ago.

'Please –' I began, but was startled by the touch of something soft on my ear. Lips, a mouth so close the words dropped into the cavity. Not Lara's.

'You don't remember me, do you?'

'No,' I said miserably. 'Remember you from where?'

'Stoneborough, of course.'

'I thought this was nothing to do with that?'

'She thought it was me,' Lara told him. 'Can you believe it? She can't even remember who she destroyed.'

'I didn't destroy anyone,' I cried. I seized something solid, Miles's upper arm, and squeezed, as if to wrest understanding from him: '*You're* from Stoneborough? I thought you said you grew up in Kent.'

'I did, after my family left the area. Because of you.'

'I don't understand.' He must have known Nessie, then. She had not been his future wife or his sister-in-law, but his own sister or a close childhood friend. And Lara . . . I could feel her fingers, spiky with disgust, tugging my knickers down my legs. She was here because he was.

She'll do anything for him. Angie knew them far better than I did. The thought of kind Angie on the other side of the pool, giggling with Douglas and Andrew, looking out for our kids or phoning to check on Eve, made me whimper. She wouldn't go along with this, she'd know it was lunacy. Stripping a woman naked and holding her captive in a changing hut! And Ed, Ed would stop them — he'd protect me from their bullying.

You're my wife. At least I thought you were.

'You almost killed me,' Miles said. 'Do you realize that?'

Me. Not Nessie, him. And, with a surge of relief, I was back to the idea of a terrible misapprehension.

'Please, can we straighten this out?' I said, hearing the shake in my voice. 'I know the village, and there was an incident, yes, when I was young. It was with a girl, the one I mentioned to Lara. But there was no boy involved. So maybe you're talking about a different place, some other person?'

As his voice came close to my ear again, his hand pressed my head against the wall, flattening my cheek and mouth. 'The fact that you have no idea what you did makes it even more despicable.'

'But what is it you think I did?' My voice was not mine, my sense of myself quite lost now.

'You did what we're going to do to you.'

'Almost finished,' Lara said, in a confirming tone, and I felt her stoop, squat, elbow bony against my leg, before roughly gripping my ankles as she removed my sandals.

As tears fell, my mind made a connection, plucked an image that might make a match.

Everyone hates you. Everyone. All the boys.

He must have been one of them. The ones we'd stripped and mocked so casually we'd considered our victims interchangeable. For they had been a pack, a litter, their pubescent bodies and incomplete faces standard issue, everyday fare. I couldn't remember a single individual, only their massed wayward voices, their universal kicks of wildness and rage. Far more powerful in my memory were Mel's snorts and the sudden delicious weakness inside my ribcage as I caught her laughter and felt the howls escape me. It had not haunted me as Nessie had. It had not come close.

'That was . . .' I stammered '. . . that was just a prank.'

'A *prank*?'

And now my face was shoved against the wall, my cheekbone connecting hard, pain coursing through my head and neck.

'Let me remind you about your *prank*, you whore. You left me alone in the woods without any clothes. I had to walk home through the village naked. Two fucking miles. When I got to the high street, people came out to laugh. Everyone I knew, my friends, my brothers.'

'But . . . but we thought . . .' I was, struggling to suppress sobs.

'You thought someone would help? Well, they didn't. It was the worst humiliation of my life. I didn't leave the house for weeks. It was the holidays, I could hide. But then school started. I thought if I survived the first day of school I'd survive for ever, but I didn't. Every single child knew about it. It was a witch-hunt. I was bullied, I was destroyed. I was sent to a psychiatrist because I tried to take my own life.'

I was unable to process this, to accept any part of it. All I could do was snivel my excuses, 'Honestly, Miles, I swear I had no idea. It didn't . . .' I stopped myself, but he reacted as if I'd continued, roughly pulling my face closer to his by my hair.

'Didn't mean anything to you?'

I thought of Mel, who had likely attended the same school. Had she been aware of his suffering? As his tormentor, had she been, in the warped childhood hierarchy, a hero? Gulping, I reached for the last cowardly protest at my disposal: 'It wasn't just me. What about Mel —'

'I don't care about the other one. I remember *you*. I remember how you enjoyed it. You were sadistic – I saw it in your face.'

'I didn't enjoy it!' This was overwhelming and yet, aware now of my crime, I could at least think more clearly, could begin to assemble a defence. 'I can't believe it affected you like this. It was over thirty years ago!'

'Maybe in thirty years' time you'll still be thinking about tonight. I hope so.'

'She will,' Lara said.

'I don't understand what you want from me!' I cried.

A slap to the side of my head shocked me into silence.

'Shut up and listen. This is what you're going to do,' Miles said. 'We're going to get you to the turnstile and you're going to go through it into the park. You're going to walk home naked, just like I did. You won't have your key, so you'd better hope someone's home.'

He knew Ed and Molly were here, of course. I had a vision of myself ringing Sarah's bell, or that of another neighbour, waiting to waylay someone coming or going from the building, and my mind rejected it as unthinkable. How could I explain? How could I endure humiliation like that?

'An eye for an eye,' Lara added. 'It couldn't be fairer. You're lucky there's no interest added.'

'Someone will see me, someone will help me.' Gayle, I was thinking, her house was closer than mine. But she was at the Vineyard, twenty minutes from here, almost on my own doorstep. Then I thought of Eve, at home on her own with Milena, just a street away. I'll go there, make up some story, get her to lend me some clothes.

'If they do, you'll be luckier than I was,' Miles said. 'Or maybe you'll be unlucky and someone will film you and post it where your pupils look – and their parents. Your colleagues. Your daughter.'

'I refuse,' I said, locking my legs, stiffening my body, like an animal. 'This is ridiculous. You're both mad.'

Lara grasped my bare arm, hurting me. 'Now, listen to me very carefully: if you make a sound when we go out there, if you do anything to get out of this, then tomorrow we will be making a complaint to the police.'

In the dark, I swung blindly from one to the other: they really were demented. How were they holding down jobs, running a household, raising kids? At last I found my fire: 'They won't take you seriously. How could they?' The police hadn't been involved in our assault of Nessie, a crime far more serious than any skirmish with Miles; it was laughable that they would be interested in pursuing what we'd done to him. 'We're talking about a different age, three decades ago!'

'Not about that, you moron,' Miles said. 'A complaint against your husband for the sexual harassment of a fifteen-year-old girl.'

My face and neck flooded with a heat so febrile, so suffocating that only adrenalin could stop me passing out. 'What? There's been no harassment.'

'I think only the victim can make that call, don't you?'

I was speechless, utterly broken. I had no idea what Georgia would be prepared to fabricate at her parents' behest or – in the hysteria of the moment it occurred, I admit it – if there *was* any truth in it. But what I did know was that it would not come out of the blue: there'd be a paper trail, screen grabs of messages taken out of context, evidence of doubts raised to third parties, an account to someone convincing of Lara having had a warning word with the wife. They'd laid the trap.

'Have you been planning this the whole summer? The tutoring, our friendship . . .?' I was sobbing, speaking in gulps.

'There is no friendship,' Lara said.

'This is why you were so keen to get me to the party . . .'

A new suspicion was dawning: last Saturday, at La Madrague, had they been going to do this then? Strip me, send me out into the night? Or had it been sexual, after all, to enslave me, guarantee my attendance at the party in spite of the planned alienation of my husband? But I'd left. I'd thought I wasn't ready for their advances, and when the seed had been planted about Georgia I'd announced I wasn't coming to the party after all. And then Lara . . .

Everything I'd felt, she had not. She had only acted.

Because tonight was perfect. At a drunken pool party, it was not beyond the realms of possibility that there would be some skinny-dipping, some shameful middle-aged character who'd drunk too much and made a laughing stock of herself. But it was more than that: it was public humiliation, the kind of thing that burned for a lifetime . . . Word would spread even without the incendiary of social media. I would be suspended or fired from work. What would Molly say?

Molly. Where was she now? Was she safe with Ed, helping put candles on a cake? How long had I been held in this hut? Had I been missed? Was she, right at this moment, picking her way around the pool, her demons reawakening, her step faltering? I felt myself begin to hyperventilate.

'Let's get on with this,' Miles said, and at once a vertical crack of blue-tinged light appeared, enough for me to see his face, his eyes frigid, emotionless.

Far away, I thought I heard voices raised above the chatter, first Liam's, 'Where is she?', and then Ed's, 'Let me find Molly . . .' but I no longer knew if the sounds were real, if the experience I was having existed or was simply phantasmic.

Then, confusingly, I could no longer see Miles's eyes: the column of light had gone black.

'They've turned out the lights in the café,' Lara was telling him. 'I don't know why.'

My birthday cake, I thought.

As the door opened fully, there was complete darkness beyond, an eruption of gaiety from across the water, a succession of distinct calls: 'Not *all* the lights, just these ones!'

A male voice raised above the others: 'Can someone sort this out? I can't see a thing!' Then, alcohol-fuelled jeering, laughter spraying from all directions.

'Must be a power cut or something,' Lara said. 'Even better.'

And now her body was wrapped around me like a towel and she was steering me through open air, chill after the closeness inside the hut. My bare skin was pale, hairs raised. Now Miles was alongside us, his grip digging into the flesh of my arm.

A grave corrective tone carried towards us: 'Don't let anyone near the pool. Rog, can you patrol?'

As voices responded, too numerous to be distinct, we reached the caging of the turnstile, the sinister blackness beyond. I thought, if they force me through, I'll wait, I'll call over the wall, I'll go down to the main entrance and try to get someone's attention, I'll –

Miles's breath was hot in my ear. 'If you turn around and come back, the deal's off.'

'It's not a deal! Stop this nonsense, please!' But I was in the triangular grip of the turnstile now, the press of cold metal against my shoulder and arm, ready to be ejected into the park. The reality was registering, the absurdity fading: this was happening or Ed would be discredited, investigated, perhaps arrested.

Then came a sudden commotion of cries, names called out with urgency, even fear. There was something wrong – something beyond the wrongness of *this*.

Miles felt it too. 'What's going on?' he said, his voice tense and imperative, and I felt a final flare of hope.

Now, a single distinct cry in a voice all three recognized: '*Mummy!*'

'Is that Everett?' Lara said. 'He's supposed to be inside with David and Suki.'

Now voices, cries, one above the rest, coming closer, its owner moving in our direction, a female voice too shrill to identify: 'Lara! Lara, where are you? You need to come, it's an emergency!' Then, obliterating the rest, consuming all other sound within the site, the giant swooping noise of an alarm.

And in that instant, a click away from expulsion, I was forgotten, as the Channings dematerialized, drawn from one darkness to another.

36

Monday, 31 August, 9.40 a.m.

We stand facing each other, neither speaking. Less than twelve hours ago, we were crushed together, confined, breathing as one into the blackness, and he hated me as a lifelong enemy. My instinct should be to flee – he represents a threat to me, a bodily danger – but there is a twisting sensation at my softest core that I recognize as mercy.

It is his daughter, not mine, who is critically ill in an intensive-care unit above us. He told me I'd destroyed him, but he was wrong. *This* is what destroys us, a child's life in jeopardy. The problem is that his is in jeopardy because she saved mine, which means it's possible he hates me now with a depth he didn't know existed last night.

Yes, my instinct should be to flee.

'Lara said she'd seen you,' he says. 'You shouldn't have come here.'

In my hand I feel Molly's phone come to life and I slide it into my bag, feel it drop at exactly the moment my own starts to ring. Friends, having waited till a civilized hour to make contact; I haven't answered the texts and they're worried. Other people care. Other people in my life besides the Channings.

'Can we talk?' I say. 'I know you need to get back upstairs, but just two minutes. Please.'

Miles says nothing, but gestures to the table where I've dropped my water bottle and pulls out the chair nearest him. I sink into the seat opposite, eyes lowered, aware of him placing his coffees in front of him. The second must be for Lara, upstairs at Georgia's bedside. I picture their usual drinks of choice: champagne, Negronis, tumblers of whisky.

When I raise my eyes again, I find his already fixed on me. I read loathing, of course, but also anguish and terror. He's never been more human to me, never less enigmatic – and yet I still cannot connect him with the boy he says he was. The boy whose face I cannot dredge from memory because I didn't care to look at it at the time, not properly. Too busy seeking Mel's approval; too busy laughing. In thirty years, none of my residual guilt has been attached to those pale and anonymous boys whose faces had blurred into one.

And yet mine had remained clear to him, his experience of my cruelty a component part of the life that followed.

'Whatever you want from me, you can have it,' I say, just catching in time the gulp in my voice that would be sure to incense him for I have no right to distress. 'You must know I would trade anything, *anything*, for this accident not to have happened.'

His reply is not immediate, but when it comes, stark and unyielding, it makes me shudder: 'You've got nothing to trade.'

I bring my hands in front of me, pleading. 'Tell me what you want from me, but please, please leave my family out of it.'

'Your family is why we're here,' he says, in the same bleak tone.

I had meant Ed, but he means Molly, of course. Dare I hope that his threat regarding Ed has passed, the sword lowered? I drop my hands. On my lap I knit my fingers together, scrape the left palm with my right thumbnail until it's too painful to bear without crying out.

In my bag, the ringing begins once more.

'I told Lara how grateful we are to Georgia, and so incredibly sorry. I know Molly will want to thank her too.' I pause. 'And Ed.'

I watch him. He has not forgotten.

'So that's why you're here,' he says. 'Not for Georgia.'

'Of course for Georgia –'

He interrupts, more curious than cold: 'You must think there's something in it.'

'Think', not 'know' or 'agree': an admission, surely, that the accusation is fiction.

'I assure you I don't.' A memory flickers then, a short-term memory, some time in the last week. I'd come into Ed's office without warning and, as I did, I caught the click of his laptop closing, a sharp look my way. Had he been covering his tracks, deleting those emails to her, emails worth inspecting after all? I'd eradicated the thought, of course, but that wasn't the same as not having had it in the first place. 'Georgia's what's important,' I say very firmly. 'Her recovery, her future.'

As Miles and I stare at each other, it seems to me that a shadow lifts. For the first time we see one another not as new acquaintances and not as old enemies, or even as adults who were once children, together for a summer, but as the parents of two girls who are friends.

'Save her for me,' he says, speaking in a new voice, a gruff and desperate one, and he looks at me as if he honestly believes I have the power to effect a miracle. 'Save her for Lara.'

I flush. He knows about us. Everything worth knowing, he's known. I inch my hand towards his and I say, 'I'll try.'

But his hand withdraws as mine approaches, the shadow resettles and all at once he's on his feet, he's snarling. 'Try what, Pock-face? *You* can't save her. You can't even save yourself.'

37

In the dark, unclothed and defenceless, I was both frighteningly close to and mercifully removed from the human clamour, audible only with each split-second plunge in the alarm siren. Trembling badly, stubbing a toe on the stone, I staggered back to the hut, my nostrils finding the lingering body heat of the Channings, the scent of my own terror. I stepped into my underwear, and then the dress, damp from the day's pool water on the floor. I heard the tear of fabric as I rushed and lost balance.

My thoughts were in uproar, my mind strained to the brink of endurance. Had that really happened? Had I been inches from tumbling nude into the park, a wretch, a savage? Did the Channings really hate me – me, Natalie Steele, wife of Ed, mother of Molly, middle-aged teacher and Elm Hill stalwart? When the alarm stopped screaming, would they come back for me and finish what they'd started?

It was only when I was outside again and tripping in unstrapped sandals towards the crowd that my thoughts re-ordered themselves, the crucial phrases fighting through the self-obsession: *Something's happening . . . Emergency . . .*

Molly! *Where's Molly?*

Then: *She's with Ed.* Ed, who an hour ago I'd battled and mocked and disrespected and for what?

'What's going on?' I'd reached the edge of the mêlée, yelled my questions to the first person I came to. 'Why is the alarm on? Why have the lights gone out?' I pulled at the nearest arm, a man's, claiming his attention.

'There was a boy in the water.' His eyes registered my dishevelment. We didn't know each other. 'They've just pulled him out.'

A boy? Everett? Hadn't we just heard him calling? Had he been in the water at the time? While his mother attacked another adult, had he broken from the multitude and stumbled into the blue?

'But the pool's out of bounds,' I said, a redundant observation since most of the party guests had spilled from the café terrace into the pool area; those who hadn't watched from railings as if from a ship's prow. A breeze had picked up, the balloons straining at their ties.

Then, startlingly close, I saw Angie crouching on the ground, her gingham skirt spread out on the stone, and in front of her, lying on his back in his swim shorts, bare chest heaving, not Everett but Josh. Then Stephen stepped forward, white and bulky, and blocked my view.

'Is that *Josh*?'

'You know him?' The man next to me nodded, grave, almost remorseful.

'Is he unconscious?'

'No, he was speaking just now. He looked alert.'

'Has someone called for help?'

Yes. An ambulance was on its way.

That was when I saw Everett, clinging to Miles and sobbing into his stomach, and Lara, too, her hands gripping Matt's shoulders, her mouth moving fast, screaming at him, and my brain, overloaded, scrambled, assumed they were upset about Josh, Lara for some reason blaming Matt for his having been in the water. I must have imagined being in the hut with them, I thought. Like I'd imagined Stephen wanting to harm me. I had some sort of death wish, a morbid desire to be victimized. *Guilt messes with your brain.* Don't say anything to anyone, I warned myself. You're the crazy one. You need psychiatric help.

'But Josh is an amazing swimmer,' I heard myself protesting to my new companion. 'I don't understand how he could have got into trouble.'

And now a nearby woman was telling us something through the din; I could not lip-read and held my ear to her mouth. 'There was someone else in the water,' she repeated, 'so maybe he got dragged under.'

'No, they're both out,' a new voice said. 'They've got her out as well. I saw that a minute ago.'

Her, I thought. Molly. *Molly.*

Two things happened then: lights came on – dim, back-up lights, not the underwater ones or those in the café – and the alarm stopped. Into the sudden silence, into our ringing ears, a voice boomed: *'There's someone still in there!'*

And, as if animated by the new light, there was an instant collective spinning as parents gripped children tighter or pulled them backwards; others screamed names and the air shook with the collision of a hundred individual fears.

'Molly!' Mine was a howl, not a call, obliterated at once by the frantic sound of another parent wailing:

'Has anyone seen her? Where is she? Georgia!'

Lara.

'Matt,' a voice was yelling, or maybe 'Nat', but I couldn't tell because I was mesmerized by the sudden sight of Miles kicking off his shoes and preparing to leap into the water.

'Don't jump,' someone told him. 'You might hurt her!'

And hands seized him from the edge just as others pulled a girl from the pool, a girl in a swimsuit, her slender limbs limp, long hair glued to her neck and back, the same shade as her skin. Lara screamed, a sound lost in the bedlam of people rushing forwards to assist or tumbling backwards to create space, until the girl and her rescuers were settled at the side of the water. The liquid streamed from her, silver in the light, and she looked . . . she looked lifeless.

It was Georgia. My legs buckled. Only in sinking to my knees did a gap appear in the throng that allowed me to make out a third figure, another girl, this one prone but clearly conscious, soaked and spluttering, speaking to the man who cradled her. Ed.

I tore to their side, my mouth open but my vocal cords disabled.

'Where've you been?' Ed cried. 'Did you not hear me shouting for you?' His face was disfigured with fright and something close to hatred.

'I couldn't hear anything over the alarm. Was she in the water as well?'

'Of course she was – look at her!'

'Darling, darling, are you OK?'

Molly's eyes were open and moving and she was breathing well, but at the sight of me she burst into sobs, which caused coughing, streams of water and phlegm gushing from her mouth and nose. Unlike Josh and Georgia, she was fully clothed. I could make no sense of this.

'What was she doing in there?' I asked Ed.

'I have no idea, but once she was in, this dress must have dragged her down. Look how heavy the skirt is! She won't let me take it off. Can you find a towel or something dry I can wrap her in? Ask Liam or one of the staff. Help, will you? Look how she's shivering!'

But hands were helping ahead of mine, bringing towels and emergency equipment. Shoved aside, I began to feel lightheaded again, recognized the whisper that would become a roar, once more losing the strength in my legs.

Ed lunged to break my fall, mad with exasperation. 'Stop it, Nat. Seriously, you need to hold it together. For once, hold it together!'

And I did, not just for Molly but also for him, for all of us: I pulled myself back from the brink and, in doing so, experienced the profound conviction that I would never go over it. I never would forsake myself and fall out of reach, not as long as I remained this girl's parent.

So, when she grew hysterical, as she now did, it was not from having been infected by me. It was because she could see Georgia. Propped against Ed, she could see as well as we could the blue light flashing through the glass walls of Reception, casting a sickly glow on all our faces but especially on Georgia's as she was borne through emergency exits, strapped to the gurney to keep her from falling.

It was a long time since I'd seen Molly hysterical like this. She thrashed and raved and howled, a creature from Purgatory, a devil from my own imagination.

38

Home, I think. I can do nothing to help Georgia and now is no time to plead my case – or Ed's – to her parents. I should not have brought myself here, without invitation, without welcome. I've neglected Molly and I've implied a level of guilt on Ed's part that I don't actually believe and all because . . .

I'm filled with shame to admit that, whatever my justifications, I came here at least partly because I am still, *still*, determined to be a part of the Channings' world. Even when they no longer want me, even now I know they *never* wanted me, not as I'd thought.

I retrace my route around the side of the building to the main road, and all at once the details are acute, significant: the black flecks of dirt on the double yellow lines, the running engines of the stationary ambulances, a trio of staff in flat, wide shoes, coming off shift, checking their phones. One right turn, and the Emergency Department looms, its sign huge, white on red, and more red painted in criss-crosses on the grey of the road.

The fresh sun in the sky.

I watch as an ambulance approaches, its siren shutting off before it enters the bay. I didn't see the vehicle that took Georgia away last night. She was the last out of the water and the first to be removed: the unconscious one, the true emergency. All my attention had been on Molly, on calming her distress, on persuading the paramedics that she should be allowed to come home, that we should avoid further attacks of mania at the hospital.

My Mazda is where I left it, lonely on its yellow line, ordinary, reliable, symbolic of all I want and need. As I open the driver's door I continue to watch the emergency bay: the ambulance has pulled up and already has its rear doors open, its ramp lowered. There is a sense of calm as the trolley comes wheeling down, smooth and virtually silent, not clattering in the way I'd expect, not surrounded immediately by receiving staff calling out urgent questions. I catch no more than a sliver of the arriving patient – plastic mask and tubes obscure all clues to gender or age – but I understand, with the deepest humanity I possess, that this is someone's sister, mother, uncle, son; this is another family ravaged and reconfigured, just like Georgia's. And this family's enemies will not celebrate.

I settle in the driver's seat, ready for my future, grateful for it. Inexplicably superstitious, I'm unable to start the engine until I know the arriving patient is safely inside the hospital so I watch the trolley's short journey into the building. The sunlight on the arriving party is so clean and whole that I can't help but be optimistic, even certain, of full recovery for the poor stricken person. Not like last night, when Georgia was removed from the lido, when the light was blue and thin and wretched.

No, it's not like last night at all.

Because now I see who steps out of the ambulance next.

39

'It was only supposed to be a scare,' I told Mel, with bravado, as we strolled to the newsagent's for a final ice cream. We would pay for it, too, not steal it from the chiller cabinet as we had many times before, scuttling from the premises in stitches. Today we would do the right thing.

'Just a laugh,' she agreed. 'At least she had her swimming costume on. That's more than some of them.'

We knew by then that Nessie hadn't drowned; we weren't murderers. That she'd somehow clawed herself out of the pond and made her way back through the darkening woods. Word had come this morning via a neighbour that she'd got into trouble swimming on her own and had arrived home extremely distressed. It had already been agreed that next summer an adult should supervise the kids at the pond – either that or forbid them to go there.

'Do you think her mum called the police?' I asked Mel.

'Doesn't sound like it. Think we'd know by now if she had.' Mel mimed her wrists being locked into handcuffs.

'What about her hair? How d'you think she explained that?'

'No idea. She must have said she wanted it like that.'

'I wonder if she told her mum it was us.'

Mel just shrugged.

I mustered a chuckle, but it was a hollow one. I knew it had been wrong. I knew it had been cruel. Even our idle pace as we headed for our treat was disrespectful, as if we were sauntering to a graveside or the wreckage of an accident purely to pass the time. 'Should we at least get our stories straight? In case the police come?'

'Just say we left the pond before her and didn't see a thing. Besides,' Mel added, 'you're going home this afternoon, what do you care?'

I cared. I cared enough to have lain sleepless in my bed the previous night, skin slick, nightie damp; I cared enough that the farewell dinner my grandmother had cooked sat indigestible in my stomach. It was not just the last day of summer as far as I was concerned, it was the last day of for ever, the day I stopped breathing easy.

'Come round and say goodbye before you go,' Mel said, when we'd finished our ice creams. She touched my hair, let her fingers rest in it, her thumb brushing my earlobe.

I eased away. 'I don't like it when you do that.' Seeing I had offended her, I tried to make amends: 'I'll write. As soon as I get home. Will you write back?'

Another shrug, different this time, as if she had no other way of expressing to me that a letter would not be enough for her, that I'd missed the point.

The police had still not come by the time my father arrived to collect me. He hadn't left us; my parents weren't getting divorced. I wonder sometimes how much keener the joy would have been when I answered the door had there not been the overwhelming dread that the man on the other side was in uniform.

'Can we go?' I kept asking him, refusing to notice my grandparents' bafflement, their hurt expressions. 'Please can we go?'

I wrote to Mel, as I'd promised. I wrote three times before I received a reply. She told me that a day or two after I'd left she and her parents had received a visit from Nessie's parents. The basic message was that the police would not be involved on the condition that Mel confess her crime and apologize. When she tried to deny it, she was threatened with a dredging of the pond for the weapon and quickly caved in. Though she had protected me – she had a rogue's honour, Mel – and I was grateful for that, it was in reality little more than a stay of execution, for Nessie would, of course, have been able to name me with ease. (Who of life's victims is not familiar with the identities of her tormentors? It is only the tormentors who let the names go.) And yet I heard nothing from my grandparents of any equivalent visit or any request for my permanent address.

Unlike Mel, I was a coward as well as a criminal.

I waited days, weeks, months, for the rap at the door. I watched the phone on the kitchen wall until my eyes grew sore and scratchy, until I could turn away and still see its ringleted cord coiling back on itself like a tail. Had Nessie's parents tricked Mel into confessing only to take their grievance to the police after all?

The age of criminal responsibility in England and Wales was ten, I discovered from a law book in the library, and from what I could understand there was no statute of limitations. Which meant they could at any time change their minds; the police could at any time pursue me.

Which meant I could never stop waiting. I could never stop waiting for the worst thing in the world to catch up with me.

To have done to me what I had done to her.

40

Monday, 31 August, 10 a.m.

Even as I watch, the pictures appear two-dimensional – his outline is flattened, the colours tinged with yellow – and my response feels artificial, a cinematic likeness of my fear.

You're tired, I remind myself. *You haven't slept. You've been imagining things lately; this whole summer, you've been misconstruing people, encounters, conversations. Blink and look again.*

I blink. I look again. I see his retreating figure, his deft, almost dancing steps as he hurries to catch up with the trolley. Only then do I abandon the car and tear back towards the building; only then do I raise my voice to yell his name: 'Ed!'

He turns in a jerking frantic way, his face exactly as it was last night at the pool: terrified and furious. 'Nat, I've phoned you about a hundred times! Where the hell have you been?'

'Please, what's wrong? What's happened to her?'

I sprint to reach the still-rolling trolley. Her face is masked in plastic, sealed inside, eyes closed. The smudge of mascara is still visible on palest cheek, her lips bluish white. Where is blood, where is the life? I reach to touch her arm: she is warm and solid. Alive.

417

The innermost part of me convulses and I swallow vomit.

'She didn't wake up,' Ed says.

In a windowless, strip-lit zone a team is waiting, information exchanged between ambulance staff and receiving team. What I catch destroys me: a drop in oxygen levels, ICU, ventilation, intubation. Ed is being questioned, details he has already addressed at least once, I gather, from his growing impatience. The person in charge is a consultant emergency paediatrician, who is on his way down; he won't be able to speak to us now but will find us as soon as he is able to comment on an outcome.

Outcome: a terrible word, sparking memory of a line I've read that flitted below the surface when I spoke to Lara: *Victims who arrive in the Emergency Department comatose have significantly poorer outcomes . . .*

Georgia was, and now so is Molly.

I've lost track of our route through the building. A corridor has opened into a larger space, like a passing place on a busy single-track road, and we're asked to wait here on our own. The walls are the sun-yellow of hope, the furniture the storm-cloud-grey of fear. Is this where they put the people to whom they expect to have to give bad news? The worst news of all?

Stop. 'Tell me from the beginning,' I say to Ed, and his need to articulate his agony triumphs over his anger towards me.

He looks as if he has aged ten years since last night.

'It was getting too late for her to still be sleeping, so I shook her, just gently, but she wasn't waking. Her breathing sounded weird.'

When did I last check on her breathing? Before I left, at 8 a.m. It was normal when I left, I'm sure of it. 'You said she was fine. On the phone, when we spoke, you said –'

'I know what I said, but I talked to Liam after you, and when I went back in to check on her, she was different. Something must have happened.'

'She couldn't have been choking on something?'

'No, it wasn't dramatic like that, like the airways were blocked. It was more like wheezing, like she was struggling to get the right amount of air but was getting some. When the paramedics came they gave her oxygen straight away.'

On the borders of his anger there is guilt and there is also grief. Don't grieve, I think, *believe*.

'What did the doctors ask you just now? I couldn't follow.'

'It was about the pool temperature last night, who was supervising, how long she was in the water. The same stuff as before.'

I can't remember the questions from last night. Ed handled them while I held Molly, subdued her, reassured her she was in safe hands – ours.

'They said it will help that they've already done tests on Georgia,' he adds. 'You can get diseases from chemicals in the pool, chemical pneumonitis, did they call it?'

'I should warn Angie, in case Josh is at risk as well.'

'No, he didn't inhale any water. He got himself out. He was conscious and lucid.' Ed breathes deeply. 'Thank God, otherwise there would have been nobody left to raise the alarm.'

Nobody left: the words make me shudder.

'What happened in the ambulance? Did she come around?'

'No. Her oxygen levels were low, she had the mask on.' His voice cracks. 'They said she needed a ventilator, a hundred per cent oxygen. They talked about stuff to do with airway pressure, I don't know what exactly. I didn't want to ask questions and distract them. We got here so quickly – there was hardly any traffic.'

I nod. 'I don't understand – last night, how did the paramedics not anticipate this? This relapse.'

Relapse is a safe word, it is not catastrophic, but Ed isn't buying it. His fury rises again, his jaw clenched as he replies: 'Maybe they did, but you were so adamant we were taking her home. They probably didn't get a full picture of her condition – no wonder they wanted to take her to A & E. But *you* insisted.'

History repeats itself; again I am to blame. I've made the wrong decision. I'm responsible for the lapse of judgement.

But history is not quite repeating. I wish it were. Because the first time I *did* take her straight to hospital and she was discharged within a few hours. The first time she was cleared, just as Harriet was, just as the vast majority of people in pool accidents are.

'She was conscious,' I say helplessly. 'Last night, I thought that meant she was OK. Like Josh. When did she stop sleeping and go into a coma? Is that what this is?'

'I don't know, Nat.'

'She must have damage to her lungs. We need to look this up online. What was that disease you just said?' My hand is in my bag, fishing for my phone, but Ed stops me, snatches the phone with unexpected force.

'No. I'm not listening to your cyberchondria. I've had years of this and I'm not having it now. Wait till the doctors come and tell us what's going on. *Then* we'll look up what needs to be looked up.'

Cyberchondria; years of this. His words chill me – because there is truth in them. For so long I have obsessively informed myself when there has been nothing new to know yet I've allowed us to be fatally casual when something has gone terribly wrong. Letting her sleep herself into a coma while congratulating myself on having evaded medical care. Leaving her, *leaving her*, so I could stalk a family I hardly know, a woman who only pretended to like me. I told myself this morning I was here to protect Ed, to ensure the Channings' silence, but was that truly my motivation?

'How long before they let us see her, do you think?'

'I don't know,' Ed says. 'It'll depend on how she responds. Once they've got her all hooked up to what she needs and done the tests I'm sure they'll let us go in. We have to wait.'

There is no window here. I look again at the yellow and the grey. *Focus on the yellow.* Waiting has a different definition from any I've known or imagined before. Five minutes is an hour. An hour will be a day. And life, without her, will never end.

I begin sobbing, tears stinging my hot, raw skin.

'Crying won't help,' says Ed, neither cruel nor comforting.

It's incredible now to imagine I found the atmosphere between us difficult in Molly's bedroom. That was swinging in hammocks in a sunny meadow compared to this. This is like we're in a sealed room that's filling with gas and all it will take to ignite it is a single word from either of us.

I blow my nose, compose myself. At any moment news will come and I must be calm for Molly. I did it last night and I'll do it again.

'Where is Georgia, anyway?' Ed asks. 'Is she in this unit as well? Where are Miles and Lara?'

'They're on the fourth floor in Critical Care. We won't bump into them down here.'

Will Molly be moved up there? I wonder. She might already be there for all we know, side by side with the girl who tried to save her.

'Why weren't we with her?' Ed groans, as much to himself as to me. 'At the lido, after the band. Why weren't we watching?'

'Because she's not a small child,' I tell him. 'Because we're constantly being advised to let her find her own way.' I speak with new urgency: 'We have to agree that no one is to blame for her falling in. It was a horrific accident. None of us could have seen her, not with the power out. When I saw her by the water earlier, it was still light, but later it was so dark, even before the blackout –'

He interrupts me. 'You saw her there earlier?' His voice is thick with blame, so much blame the room hums with it. 'When, exactly?'

'Before you arrived,' I say, stretching the truth. 'She was on her own. I thought she was testing herself, maybe doing some sort of exercise for Bryony.'

'You called her away, though?'

'Of course I did. She promised she wouldn't do it again. The pool was out of bounds, we all knew that.'

We're being a bit naughty, going off limits . . .

Inside me I feel a tremor, its source more complex than remorse.

'You should have told me this last night,' Ed says.

'I'm telling you now. The point is, maybe she was trying something similar when she fell. With the underwater lights, she would have been fine, but to be plunged into blackness . . .' My body language opens in direct appeal. 'A power cut, Ed, it was the worst kind of bad luck, but that's what it was. Whatever random thing caused the lights to fail, *that's* to blame, not us, not the Channings.'

But Ed is just staring into thin air, distracted, tormented. 'Liam,' he murmurs.

'What about him?'

'When he called me, just before . . .' His voice breaks and I think, *Just before he discovered our girl half dead in her bed* . . . For all his denouncing of me, he's torturing himself because he should have stayed by her bedside, forgone the second call.

'What did Liam say?'

Ed lets out a groan, crushes my phone tighter in his fist. 'He'd looked at the CCTV footage of the camera at the shallow end.'

'And? Does it show her falling in?'

'No, there's nothing of what happened in the water, it was too dark without the underwater lights, but there was an emergency light on above the exit by Reception and there's just enough illumination to show the kids getting into the pool, before the blackout. Georgia and Josh, I mean.' His gaze locks mine. 'It's not like everyone thinks, Nat. They didn't get in because Molly fell in. They'd planned to go in all along. The clothes in the changing hut were theirs. It was the one at the end nearest the main entrance.'

My brow creases as I reshape the story. 'All right, then. So if they planned to go in the water that must mean Molly went with them to watch, hang out. But when the lights failed . . . Did Liam not see her on the film at all, then?'

'Yes, this is what I'm coming to. Georgia and Josh had just gone in down the steps, then Molly came through the door and walked towards the edge of the pool. After that, all three move out of range of the emergency light and he can't see them, not without being able to enhance the visuals in some way.'

'Maybe Molly was trying to persuade them to get out. Then she got too close to the edge and was disorientated in the dark and overbalanced?'

My poor girl, how it must have felt, swallowed blind by the monster she'd spent most of her young life escaping.

I continue, picturing it clearly: 'Still, thank God the other two were already in the water. Imagine if they'd still been changing and she'd fallen in first. In the dark they wouldn't have seen where she was, would have been much slower to react. What are the chances? A power cut right at the moment a non-swimmer gets too close to the water? It's like an act of God.'

An act of a vengeful God. A punishment not of the daughter, but of the mother.

'I don't think so, Nat,' Ed says. 'There's something else.'

'What?'

'That's not the only footage Liam looked at. He also checked the camera in Reception. That's where all the electrics are, behind the front desk.'

He pauses. The hum of blame is quieter now.

'It wasn't a power cut, like we all assumed. He thinks someone deliberately turned off the lights.'

'Deliberately?' I'm knocked sideways. 'Why would anyone do that?'

But the narrative is writing itself in parallel, the answer clear and true: to create darkness, to conceal the trespasses of a friend, two friends.

Ed goes on: 'The light wasn't great, but he's fairly sure he recognizes the person who turned off the power.'

'Who?'

And I hear the suck of his breath before he says what scarcely needs to be said.

'It was Molly.'

4I

The only positive effect of Ed's revelation is that a full ten seconds pass when I'm not thinking of Molly being pumped artificially with air and fed fluids and nutrients directly into her bloodstream. I'm not thinking about cuffs and pads and IV lines and drains. I'm not thinking of what happens when the machinery stops, whether her body can remember how to do it all alone.

No, I'm thinking now about a thirteen-year-old girl who intentionally plunged an event into darkness and put herself and others in mortal danger. Two minors were voluntarily in the water, yes, but there were other, much younger children at the party, never more than a railing away from deep water. Without light, the risks increased incalculably.

'Why would she do that?' I ask at last. Why would a lifelong aquaphobic remove the crutch of light and move willingly towards water? And then I answer before Ed can: 'Because Georgia asked her to.'

'What?'

'It's always a friend, Ed, always. In a year or two it will be a boy, but now, it's a girl.'

He's not about to argue the validity of my statement. He teaches teenage girls so he knows theoretically how the hive works, but he doesn't know, as I do, how it feels to be in it. 'But why would Georgia ask her to do that?'

'So they could swim unseen, Josh and her. Like you say, they had their swimming kit with them. They'd planned it in advance.'

'But why? It makes no sense,' Ed says.

'Only because it went wrong. But if we can figure out what they were *expecting* to happen . . .' My pulse stutters as a possibility presents itself, a possibility I cannot share with Ed: if Georgia was willing to lie about him to the police for her parents – assuming she has even been made aware of that particular scheme – then was she also willing to stage a diversion while they dealt their punishment to their primary victim?

But, no, the party itself was the diversion, and I cannot believe Lara would allow her daughter to put herself at physical risk.

I retrieve Molly's phone from my bag and seat myself closer to Ed's side. 'Let me show you her recent messages. You see all these numbers? I thought they might be the times of Georgia's and Josh's laps in the pool. In which case, maybe last night was a race. They wanted to do it when the pool was empty. Most of the time it's too packed to get two free lanes.'

'That's crazy,' Ed says. 'What about all those balloons?'

'They were tied to the dividers. The lanes themselves were clear. If anything, the balloons would have been useful camouflage.'

'But why last night? Why not just do it first thing in the morning? The pool can't be heaving all the time. And why turn off the lights? How long does it take to race up and down? They'd have been able to do it with the lights on before anyone reacted fast enough to haul them out.'

He's right. By the time the offenders were spotted they'd be shaking themselves off, rejoining the party. Darkness wouldn't have been crucial.

'Besides, even in the dark they would have been heard, wouldn't they?' Ed says. 'No one swims *that* quietly, unless they're under water. Let's see the rest of these messages.'

The power is low: another few minutes and the phone will go dead. Another few minutes and the consultant will come to find us.

We trawl through.

Molly, you ready for your bit?

Remember everything the nice man told us? #Schtum (This with an emoji of a face with a zipped mouth.)

Yes. (The same emoji from Molly.)

Eve, you're all set, right? #TopSpotter

Too freakin right. #YourLifeInMyHands

'What's this spotter business?' Ed asks.

'I don't know. A lookout, maybe?'

Head to head . . .

Beauty v. the Beast . . .

'You're right, it's definitely a race,' he says. 'Between Georgia and Josh. The times must be minutes and seconds.' He scrolls back. 'Two minutes fifty-one, two minutes twenty-nine. Does that sound about right?'

I consider. 'Depends on the distance. Two lengths would be a hundred metres, and I would have thought they could do that in under a minute. Maybe they race two hundred metres or even further. We might need to wait to ask Josh.'

There is silence as we absorb the implication: not Georgia, not Molly, only Josh can be relied on for a witness statement.

Ed is frowning. 'It's odd, but the times that get the best reactions are the slower times, not the faster ones. It's like they're counting *down* from something?'

We both look up as our ears catch the sounds of doors opening and closing. Time suspends as we identify whether the footsteps – rapid, urgent – are coming towards us. They are not. Intuition tells me that the longer we wait, the better the news, but I can't say why and I don't share the instinct with Ed.

And then suddenly I know. With sleep, I would have known sooner, but it would have saved us nothing. 'I think the longer times *are* the better ones,' I tell Ed. He said it himself: *unless they're under water* . . . 'I think they might have been having a breath-holding competition.'

'What?'

'You remember I told you about shallow-water blackout? It happens when you hold your breath for too long. Sometimes you need to, in a dive or for a length under water, but sometimes you do it as a challenge.'

Other than that single complaint of Matt's, I've never had any evidence that Josh and his mates were engaging in breath-holding games, and I'm not convinced I have the evidence now. Why, then, do I feel so utterly certain?

'I think the kids were competing to see who could hold their breath under water the longest. It's very dangerous, which is why it's banned at public pools. It's banned at the lido, Matt told me.'

I do not confess that he did so in direct reference to this very group – and I didn't pass that detail on to Ed. I'd made my own decision that Georgia had had nothing to do with it. Then, last night, I let Molly be summoned to the side of the very boy who'd been reprimanded, because I'd feared she was going to ask to go home when I wanted to stay. I'd wanted to have my moment in the spotlight, a sad, middle-aged woman craving attention, missing desire. Alive to every glance and word from a friend, another woman.

I feel nauseous.

'Last night was the grand final,' I tell Ed. 'They knew they'd be seen with the underwater lights on so they got Molly to turn them off. Hence the tour with Matt. He must have shown them where the electrics are, the master switches.' It is easy to imagine Georgia extracting from Matt – or any of the staff, frankly – the necessary security codes to gain access alone. 'They must have been planning it for weeks.'

But Ed is not convinced. 'I don't get it. Turning off the power was what made everyone take notice. If they wanted to do it secretly, they'd have been better leaving the power on and sneaking in. Or just turning off the underwater lights.'

'Maybe that was the aim. Maybe Molly got it wrong, hit the wrong switch. She would have been very nervous, sneaking into Reception on her own.'

My mind has come alive, releasing new facts, identifying clues. 'When I saw her by the pool earlier, she was pacing. She must have been counting steps to help her later in the dark.'

'I can't believe she'd go along with something so obviously dangerous,' Ed argues. 'She's never done anything remotely like this before.'

'Not to our knowledge, no. But it's been an unusual summer. She's made new friends. She idolizes Georgia and Josh and Eve.'

'That's another thing. Why would *they* be so reckless?' Ed says. 'They've been on lifesaving courses, spent their lives in pools – they know the risks better than anyone.'

'I'm guessing they thought they were immortal, that nothing bad could ever happen to *them*. Oh!' My heartbeat accelerates. *TopSpotter . . . MyLifeInYourHands . . . Georgia and Josh and Eve . . .* 'Eve wasn't there last night. She must have been going to time them but she was ill so Molly took her place. That must be what the spotter is. Let me just check something . . .'

Molly's screen displays a warning about the battery being about to run out. Dismissing this, I tap it on the clock icon at the top, sensing what I'll see next before I even see it: huge changing numbers, the stopwatch still ticking: *13:03.19 . . . 13.03:20 . . . 13.03.21 . . .* She'd hit 'Start' just over thirteen hours ago at about 10.30 p.m. When I was in the hut with the Channings, when Ed was sticking candles into my birthday cake.

'Do you know what I think? I think she was by the pool doing this spotter role, but her friends being under water for so long made her panic. Maybe she saw that Georgia was in trouble, or thought she was, though of course she couldn't see much because of the lights. It makes sense, doesn't it? Only a dire emergency like that could give her the courage to go in and help. Some instinct overrode the fear. Georgia wasn't rescuing Molly, Ed. Molly was rescuing Georgia. Or *thought* she was.'

We stare at each other in horror.

'Wouldn't she have been better to call for help?' Ed says. 'There were a hundred adults just shouting distance away. A hundred people who knew how to swim.'

'She might have been sworn to secrecy. And you don't go to authority figures when you're already in the middle of a criminal act.'

'Josh did.'

'He's older, more confident. And by then it was an out-and-out emergency, whereas she had just shut off the power, was terrified, not sure she could trust her instinct. This feels right, Ed.'

And it does: our daughter trespassed in a prohibited area of a closed building, turned off the lights to the entire complex and then, confused by the activity taking place, blundered into the water to try to help her friends, dragging the strong swimmers under.

'Nat?'

'Yes.'

'If this is right, she could be in trouble with the police. The CCTV evidence will count against her.'

'No,' I protest. 'She's only thirteen. They're fifteen and almost sixteen. There'll be evidence somewhere in this phone that she was influenced. And there's her phobia. She can't think rationally around water. That's well documented.'

'It's not how the Channings will see it,' Ed says bleakly. 'They'll twist it. Whatever it is, they'll twist it. This is a nightmare.'

'It's just a theory,' I tell him. 'It may not be right. And the police may not get there themselves.' Already it feels as if we're conspiring to pervert the cause of justice. The cause of the Channings.

At the sound of doors swinging open and shut, we abort our discussion and listen. This time the footsteps are approaching and we stand together a split second before the doors are pushed open. A member of staff comes through: male, late forties, dressed in green scrubs. No clipboard, no notes, no smile. When he steps towards us, there is nothing in that step to tell me what he will say.

But I know it is terrible news because my whole body prickles, a corrosive, almost dissolving feeling, as if I'm being eaten alive.

I reach for Ed's hand, but he is no longer in range, has moved forward independently. Then he glances, sees my hand outstretched, palm open, and he does not take it. And I think then, I've lost both of them. *I've lost everything.*

I've lost everything and I've got no one else to blame but myself.

Not even the Channings.

42

2016 — one year later

You could say it was a perfect storm of elements, what happened last summer: Molly's bid for independence and the sudden breaking of her deadlock with a serious lifelong affliction; the release of tension from my having successfully completed my first year at straitlaced Elm Hill Prep and the excitement of being back in the wild for the summer; Ed being preoccupied at a time of year when I usually counted on him as my daily companion (and, let's face it, moral guide); seeing Mel again; the August heatwave with its rising temperatures, its air heavy with temptation.

And the reopening of the lido. That, mostly, because its impact was utterly profound. It was not so much an opening as an arrival, a landing — as if it materialized one day fully formed, an oasis in the suburban deserts, a watery paradise complete with its own deity.

You know, I looked up water goddesses once, read all about Thalassa, the woman who rose from the depths, and Neptune's queen Salacia, with her crown of seaweed, and Ran, the Norse sea goddess of love, who collected the drowned in a net.

Of course the ones we know best are Hydra, Medusa, the Sirens: villains of the water all.

The first thing I'm going to tell you is that Georgia is alive. She is both a survivor and a hero. She was unconscious for almost twenty-four hours, but they fished her from her oblivion and the neurological damage was both minimal and treatable.

Her memory of the incident is incomplete, but she knows she was in the pool to compete with Josh in a breath-holding contest and she admits she recruited Molly to turn off the underwater lights so they might avoid discovery. It was a high-spirited lark agreed after the event to have been woefully misconceived. But when Molly toppled in after her, she tried valiantly to save the life of a non-swimmer – a non-swimmer whose parents should have been supervising her more closely, frankly, not pouring cocktails down their throats and fussing about candles on cakes. Not arguing, as they were seen publicly to be doing earlier in the evening. My suggestion – or can I admit it was a hope? – that it might have been Molly who was saving Georgia has been forgotten, if it was ever circulated in the first place. But that's OK. That's what expensive PR buys you and no matter what the rest of the world believes, I know what *I* think.

The Channings have moved out of La Madrague. They couldn't continue to live a stone's throw from the place their daughter almost lost her life.

Gayle told me the house has been bought by a family from north London. She and the mother got chatting in the lido café and somehow Gayle found herself being talked into doing some tutoring for the older son, who's going for the eleven-plus to get in to a grammar school just down the train line (like Gayle, the family doesn't believe in private education).

I haven't seen Lara again, not in the flesh. I see her sometimes on TV and my hair stands on end before my brain has even processed the visual evidence of her. It must be her voice: its smoky, intimate cadence is in me for ever now. She's been hired as a consultant to the Department of Health – or is it the World Health Organisation? Anyway, she's spoken across the media about her family's scare and the campaigning it has inspired. She was on *Newsnight* a few months ago when it was in the news that a nine-year-old boy in Surrey had drowned at a birthday pool party after dropping his mobile phone into the water and going in after it. She is a natural spokeswoman, an excellent advocate for safe swimming. In one speech, she revealed that she had been offered a modelling contract with a leading swimwear brand and had decided to accept the work only after making it clear her fee would be donated to the STA, the world's largest independent swimming teaching and lifesaving organisation.

Mermaid on Mulberry Street has been salvaged from the ocean bed and released on Netflix.

In interviews, Lara is always careful to respect her daughter's privacy. Georgia was the inspiration for her activism, that she freely concedes, but the last thing she wishes to do is exploit her in any way or cause a setback to her recovery. Occasionally, though, a photo will be released on social media or she'll let slip a snippet about the teen heroine. Like how she's doing her GCSEs a year late and hopes to follow up with A levels and then drama school. Or how she's been back in the water, yes, but will never be as confident as she once was. Make no mistake, Georgia is as passionate as Lara about letting young people know that breath-holding games can end in tragedy. Senseless tragedy, Lara calls it, stressing that however strong you are, the water will always win.

She never says that when Heaven falls that's how *she'd* like to meet her maker.

Georgia is still in touch with Josh and Eve. I discovered that, as I did many of the other details, on the one occasion after the accident that I met Angie. Before she was made aware that she had to pick sides.

Josh's recovery was immediate. The first out of the water, he was the one who called for help when he came up for air and could find neither Molly nor Georgia poolside. He'd felt a strong current under water, he reported, which must have been Molly falling in. It's thought she collided with Georgia, her voluminous clothing weighing both girls down and trapping them, possibly with the added hazard of a tangled balloon ribbon. Josh estimates that almost two minutes had already passed before this happened and the state of relaxation he'd settled into under water made him slow to grasp the situation and lose precious seconds before raising the alarm. He feels guilty about that; he feels personally responsible for what happened to his friends.

Angie was appalled to learn from Josh that he and Georgia sometimes engaged in hyperventilation to remove carbon dioxide from their blood. They knew enough about the risks of this to use a spotter, a trusted teammate who timed their submersions and checked closely for suspicious immobility. Eve was their preferred and practised spotter. Why they thought to recruit an aquaphobic child in her absence remains unexplained. Maybe they felt sorry for Molly or were acting on pressure from Lara to include her; maybe Georgia had been asked to keep her distracted at the party and this was simply the killing of two birds with one stone. Maybe Molly had begged to be given a role, a chance to belong. I'm as certain as I can be that Georgia befriended Molly in the first place at Lara's command, that mother involved daughter in her scheming, but a part of me also still believes that Lara liked Molly. She genuinely wanted her to experience the joy of the water. She thought, perhaps, that she didn't deserve a mother like me. A sadist.

The Channings never pursued their threat to report Ed to the police and I never told him about it, or about what had happened in the hut that night. I try to convince myself that my secrecy is to spare him the anguish of what might have been, but it doesn't work. I know the true reason:

I'm too ashamed.

Though Miles never joins Lara at her media appearances, there is no evidence to suggest that they have parted ways. If they have, Wikipedia has not yet caught up.

As for what I did to him in Stoneborough, so carelessly, and yet with so long-lasting an effect, I know now that it was the worst kind of bullying. Given the chance, he might have preferred the brief, containable scare of having his head held under water, like poor Nessie. Being stripped against your will, being forced to appear naked in public, it's one of the most humiliating and traumatic episodes anyone can suffer, and this was a pubescent child with a developing body and a mind at its most formative. It is a staple of anxiety dreams even for those who've never suffered the daylight reality of it. Hence my own recurrent dream, the one where I'm running naked through Elm Hill. It's so real that I wake up with the chill of the night air on my skin even as my face burns and my heart pounds. I check my feet for blood. I wonder if there is a cardigan in my wardrobe that isn't mine or a woman called Beverley living on the other side of the high street on Broadwood Road.

For those, like Miles, who have had the misfortune actually to suffer it, it is almost without exception cited throughout their lives as the most damaging, the most demeaning of all childhood bullying. It is *never* forgotten. I read a case study of a successful figure in the corporate world who'd sought treatment for drug abuse and had had his troubles traced to a boyhood trauma involving being stripped and humiliated by bullies. You can grow up successful, but you will not feel successful. You may need prescription drugs or the self-medication of alcohol. You may harbour desires for revenge and you may even act on those desires in the hope of laying your ghosts to rest.

But whatever you do, you cannot undo it. It never disappears. You'll always be that child mocked as a savage by the civilized world.

Inside your head, the laughter will never fade.

Before I forget: not so long ago, I saw Stephen on the high street. He was at a table on the Vineyard terrace, drinking with another couple of guys. 'All right,' he called to me, and that was all. Not short but not effusive, just a standard level of interest for a standard neighbourly greeting. That weirdness between us had been no more than casual opportunistic bullying by an unpleasant man. A bored one. He'd found it amusing to watch me squirm. And, presumably unwittingly, he'd been a diversion from his friend's darker and more systematic agenda.

A red herring.

You are probably wondering about Molly. About what the doctor told us when he came through those doors that bank-holiday Monday morning in late August, when Ed hated me almost as much as Miles did. When everyone hated me.

She was suffering from what is known as dry drowning, which means she'd inhaled enough fluid to cause pulmonary oedema, the extrusion of liquid into the lungs, which reduced her ability to exchange air. Apparently this can take place up to seventy-two hours after submersion.

If Ed had not called for help when he did, she would almost certainly have drowned in her own body fluid within the next twelve hours.

If the consultant in respiratory paediatrics hadn't been on site, having been called to attend to Georgia late the previous night, the care might have been neither as prompt nor as excellent as it was. In the end, the two families were linked by the team that saved their daughters.

Molly still has the emphysema-like symptoms associated with recovery, will likely have them for the rest of her life, but she is alive and – as far as we know to date – her brain has suffered no damage. She continues to attend the same school and has an exemption from all excursions and activities involving water.

We remain in our flat in Elm Hill and Ed and I are still together. It's a different together from before last summer, but at least it's a different together from the one during it. We no longer consort with glamorous people. I hear the occasional story of superior lives from Gayle, but I do not wish to sample them for myself. I prefer old friends. Sarah is walking well again and we have a standing date to take Inky down to the Kent borders for a woodland ramble.

With her encouragement, I'm visiting Stoneborough more regularly. I may not think I would choose my mother in a fantasy-parents game, but I know where I am with her. She will not surprise me and I can safely say I love that about her. Since my grandmother passed away in January, Mum has been especially close to Molly. They have a bond all their own and it's a good, healthy one.

Ed and I are still not home owners and most of our savings have been used to pay for private medical services for Molly. But we are husband and wife, parents, constants, and that is enough for us.

Neither of us was able to start work when the new school year began last September. Ed's job at All Saints was held open for him, but mine was too new for me to have earned that sort of privilege so I made the decision to resign. I am a supply teacher now; I go where I'm asked, for the most part where nobody knows me and my story. I try not to have favourites in my class, try not to notice the more charming parents.

Other than poor Matt, the lido staff were cleared of any suspicions of wrongdoing on the night of the accident, and the place opened its doors again just a few days later. Of course, by then, the neighbourhood children were back at school, the term-time routines under way, and attendance fell sharply. It was growing cold, starting to creep into autumn.

For eleven months I avoided returning there. Then, just a few weeks ago on a sticky August day, I faced my fear and went for a swim with Gayle. Can you believe that it was almost as if nothing had changed? We crammed ourselves into a postage-stamp-sized square of unoccupied stone, struggled to manage a length without ploughing into a gaggle of shrieking kids, queued for an age at the kiosk for soft drinks. Even some of the lifeguards were the same.

For most of the outing I consciously avoided looking directly at the café deck, but just as we were leaving I succumbed. And I admit I did a double-take when I saw our table because a glamorous blonde was sitting there, her mouth wide with laughter, her arms flung in the air as she entertained her friends. Maybe she was even singing along to the eighties song playing on the PA system.

Of course, on second glance I saw that her looks were quite crude. She was too young to remember the song. I guessed she was simply one of those very effusive types who can only get the attention they crave by acting crazy.

She was no Lara.

Epilogue

Molly Steele, 2016

This is private. If you are reading this without my permission, then you will be cursed. Which means you will *definitely* be cursed because you totally *do not* have my permission. No one does and no one will, *ever*. So stop reading before your eyeballs start to burn and you turn blind!

I fantasize sometimes that I'm being interviewed, not by the police but by a reporter or maybe someone researching a book about me. Or I imagine I'm watching an actress playing me in a film and this is the scene where she's explaining everything that happened. It's all in the distant past now and my name has been changed, no one knows it's me, which is why I'm free to tell the truth.

You know, the truth is not one single thing, I've learned *that* much. It changes, even within your own mind. Even now I'm not totally sure what I was hoping would happen that night at the lido.

Everyone knows it was Georgia who ordered me to turn off the lights (she 'tasked' me, that was how she put it) – it was the only way they could stage the grand final undetected. OK, so with the pool lights on, she and Josh

445

might have been able to slip under water without being seen, especially with that wall of balloons (the balloons were her idea, by the way, but she was happy for her mum to take the credit). But Eve would have stood out like a sore thumb crouching at the side, so it had to be dark. And it *had* to be that night, it was the season finale, and Georgia was going on holiday the next day so she'd get out of practice and then Josh would have an unfair advantage.

She didn't admit it, she's too cool for that, but I think she had another reason: she wanted to sabotage her mum's perfect party, even if it was just in a secret way only we knew. She wanted to remember it for *her* triumph, not Lara's.

So my 'task' was to sneak through the building to Reception, find the electrics cupboard behind the desk and shut down the underwater lights, go to the fire doors, wait for Eve's signal (an owl hoot, pretty unoriginal), then go back in and turn the lights on again. It wasn't so complicated and at least I didn't have to go near the water.

Obviously I still had my doubts. I'm not *that* retarded. 'Won't someone come and try to fix it?' I asked Georgia.

'It's only the pool lights,' she said. 'I'm thinking they might not even notice, they'll all be so wasted, or they'll think they're set on a timer to go off at the end of the evening. It's not like they'll see it as some big emergency. And when the lights come back on again after five minutes they'll assume it was a temporary power cut.'

'The guests, yes,' I said, faltering, because I didn't want to argue with her. She didn't like that. 'But what about the staff? Won't they know there's no timer? Won't it be their job to sort it out?'

Georgia looked at me like I was starting to bore her. 'If you're not going to do it, Molly, then just say and we'll find someone who will.'

And so I agreed. I loved her then. I would have done anything she asked, even that.

On the night, there was a hitch.

'We have a *situation*,' Georgia told us, doing quote marks in the air with her fingers. Eve was ill and had been kept at home. She was their regular spotter: she knew when to get worried, when to pull them up and get them out.

'You,' Georgia said to me. 'You can do both. Turn off the lights and come straight to the pool. Wedge open the fire doors so you can get back in. Then, as soon as we've finished, go back in and turn the lights on again.'

My mouth fell open like a fish. A fish that can't swim.

'Maybe we should postpone the whole thing,' Josh said, noticing my horror, but Georgia gave him that look, like he'd really disappointed her by being lame, and he agreed: of course I should stand in for Eve. It wasn't like I had to get into the water or even touch it. All I had to do was go to the edge of the pool, where they'd be waiting, give them the ready-steady-go and start the stopwatch.

'I'm not sure,' I said.

447

'What's *wrong* with you?' Georgia said. I think she knew by then that the way I felt about her had changed, but with Eve out she needed me more than ever and couldn't risk being too nasty to me. 'It won't be *that* dark,' she added, coaxing now. 'Plus you'll have your phone. The main thing is the stopwatch. Not just his time when he comes up, but mine. I want to know to the hundredth of a second how long I've whipped him by.'

'In your dreams,' Josh said.

They were so desperate to win it was like they'd rather die than come up first.

'What if . . .' I hesitated '. . . what if you *don't* come back up?'

They looked at one another and burst out laughing.

'Of course we will. This isn't *The Virgin Suicides*, Molly.'

'It's not the virgin anything,' Josh added, and I blushed. They'd hinted at other times that they'd had sex together. They weren't going out or anything, it wasn't a big deal. Josh, Matt, Ethan, they all wanted Georgia.

'Don't look so nervous, Mollster,' she told me. 'You'll give the game away. You know how paranoid your mum is.'

As soon as I was on my own I just wanted to cry. I couldn't help it – it was completely different now I was going to have to go near the water. I tried to practise the steps, but Mum saw me, yelling like a lunatic for me to get back, which made the others come and find out what was going on.

'What were you *doing*?' Georgia said. 'Do you *want* this to fail? Come and have a drink. You need something to calm you down.'

But there was no way I could sit with them drinking mocktails and listening to Georgia arguing with Matt because he wouldn't get her the vodka she wanted. In the end she found someone else to get it. She said a shot gave her the edge she needed before she eviscerated Josh. She liked the word 'eviscerate'.

I tried to talk to Mum, but she had that glittery look she'd had all summer, like she thought she was famous or something. Drunk, basically. I wished she wasn't so wasted, that she would stop looking around and listen to me, but it wasn't like I didn't know *why* she was so jumpy. It was the same reason everyone was: Georgia.

God, I hated her by then.

I hated her because I'd discovered my dad was obsessed with her, just like they all were, even Mum.

She's special.

She's a beauty all right.

At least he admitted it: *She's destroying us.*

He was right – even if Mum was too stupid to see why: she *was* destroying us. She was the maggot that was eating my apple from the inside. Something was going on between her and Dad and it was breaking up my family.

It was the Tuesday before the party that I realized. I'd been in Stoneborough the previous week, and before that I'd been deluded, just like everyone else.

449

It was something our neighbour Sarah said, though she didn't know she had.

'Molly, I was just telling your mum I saw your friend when you were away at your grandma's. The pretty one, Georgia. Poor thing, having to have so much tutoring. It didn't exist in my day, you know, or at least not that *I'd* ever heard. But every day she came. In her holidays! And so good-tempered about it, gave me a huge smile when I bumped into her on the stairs. Asked me if I needed any help with Inky while you were away.'

I looked at her, trying to work her out. She's old, sure, but she's not dumb. 'Georgia came every day?' I said.

'Yes, on her bike. I saw her from my window. I hardly saw your mum at all. She was out most of the time.'

Every day. Georgia was only supposed to come on Wednesdays and Saturdays. And Sarah had 'just' told my mum this as well, but Mum was so self-obsessed she hadn't even picked up on the clue.

Actually, maybe Sarah *did* know what she was saying. Maybe I was her messenger.

At the party, I knew for sure. Mum and Dad were splitting up. I heard it with my own ears – and *he* was leaving *her*. That was the crazy unfair part.

We've been married for sixteen years, Mum said. *We have a daughter together.*

We're agreed, then? Dad said. *After tonight, it's over?*

It doesn't seem like I have a choice, Mum said, and she sounded so sad and defeated, like her heart was breaking on the spot.

Everything was going to change. I would go with her to live in a new flat, probably change schools as well. She would get even more insanely protective than she already was. My life would be a misery.

Maybe that was when I had the idea that I could do what Georgia was asking, but I could do it in a different way. If I could get her to leave my dad alone, *he* wouldn't leave my mum.

The mad thing is that it was Dad who almost got in the way. Just as I was about to enter the security code – Georgia wheedled it out of lover-boy, of course – and sneak through the building to Reception, he stopped me and said it was time to light the candles on Mum's cake and it might be nice if I carried it in, not him.

In case she threw it in his face, I thought. 'Can we do it in ten minutes?' I asked, and he said fine, he didn't know where she was anyway.

'I've lost her,' he said, and he looked so worried, as if he might be regretting what he'd done.

I felt sorry for him then. He just needed some help in making the right decision, in making things all right again.

It was easy to find the light switch and to push open the fire doors to the pool area. It was much darker than I'd expected – they must have dimmed the lights in the café at the same time – because I could hear people laughing about how spooky it was, but I had measured the steps and I knew where Georgia would be and, anyway, as I got closer my eyes adjusted. I could see their heads above the surface of the water a few metres apart. I had my phone in my hand with the stopwatch app open.

'Say when you're ready,' I whispered.

'We're ready,' Josh said.

'May the best bitch win,' Georgia said, and I thought, *Yeah*.

'Three, two, one, go,' I said, and I hit 'Start'. They dipped under, perfectly synchronized. They trusted me, I was the judge, and that made me feel powerful.

But I didn't watch the ticking digits. I put the phone in my bag and took my bag off my shoulder and pushed it to the side. I could make out Georgia's hair floating just under the surface and I leaned over and put my hands into the pool. It wasn't like putting my hands in the basin in the bathroom at home, the water felt big and greedy and sucking, like it had no bottom to it. Then I put my forearms in.

She must have detected motion, the push of water, but she remained still. Maybe she thought it was Josh moving towards her or even surfacing already, or maybe pretending to surface so that she would be deceived and come up first – they had all these strategies and ploys and double bluffs. I imagined the competitive twitch of her face as she considered these possibilities.

I reached towards the top of her head and placed my hands on it. I didn't push it down, I just didn't let it push back up. I didn't let it move to the side either and when it tried to duck lower, out of my way, I gripped it by the hair.

I'm taller than her, stronger than her, I thought.

She's like a sprite compared to Molls.

Someone like Georgia Channing isn't going to befriend Molly for no reason, is she?

If you're not going to do it, then we'll find someone who will . . .

Suddenly something lashed at my arm and gripped it, pulled at it. I struggled and lost my balance and then I was freezing cold all over, though my brain didn't know at first if I was hot or cold. I swear it didn't even know I was in the water. But I was. The whole of me was in the water. It was like being in catacombs, in sea caves, wallowing and swallowing, filling and sucking and sinking.

I reached for something solid and I grabbed a body part that might have been a leg. Then the leg kicked from my grip and I had no awareness of anything. I was a yolk suspended in white, inside the shell. There was no way out, the shell could not be cracked from the inside.

I opened my eyes and there was nothing to see. It was like I'd read when people fall through ice and they can't find the hole, or when they get buried in an avalanche and they don't know which way is up. Then there were hands that weren't Georgia's, hands on me from above, lifting me.

'She's breathing. Someone get her parents. What's your name, love?'

'Is she unconscious?' It was Matt — I recognized his voice. 'It's Molly — Jesus. Get the fib, someone, quick!'

'I'm here, I'm alive,' I said, and the words were made of liquid, making me cough. My chest hurt so much.

'She's conscious, thank God.'

I grew aware of a horrible noise, an alarm, and everyone was shouting. I wasn't shocked into remorse or anything like that. I don't remember even thinking Georgia might still be in the water, let alone caring. What I felt when I lay by the pool was not *I wish I hadn't done that*, but *I hope I've done enough.*

My breath was coming back and I was feeling very cold.

Then Dad was there, gentle and serious and steady. He had to speak close to my ear because of the alarm. 'You're all right, sweetheart. You're going to be fine. We need to get you out of these wet clothes.'

'Don't leave,' I said, my voice all wet and bubbly.

'I'm not going anywhere.'

'Not that, I mean . . . Georgia.'

And he looked at me and I could see he got it. He knew I knew. Then he pretended he didn't. 'Don't worry about the others,' he said. 'They've got their own parents with them. Let's try and get you dry, shall we? Help is on its way.'

Then the alarm stopped and the lights came on and Mum was there. I thought she was going to go mental but she was fine, she was great. She said I would go to sleep that night and in the morning I wouldn't remember a thing about it. Her voice was really calm, like Bryony's. Then I heard the ambulance sirens and I saw

Georgia on the stretcher and remembered what I'd done. There was the most terrible screaming, I felt like I was being crushed by the sound of it, and then they said it was me, it was me who was screaming.

'I want to go home,' I said, and I kept repeating it and repeating it, like I was the alarm now, and they said to stop, please stop, they would sort it out.

'She needs to be with just us,' Mum said. 'Josh is being allowed home. I'll insist she is too.'

They took us in a kind of ambulance car and I felt better when I was in my bedroom, just me and Mum and Dad. And then I woke up and they weren't there and it turned out I was in a ward at Trinity Hospital, and the pain in my chest and throat was so bad I started crying.

No wonder I felt like I was in a film. It kept cutting from place to place, face to face, like someone was editing my story for me, telling me which lines to say. It was like it wasn't real, even though I knew it must be.

I have never been questioned by the police or any of the authorities; Mum and Dad protected me from that.

They've asked me, of course. Question after question, angle upon angle.

Why did I need to follow Georgia and Josh to the water's edge? Couldn't I have operated the stopwatch from a safer distance?

'I couldn't see their heads well enough. It was darker than I expected.'

Didn't you realize you'd turned off *all* the lights?

'No, I made a mistake.' (True.)

Did you slip?

'I think so.' (In a way.)

Were you trying to stop them? Mum said.

Were you worried one of them had got into difficulties? Dad said.

What were you doing? What were you thinking? Do you have any idea what could have happened?

I think quite enough *did* happen, the other says. It was sometimes hard to tell who they were accusing, me or one another.

And then, after days or weeks or months, they stopped asking. They'd been advised by one of their experts to lay off.

Sometimes I think Mum knows, or has at least guessed that it didn't happen the way everyone's agreed it did. She's been bad herself. She knows the feeling when you're not in charge of yourself, when you're possessed by something wild and vicious and headlong. When the right way to act is completely ignored; it's just some meek, lame voice you pretend you can't hear.

Georgia's forgotten it, I'm sure of that. Or else she's decided not to tell. Just like she's decided not to contact my dad since she moved away. I know that for sure because Izzy's brother helped me hack into Dad's email and there was nothing from her, not even from last summer. He's erased her, like she never existed.

Of course, Dad and I haven't ever discussed what they did together. It wasn't like I actually *saw* anything, so

456

he would only deny it anyway. But when you know, you know (that's one of Bryony's sayings). I think Georgia's mum knew too. I saw her watching my dad watching Georgia at the party and there was a flicker in her face that looked like understanding, like she wasn't noticing any more that he looked like that old actor. She was way better at reading people than *my* mum, way better at spotting clues.

Sometimes, I think of Elm Hill last summer as the Cluedo board, the new one Dad hates so much, where you don't go to the cellar to make your accusation but to a bright-blue swimming pool at the centre of the board.

Of course, the game's exactly the same, either way: before you can make your way to the middle, you have to work out who the villain is.

Unless you're prepared to risk your hand and guess.

Acknowledgements

My thanks to the team at Michael Joseph/Penguin for their expertise and dedication, in particular to Maxine Hitchcock, Kimberley Atkins, Eve Hall, Francesca Russell, Claire Bush, Sophie Elletson, Lee Motley. And to Hazel Orme for an impressively eagle-eyed copyedit.

Heartfelt thanks to all at Curtis Brown who've supported this novel (and its writer) with such commitment and energy: Sheila Crowley, Becky Ritchie, Abbie Greaves, Luke Speed, Alice Lutyens, Johanna Devereaux, Claire Nozieres. Also Deborah Schneider at Gelfman Schneider in NYC.

A big thank you to Lily Johnston for her very helpful research and to Tara Fisher-Harris at Brockwell Lido in south London for answering my many questions. (For the record, Brockwell Lido is in no way a model for Elm Hill Lido but is instead quite exemplary in its running.)

Lara Channing's book is *Poolside With Slim Aarons* (Harry N. Abrams, Inc., 2007). The film she loves is *La Piscine*, directed in 1969 by Jacques Deray and starring Alain Delon and Romy Schneider. *Mermaid on Mulberry Street* is of course fictitious.

Discussion Questions

* Contains plot spoilers *

- What is the relevance of the swimming pool as the 'stage' for the action in the novel? If the lido had never opened, do you think Natalie's behaviour that summer would have been different?

- To what extent do you think Natalie has contributed to Molly's aquaphobia? Does Molly want to get better?

- 'Might being pretty be important, after all?' How significant are physical appearances in the novel?

- Discuss the mother/daughter relationships in the novel. To what degree are the mothers and daughters in competition with each other?

- When discussing her friendship with Lara, Ed tells Natalie: 'You're out of your depth'. The female friendships in the novel are defined by a delicate power balance. What factors affect this balance, and how does the power shift at different moments in the novel?

- Natalie's determination to make her marriage to Ed stable is, in part, to avoid making the mistakes of her own parents. To what extent do we see history repeating itself in the novel? Do characters learn from the past, or from each other?

- Do you think Natalie is sexually attracted to Lara, or, rather, does she want to be her?

- What do you think is the significance of Natalie and Ed's jobs as teachers?

- Do you think that Ed was really having an affair with Georgia? Why is the author not explicit in telling us either way?

- Is there any way to excuse Molly's actions at the party and Natalie's behaviour in the past on the grounds of their age? Was it fair of Miles to be seeking revenge after so many years?

Read on for a sample of
Louise Candlish's thrilling
and intriguing novel

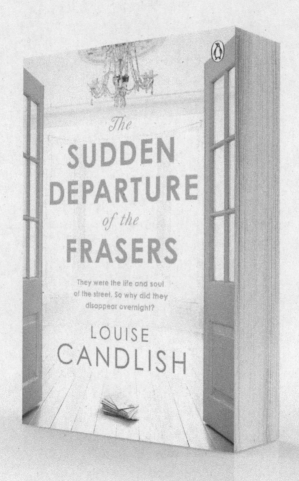

*The Sudden Departure
of the Frasers...*

Chapter 1

Right from the moment she first held the keys in her hand, something felt wrong.

Later, she would regret ignoring that instinct, but at the time she put it down to the simple fact of Joe not being there with her. It couldn't be helped, of course, it was just one of those things – or several of them. A rescheduled client meeting that could under no circumstances be missed; the estate agent's half-day closure for staff training (or, as Joe suspected, plans for a long lunch courtesy of the commission earned on *their* house); her own eagerness to get into the property and start their new life: all conspired to bring her there that morning to pick up the keys alone.

'Well, congratulations, Mrs Davenport,' said the agent, and he placed the keys with a ceremonial flourish on the release document for her to sign. There were two sets, one attached to a costly-looking silver key ring with a pretty dragonfly charm – the previous owners', presumably.

'Thank you.' Hand shaking, Christy scrawled her name before snatching up the keys and defending them in a clenched fist – as if someone might step forward and battle her for them! For these were the keys to a house on

Lime Park Road, and never in her wildest dreams had she thought she would come to own a property on that street. Yes, she and Joe had always aimed high, but this, this was rags-to-riches stuff, the fairy-tale ending you wouldn't normally trust.

'I hope you and your husband have many happy years in your new home,' the agent said. He was different from the one who'd handled the sale, younger and less sincere: could that be why the encounter felt, somehow, illicit? He could be a con artist, she and Joe the innocent victims of some elaborate sting. Or maybe it was the previous agent who'd been the fraudster?

Illicit? Con artist? Fraudster? What had got into her? She could tell by the way the man was frowning that her smile looked as problematic as it felt; it was causing disquiet, the way it might if a clown put his face too close. Managing a last choked thank you, she made her exit to the street. It's just nerves, she told herself; or excitement, the pure, debilitating kind that was hard to distinguish from terror.

Either way, she could have walked the route in her sleep, for she knew Lime Park as well as any postman from the countless occasions she and Joe had roamed it together since first viewing the house. She knew the short parade that masqueraded as a high street, with its mix of cafés, boutiques and estate agents, and the florist's on the corner that spilled its colours far across the pavement, as if cans of paint had been flung from the windows above. She knew the famous old art school that had stood empty for years before being redeveloped into the complex of luxury flats it was today. She knew the little park, the main gates of which she passed through now, walking in the shade of the old limes that lent the area its name, catching the scent of cut grass on the breeze. And she knew the web of streets beyond, including the one that curved around the park's southern edge, the one that contained the house to which she held the keys (she was gripping them in her hand still, as if to relax a single finger would be to render the whole business null and void; the fine edge of a dragonfly wing cut painfully into her palm).

And here it was: Lime Park Road, lined as far as the eye could see with cherry trees in full bloom, like giant sticks of candyfloss, casting dancing black patterns on the sun-bleached car lanes. It was a festive sight, could almost be the gateway to a carnival – until you noticed there wasn't a soul to be seen. No one was parking a car or closing a gate; no one was pushing a baby or walking a dog; no one was arriving or departing.

There was only her.

As the road swept eastward, the façade of their new home came into view. The houses on Lime Park Road were brick villas built in pairs in the late nineteenth century, their matching chimney stacks positioned at the outer edges of the roofs like cocked dog ears, and number 40 was the right hand of its twosome. Hers now, hers and Joe's, and yet it was with the furtive air of a trespasser that she pushed open the gate and teetered towards the glossy Oxford-blue door. She lifted the key to the lock, her breath held. How unfamiliar each element of entry was: that brief resistance followed by a sudden sweet give, the weight of good timber against her palm, the cool hardness of tile underfoot, and the smell in the broad hallway of ... not so much temporary disuse as reckless abandonment.

But maybe that was because she knew the previous owners had left in a hurry. Virtually overnight, in fact. Lord Lucan's got nothing on this pair, the agent had joked.

She wished she hadn't remembered that detail, for the sight of the bare hall walls and closed internal doors caused wild thoughts to surface: what might she find behind these doors? Bloodstains on the floor? A decomposing body? Some sort of weapon that linked the murder to Joe and her?

Ashamed, she turned brisk, throwing open the first door she came to, the one to the large square sitting room at the front. Everything was perfectly in order, of course, and quite devoid of signs of crime. There was the grand and glamorous marble fireplace they had so admired; and the pair of thickset ribbed radiators, the type torn from Victorian schoolhouses and reconditioned for the nostalgic wealthy; and the deep bay with its shining triptych of panes. She'd forgotten its original oak seat, newly upholstered in a textured linen print that looked far too expensive to actually sit on.

Christy marched across the room and hurled herself onto it, if only to prove that she was not the kind of person you could intimidate with *fabric*. The view onto the street was glorious, a collage of green leaf and golden brick unfettered by the low-level planting in the front garden; it was like looking through a giant camera lens at a scene lit to perfection by a master cinematographer. This was where she would come to watch the seasons change, she thought, during those many happy years the agent had wished her.

On her feet once more, she moved to the rear of the ground floor, actually gasping at the sight of the vast kitchen, just as she had when she'd first seen it. The fittings were high-end and handmade (the agent had mentioned a designer neither she nor Joe had heard of but whose name, when invoked in earshot of her boss, Laurie, had caused swooning), the cabinet doors made of opaque glass with brass fittings, the worktop a glittering slice of quartz. Family and friends were going to be not so much impressed as astonished, she thought, and to picture them assembled amid the hard, gleaming angles was like imagining villagers circling a spaceship that had just landed in their field, lights flashing in colours never before seen on earth. With the image came a fresh swell of unease, a recognition of its true source. Who are we fooling? she thought: this house is worth far more than we paid for it. There *must* be a catch.

She remembered with perfect clarity the day the agent had rung with news of an unusually well-priced house in Lime Park, a once-in-a-lifetime deal for a buyer who could act fast – so fast that only the chain-free were invited to bid. How she and Joe had patted themselves on the back for having already sold their two-bed in New Cross and rented just before the market had suffered a fortuitous downturn. But even so, this house was beyond 'well-priced', it was a gift, and in the whirlwind of the transaction they had perhaps not been diligent enough in asking the crucial, central question:

Why?

'They're leaving for personal reasons,' was all the agent had been able to tell them of the sellers, which made Joe suspect financial ruin.

'No,' Christy said. 'Why would they sell at such a good price if they need the money? They'd hold out for top whack.'

'Not if they need the cash quickly,' Joe said. 'Maybe a debt's been called in and they have to cut their losses. It must happen all the time in a recession.'

The agent agreed that times were harder in the outer suburbs. It wasn't Chelsea, after all.

But Christy's instinct pulled in a different direction. 'No. This is something emotional. It must be divorce or illness. They need to pay for treatment, perhaps.' Whatever it was it had to be something catastrophic for a couple to give up a home they'd plainly only just finished renovating, for the place was box-fresh throughout; you could smell the newness of it, hear it squeaking. 'Are they leaving London?'

But the agent didn't know, had no forwarding address on file, the sale being conducted by the couple's solicitor. He admitted he'd not met the couple – Jeremy and Amber Fraser, they were called – face to face.

A sharp rap at the front door startled her and, laughing at herself, she opened up to the postman. He had an item too big to fit through the letter box, an oversized brochure of some sort for Mrs A. Fraser. There was other post, too, all of it for the outgoing couple.

'Didn't the Frasers redirect their mail?' she asked.

'There's sometimes a bit of an overlap,' the postman said, 'but it'll kick in in a few days, don't worry.'

'I'll collect it all up and send it on to them in one batch,' she promised.

Alone again, she inspected the items. Only two were not junk or publicity mail-outs and both were addressed to Amber Fraser: one was a postcard with a picture of an old *Vogue* cover, the model an alluring redhead with a plum-coloured pout; the other a white envelope with 'Private & Confidential' stamped on it. Christy experienced a sudden desire to tear the letter open – an extension of that peculiar sensation of being in the house unlawfully – but resisted the urge and satisfied herself by reading the postcard:

Hi Amber,

How are you? Hope you're still loving your forever home! Have tried emailing and phoning you, but no luck. Couple of loose ends to tie up – call me when you have a spare moment?

Love, Hetty xxx

Below the name a mobile phone number had been scribbled, 'just in case'.

On cue, Christy's phone began ringing: Joe.

'Your meeting's finished?'

'Just this second. How's the house?'

She was honestly not sure how to answer this. 'It feels a bit strange, like I'm going to be arrested for breaking and entering. Does that sound crazy?'

Joe chuckled. 'That's just Imposter Syndrome. Happens to everyone.'

Well, not *everyone*, she thought, not the entitled Oxbridge types with whom he worked and routinely lost out to in promotions, but she knew what he meant: everyone ordinary, like them.

'But don't worry, the solicitor sent the confirmation email, we've definitely completed, otherwise they wouldn't have released the keys. We're the owners now.'

Christy felt her heart contract, and with its unclenching came the first flood of joy. 'It just seems too good to be true, Joe.'

'I know.' But his tone was unambiguously triumphant because as far as he was concerned all good things came true if you worked hard enough to get them. In the seventeen years that had passed since they'd met at university, he had never stopped remembering that he had something to prove.

'Are you on your way?'

'Leaving right this minute, just setting my stopwatch to time the commute. One minute longer than an hour and we're giving the house back.'

Laughing, Christy hung up and looked once more at the handful of post for the Frasers. Then she slotted the postcard and the 'Private & Confidential' letter between two larger envelopes, out of sight. Joe's right, she thought, you're not an imposter.

You're just lucky.

'And look what else I've got!' Along with a chilled bottle of Veuve Clicquot, a gift from Marcus, the partner at Jermyn Richards who was his boss and long-time mentor, Joe waved a copy of *Metro* under her nose. It was open at an article titled 'Top Ten London Streets for Families':

6. LIME PARK ROAD (NEW ENTRY)

It's a miracle that this Victorian beauty has kept itself below the radar for as long as it has – blame the Lottery-funded revamp of the park last year and the newly opened Canvas restaurant for its breakout moment. This is the most sought-after street in the neighbourhood thanks to its handsome brick villas, once chaotic shares for the students of the Lime Park Art School. While there's still a smattering of the old boho crowd amid the incoming well-heeled families, don't let that deceive you: the days of snapping up a property for the price of a couple of watercolours are long gone.

'Talk about being in the right place at the right time,' Joe crowed. 'We've probably made a ten per cent capital gain on the house since this morning! Shame we've hardly got anything to put in it, mind you.'

'I know. It's a bit embarrassing.' Christy's glance swept the spacious zone between kitchen units and garden doors that had been furnished by the Frasers with such memorable elan. There'd been a vintage dresser stacked with coloured glassware and a leaf-green velvet sofa with wittily mismatched cushions. The dining table and chairs had been of the same bold contemporary style she'd seen through the window of Canvas, all curved lines and vibrant hues.

Wherever they'd gone, the Frasers would not have arrived, as she and Joe had, with nothing but sleeping bags and a change of clothes. The cut-price van-hire company the Davenports were using to transport their possessions from the storage facility did not have the smaller van size available till the next day. Perched now on bar stools to eat the cheese-and-tomato sandwiches Christy had made that morning – it seemed too prosaic a snack for so glossy a setting – they were grateful to their predecessors for having left them and saved them from sitting cross-legged on the floor. (Another reason to discount the theory that the Frasers had fallen on hard times: the stools looked like design classics; you could probably get hundreds of pounds for them on eBay.)

But none of that worried Joe as he poured the champagne into plastic beakers. Smart in his office suit and only a few days into a new haircut, he looked like a man who'd earned his spot on that designer stool; a man entering his prime. His eyes, the colour of cognac and the only exotic touch in a solidly Anglo-Saxon face, glowed warm with glee as he touched his cup to hers and popped the discarded ends of her sandwich into his mouth. 'Here's to a new life of bread crusts and eye-watering debt!'

Christy grimaced. 'Let's not think about debt today. Let's pretend we own the house outright.'

In reality, she would not forget as long as she lived that adrenalin-drenched sprint to pull together the finance for the house, how they'd tossed into the pot the proceeds of their flat, life savings and a loan from Christy's parents (Joe's had nothing to lend; her own, little enough to cause her guilt pangs for having had the nerve to take it), not to mention a mortgage brokered in haste by a friend of a friend and regarded thereafter by the couple as too horrifyingly colossal to be real. Even then, they'd fallen short, had had to resort to punishing forgotten credit cards to cover their solicitor's fees.

'Cash-poor' didn't scratch the surface of it.

And then there was the other sacrifice, agreed between the two of them in what already felt to Christy like a deal with the devil: babies. There could be none yet, not until one – or both – of them had been promoted. After all, you could decide to have a family any time, couldn't you, but a house like 40 Lime Park Road was a rare and special thing and they might never have had this chance again.

Yes, they were agreed on it.

He just wanted a decent book to read ...

Not too much to ask, is it? It was in 1935 when Allen Lane, Managing Director of Bodley Head Publishers, stood on a platform at Exeter railway station looking for something good to read on his journey back to London. His choice was limited to popular magazines and poor-quality paperbacks – the same choice faced every day by the vast majority of readers, few of whom could afford hardbacks. Lane's disappointment and subsequent anger at the range of books generally available led him to found a company – and change the world.

'We believed in the existence in this country of a vast reading public for intelligent books at a low price, and staked everything on it'
Sir Allen Lane, 1902–1970, founder of Penguin Books

The quality paperback had arrived – and not just in bookshops. Lane was adamant that his Penguins should appear in chain stores and tobacconists, and should cost no more than a packet of cigarettes.

Reading habits (and cigarette prices) have changed since 1935, but Penguin still believes in publishing the best books for everybody to enjoy. We still believe that good design costs no more than bad design, and we still believe that quality books published passionately and responsibly make the world a better place.

So wherever you see the little bird – whether it's on a piece of prize-winning literary fiction or a celebrity autobiography, political tour de force or historical masterpiece, a serial-killer thriller, reference book, world classic or a piece of pure escapism – you can bet that it represents the very best that the genre has to offer.

Whatever you like to read – trust Penguin.